This isn't happening.
Dogs don't turn into men. They don't!

But even as the argument roared in her head, Natalie's gaze took in the sight in front of her. The man was *built*, his waist narrow, his abs ripped, his biceps as thick as tree trunks, one adorned with a thick golden armband with what appeared to be the head of a wolf. His shoulders were easily half the width of her sofa. Her gaze continued up, reaching his face, and her heart clenched. Scars crisscrossed the flesh every which way, tugging down one of his lips, cutting across one eye. His body might be prime, but his face was made for nightmares. Within that ruined face, eyelids lifted revealing dark eyes that turned to her, contracting on a sheen of pain, radiating a dismay so raw it almost made her ache.

"I'm not going to hurt you, Natalie." His voice was low and urgent as he struggled to his feet, grimacing. Towering over her, he watched her with eyes filled with the same intelligence, the same *gentleness* she'd seen in the dog's. "I would never hurt you."

She was shaking, her pulse racing, her stomach cramping from shock. But not from fear. Because as she stared into those dark eyes, she saw only truth and honor and kindness. She recognized the essence of the dog in the man.

"I would never hurt you," he said again, his voice throbbing with sincerity and desperation that she believe him.

"I know," she told him.

And she did.

By Pamela Palmer

Vamp City Novels
A KISS OF BLOOD
A BLOOD SEDUCTION

Feral Warriors Novels
WULFE UNTAMED
A LOVE UNTAMED
ECSTASY UNTAMED
HUNGER UNTAMED
RAPTURE UNTAMED
PASSION UNTAMED
OBSESSION UNTAMED
DESIRE UNTAMED

PAMELA PALMER

WULFE UNTAMED
A FERAL WARRIORS NOVEL

AVON

An Imprint of HarperCollinsPublishers

AVON BOOKS
An Imprint of HarperCollins*Publishers*
10 East 53rd Street
New York, New York 10022-5299

Copyright © 2014 by Pamela Palmer
ISBN 978-0-06-210755-8
www.avonromance.com

First Avon Books mass market printing: February 2014

10 9 8 7 6 5 4 3 2

*This one is for Laurin Wittig
and Anne Shaw Moran,
my sisters in all ways that matter.*

Acknowledgments

Many, many thanks to all the people who've helped me tell the Ferals' story, especially my critique partners and best friends, Laurin Wittig and Anne Shaw Moran, and my wonderful, dear, and talented editor, May Chen, all three of whom have been at my side every step of the way. We did it, ladies. This one's a wrap.

I also want to thank all the hardworking and incredible people at Avon Books who've had a hand in getting this and my other Feral Warriors books onto the shelves and into the hands of readers, especially Pamela Spengler-Jaffee, Jessie Edwards, Chelsey Emmelhainz, Amanda Bergeron, and Tom Egner and his team.

In addition, many thanks to my copy editor, Sara Schwager, my assistant, Kim Castillo, my agent, Robin Rue, and to Carla Gallway and my street team, Palmer's Pack. You guys rock. Thanks, too, to Denise L. Paquin, O.D., my daughter's optometrist and lifesaver, for helping me better understand the part the brain plays in vision and for giving me the right words. Any errors in the manuscript are my own. And a warm hug, as always, to my family for your unwavering support.

Most of all, thanks to my readers. I might write the words, but it's your minds and your imaginations that have brought the Feral Warriors to life. With your e-mails, reviews, tweets, Facebook posts, and your efforts to come see me at book signings and conventions, you delight me and inspire me. You've touched and brightened my life in more ways than you know, and I'm incredibly grateful.

WULFE UNTAMED

Chapter One

The Earth opened before her with a bloodcurdling scream. Day turned to night.

There was no escape.

Mere feet in front of her, an unearthly red-orange light burst from that wide, gaping hole. Still, the Earth screamed. Tied to a stake at the edge of that abyss, she could do nothing but watch. And tremble.

She was not alone and, oh, if only she were. Because one of the other four tied around that gaping maw with her was her brother, Xavier. All her life, she'd watched over him. Now she could do nothing to help either of them. And they were surely going to die.

Around them, half a dozen large, muscular males—half of them clothed, half naked, ran, shouting, drawing blades, as a second group of men descended on the circle and drew them into battle.

As steel clanged, one of the naked men disappeared suddenly in a spray of sparkling lights to be replaced by a large, maned African lion. Another lunged at one of his attackers and, in a similar spray of lights, turned into a huge wolf.

Impossible.

Thunder rolled across the sky.

A horrible stench met her nose. Fire tore down her cheek as if one of the warriors had turned his blade on her, but there was no one close.

And then suddenly there was.

She cried out in pain and shock, staring at the monster that stood . . . that hovered . . . in front of her—more hideous than anything she'd ever imagined. He was the size of a man, black hair floating around his head as if each lock were alive, gleaming in the unholy red-orange light. A black cloak hung around his indistinct body. And his face . . . his face . . . Features hung at odd angles, his flesh like melted wax, wicked fangs protruding unevenly from a slash of a mouth.

She froze with terror, her heart pounding out of her chest, as his hand . . . his claw . . . lifted, red with her blood.

Natalie Cash woke with a start, her heart pounding, her body damp with sweat. An early-dawn glow lit the window shades of her bedroom, and she blinked, trying to catch her breath from the nightmare that even now scampered back into the shadows of her mind, leaving behind only wisps of horror and fantasy—a man shifting into a wolf, a terror too awful to remember.

With unsteady hands, she raked her hair back from her face.

A hell of a way to start the day.

Xavier had been in the dream, she was almost certain, though in what capacity she had no recollection, now. Every night was the same—the nightmares that slipped away upon waking. They'd been plaguing her ever since *the incident,* the week of her life that had vanished a month and a half ago, leaving three of her friends dead and her brother missing.

The cops didn't have a single lead.

Easing from the bed quietly, so as not to wake Rick, she padded to the bathroom down the hall, then to the kitchen for a cup of hazelnut coffee. Mug in hand, she let herself out through the sliding glass door onto her deck. A pleasant breeze brushed her cheek as she settled onto her favorite cushioned chair and soaked in the beauty of the woods behind her house, drenched in the light of dawn.

As the sky lightened, as the birds woke and began to sing, she sipped the fragrant brew and slowly found the equilibrium that was usually such a natural part of her. Before six weeks ago, she'd felt settled and satisfied, her life on track, everything falling into place. Her optometry practice, a year old now, was thriving—she had a full patient load, and she loved it, especially working with the kids. Her mom was thrilled that she was out of college and back in town. And she was engaged to marry Rick, her longtime boyfriend and best friend.

Everything had changed in a single day—the day two of her friends from high school suggested a day-trip to Harpers Ferry. Rick had made plans to help his dad, and since one of her friends had invited her own younger brother and his girlfriend, Christy, Natalie had brought Xavier.

Her stomach clenched with the grinding, constant yearning to go back in time and change that decision. If only she hadn't invited him. If only they'd chosen the outlet mall in Leesburg instead.

The morning had been pleasant as they'd traipsed about the quaint, historic town. And then her memories just blanked out. A week later, she and Christy awakened in a field nearby with no memory of the time between. The bodies of three of their companions had been recovered that first afternoon. Only Xavier remained missing.

And her life had careened off the rails.

Taking a small sip of the hot brew, breathing in the hazelnut and warm coffee scents, she tipped her head back and watched the pink clouds amble slowly across the dawn sky.

Somewhere, somehow, Xavier still lived, she was sure of it. She'd awakened in that field to find a quarter-sized circle on her palm, drawn in pen. A circle with a small curve in the middle—a smiley-face without the eyes—one of her blind brother's favorites. She felt certain Xavier had put it there, a message that he was okay. But where was he? Where had she been? And why hadn't he come home, too?

As the weeks passed, her fear grew that she might never see him again.

She had no choice but to carry on. But that missing week haunted her. Grief at the losses she'd suffered had settled like a fist beneath her breastbone, an ache that throbbed constantly, refusing to abate.

Natalie took another sip of coffee, envying the clouds that floated free of the cares of the world.

A low sound caught her ear, and she straightened. A movement in the trees caught her eye, and her heart lifted on a thrill of pleasure as the huge wolf who'd visited her a few weeks ago, bounded into view. He was a magnificent animal, easily the size of a bear, with a thick coat—variegated black and gray—on his back and head, sable on his legs and belly. He wasn't really a wolf, of course, though he might have some wolf blood. He was too friendly. At least, he had been the last time.

She watched him carefully, her more primitive instincts urging her to retreat to the house, just to play it safe. But as he crossed her yard, as she peered into that beautiful, intelligent face, she once again felt no fear. Exhilaration, yes. And awe. But not fear, not when those golden eyes of his radiated a warm, joyous welcome.

She smiled, his arrival lifting her heart and easing the burden from her shoulders, holding it aloft for a few precious moments. Setting her mug on the table beside her, she turned to him as he leaped up the few steps to the deck with a grace that belied his size.

At the top of the deck stairs, he stopped, gazing at her like a human might rather than rushing forward like a dog. Still, unbridled pleasure filled his eyes, a pleasure that burst in her chest with utter delight. Grinning, Natalie held out her hand.

"I'm so glad to see you," she said quietly, not wanting to wake Rick or the neighbors.

The dog's hesitation lasted all of two seconds more before he strode forward, sliding his massive head between her waiting hands. How was it possible she'd missed him so profoundly when she'd only met him once before? Yet that's exactly how she felt.

Stroking the thick, soft fur on the sides of his neck, emotion welled up inside of her, a strange mix of grief and sorrow, and peace. As if the sheer power of his soul tore away the protective defenses she'd been struggling to build around her misery, then lifted the grief itself, helping her to carry it.

A fanciful notion. And yet stroking his fur, gazing into those intelligent eyes, she felt as if she'd somehow grabbed hold of the anchor she'd been struggling so unsuccessfully to find. She'd always heard that pets had an amazing ability to ground and calm humans, but she'd never expected to feel such a visceral reaction to an animal she barely knew.

"I needed your visit, today," she said quietly. "I already feel better. Lighter. Stronger."

If possible, the look in those golden eyes deepened.

"Who are you? You don't wear a collar or dog tag, yet you can't be wild, can you? You're far too comfortable with humans." As he sat, she ran her fingers between his forelegs, scratching his chest. "Whatever your situation, you're certainly thriving. Look at you. You're well fed. Truly gorgeous."

While she stroked his head with one hand, Natalie sipped her coffee with the other, marveling that what she'd told him was true. She felt one hundred percent more capable of handling the day than she had when she'd first awakened. She felt almost calm again.

Or she did until the big animal stiffened, suddenly, and leaped to his feet. Hackles rising, he turned toward her back door, a low, deadly growl rumbling from his throat.

Wulfe smelled the male before he saw him through the screen door. The fiancé.

Instinct, or maybe jealousy, had him growling.

"For God's sakes, Natalie," the man exclaimed. "He's a wolf!"

Natalie's soft hand slid through the fur on Wulfe's neck. If he were a cat, he'd be purring. Deep inside, the wolf animal spirit that had marked him howled with pleasure.

"He's a dog and a friend. He won't hurt me, Rick."

Hell no, he wouldn't hurt her. He'd kill anyone who tried to hurt her. He'd just come to check on her, to make sure she was okay after all she'd gone through in Harpers Ferry. Xavier worried about her. They both did.

His gaze shifted back to the man behind the screen door. The prick just stood there, making no move whatsoever to protect his female. And, okay, that wasn't entirely fair since Wulfe had made it more than clear he wouldn't hurt the female. And more than clear he didn't like the male. It wasn't that he didn't like him. He just didn't like it that, standing there in nothing but boxers, the male had almost certainly come from Natalie's bed.

"Natalie, please. Come inside? You said you didn't want to talk about it last night, but we need to. I feel like I'm losing you."

Wulfe felt Natalie's tension through her hands, and it was all he could do not to growl at the fiancé again because he really, really wanted the man to go away and let him enjoy these few minutes with Natalie. He loved having her hands on him, even if it was just in his furred state. Only in his dreams was he free to touch her back. Not only was she engaged to the prick, but Wulfe would scare her half to death if he revealed his human face. So he'd take what he could.

It was so good to see her again, to smell her sweet scent and to drown, even for a few moments, in those calm gray eyes. She was so lovely, the morning sun turning her hair a bright gold, bathing her entire body in rich color. Even with his wolf's far-less-color-sensitive eyesight, he could see the sun's light creating the illusion of an aura—gold, blue, and green.

"Nat, I understand you've been through hell. I know you're grieving for your brother and your friends. I'm trying to be here for you, but you're shutting me out."

Still, she didn't answer, but Wulfe had a front row view of her expression, and he saw the sorrow in her eyes. The sadness. And his heart gave a painful squeeze.

Finally, with a sigh, Natalie rose. "Go home, boy."

Instead, he sat, staking a claim, though on what . . . or who . . . he wasn't sure. Natalie was not his.

With a wry smile, Natalie stroked his head, then brushed past him and walked inside, closing the screen door. As Wulfe watched, she pressed her palms to the other man's face, filling Wulfe with a sharp, piercing jealousy.

"I love you, Rick. I just need time."

"You're different, Nat."

Mentally, Wulfe blinked. She *was* different. And not in the way her fiancé meant. That sunrise glow—the gold, green, and blue aura—had followed her inside. Even out of the sunshine, it clung to her flesh, bright against the dark shadows of her living room.

What the hell?

Natalie dropped her gaze to the other man's bare chest. "Rick . . ." She shook her head. "You'd be different, too, if you'd lost days, and friends. If your brother was missing." She looked up, meeting the man's gaze. "I have dreams . . . the most terrifying dreams. Sometimes I think I'm beginning to remember some of it, but the things I remember . . . aren't possible."

Wulfe gave a loud mental groan. The *last* thing they needed was for Natalie Cash to remember seeing shape-shifters and wraith Daemons and the inside of Feral House. Not that she'd be able to find it. Probably. And not that anyone else would believe her. Still . . .

"Nat, if you remember something, you have to tell the cops."

"They're just dreams, Rick."

The man ran a frustrated hand through his hair, mussing it even more, then held out that hand to her. "Come back to bed, Natalie."

For a moment, Wulfe thought she'd say no. Instead, she turned back to the screen door, to him, that odd aura clinging to her. "Go home, boy."

Was he really seeing something, or were the changes that had been coming over him of late affecting his vision, now, too? Maybe it was just his wolf's eyesight that was affected, but he couldn't very well shift to human form to check. Not when his clothes were in his truck on the other side of the woods.

With a growl of frustration, he leaped off the deck and headed back into the trees. Natalie's odd glow was probably just a factor of his own vision—either a side effect of the Ferals' endangered immortality, or the Daemon blood within his own heritage that had begun to stir to life.

But his gut gnawed at him, the possibility raising its head that she really was glowing. That perhaps she'd been changed in some way by the Daemon who'd attacked her six weeks ago. He needed to get someone out here to take a look at her without alarming anyone. Because if Natalie Cash *had* been changed, and the humans started to see it, she could endanger the anonymity of the immortal races. Which could endanger her life.

Hell. She didn't deserve this.

Leaping over a rotting log, he ran through the woods, his wolf's paws quick and sure. The forest scents played in his senses, the smell of moss and leaves, of rabbit and spring dawn, pleasing the animal. But his mind remained firmly on Natalie.

He'd first met her on that field of battle where the evil Mage had captured her and her friends to use as Daemon bait. He'd noticed her because she was pretty, but also because her stoicism in the face of such horror had drawn his respect. In the end, only three of the six humans had survived, and the Ferals had taken them back to Feral House and locked them up until they could steal their memories of all they'd seen. They'd only succeeded with the two women, and had subsequently sent them home. But Xavier was blind, and memories were stolen through the eyes. He could never go home again. And Natalie could never know that her brother remained alive. No one could.

Her grief made Wulfe ache.

Clearing the woods on the other side, he loped down the hillside to the deserted warehouse outside Frederick, Maryland, where he'd parked his truck. Sending his wolf's senses outward, he reassured himself no humans lurked about, then shifted, calling on the power of the animal spirit that lived within him

to change back into a man in a rush of joy and sparkling colored lights. The June morning was warm,
the birds twittering in the trees above as the sun
slowly rose in the east.

As he rounded the cab to fetch his clothes out of
the open bed, he caught a glimpse of himself in the
window—the crooked nose set among nearly two
dozen scars, one of which slashed across his mouth,
tugging his lip downward, giving him the appearance of a perpetual scowl. His was a face that made
women scream, a face that sent children running into
the night.

With a sigh, he tugged on his jeans. He hadn't
always been this way, of course. Centuries ago, in
his youth, women had sighed over his beauty, claiming him the most handsome of males. At seven feet
tall, he'd towered over his competition in every way.
Despite that, he'd never thought himself vain or arrogant, which in hindsight had probably been the
height of conceit. The fates had punished him for his
hubris. In a single day he'd lost it all—his looks, the
admiration of his peers, his self-respect. The goddess
had, in her terrible wisdom, declared his soul flawed,
then marked him so that everyone would know it.
Marks he'd carried for centuries now, and would for
the rest of his immortal life.

He shrugged into his T-shirt, then pulled on his
boots. At least the wolf animal spirit hadn't found
him lacking. Three years after the scarring, the sole
wolf shifter had died, and he'd been marked to be
the next. It was said that the animal spirit always
chose the individual it considered to be the strongest and most honorable among those of the Therian
race that still possessed wolf-shifter DNA. So Wulfe

had learned to give thanks for the goddess's painful lesson. He'd been taught a terrible humility, then been rewarded for embracing it.

The lesson had been a steep price to pay, but he'd pay it again a hundred times over if it meant remaining a Feral Warrior, one of only a handful of shapeshifters left in the world. At the moment, the Ferals were all that stood between the races of the Earth, both immortal and human, and destruction by the Daemons, if the soulless Mage succeeded in freeing the fiends, as they were determined to do.

Wulfe dug his keys out of the pocket of his jeans and let himself into the cab.

If only he could keep Natalie safely out of this war. But the way she was glowing . . .

He shook his head, his heart heavy as he started the truck and headed home to Feral House.

Natalie Cash wasn't safe at all.

Chapter Two

Wulfe pulled his truck into the wide circular drive of Feral House in Great Falls, Virginia. The three-story brick mansion was set among the trees in this upscale neighborhood near the Potomac River a dozen miles outside of Washington, D.C. Vehicles lined the drive, the house itself overflowing with people now. Lyon had recruited a large contingent of nonshifting immortals, Therian Guards, to back up the Ferals in their rapidly escalating battle to keep the Mage from freeing the Daemons.

Most of the Therian Guards hailed from the British Isles, and the strongest twenty had been moved into Feral House to help protect the Radiant. They'd quickly filled the extra bedrooms, the rest bunking on sofas and pallets in the living room, media room, and basement. Another 137 took up every spare bed in the local Therian enclaves and in the safe houses dotting the area.

While it rankled that the Ferals needed backup, not a one had argued against the move. Not when the enemy had Ferals of his own, now—fully functioning, if evil, immortal shape-shifters—while the original Ferals' immortality had been badly compromised.

As Wulfe parked behind Kougar's Lamborghini, the early-morning sun reflected off the dew still coating the roof shingles, making them sparkle. If only he'd find the mood inside as bright. If only they'd made a breakthrough in finding a way to reclaim their immortality while he was gone. But as he walked through the front door and saw the haggard faces of Tighe and Paenther as the pair descended one of the twin curved stairs that bracketed the huge foyer, that hope was dashed.

"Where've you been?" Paenther asked, his tone only mildly curious.

Several men and two women nodded as they passed. He recognized them only because Lyon had made them memorize the faces of the Guards. The house was full of the low murmur of voices, but the Guards were well disciplined and eminently respectful of the Ferals, and the place had not become the madhouse they'd feared. So far, the only real problem had been keeping them all fed.

"You went to Frederick, am I right?" Tighe's short blond hair gleamed brightly beneath the light of the chandeliers as he reached the bottom step and reached out an arm, clasping Wulfe's at the elbow as their forearms slapped in the greeting of the Ferals.

Wulfe didn't deny it. "I couldn't sleep."

Paenther greeted Wulfe in the same fashion, his jet-black hair framing a face that looked one hundred percent American Indian, though the warrior was only three-quarters. Slashed across one eye were three long scars, what appeared to be claw marks and were in fact feral marks. Each of the warriors had them somewhere on their bodies, the mark of the animal spirits that lived inside them. Wulfe's own feral marks were on his forehead above his left eye. But he doubted even his brothers knew that. What were three scars among so many?

"Did you see Natalie?" Tighe asked. All Wulfe's brothers knew why he went to Frederick.

He opened his mouth to confide what he'd seen, then closed it again. The Shaman would know better than anyone else if there was something wrong with Natalie. Or with *him*, for that matter. Until that ancient male had a chance to look at her, he'd keep it to himself. The last thing Natalie needed was to be dragged back into his world and this mess, even if the thought of her in his life again sent a thrill of excitement winging through his mind. Xavier seemed content enough helping Pink in the kitchens and remaining a virtual prisoner of Feral House, but Xavier was a rare case. Most humans would never accept imprisonment for a lifetime. And Wulfe didn't want that for Natalie. If for some reason they couldn't take her memories and let her go again, she might wind up with the same choice Xavier had been given—life as a servant of the Ferals, or death.

She had a life, a home, a fiancé, and he wouldn't steal those things from her, not if he had any other choice. He prayed that glow had just been his own vision messing with him.

"I saw her," Wulfe admitted. "She's developed a soft spot for the wolf." The memory of her sweet smile as she'd greeted him, her soft hands in his fur, tugged the corners of his mouth upward. Until he remembered . . . His mouth turned hard. "She wasn't alone."

"Her fiancé?"

"Neither of them seemed very happy. He accused her of changing."

Paenther snorted. "The woman went through hell. Of course it changed her."

Tighe peered at Wulfe. "Is she starting to remember anything?"

"I don't think so though she may be reliving some of it in her dreams. But even if she doesn't remember, she knows her friends are dead. She knows her brother's missing."

"So she knows something terrible happened during the days she lost." Paenther's mouth tightened. "Sometimes the not knowing is the hardest." He clasped Wulfe's shoulder. "She'll be okay."

"It's nice of you to keep an eye on her." Tighe clasped his other shoulder.

"Have you seen the Shaman?" Wulfe asked, as Paenther started toward the dining room.

Tighe's eyes narrowed. Stripes always saw too much.

"He's still asleep, I imagine," Kougar said, entering the foyer from a different hallway behind them. "He and Ariana were up until dawn."

Kougar's mate, Ariana, and the Shaman had been working tirelessly to figure out a way to counter the effects of the dark charm the evil Mage, Inir, had somehow snuck into Feral House, a curse that was rendering them mortal. They'd found the charm—a chunk of crystal of some sort—and destroyed it. But the damage had already been done.

"Any luck?" Tighe asked.

Kougar shook his head, not bothering to elaborate as he strode past them, following Paenther down the hallway to the dining room. No elaboration was necessary. How many ways were there to say, *We're fucked*?

As Wulfe moved to follow Kougar, Tighe stopped him with a hand to his arm, his gaze sharp. "What's up, buddy? What's really going on with Natalie?"

"Would you quit being so damned perceptive?" Wulfe growled.

Sympathy tightened Tighe's expression, but he didn't give way.

Wulfe sighed. "She has an aura, a bright blue, green, and gold one. I've never seen anything like it, on her or anyone else."

"Have you ever seen auras?"

"No. Maybe it's just another of my newly awakened, strange-ass Daemon talents."

"But you're worried something's wrong with her."

"Yeah." Hell, it was twisting his gut in knots.

Tighe nodded with quiet understanding and clasped his shoulder again. "Maybe we can convince the Shaman to drive out there with us later and take a look at her."

Wulfe stiffened. "I'd scare her half to death."

"You don't know that. She wasn't scared of you the last time she saw you."

"She'd just been attacked by a Daemon. And she doesn't remember any of that, now. Or me."

Tighe's expression turned thoughtful. "It might be

safest if the Shaman knocked on her door alone. He can pretend to be a kid selling popcorn or cookies or something. Kids are always coming by here selling popcorn or cookies." The Shaman might be thousands of years old, but thanks to a Mage attack in his youth, he still looked fifteen.

"Okay. Thanks, Stripes."

Together they headed to the dining room, stepping through the archway into the large, formal room. Around the mammoth dining table sat most of the other Ferals and their wives. Only Lyon was missing. And his mate, their Radiant, Kara.

Zeeland alone among the Guards sat at the dining table with the Ferals. One of the highest-ranking, he was a close personal friend of a couple of the Ferals. To Wulfe's knowledge, no one had ever told the other Therian Guards that they weren't welcome at the main table, but they seemed happy enough out on the patio where the morning sun filtered through the summer trees, or at one of several card tables that had been set up in the open space between the main table and the hallway.

As Wulfe and Tighe started across the dining room, Tighe's mate, Delaney, strolled out of the swinging door to the kitchen, a tray of sweet rolls in her hand that she placed on one of the card tables. Seeing Tighe, she smiled and joined them.

Tighe hooked his arm around her shoulders. "How's it going in there?"

Delaney's smile turned rueful. "As well as can be expected with five women and one blind male in the kitchen. Pink's not happy, but with so many mouths to feed, she needs the extra hands, and she knows it. Some of the Guards have offered to help with the cooking, but that was a complete nonstarter. Pink won't even let them in the kitchen." She shrugged. "We're handling it."

Tighe gave her a quick kiss. "Don't overdo it."

She grinned at him. "I may be pregnant, but I'm immortal, now, remember?"

Tighe grinned back at his wife. "And I thank the goddess every day for that."

With a low laugh, Delaney headed back to the kitchen. As Wulfe and Tighe neared the main table, the other Ferals rose, greeting them as if it had been weeks and not hours since they'd seen one another. Humans rarely understood the need that the animals—most of the animals—had for touch. Hawke and Falkyn could take it or leave it, as could Vhyper. But the cats and canines were another matter.

Despite the warmth of the greeting and the sunshine pouring in through the back windows, the mood in the room felt heavy and thick with frustration. No one at the main table spoke as Wulfe grabbed a plate from the stack in the middle and began stabbing thick slabs of smoked ham off of one of the platters. Out of the corner of his eye, he spied Xavier coming toward the table from the kitchen, a pitcher of juice in one hand, a blind man's cane in the other. Wulfe's gut tightened at the sight of Natalie's brother.

"Three more steps head-on, X-man," Jag said.

Xavier, the only bright spot in the room, grinned and took three more steps. Jag lifted the pitcher out of his hand. "Thanks, dude."

"X . . ." Wulfe said, pushing himself from his seat and joining Xavier as the young man made his way back to the kitchen. "I stopped by to check on Natalie this morning."

Xavier's face fell, his expression hiding nothing. "Is she okay?"

"She looked good. Her fiancé was with her." Not lies, not really. Natalie had looked lovely. And her relationship with her fiancé would probably be fine.

"That's good. I'm glad she has someone to help her through this."

"Me, too. Just thought you'd like to know."

The kid grinned. "Thanks, dude." Dude, always dude.

"You're welcome, dude." And now he had them saying it.

He saw no need to share his worries with Xavier since the kid could never leave Feral House to see his sister again; nor could she ever know he still lived. They occupied two different worlds, now. Xavier and Wulfe one, Natalie the another. It was a fact Wulfe would do well to remember himself.

Returning to the table, he took his seat across from Fox and his new mate, Melisande, and dug into his meal.

"Everyone still able to shift?" Paenther asked, his tone nonchalant even as a thread of tension ran through his words.

It was no idle question. The Ferals had been at war with the Mage pretty much from the dawn of time except for a small period five millennia ago when the two immortal races had pooled their combined power and magic to defeat the High Daemon, Satanan, imprisoning him and his entire Daemon horde in a magical prison, the Daemon Blade. But some years ago, the powerful Mage, Inir, had become infected with a wisp of Satanan's consciousness left behind all those millennia ago, a consciousness that had grown within Inir until they suspected that Satanan himself now directed the Mage in the battle to free himself and his horde from that blade.

The primary thing needed in order to accomplish that was the unanimous consent of all the Feral Warriors, a thing the real Ferals would never give. But Inir had found a way around that. He'd created a small band of evil Ferals, and now slowly destroyed the good ones through the curse that was turning them mortal and would soon, they feared, steal their ability to shift into their animals, if not steal their lives. They suspected that the charm had been made with Daemon magic, the most powerful force on Earth. Unfortunately, none of the usual methods of clearing the magic had worked. All they could do now was search for a cure. And pray they found it in time.

Wulfe was shoveling his last bite into his mouth when Lyon strolled into the dining room, Kara in his arms, tucked neatly against his chest. Though of average height, the woman looked tiny within the arms of her powerful mate. And very ill thanks to another of Inir's diabolical attacks. But her arm was hooked around Lyon's neck, her tired eyes bright with pleasure as she spotted the rest of the Ferals. As one, they rose and went to greet her.

Wulfe kissed her on the forehead, squeezing her hand, as Kougar patted her knee. One after another, they silently told their beloved Radiant how much they cared until her eyes were shining with unshed tears.

The Radiant was the one woman in all the world who could pull the energies from the earth that allowed the Ferals to access the power of their animals, to shift. Without that radiance, even without a dark charm fucking up the works, they'd eventually weaken and die, though it would take time—a couple of years.

But Kara had come to mean far more to them than simply their provider of radiance. Though she'd only been with them a short time, and had come to them believing herself human, she'd proved herself brave and loyal beyond compare, stealing all of their hearts, not just the heart of their chief, to whom she was now mated. If anything happened to her, they would all suffer. Lyon would be destroyed.

Lyon pressed a kiss to the top of his mate's head, then joined them at the table, seating Kara to his right.

Kara smiled wearily. "I needed a change of scenery."

"Twenty minutes, no more." Lyon grabbed a plate. "Eggs? You have to eat."

Her smile turned soft as her gaze met her mate's. "You're a tough nurse. But, yes, eggs would be nice."

Lyon's eyes filled with such love as Kara's hand covered his much larger one, that Wulfe almost felt compelled to look away.

Around the table, the Ferals turned to their wives with a kiss or a touch, all moved by the deep love between their chief and his mate, all sharing the fear that the Ferals' days were numbered. Only Wulfe and Vhyper remained single, which was a startling change from a year ago, when Wulfe had been the sole mated male. Nine months ago, his mate Beatrice, their previous Radiant, had been killed in a Mage attack. He'd mourned her, of course. Mating bonds between immortals were physical things that, when broken, damaged the one left behind. And he *had* been damaged in ways he was only beginning to figure out.

The thing was, as he watched his brothers with their mates, he knew that what he'd had with Beatrice had been pale and thin in comparison. Theirs had been a mating decreed by the goddess, as the Radiant's mating always was. He'd hoped it would be a good one, like Lyon and Kara's, but Beatrice had never been able to see past his scars. She'd allowed him to make love to her, but only on occasion, and only in full dark. He'd often suspected she'd fancied herself the Ferals' queen and he the one designated to serve her sexual needs. But she'd never really wanted him. And he was certain she'd never loved him.

No, their relationship had not been satisfying to either of them, and while the severing of their mating bond had damaged him, her loss hadn't crushed him as it should have.

As his gaze roamed the table, skipping from Hawke's stroke of Falkyn's cheek to Paenther's eyes as he gazed at Skye, to Melisande's head tipped against Fox's shoulder and the soft kiss he placed on her crown, he felt an ache deep in his chest. An emptiness. A loneliness that he'd rarely felt so sharply. Because there was a woman that his heart had begun to long for. A human engaged to another. A woman who could not be his.

Natalie.

Jag dropped his fork suddenly, with a startling clatter, his face a mask of alarm.

Olivia grabbed his hand. "What's the matter?"

"My animal . . ." He shoved to his feet so fast his chair fell back, slamming against the floor. With quick, hard strides, he moved away from the table, his back to them, ramrod straight, his fists clenched at his sides. Suddenly, he whirled to face them, his face a mask of shock, quickly turning to fury.

"I can't fucking shift!"

The room went silent, even the Guards quieting. As one, the Ferals exchanged glances, the ramification of Jag's statement rushing over them simultaneously.

Deep inside, Wulfe's animal growled as if he understood. And he probably did.

"It's begun," Kougar murmured.

They were losing their immortality. Now, their animals.

Olivia rose and went to her mate, sliding her arms around Jag's waist as he hauled her close in return.

Did this mean Jag would be the first to die? Goddess help them all. The moment they were gone, there would be nothing to stop Inir and his evil band of Ferals from freeing the Daemons.

Paenther asked the question they were all thinking. "Maybe we need to attack Inir's stronghold while most of us can still shift, Roar."

Lyon eyed his second-in-command with a hard sigh. "Don't think I haven't considered it. If I really thought we'd never recover, we'd move now, but I refuse to believe that. Attacking fully functioning Ferals as mortals is akin to suicide. And I'm not leading you in there to die. Not if we have any other choice."

Kougar leaned back in his chair. "There's a good chance Ariana has the answers in her head. She just has to find them." Within the Queen of the Ilinas' mind was amassed all of the knowledge of the queens who'd come before her. "As she's fond of telling me, her personal encyclopedia of knowledge is neither indexed nor easily browsed. But if the answers are in there, Ariana will find them."

"If," Tighe muttered. "And even if she does, will it be in time?"

Fox rose and strode to Jag, gripping his shoulder, concern etched into the hard planes of his face.

There were no words of comfort, and they all knew it. Jag might be the first, but the others would follow. If they didn't find a way to reverse the dark charm's curse soon, they were all going to die. And Satanan and his terrifying horde would rise.

After breakfast, Wulfe shifted into his animal and curled up outside the Shaman's bedroom door so he wouldn't miss his waking. At half past noon, Wulfe finally heard the Shaman stir, and leaped up. As he trotted back to his own room, he called to Tighe telepathically, a form of communication only possible when one or the other of them was in his animal, and only when they were in relatively close proximity.

The Shaman's awake. If he's willing, do you still want to go with us to Frederick?

I'll meet you in the foyer in five, Tighe replied.

Reaching his bedroom, Wulfe shifted and dressed, and was just striding back down the upstairs hall when the door he'd been lying in front of opened, and the male he'd been waiting for stepped out.

The Shaman was unique in many ways—more an-

cient than the pyramids and gifted with an ability to
sense magic that most Therians lacked. He looked
like a young teenager from a couple of centuries past,
his hair long and tied at his nape, his long-sleeved
white shirt ruffled. But while his face remained
youthful, lacking even the ability to grow a beard, his
eyes held an unmistakable wisdom and compassion.

"Shaman, may I have a word?"

"Good morning, Wulfe. Yes, of course."

Wulfe told him briefly about the odd glow. At the
Shaman's frown, a fist formed in his stomach.

"I need to see her," the ancient said.

"I can't bring her here. Can you spare a little time?"

"Yes, of course. I would enjoy the drive. The road
often clears my mind."

"Good. Great. Do you want to eat first?" He was
in a hurry to get going . . . it had been *hours,* but the
male deserved to get some lunch if he wanted to.

"If you'll stop by Starbucks on the way out, I'm
ready."

"Deal. Let's go."

They found Tighe waiting for them in the foyer, an
unopened package of Oreo cookies in his hand. "I
told Delaney where we're going and why," he said,
as the three headed out to Wulfe's truck. "They can
send Ilinas for us if they need us in a hurry."

Ilina travel was a bitch. It might be fast as lightning,
since the Ilinas' natural state was mist, but it was a
head-spinning, stomach-turning ride that they'd all
rather avoid.

Wulfe and Tighe piled into the front seats of the
truck. As the Shaman climbed in the back, Tighe
handed him the Oreos. "When we get there, knock
on Natalie's door and tell her you're selling cook-

ies. Human kids do it all the time." Tighe glanced at Wulfe ruefully. "Delaney rolled her eyes when I told her the plan. She said brownies sell cookies. What the hell does that mean? When I asked if we had any brownies, D just laughed and waved me out of the kitchen."

"It's got to be a human thing."

"Clearly." Tighe glanced at him carefully. "Any chance what you saw at Natalie's has something to do with your Daemon blood?"

Wulfe's entire body went tense, the question hanging in the air like a rancid thought. "Maybe. Hell if I know." The evidence kept growing that he really did have Daemon blood, but he sure as fuck wasn't accepting that gracefully. *Daemons*, the most evil, vile creatures to roam the Earth, *and he was one of them?* Okay, maybe not entirely. Any Daemon ancestor of his had to have lived more than five thousand years ago. Even for an immortal, that had to be generations and generations ago. Still . . . how was he supposed to accept that he was part *Daemon*?

He'd thought it just a rumor that his wolf clan was descended from those monsters. He'd never believed it, not for an instant, not until a week ago, when he alone had been able to see the labyrinthine warding Inir had used to protect his stronghold in the mountains of West Virginia—warding riddled with Daemon magic. He alone had been able to get his Feral brothers through the worst of it. And even more damning, he alone had begun to hear Inir and Satanan conversing . . . *in Inir's head*. Satanan hadn't even risen yet. He still only existed within Inir's body, little more than a wisp of consciousness. Yet, Wulfe continued to hear the two of them chatting from time to time.

Finally, he'd stopped denying the obvious and accepted that he had Daemon blood. After all, good or bad, it gave him advantages the Ferals needed in this war against Inir, and increasingly, against Satanan himself. Still, what it meant for him in the grander scheme of things, he had no idea. And it was freaking the hell out of him.

Wulfe turned on the radio to his favorite country-music station, and the three lapsed into silence, each lost to his own thoughts. Twice the Shaman called Ariana, suggesting she research specific events that Wulfe had never heard of—the incarceration of the King of Marck in the Buldane pit, and the plague of Opplomere. As promised, the ride appeared to be helping the Shaman think.

All it did was make Wulfe more impatient to get back to Natalie.

They were only a couple of miles outside Frederick when Wulfe began to hear the voices again. The hair rose on his arms.

If you'd killed the Radiant when you had her, you wouldn't be having this trouble. You could have simply stolen the new one.

That's assuming I could identify the new Radiant and catch her before she reached the Ferals, my lord. An unlikelihood. Besides, I needed the current Radiant to bring my new Ferals into their animals. This will work. We have Radiant's blood. Just not unascended Radiant's blood. My sorcerers will find a way to make it what it must be. I've already felt the first of the Ferals' lights go out. One is no longer registering as a shifter. Once the others follow, and we've perfected the blood, you and your horde will be freed.

Wulfe's hands clenched around the steering wheel

at the disclosure of Inir's grand plan. The ritual to free the Daemons required the blood of an un-ascended Radiant—a newbie, which Kara hadn't been in months. As long as they kept Kara safe, they'd assumed Inir couldn't perform the ritual. Apparently, they'd assumed wrong.

"Wulfe?"

At the sharp note in Tighe's voice, Wulfe glanced at his friend.

"You're about to snap the steering wheel. What's up?"

"I heard Inir and Satanan again."

"And?"

Wulfe told Tighe and the Shaman what he'd heard. Tighe growled, pulled out his phone, and called Lyon, relaying the information.

Wulfe glanced at Tighe when he'd disconnected the call. "What did Lyon say?"

"Not much. He's still not giving up on finding the ritual to make us mortal again."

Wulfe just hoped they found it in time.

Minutes later, as they drove slowly past Natalie's house, Wulfe felt something sigh inside of him. His wolf gave a whine of excitement at the prospect of seeing her again, but both man and animal spirit were going to be disappointed this time. Only the Shaman would be going up to the door.

Wulfe parked his pickup across the street and turned off the ignition, forcing himself to stay put while the Shaman climbed out of the truck and crossed the street, cookies in hand.

"Do you think she's home?" Tighe asked.

"We've wasted two hours if she isn't. It's Sunday. Xavier says she's an optometrist with a practice in town. Sunday and Monday are her days off."

"Doesn't mean she's home."

"Doesn't mean she's not."

"She could be running errands."

"She could be doing any of a hundred things."

They were both watching the Shaman ring the doorbell, neither paying any attention to the conversation, which had devolved quickly.

Be home, Natalie. He needed the Shaman to tell him that she was fine. *Please let her be fine.* She deserved that, deserved a life without the threat of Daemons though if the Ferals didn't find a way to stop Inir, all humans would soon know that terror.

The door opened. Wulfe's heart began to thud in his chest. *Natalie.* She stood in the doorway in a pair of white shorts that accentuated her long, long legs, and a soft blue T-shirt that highlighted the blues and greens in her shockingly bright aura. At least he knew it hadn't been a trick of his wolf's eyesight. Dammit.

Tighe whistled. "That's some glow."

"You can see it."

"Clear as day."

Crud. Strike two. He'd really hoped it was him.

As he watched, the Shaman reached out his hand as if to shake hers. Natalie looked bemused, but she shook the proffered hand with a friendly smile. Probably, human children didn't shake hands with their cookie customers. A moment later, she turned away but didn't close the door, and the Shaman continued to stand there. When she returned, she handed the Shaman what appeared to be a few dollars and he, in turn, handed her the Oreos, shook her hand again, and turned away.

"Well?" Wulfe demanded as the ancient male climbed into the truck a minute later.

"I sense Daemon energy though what that means, I do not know. It may be a lingering effect of the energy all of you were exposed to on the battlefield in Harpers Ferry."

"Then all three of the humans who survived that battle might have been affected. Xavier hasn't shown any signs of it, yet," Wulfe said.

Tighe grunted. "We'll have to send someone to check on the screamer." The teen, Christy, had done little but scream the entire time she'd been in their prison. "Can we leave Natalie in the human world looking like that?"

"I believe so," the Shaman said. "Few humans can see auras. But someone should keep an eye on her."

Wulfe eyed him sharply.

The Shaman held up his hand. "Just keep an eye on her."

Tighe glanced over, met Wulfe's gaze. "It might be safer to bring her back to Feral House."

"No." The word left his throat like a shot. Lyon would only command her locked up in their prisons again. While the Ferals never took human life without reason, Daemon energy might be deemed reason enough. He wouldn't risk it. "She stays here."

Tighe nodded, sympathy in his eyes as if he'd heard the thoughts rolling through Wulfe's head.

Wulfe turned to the Shaman. "How do we cure her?"

"I have no idea." The Shaman sighed. "I'm sorry, Wulfe. My expertise is Mage magic, not Daemon."

Tighe reached over and clasped Wulfe's shoulder. "You've had worse assignments than keeping an eye on a beautiful woman."

In truth, there was nothing he'd enjoy more than

watching over *this* woman even if he'd have to remain in his animal to do it. "I wonder if she'll let a wolf in the house," he mused. It might be worth a try. Tonight, he'd find out.

When they got back to Feral House, Tighe took him aside. "Be careful, buddy."

Wulfe lifted a brow.

"She's human."

"So?"

"I'm just saying, you're strung tight about this. I knew you had a soft spot for her, but I think it's more than that. A lot more."

Wulfe's jaw tightened. "It doesn't matter. She belongs to another male, and even if she didn't, my severed mating bond has screwed me up good." Not to mention, he didn't know what in the hell was going on with his Daemon blood. He shook his head. "I'd never pursue her."

Deep inside, his wolf whined unhappily.

Tighe nodded. "It would be best if you kept your distance. Then maybe, when this is over, you can forget about her."

That was just it, though. He couldn't forget about her. Not for one damned minute.

Tighe shrugged. "I'm just saying, humans don't live long, buddy."

Wulfe snorted. "The way things are going, neither do we."

But he understood Tighe's concern, and he shared it. The last thing he wanted or needed was to have his heart ripped out of his chest in fifty or sixty years—a blink of an eye if he managed to get his immortality back. Because fifty or sixty years was all Natalie had. Maybe far, far less.

The rain started just as Wulfe pulled to a stop behind the deserted warehouse. It was early evening, approaching sunset, though the sun was hidden behind thick rain clouds. He turned off the ignition and climbed out, tossing his keys beneath the vehicle so the rain didn't ruin the electronics. Stripping, he shoved his boots and clothes into the backseat, then locked the doors and shifted into his wolf.

A thrill of pleasure snaked its way through him as he reflected on the fact that Lyon had officially given him the job of keeping an eye on Natalie Cash. Unfortunately, there was really nothing else for him to do. Not unless word came of another newly marked Feral for them to hunt down and throw in the prison beneath Feral House. Or they got a lead on the two escaped new Ferals, Grizz and Lepard.

Wulfe trotted through the woods, the rain soaking his fur and his mood, because there was zero chance Natalie would come out to see him this time, and slim to no chance she'd let a soaking-wet wolf into her house. Otherwise, he didn't mind the rain. The day had been warm, and the cool rain felt good against his hide.

They'd tracked down the screamer, Christy, without much trouble and confirmed that she had no odd glow. Nor did Xavier. Which meant that whatever was going on with Natalie was hers alone.

Inside, his wolf gave a howl of misery. Neither man nor animal spirit liked it, not one bit.

As he reached the edge of the woods, he eyed the house with the yellow siding that he knew to be hers. The kitchen light was on, but he couldn't see any sign of Natalie. Wait. There she was. She crossed the kitchen, the overhead light turning her hair to gold. His stomach did a little flip, but as he sat on the wet ground, the rain splattering against his snout, his heart felt heavy in his chest.

Natalie had already been through so much, even if she didn't remember most of it. She wasn't supposed to be in danger anymore, yet in his gut he felt it circling around her. The need to protect her clawed at his insides.

Somehow, he had to get her to let him in.

As the rain pattered against her kitchen windows, Natalie dropped the last teaspoonful of apple-spice cookie dough onto the baking sheet in front of her, slipped the cookie sheet into the oven, and set the timer. Baking had always been her comfort activity, that and work, and both were getting her through now. In the month since the incident, she'd made a dozen cakes, two dozen pans of brownies, and at least sixteen different cookie recipes. Her neighbors were starting to complain that she was trying to fatten them up, but she had to do something with the fruits of her crisis since she ate few sweets herself.

And there was no doubt she was in crisis. Especially after this morning.

Leaning back against the kitchen counter, she wrapped her arms around herself and closed her eyes, fighting back the thoughts that constantly flayed her— the days she had no memory of, the police investigation that continued to go nowhere. And the pounding, grinding grief. The police believed Xavier was dead, and she refused to accept that, but where was he?

She blinked back the tears that burned her eyes and turned to the sink to wash her mixing bowls. Her

gaze caught on the package of Oreos, drawing a bemused smile and a disbelieving shake of her head.
What had made the teen come to her door selling
store-bought cookies? He'd almost certainly been up
to something though she hadn't sensed anything ma-
licious. She'd detected a faint accent in his voice, so
perhaps he'd been an immigrant or exchange student
looking for a little extra cash and going about it in
an odd way. Or he might have been a drama student
having a little lighthearted fun with her. She probably wouldn't have actually bought the cookies, but
she'd always been very, very good at reading eyes,
and in his she'd seen a wealth of kindness.

She loved looking at people's eyes. Perhaps because
she was an optometrist. Or maybe that was part of
the reason she'd become an optometrist in the first
place. She'd never been entirely sure. But from the
day her youngest brother had been born blind, she'd
been fascinated with eyes.

Oh, Xavier, how I miss you.

The ache beneath her breastbone pulsed so harshly
it nearly doubled her over, the grief overwhelming
her in that instant. *Breathe. Just breathe.*

Slowly, she pushed past it and began to clean up the
kitchen. By the time she was done, the smell of freshly
baking cookies filled the air but did little to tempt her.
After what had happened this morning, her appetite
was well and truly gone. She'd done the right thing, she
knew that. But never in her life had she felt so alone.

If only her mom were in town. Picking up the phone,
she made the call she'd been putting off all day.

"Natalie," her mother said, her voice breathless
with both hope and dread as it always was these
days. "Any news?"

"Not about Xavier." If only she had some good news to share. "Rick and I called off our engagement this morning."

"Oh . . . honey."

Natalie could hear the scrape of a kitchen chair against tile and imagined her parent sinking onto it, gripping the table unsteadily against this latest blow. The unmistakable sound of sobs filled her ear, and she closed her eyes, wishing she'd been able to deliver this blow in person instead of over the phone. But her mom was in Birmingham, visiting her sister, and planned to stay there another week. Someone was bound to break the news to her long before that if Natalie didn't tell her first.

"Nat?" Aunt Deb's voice rang in her ear suddenly. "Did they find him?"

"No. I broke up with Rick."

"Oh, thank God. The way your mom collapsed I was certain they'd found Xavier's remains."

Natalie cringed at Deb's frank talk. And then her mom was back on the phone.

"*Why*, honey? Why now? You need him."

"I don't know." How could she explain that the relationship had become strained? That as patient and understanding as Rick tried to be, she found little comfort in his presence. He reminded her too much of her life before. And perhaps the real clincher was that she sensed he was working too hard to be patient. He was a good guy, there was no doubt about it. But he missed the old Natalie. He wanted her back. And that woman was gone for good.

He'd stayed over last night, and they hadn't even made love. She hadn't been in the mood. She was never in the mood anymore. Rick hadn't complained, not about that. He rarely complained about anything, but she'd seen the frustration in his eyes. Finally, as he'd dressed to leave, she'd suggested they call off the wedding. Rick had nodded, sadly, as if he'd been thinking the same.

"I need time, Rick," she'd said as she handed him back her engagement ring. "I just need some time alone."

He'd looked at the ring sadly. "If I were the right man for you, Nat, it would be me you needed."

She hadn't been able to argue.

She gave her mom the shortened version, which set off another round of sobs. "We'll talk later, Mom," she said quietly. "The oven timer's about to go off. Give Aunt Deb my love."

In a way, she envied her mother for getting away. A change of scenery would do her good, too. But she had her practice and a full schedule of patients to see this coming week, and for now that would have to be enough. *One foot in front of the other. Just keep moving.* There was little else she could do except pray that someday the ache would ease enough that she'd be able to breathe again.

As she pulled the cookie sheet out of the oven, she heard the low bark of a big dog at her back door. Her mind flashed immediately to her canine buddy and she found a smile pulling at the corners of her mouth at the thought that he'd come to see her again.

Laying the cookie sheet on the stove, she pulled off her oven mitt and hurried to the sliding door to look out. Sure enough, he was sitting in the rain, looking up at her with a hopefulness she could practically feel through the glass. Poor guy. He was soaking wet.

She hesitated to let him in—surely he belonged to

someone in the neighborhood. But why would anyone who loved him let him out to roam in weather like this? He shouldn't be off a leash at all, especially not looking like a monster-sized wolf.

"Hold on, boy," she called through the door, then ran back to her laundry room, where she kept a stack of old towels. Grabbing two fraying bath towels, she laid one on the carpet, then opened the door just enough to let the massive animal in, braced for the invariable dash and shake.

To her surprise, he didn't bound inside, nor did he shake at all. Instead, he walked forward calmly onto the towel, and stopped, watching her expectantly.

"You're amazing." She closed the door behind him, then opened the second towel and rubbed him down. "Someone's trained you well."

The dog looked up, meeting her gaze with a look in his eyes that she could swear was amusement. "You're way too smart for your own good, aren't you, boy?" She knelt in front of him, rubbing down his head and neck, watching the pleasure fill those beautiful eyes. Oddly, he didn't even try to lick her face, which most dogs did given the opportunity. "You're quite the gentleman." She dried his legs and his belly, then finished with a quick rub of his tail.

"There you go. I'm afraid I don't have any dog food, but I have leftovers from dinner. How about chicken and green beans? That shouldn't be too terrible for you. I've also got cookies. Do you have a sweet tooth, boy?"

To her surprise, he shook his head . . . or appeared to. She laughed. "You're really something."

She pulled a wide, shallow plastic food storage container out of the cupboard, then cut up the leftover chicken and green beans and heated them in the microwave just enough to take off the chill. After pouring the mixture into the plastic container, she set it on the floor in the corner.

The big animal looked up at her with an unmistakable gleam of thanks in his eyes, then turned to the food and wolfed it down while she filled another container with water.

She picked up the cake recipe she'd thought to make tonight, but no longer felt driven to continue her baking and set it down again. The animal's presence had calmed her, pulling her back from that edge of desperation that always drove her to bake.

Maybe, instead, she'd try to get some work done. While the dog ate, Natalie grabbed her laptop off the counter and settled on the floral-patterned sofa in her small family room. As she pulled up the file of the first patient she saw on Friday, and the results of the vision tests she'd run on the girl, the tension began to ease out of her shoulders. For the first time all day, she felt like she could breathe freely again. This was what she'd been born to do. It was no wonder, considering she had two younger brothers whose lives had been handicapped by their eyes' inability to function optimally, if at all. Her youngest brother, Xavier, had been born blind, but it was James, only two years her junior, who'd actually had the hardest time thanks to a pair of undiagnosed vision problems that had made it next to impossible for him to learn to read.

By the time James was seen by a developmental optometrist, a specialist who could actually help him, he'd been a freshman in high school, and it had been too late. When she thought back on it, she wanted to shake their family eye doctor who'd seen him every couple of years throughout his childhood, who'd assured her mom that there was nothing wrong with James's eyes, that James could read if he wanted to. And while, technically, he was right—there wasn't anything wrong with his *eyes*—his brain could never make sense of what he saw because he wasn't able to track smoothly across the page or keep from seeing everything slightly double.

Finally, one of his teachers talked her mom into taking him to a vision specialist, but by then James was convinced he was a dull-witted loser and refused the recommended therapy that could have corrected both problems. Though they didn't know it at the time, he'd already found drugs and alcohol. A year later, he dropped out of school and took off. The last time they'd heard from him, he was living in Florida and had been in and out of rehab repeatedly.

While she'd love to find a way to open, quite literally, the eyes of the eye-care establishment as a whole to the benefits of vision therapy, she'd settle for helping the kids she could. No child should be made to feel stupid because of an undiagnosed vision problem.

James had been lost to them for years and now Xavier was gone, too. The ache in her heart was sometimes so sharp, she thought it might rupture that critical organ. She couldn't imagine how much harder this all was on her mom.

The dog trotted through the kitchen, his nails clicking on the linoleum, then padded silently across the carpeted family room to join her.

Natalie smiled. "All through?"

He sat at her feet, then leaned forward to rest his chin on the cushion, pressing against her thigh, as if thanking her. Her heart swelled with adoration. As he looked up at her with soft, liquid eyes, she knew she was in trouble.

"Where's your family, boy?" She ran her hand over his head, stroke after stroke, as those liquid eyes watched her. "If you don't have one, you can live here."

The words were out before she really thought them through, though it wasn't like he could possibly have understood her. She didn't have time for a dog. Still, the thought of his waiting for her at night made something stir inside of her, an excitement and longing for companionship that she hadn't felt in weeks.

"Since you can't tell me your name, I'm afraid I'm going to have to give you a new one. What do you think of King?"

He gave her a disgusted snort and she laughed. "Okay, not King. How about Bruiser?"

He looked away as if he couldn't bear it, making her grin.

"Not Bruiser, then. I'm half tempted to call you Wolf, but the neighbors might think you really are one, and I'm not sure that's a good idea."

But at the sound of the name, he lifted his head expectantly and barked once, low.

"You like Wolf?"

He barked again, his eyes all but laughing at her.

"Okay, Wolf it is. Did someone already give you that name? It certainly fits." She stroked his big head again. Would he be happy here while she was at work all day? Did she really want responsibility for an animal? This animal?

Staring into those kind, intelligent eyes, she knew there was nothing she wanted more.

Her hand sunk into the fur beneath his ear as she stroked his neck. "I'd be honored if you chose to live with me, Wolf, but I understand that you may already have a family. Regardless, you're welcome to visit me anytime."

As Natalie returned to her work, Wolf curled up on the carpet at her feet, a warm, welcome presence. She'd worked for nearly an hour when Wolf suddenly leaped to his feet, baring his teeth, a low growl rumbling deep in his throat.

"What is it, boy? What do you hear?"

The animal met her gaze as if he understood every word she uttered. In those dark eyes, she could swear she read indecision, as if he felt torn between investigating and protecting her. What a wonderful dog.

She placed her laptop on the sofa beside her and rose. "Come on. We'll investigate together."

But he stepped in front of her, blocking her path.

"Wolf, move."

He glanced up at her, his eyes stubborn and determined, and damn if he didn't shake his head again. Which was impossible. He was a dog.

But when she tried to push him out of her way, he refused to budge.

"Wolf . . ."

She heard a bang at the front door, as if someone had thrown something against it. *Or kicked it.* A moment later, her front door splintered and crashed back against the wall. Shock reverberated through her body, her heart leaping with terror because she knew . . . *she knew* . . . that whatever malevolent force had killed her friends and stolen her brother, had come for her again.

Chapter
Four

Wulfe growled low in his wolf's throat as the first
of the Mage sentinels came charging into Natalie's
family room, sword drawn, triumph on his face, and
violence in his eyes.

Wulfe's mind roared with fury that they violated
Natalie's house, that they threatened her safety, even
as he thanked the instincts that had driven him to
check on her this morning. What if he'd waited until
tomorrow morning, then arrived to find her missing?
Or *dead*.

The thought barreled through him, lending furious power to his hind legs as he leaped at the first of
the bastards, crushing the Mage's skull between his
powerful jaws. The last thing he wanted was for Natalie to witness any more violence, but . . . no . . . the
last thing he wanted was for her to become a victim

of it herself. If that meant forcing her to watch him take out her attackers, so be it. He could always clear her memory of the sight later. He hoped.

A second Mage intruder rushed into the room, and a third, and a fourth, all dressed in the tunics of Inir's sentinels. Why were they here? Was it because of her glow?

Wulfe leaped for another of the Mage, killing him, too, as a blade tore through his shoulder from behind. Not good, not when he wasn't healing much better than a mortal these days. Fire licked through his muscles, the pain radiating down his limb. *Son of a bitch.*

"No, don't hurt him!"

As Wulfe turned to tear off the hand of the Mage who'd stabbed him, he saw Natalie grab the wooden lamp off the end table, rip off the shade, and swing it upside down as if she planned to use it as a weapon. Admiration and terror rushed through him in equal measure because she was going to get herself killed.

Not if he took care of these bastards first.

He lunged for the next of the Mage, going for his throat. As the pair crashed to the floor, half a dozen more ran into the room, swords drawn, eyes blank. Soulless.

"Don't kill them," one commanded. "Inir wants them alive."

Them? There was no doubt that Inir . . . or Satanan . . . had felt Wulfe's presence, and his Daemon essence, before. On the mountain, he'd heard Satanan say, *I sense one of mine. Blood calls to blood.*

Hell, the Mage might have followed him here. He might have inadvertently led them right to Natalie.

He leaped for another Mage, taking him down,

then scrambled out of the reach of grasping hands to attack another and another, taking three more blades to the shoulders and side.

In his peripheral vision, he saw Natalie swing her lamp at one of the two Mage who'd cornered her, cracking it against his shoulder. But before she could pull her makeshift weapon back for another swing, the second of her stalkers seized it, wrenched it from her grasp, and grabbed her.

Instantly, she stilled, and Wulfe knew she'd been enthralled. She wouldn't remember anything more of this fight. But they weren't taking her. Over his dead body would they take her.

In a spray of sparkling lights, he shifted to human form, swiped one of the dead Mage's swords off the bloody carpet, then ripped the blade out of another of his attacker's hands. Swinging two blades at once, he took on the remaining Mage. The Ferals avoided killing Mage whenever possible since Mother Nature took their deaths so personally, but he didn't have a choice this time. It was either kill them or escape, but with Natalie enthralled, he'd have to remain human in order to sling her over his shoulder and run. Unfortunately, the draden would almost certainly find him before he could reach his truck and safety, and he'd be forced to shift back to wolf or die, simply delaying the inevitable fight to the death with the Mage. Better to do it here, now. Mother Nature was just going to have to be pissed.

One by one, his attackers died beneath his blades. Outside, the wind began to howl like a freight train bearing down on the house. By the time only two Mage remained, his opponents circling him, his vision was beginning to waver, his arms starting to feel like anvils thanks to the stab wounds that still bled freely. If he didn't kill these last two quickly, it would be too late. For both him and Natalie.

As they leaped at him, carving slices into his side and thigh, Wulfe called on the last of his considerable reserves and took them on with desperate efficiency, hacking, stabbing, until only one remained.

Wulfe faced the last of the sentinels sent to attack them, the leader of the band. Fury tore through him, fury that these soulless monsters had followed him here. *Here*. That they'd desecrated the home of one of the brightest spirits Wulfe had ever encountered and threatened her life. Inside, his animal gave a furious growl.

Fangs sprouted from his mouth, claws erupted from his fingertips, and he went feral, that place half-way between man and beast. As the sentinel lunged at him with his sword, Wulfe cut off the bastard's remaining hand. The last thing Wulfe needed was to become enthralled, too.

Digging his claws into the sentinel's neck, he slammed him against the nearest wall. "What does Inir want with us?"

Real fear shone in those soulless eyes. "I don't know. Our orders were to capture you both and bring you in."

Wulfe believed him. With one clawed hand, he ripped out the Mage's heart, then dropped it to the floor, along with his body. A harsh wave of dizziness rolled across his vision, and he sank back against the wall, sweat rolling down his temples, blood down his chest.

A gust of wind blew through the house, whipping the curtains and scattering papers every which way.

Hail pounded against the siding and windows. He needed to get Natalie out of here before Inir sent more men, which he'd undoubtedly do when this batch failed to return.

His head felt helium-light, his shoulder as heavy as burning iron as he pushed away from the wall to search for a phone. If he could get ahold of Feral House, his brothers would send Ilinas to pick them up. He'd be home, with Natalie, within seconds.

He spied a cell phone on the kitchen counter, but when he turned it on, he found it password protected. Hell. And he saw no sign of a kitchen phone.

The lights flickered and died, casting him into a darkness broken only by the lightning that slashed across the sky every few seconds. He turned back to find Natalie standing as if frozen, right where the Mage had left her. Enthralled. His heart cramped at all she'd seen, at all she'd endured . . . again. She'd snap out of the enthrallment in an hour or two, maybe less. Until then, they were trapped here. And he desperately needed to lie down and give his body a chance to start the healing process.

He was afraid he might pass out, and the last thing he wanted was Natalie waking to this scene of carnage. As a warrior, he'd become far too used to such sights, but although Natalie had seen worse—she'd watched her own friends die—she didn't remember. The least he could do was get rid of the bodies, or at least move them out of her sight until they disintegrated in a few days. The basement would have to do.

After three tries, Wulfe found the right door, then bent to scoop up the closest body and nearly sank to his knees as pain screamed through his shoulder and side, and weakness tore at his muscles. His vision swam.

Straightening slowly, he slammed his palm against the wall, willing his vision to clear. When it did, he made his way to Natalie, lifting her carefully. The bodies would have to wait. Clenching his jaw, he made his way slowly up the stairs, Natalie tucked against his chest.

He was nearly to the second floor when a razor-sharp bite tore into his injured shoulder wrenching a bloodcurdling yell from his throat. *Draden.* He'd known the little fiends, no bigger than an average man's fist, would find him sooner or later, drawn to his Therian life force. If he didn't shift soon, they'd steal it all, killing him. But he couldn't carry Natalie in his wolf.

Pushing himself past the point of endurance, he climbed the last couple of steps, sweat rolling down his temples. Another draden found him, then another, and another, all tearing at his flesh until his sight blurred, until it was all he could do to put one foot in front of the other.

As he stumbled into the nearest room, a flash of lightning lit the bed and he pushed himself toward it, managing to lower Natalie onto the soft mattress and not . . . quite . . . follow her down. The moment she was out of his arms, he shifted back into his wolf, listening with satisfaction as the draden squawked their anger at the loss of their meal and flew away.

His vision tilted. If he were still immortal, the weakness would be a temporary thing. But he wasn't, and there was no telling what would happen.

Goddess, he had to survive this. He had to. Natalie needed him.

Lurching toward the bedroom door, he managed to butt it closed with his wolf's flank, then sink down in front of it, blocking her escape. Hopefully, he'd awaken if she tried to move him.

Hopefully, he'd awaken again period.

A loud crack of thunder startled Natalie awake. Lightning flashed across the room and she caught sight of the pictures on the wall.

"What am I doing in the guest room?" she muttered groggily. Confusion clouded her mind as she sat up and swung her legs over the side of the bed. She reached for the lamp, but though her fingers turned the knob, nothing happened. The electricity was out. And the closest flashlight was in the master bedroom.

Utterly confused, she pushed to her feet just as another flash illuminated the room and the large dog lying in front of the closed door, his fur caked with . . . *blood.*

It all came back in a rush—the men breaking into her house. The dog, Wolf, attacking them . . . *killing them* . . . as he protected her. She swayed, her forehead heating at the memory of the violence, her stomach lurching. Had he killed them all? Heaven help her, she hoped he had, because they'd stabbed him, over and over, in return.

Stumbling forward, she sank to her knees on the carpet beside the beautiful animal and reached for him. *Please don't let him be dead.* Her palm pressed against the warm fur of his shoulder and felt the steady rise and fall she'd hoped for. *Thank God.*

Downstairs, something crashed, stopping her heart. *The intruders are still here.* Her pulse began to thud hard enough to shake her entire body as she waited for the sound of boots on the stairs, a sound she might not hear over the howling wind and the rain slashing against the windows.

Lightning again illuminated the dog's blood-soaked fur. Thunder cracked, startling her out of her momentary paralysis. She had to do something to stop the bleeding, or Wolf was going to die right here, right now. If the intruders broke through the door, so be it. They must know she was up here. Which made no sense.

Pushing to her feet, she moved quietly to the dresser where she kept the stack of old T-shirts she wore to exercise in. They'd have to do. Grabbing a handful, she sank down beside the animal and whispered softly.

"It's me, boy. This might hurt, but I've got to staunch your wounds."

Her fingers pressed gingerly, burrowing through Wolf's fur, as she sought the site of the stab she'd seen him take to the shoulder. Warm blood coated her fingers and she knew she'd found it. As gently as possible, she pressed one of the shirts against the wound, then started searching for any others.

"Poor guy," she whispered. "You chose the wrong night to come see me, but you probably saved my life." She needed to get him to a vet. The beautiful animal made no sound, gave no indication of consciousness. He might be alive, but for how much longer?

Something skittered across the floor downstairs, stopping her heart for another moment. Why hadn't they followed her upstairs? For that matter, how in the heck had she fallen asleep on the guest bed in the middle of an attack on her house? None of it made a bit of sense. The last thing she remembered was hitting one of the nasties with the lamp and the other one grabbing her. Had he hit her, then? She didn't hurt anywhere. Somehow, she must have stumbled up here and passed out.

As she probed the dog's side, she felt more warm blood and knew she'd discovered another wound. If only she could see them. If only she had a flashlight. Or . . . a camp lantern. *Yes.* Her camping supplies were stored in the closet in this room. Rising, she dug the lantern out of the bottom of the closet and turned it on only a little, bathing the injured animal in a soft glow.

He had blood *everywhere*. Her gut cramped. How was she supposed to know how much of the blood was his and how much belonged to the men? They'd been dressed so strangely, like some kind of foreign army, in matching blue tunics. And *swords*.

She pressed T-shirts against the two wounds she'd found so far, knowing she had to find the others, yet wondering what she was going to do with them if she did. She only had two hands. And no telephone or suturing supplies.

"Hang on, Wolf. Just hang on for me. Sooner or later, they'll leave, and I'll be able to get you to a vet. What are they *doing* down there?" She heard something roll across the hardwood foyer. *Roll.* Suddenly she remembered the way they'd broken down her front door and relief left her on a hard exhale.

"It's not them, it's the wind. Of course, of course." Leaping to her feet, she stroked Wolf's head. "This is going to hurt, boy, but I have to move you if I'm going to get you help."

She scooted around to his back end and, as gently as she could, lifted his hips and lowered them again a few inches out from the door. Moving to his head, she did the same, back and forth, a few inches at a time until she nearly had him far enough from the door to open it. Once more should be enough.

Sweat beading on her brow, she took a deep breath, squatted at his tail, and lifted his hips one more time.

Suddenly, her hands were empty, the dog just . . . *gone* . . . exploding in a spray of colored lights.

Natalie fell back, landing on her backside, then stared, jaw dropping, as a man appeared out of thin air . . . a huge, naked man lying on the floor right where the dog had been.

She crab-walked back, the bed catching her in the shoulder blades. *This isn't happening.*

The man groaned and began to stir. Natalie tensed, her heart pounding violently in her chest as she pushed herself to her feet, then sank onto the bed when her legs refused to hold her.

Slowly, the man sat up and leaned back against the door, his muscular body marred by half a dozen stab wounds, one on the shoulder . . . *right where the dog's had been.*

This isn't happening. Dogs don't turn into men. They don't!

But even as the argument roared in her head, her gaze took in the sight in front of her. The man was *built,* his waist narrow, his abs ripped, his biceps as thick as tree trunks, one adorned with a thick golden armband with what appeared to be the head of a wolf. His shoulders were easily half the width of her sofa. Her gaze continued up, reaching his face, and her heart clenched. Scars crisscrossed the flesh every which way, tugging down one of his lips, cutting across one eye. His body might be prime, but his face was made for nightmares. Within that ruined face, eyelids lifted revealing dark eyes that turned to her, contracting on a sheen of pain, radiating a dismay so raw it almost made her ache.

"I'm not going to hurt you, Natalie." His voice was low and urgent as he struggled to his feet, grimacing. Towering over her—he had to be a full seven feet tall—he watched her with eyes filled with the same intelligence, the same *gentleness* she'd seen in Wolf's. "I would never hurt you."

She was shaking, her pulse racing, her stomach cramping from shock. But not from fear. Because as she stared into those dark eyes, she saw only truth and honor and kindness. And, odd as it was, she recognized the essence of the dog in the man.

"I would never hurt you," he said again, his voice throbbing with sincerity and desperation that she believe him.

"I know," she told him.

And she did.

I know.

Wulfe stared at Natalie, trying to catch his breath through the pain of the wounds that refused to heal, as realization hit him like a sledgehammer. Somehow, he'd shifted back into human form and stood in front of Natalie in all of his scarred, naked glory.

Goddess, when had he shifted? It couldn't have been long because the draden had yet to find him again. And they would.

She stared at him, white as a sheet, clearly in shock. *I know.* He'd promised he wouldn't hurt her, and she'd replied, *I know.*

"How much do you remember?" He must have

failed to take her memories of before or, at the very least, her memories of the small friendship that had bloomed between them in the Feral prison.

Sitting there, her hands clasped in her lap, she met his gaze with the calm strength he'd come to associate with her despite the fact she was visibly shaking. "I don't remember much—the men breaking into my house, Wolf attacking them, getting stabbed." She blanched. "You." The word was uttered on an exhale, the last of her color draining away as she doubled over until her head rested on her knees. "This isn't happening."

He frowned, wanting to go to her, yet afraid he'd scare her more if he tried.

"Are you okay?" If only he could see her face. Reaching for his wounded shoulder, he encountered stickiness . . . and pain. The one in his side was the worst, but the Mage swords didn't appear to have punctured anything vital, or he'd be fighting for his life by now. How did humans stand this . . . this . . . not healing?

"I feel a little faint." Natalie slowly lifted her head, then straightened. Her color was back, if only a little, her usual calm cracked, but not shattered. Even in the dark, she shone with a glow that had nothing to do with the unnatural aura. *So lovely.*

Her brows drew together. "*What are you?*"

"A shape-shifter. Man to wolf." He reached for the door, feeling exposed, feeling like a monster. "We need to get out of here, Natalie. Those men were Mage, evil, and their leader is going to send more of them as soon as he realizes the first group failed. They may already be on their way."

"You're injured."

"I'll heal." He hoped.

"I don't have clothes to fit you." She rose unsteadily. "It's pouring out there. I could give you a blanket."

Something warm and thick moved through his chest. She was worried about his getting wet. "I'm going to have to return to my wolf form in a minute. I can't remain in human form long at night, not . . ." Not unless he was in his truck or at Feral House or somewhere else that had been warded against the draden. "I'm sorry, Natalie. I know this is a lot to take in all at once." *He* was a lot to take in, the way he looked, the way he'd killed, right in front of her. "You shouldn't have seen any of this."

She swallowed, nodding, shadows of the violence she'd witnessed darkening her eyes.

"I'm not going to hurt you. But we need to go."

Straightening her shoulders, she shook her head. "I'm not going with you. I can't. There are . . . dead bodies . . ." Her voice cracked, slicing open his heart. "I'm going to the police."

His jaw tightened at all the reasons that wasn't going to happen. The last thing they needed was for her to tell the human cops a crazy tale of a shape-shifting wolf, then bring them back to her house to round up all the dead bodies—bodies that would disintegrate suddenly, in a couple of days. Bodies that were not human.

His hands clenched and unclenched at his sides as he debated how to secure her cooperation. "Come home with me, Natalie. I can give you something the police can't."

Her expression turned wary, fear alive in those no longer calm, gray eyes. "And what is that?"

He met her gaze, his mouth twisting in a semblance of a smile. "Xavier."

Natalie swayed, her heart suddenly in her throat.

"Where is he? What have you done to him?" She'd started to trust this man, this . . . *werewolf.* Was he nothing but a kidnapper? A *murderer?* "The week I lost, was I your prisoner, too?"

"We didn't hurt you. We let you go."

"But not Xavier."

"We couldn't take his memories of all he'd seen. We can only take memories through the eyes."

She stared at him, the sudden feeling washing over her that they'd had this discussion before. "And his don't work."

"He's fine, Natalie. He's safe. And he'll be glad to see you."

Safe. How could he possibly be *safe?* Her pulse raced, her muscles tensing with the need to run. With him injured, she might be able to get away. But what if he was telling the truth? What if he really could take her to Xavier?

She pressed a trembling palm to her pounding head and met the werewolf's gaze. The warm light of kindness emanating from his dark eyes slowly burned through her own haze of fear, reminding her why she'd been drawn to the animal in the first place. Despite every logical thing to the contrary, her instincts told her she could trust him. He wouldn't hurt her.

And she would risk being wrong, risk anything, to reach Xavier.

"Okay."

He watched her for a moment more, then nodded and turned. "We'll leave through the front door and circle to the back. I don't want you having to see . . ."

"The bodies."

"Yes."

She grabbed the lantern. "Why the backyard?"

"My truck is on the other side of the woods."

The wolf always came to her through the woods. He drove a *truck*? Of course he did.

The man opened the door. "Pack a bag. Quickly. Essentials only, and just for a few days."

A bag. With a shake of her head, she focused on that, just that, and slipped past him to run to her bedroom. "Does Xavier need anything?" she called as she grabbed the small, hard-sided, yellow suitcase out of her closet.

"Not that I know of." She turned to find him standing in her doorway, watching her. "We'd have gotten him anything he asked for. Pink makes the shopping lists, and he's become her best friend. *Fuck*."

The man exploded into sparkling lights, and suddenly the wolf was back.

Pardon my language.

At the sound of his voice in her head, she met his wolf's gaze and saw the man's intelligence and personality in the wolf's eyes. Chills ran down her arms, making the hair rise. He was speaking to her. Telepathically.

The draden are back, and I have to stay in my wolf. I'll explain that later. Pack, Natalie. And change your shirt.

With a shake to clear her head, she glanced down to find her clothes and arms streaked with blood. For a moment, she just stared. Then, taking a shaky breath, she pulled herself together again. They needed to get out of here quickly, before more of those soldiers came. The thought spurred her to move. Grabbing a clean tee, she ran into the bathroom to change and grab a few toiletries, then packed quickly.

Feral House is full of women, these days, the wolf said as she added the last items. *Most of my brothers are married. If you forget anything, you can borrow it.*

Married werewolves. Her head was going to explode. "How many of you are there?"

One wolf shifter. More than a dozen other Ferals . . . shifters . . . each of whom shifts into a different animal. I'll explain more later.

So not werewolves. Not exactly.

She zipped the suitcase, then grabbed the flashlight off the bottom shelf of her nightstand, deciding the lower light would attract less attention. Turning to the wolf, the *shape-shifter,* she said, "I'm ready."

He rose and trotted to the stairs.

"I'm going to need my purse. It's on the desk in the kitchen." She really wanted her laptop, too, but she was afraid the rain would destroy it.

I'll get the purse and your phone. Grab a raincoat. It's pouring.

The wolf ran down the stairs ahead of her as the wind and rain blew in through the open front door. By the time Natalie snatched her raincoat out of the coat closet and pulled it on, her pants were already damp. As she turned her back to the buffeting wind to zip up the raincoat, she made the mistake of glancing toward the family room just as another bolt of lightning illuminated the house. Bodies . . . body *parts* . . . lay everywhere, blood streaking the walls and soaking the carpeting. The sight burned her eyes and made the bile rise in her throat. Swallowing it back down, she spun away.

Her house was ruined. Her life was in shambles. But Xavier might still be alive. The thought raced through her like a live wire, filling her with hope and excitement, strengthening her against all she'd lost. Because if she could really see him again, if she truly found him safe and well, none of this mattered. None of it.

Straightening, she pulled up her hood and waited. A moment later, the wolf returned with her purse dangling from his mouth. She took it from him, slung it over her shoulder, and braced herself against the wind as she stepped through the wreckage of the front door and into the driving rain. Without a backward glance, the wolf at her side, Natalie left everything she knew behind.

Chapter Five

As Natalie followed the massive gray wolf around the corner of her house, through her backyard, and into the woods, the wind buffeted her, dragging at the hood of her raincoat. She clung to her suitcase with one hand, her flashlight with the other.

Her hand shook as she struggled to assimilate all that had happened. How was any of this real?

"Do you have a name?" she asked the huge animal, desperate for any pretence of normalcy.

You already guessed it. I'm Wulfe, spelled W-U-L-F-E. All the Ferals, the shape-shifters, have taken the names of our animals. It's tradition.

"You're the only wolf." Twigs snapped under her soles, the leaves torn free of the trees flying and swirling around her. The woods smelled of rain and damp fur this night.

Yes. The others include a tiger, hawk, lion, jaguar, cougar, panther, fox, snake, and falcon. There aren't many of us anymore. Maybe as many as twenty-six, but that's it. We're Therians, a race that used to be all shape-shifters. Five thousand years ago, we were forced to mortgage most of our power to defeat and imprison Satanan and his Daemon horde. When the dust settled, one member each of only a fraction of the animal lines reclaimed the power of their animal and the ability to shift. They banded together and became known as the Feral Warriors, the defenders of the race and the protectors of the Daemon Blade, in which Satanan and his horde are imprisoned.

He described something from a movie or urban fantasy novel. If she hadn't seen him shift with her own eyes, she'd never believe any of this. Now, she had no reason to doubt him. Still, despite his fantastical tale, she had more pressing worries.

"What's going to happen when the police find the mess in my house, Wulfe? They're going to think some of that blood was mine." Her stomach cramped. "My mother's going to think she's lost me, now, too."

Once we get a little deeper into the woods, I'll use your phone to call for cleanup. We can ward the house against intrusion so that no one will see the damage until we have a chance to fix it. The bodies and blood will disintegrate on their own in a few days.

How could that be? How could any of this be?

The wind began to die down, the rain changing to a mere drizzle. Ahead, the wolf trotted, favoring one leg.

"You need to see a doctor," she said. "Or a vet."

In her head, she heard him chuckle. *We have a healer staying with us, now. She'll be able to help me.*

"Are you in pain?"

A little.

"Did those soldiers know you were a werewolf?"

I think so, yes.

She thought about that, felt relief at his words. "So they were after you."

Yes. They may have been after both of us. I'm sorry.

Natalie frowned. "Why?"

It's complicated.

"Isn't everything? Did you . . . did shape-shifters . . . kill my friends?" There. She'd asked it.

His head whipped back, the flash of horror that lit his wolf's eyes revealing the truth before the *No* exploded in her head.

They were killed by Daemons and Mage. He made a sound of frustration. *I guess there's no reason not to tell you the rest. The six of you were captured to be sacrifices. You, Xavier, and Christy were the only ones we were able to save.*

"I thought you said the Daemons were imprisoned."

They were. They still are, though the Mage managed to free three of them. We killed those three, but during that battle—a battle you witnessed—you were exposed to an energy that, for about a week, kept us from stealing your memories of the event. The Mage leader, Inir, is evil. Worse, Satanan is now controlling him. We're trying our damnedest to stop Inir from freeing Satanan and his entire Daemon horde, but we're struggling.

"I still don't understand where I come into all this. What do they want with me?"

I'm not sure.

"Wulfe . . ."

That's the truth, Natalie. All I know is that yesterday morning, when I came to check on you, you'd developed an odd glow.

He'd come to check on her . . . Wulfe. Not the wolf-like dog, but Wulfe, the shape-shifter. Good grief. "What do you mean by 'odd glow'?"

You've acquired a bright aura, an unnatural one.

"And you think the attack last night had something to do with that?"

I don't know what else it could be.

"Xavier?"

Neither Christy nor Xavier is experiencing it, so far.

As Natalie made her way through the dark woods, the rain slowly eased to a drizzle. Exhaustion rolled over her as she tried to take in all that he'd told her, all that had happened. A little of the tension she'd been living with eased out of her shoulders as those lost days began to emerge, ever so slightly, from the fog. She'd been with Wulfe. And Xavier. Presumably safe. But there were still so many things she didn't understand.

Emotion welled up as the adrenaline of the past hours slowly drained away, burning her eyes. *Please let Xavier be at the end of this journey. Please, please, please let me see my little brother again.*

A rain-soaked branch snapped dully beneath her shoe, and the scent of the night woods filled her senses as they walked in silence.

Wulfe stopped suddenly, his ears going rigidly alert, his hackles rising. *Natalie, turn off your flashlight and give me your cell phone. Fast.* With startled eyes, she watched as he exploded in a million sparkling lights, turning back into a man.

Dropping her suitcase, she flicked off her flashlight and shoved it into her pocket, then fished her cell phone out of her purse, swiped the screen, and punched in her security code. Wulfe's dark form rose large before her as he reached for the phone and snatched it from her hand.

He tapped a number, lifted the phone to his ear, and grabbed her hand. "Let's go. Quickly."

She picked up her suitcase and together they hurried through the dark woods. Without a flashlight, she could see virtually nothing, but Wulfe's tight grip kept her upright each time she stumbled.

"Natalie and I are in the woods behind her house," he said into the phone. "We've got Mage sentinels on our tail. I'm guessing more than two dozen." Disconnecting the call, he released her hand long enough for her to slide the phone back into her purse, then took it again.

"They're on their way," he assured her.

"Where are they?"

"Great Falls. Virginia side. Give me your suitcase."

She handed it to him and his hand tightened on hers as they half walked, half ran.

"That's an hour from here."

"Not the way we travel. But our transport has to find us, and that could take time."

Which made little sense. "Can you see where you're going?"

"Well enough. My human night vision isn't nearly as good as my wolf's, but it's better than yours."

A dull thud reached her ears, vibrating up through the ground. Footfalls. A lot of them. Terror crawled slowly up her spine.

Suddenly, Wulfe made a low sound of pain. "*Fuck.* Sorry. Natalie, I'm going to have to shift. The draden . . . I can't explain but I have to shift. Take your suitcase."

He shoved her small case into her hand, then stepped away from her and in another spray of colored lights, again became the wolf.

"Wulfe, I can't see," she whispered. He was little more than a dark smudge against the nearby trees.

I'll guide you.

The smudge moved to her side, his warm body pressing against hers. Natalie slid her hand into his fur, then followed as he started forward. But the ground was wet and uneven, small branches strewn about everywhere from the storm, and she could only move so fast.

Behind them, the footfalls grew louder.

Natalie, we need to run. Hold on to me and do the best you can.

Her pulse began to race because she knew they were in trouble. Dropping her suitcase and her purse, she bent over to grip Wulfe lightly around the neck, not wanting to add weight to his already wounded body.

"Be my eyes, Wulfe."

She nearly lost her grip on him as he took off, but she managed to hold on and run alongside him, at a slow and awkward gait. Behind them, the pounding grew louder until Natalie's spine crawled, and she kept imagining she felt the steel of a blade piercing the back of her neck.

"How much farther?" she whispered.

Too far. But all we need to do is stay ahead of them until the Ilinas find us.

But in the next instant, her foot snagged on a fallen limb, and she went down, hard.

Natalie.

She saw the sparkling lights, though even those were barely visible in the dark, and a moment later, strong arms scooped her up, then almost as quickly, released her legs, setting her back on her feet. She understood why as the clouds broke apart and moonlight illuminated the Mage running to surround them on every side. As before, they wore blue tunics and carried swords. As before, they meant trouble.

"Wulfe!" a woman's voice called in the distance.

"Here!" Wulfe shouted in return. And before Natalie could wonder, two dark forms, two women, appeared beside them. Out of thin air.

"Stop them!" one of the enemy shouted.

Wulfe whirled and grabbed Natalie by the shoulders. Though she couldn't see his eyes, she felt the force of his gaze. "You're safe, Natalie. Don't be afraid."

Then he released her and stepped back. And her world went into free fall.

Natalie swayed, stunned.

The sudden lights blinded her. Voices erupted all around her. One moment she'd been in the pitch-black, rain-soaked woods. The next, here, behind this house, this . . . *mansion* . . . lit up like a birthday cake. People everywhere.

Impossible.

Her vision swam, her pulse thudded as her body turned cold and clammy.

Strong feminine hands grabbed hold of her arm. "Don't faint on me, human," the owner of those hands said, not unkindly.

"I need to get my head down." Close by, she heard

the sound of vomiting, but she struggled too hard to keep from passing out to worry about anyone else. Sinking to her knees, she folded over until her forehead nearly touched the dry grass. A soothing, slender hand stroked her back, filling her with warmth, easing back the dizziness, the shock.

As the vertigo passed, Natalie took a deep breath and sat up, glancing at the woman—a petite blonde with sharp, bright blue eyes. "Thank you."

The woman smiled. "My gift comes in handy every now and then."

"What happened?" Natalie asked, pushing herself slowly to her feet.

The woman grabbed her arm, helping her up. "I brought you to Feral House. You'll be safe here."

"*You* brought me?" Behind her companion, she saw Wulfe rising from his hands and knees, the light from dozens of windows playing over the muscles and contours of his perfect form.

"I was your Ilina transport. Wulfe's fine, by the way. Humans handle Ilina travel much better than the immortal races, for some reason. I'm Melisande, the wife of one of the Ferals."

Wulfe turned and saw her, his face a mask of concern as he started toward her. "I'm sorry," he said, grabbing her shaking hand, his large fingers wrapping tight around hers. "I didn't have time to fully warn you."

Natalie nodded, swallowed. But her mind kept blanking from overload, screaming, *This isn't happening!*

She clung to Wulfe's hand, squeezing hard as his warm fingers settled more firmly around hers.

Slowly, her gaze eased around him, to take in her

surroundings. On one side, at least a dozen people, both men and women, sat at tables scattered across the patio, watching her curiously. All appeared dressed similarly, in casual training pants and tanks. They looked like some kind of military fighting unit. Looking the other way, she saw several more of the fighters standing in the grass, watching her, swords at their sides.

The sound of a door had her turning back just as three muscular men strode from the house. The one in front, a male with a distinct air of authority, looked from Wulfe to her, and back again, scowling. The other two were a contrast—one with long black hair and the features of a Native American, a trio of scars slashing across one eye. The other as fair as his companion was dark, his blond hair cut short.

Wulfe turned to face them, his hand still tight around hers.

One by one, the three greeted Wulfe, clasping his arm at the elbow, slapping forearms.

"What happened?" the leader demanded, his amber eyes once more flicking unhappily toward her.

Wulfe glanced pointedly at the throng on the patio. "Can we talk inside?"

The leader nodded. "My office." As he and the Native American turned back toward the house, the remaining man tossed Wulfe a pair of workout shorts then turned to her.

"I'm Tighe," he told her, dimples appearing briefly in his cheeks. His eyes, warm and kind, ratcheted down her racing pulse a couple of notches.

As Wulfe released her hand to pull on the shorts, she nodded. "Hi, Tighe."

"I'm sorry you got caught up in all this."

"Me, too."

Wulfe nodded toward the house and started forward, waiting for her to fall into step beside him, but he didn't reach for her hand again.

Tighe brought up the rear. "You look like hell, Wulfe."

"The bleeding's stopped."

"Thank the goddess for small favors," Tighe murmured, as they crossed the patio. "Natalie appears unharmed."

"One of the Mage enthralled her. I'll tell you the rest when we get inside."

Natalie glanced toward Wulfe. "Enthralled?"

His expression turned grim. "The Mage can . . . and did . . . capture your mind with a touch. Once I'd dispatched them, I carried you upstairs and laid you on the first bed I could find before I passed out."

Dispatched them. A vision of blood and body parts flashed through her head, and she drew in a trembling breath and shoved the memory aside, focusing on the rest of his revelation. He was the one who'd put her in the guest room. Waking up there finally made sense. As much sense as anything tonight.

Wulfe led her into the house, into a huge room with the biggest, most ornate dining table she'd ever seen. A pair of crystal chandeliers hung above the table, casting light on walls covered in blue-and-gold wall-paper.

Somewhere nearby, a peel of high-pitched laughter was answered by a laugh she recognized instantly.

"*Xavier*." Her body tensed, her heart jolting, as her gaze flew to Wulfe. "*Is he here?*"

A funny look crossed the big man's face, a hint of a smile. "X!"

"Coming!" Xavier called back.

Natalie swayed, and Wulfe pulled her against his side, his arm around her shoulders. Her heart began to pound, tears burning her eyes. As the far door swung open, and her youngest brother pushed through, a cane in his hand, a smile on his beloved face, joy burst inside of her, powering her feet.

"Xavier," she breathed, pulling away from Wulfe to rush toward him.

"Nat?" Xavier's smile erupted into a full-out grin and he stopped, opening his arms for her.

Tears running down her cheeks, Natalie closed the distance between them and hugged her brother, who stood only a couple of inches taller than she, euphoric at the feel of his arms around her, at the sound of his heart beating against her own. *Alive.*

The events of the past hours ripped away the last shred of her control, and she began to sob as she held him, as she shook and rejoiced and thanked the heavens over and over and over again for giving him back to her.

Xavier patted her back. "Nat, are you okay? You smell like blood. What happened?"

"I'm fine. I'm just so . . . glad to see you."

Finally, she pulled herself together and let go of him, stepping back enough to examine his face. Someone pressed a couple of tissues into her hand, and she used them to mop up her tears and blow her nose.

"What happened, Sis? What are you doing here?"

She felt a large hand settle on her shoulder and knew, without looking, that it belonged to Wulfe. The feel of him beside her helped settle her.

"The Mage found her again, X, but I was there. I

took care of them, and they didn't hurt her. She got a little bloody trying to staunch my wounds. She's going to stay here for a while."

"Wow. You're okay, Wulfe?"

"Yeah, I'm fine."

"Not cool that the Mage found you, Nat," Xavier said. "But cool that you're back. I've missed you."

Natalie laughed, the sound watery. "Oh, Xavier, how I've missed you, too."

"How's Mom?"

She grimaced, unsure how to answer that. The last thing she wanted to do was hurt her brother. But sometimes, only the truth would do.

"She's grieving."

His face fell. "She thinks I'm dead."

Natalie met Wulfe's gaze, holding on to the soft understanding she saw there. "Mom clings to the hope that you're alive, but the cops . . ." She shook her head. "I'm afraid no one else thinks you survived."

"I guess it's better that way. No one's looking for me."

"Everyone's looking for you. They've scoured the Harpers Ferry area over and over again. But they're past the point of believing they'll find you alive."

"This has to be killing Mom."

Natalie gripped his hand. "It's been hard on her. You know how much she loves you. But she's tough, Xavier. She'll be okay."

Sorrow cast a sheen in his eyes, and he squeezed her hand in return. "As long as you don't disappear, too."

The truth of his words cut deep. "I won't." Her gaze found Wulfe's again. "I have to believe I'll get home again."

Wulfe nodded. "I'll make it happen."

And she believed he would if the power lay in his hands.

Wulfe clasped Xavier's shoulder. "Lyon's waiting for us in his office, X. You two can talk more later."

Natalie hugged her brother again, drinking in the feel of his wiry body, and the sheer miracle of his survival before forcing herself to pull away. "I'll see you later."

"I'm glad you're here, Nat, for however long you stay. You have to meet Pink. She's half-flamingo, but she can't shift like the others can, she's stuck that way. But she's awesome." Xavier frowned. "You'll like it here, Nat. But do whatever they say. They're the good guys, just do whatever they say."

"I will." But the gravity of his words sent a chill down her spine. *They're the good guys, but* . . . She wasn't safe here. Not entirely.

She squeezed Xavier's hand, then turned back to Wulfe, surprised by the softness in his eyes as he watched her.

"Ready?" he asked.

"Yes."

His fingers curled lightly around her upper arm as he led her through the dining room and into the hall. His touch, his presence, steadied her. Strengthened her. Despite Xavier's warning, she felt safe with Wulfe as she had from the moment she'd met him in his animal form, though she probably shouldn't. In so many ways, he was a total stranger. And yet . . . he wasn't. In his eyes, she recognized the same spirit, the same sweet yet fierce soul who'd pressed his wolf's head against her thigh, then taken knife wound after knife wound to defend her. The man's face was still new to her—the scars disturbing, mostly because they spoke of great suffering. But beneath those scars was a strong face, a handsome one. And his body, which she'd seen more of than she had any right to, was nothing short of breathtaking. His scent invaded her air, a warm, masculine aroma that wove a spell over her, easing the tension from her muscles even as it quickened her pulse.

Everything about him called to her on the most primitive level, leaving her feeling secure but not calm. No, not calm. His half-naked closeness excited every molecule in her body.

As he ushered her down the hallway, his thumb began to rub her upper arm gently. "You're still shaking," he said quietly.

She laughed, a single burst of air. "I'm still reeling from all that's happened, but I'm fine, Wulfe. More than fine." She turned and met his gaze, the joy barreling up and out of her in a grin that split her face. "My brother's alive." Tears pooled in her eyes all over again, but she blinked them back, watching as an answering smile lit Wulfe's eyes, igniting a sparkle within those dark depths that set up a warm, lively dance in her chest. His scarred mouth twitched, then widened, his crooked smile nothing short of stunning. Her pulse took off in a crazy flight.

"That went down just as I had hoped it would," he murmured.

"What do you mean?"

If possible, his eyes softened even further. "You've been sad. Seeing X made you happy."

As gratitude and affection surged up inside of her, Natalie rose up and placed a quick kiss on his cheek. "Very. Thank you."

To her dismay, Wulfe jerked back, the light dying from his eyes. "You're welcome." But his tone turned flat, and he released her arm and turned away, continuing down the hall.

Natalie hurried to keep pace with him, wondering, unhappily, if she'd breached some kind of werewolf...shifter...etiquette. The last thing she wanted to do was displease the man who'd been nothing but wonderful to her. Taking a deep breath, she steeled herself for the meeting ahead and whatever followed, because it was obvious she didn't understand this world. Or, for that matter, the people in it.

She was in over her head, that was all too clear.

And she might have just alienated the only one standing by her side.

Chapter Six

She'd kissed him.

Wulfe led Natalie through Feral House to Lyon's office, feeling knocked on his ass.

She'd kissed him.

Just his cheek, of course. But she'd touched his scars. *With her lips.* A thing Beatrice would have never done.

Goddess, this woman was turning him inside out. Watching her with her brother had ripped his heart out. Hearing her sobs, even if they'd been of joy and not sorrow, had utterly slain him.

Then she'd kissed him.

His hand itched to reach for hers again. His arm tensed with the need to curl around her shoulders and pull her close, but he wouldn't do that. Not when she was steady on her feet again and no longer needed him. She might have kissed him, but he knew a peck of gratitude when he felt it. If he tried to draw her close for no reason other than that he couldn't think of anything more wonderful than holding her close, she'd probably stiffen, then pull away. Nicely, of course. He didn't think Natalie knew how to do anything except nicely. But they'd both be left feeling intensely uncomfortable, and he didn't want that.

As they strode through the foyer, side by side, Natalie's soft scent wafted to his sensitive nose and he drank it in, feeling it slide through him, warming him, settling into his blood, his chest, calming him. Her scent reminded him of wild roses beneath a summer sun—at once lovely, warm, and tenacious. Being near her was like walking into an errant shaft of sunlight on a cold, overcast day. Or like stepping into cool shade in the middle of a summer scorcher. It made him sigh, deep inside. It made him feel good all the way to his soul. His wolf agreed, giving a low bark of satisfaction.

As they neared Lyon's office, Natalie gasped, her hand flying to her cheek.

"What's the matter?" Wulfe asked.

She shook her head, then slowly relaxed again. "It's nothing."

He peered at her doubtfully, but she seemed to be okay, so he turned forward and opened the door to Lyon's office. He motioned for her to take a seat in one of the chairs in front of Lyon's desk, and she did, moving with that innate grace of hers to settle onto the chair, her back straight, her hands in her lap, her expression calm and alert, as always, despite the fact that he knew she was still shaking.

His instincts told him to stand behind her, to protect her back, even though he knew Lyon would never make a move against her without discussing it with Wulfe first. Lyon didn't work that way. The Chief of the Ferals was ruthless only when he had no choice, and, in all things, utterly fair. But before Wulfe could take his place behind Natalie, the healer, Esmeria, headed him off, gliding forward to meet him with a sound of sympathetic dismay. Wulfe stood still, just inside the door, as the Therian healer pressed her hand to the wound on his shoulder, closed her eyes, and slowly stole the pain.

As he submitted to Esmeria's ministrations, Wulfe's gaze moved to Lyon where he sat behind the large desk that dominated the room. Floor-to-ceiling book-shelves covered the walls except for the space occupied by the hearth, where Paenther stood. Tighe propped one hip on the corner of Lyon's desk and waited.

Lyon rose and held out his hand to Natalie. "I'm Lyon, Natalie. Chief of the Ferals. We met weeks ago though you don't remember."

Natalie shook his hand. "I'm pleased to meet you . . . again."

Paenther stepped forward, his black hair swinging forward to partly obscure the feral marks across his eye. "I'm Paenther, the black panther shifter and Lyon's second-in-command."

She nodded, shook his hand, and settled back onto her chair, her posture slightly less tense than before. Humans generally responded well to shows of re-spect and friendliness, and Wulfe appreciated Lyon and Paenther taking the time to show her both.

Lyon's gaze turned to Wulfe. "What happened?"

Esmeria moved behind him, and Wulfe stepped forward, allowing her access to the wounds on his back. "Ten Mage sentinels kicked in Natalie's front door. Inir had ordered them to bring us . . . both of us . . . to him alive."

"Why?" Paenther asked with a frown.

"How did Inir know you were there?" Lyon asked at the same time.

"I don't know. On Inir's mountain last week, Satanan sensed me. I'm wondering if he always knows where I am, now."

Lyon frowned. "So they waited until you were far from Feral House before trying to take you. Why Natalie?"

"No idea."

"Did you kill them?"

"The ten who breached the house. Unfortunately, the front door was kicked in and there was no fixing it before we left. We need to send a cleanup crew before the humans find it."

"I know where the house is," Tighe said. "I'll go."

Lyon nodded. As Tighe rose to leave, Lyon turned to Wulfe. "More sentinels came after you later."

"They followed us into the woods, more than two dozen of them. Either the first group jumped the gun and attacked us without waiting for their backup, or the Mage are stationed close enough to Frederick that Inir was able to send reinforcements quickly. Within about an hour."

"They knew you'd go back there." Lyon sighed. "Until we know why they want you both, Natalie stays here."

"I agree."

Lyon turned to Natalie. "I'm sorry, but we're going to have to lock you up."

Natalie jerked.

Wulfe's muscles bunched, a hard *no* burning in his throat. Deep inside, his wolf leaped up, snarling. "You can't put her in the prisons, Roar. Not again. Not when we've got men down there that we're not sure about."

"Wulfe . . ."

He slammed his fist on Lyon's desk. "She doesn't deserve the prison again!"

"She was never down there because she deserved it." Lyon sank back onto his chair wearily. "If she gets away from you and shares what she's seen with other humans, the result could be catastrophic, especially with the human cops already stumped by the deaths and disappearances of her companions last month. You know that. I can't risk it."

Dammit. He knew Lyon was right. Still . . . what if . . . ? "She doesn't have to be locked up in the prisons." Enthusiasm quickened Wulfe's speech. "Natalie can stay in the bedroom between yours and mine. I'll put locks on the windows and on the outside of the door. She'll be comfortable. And if she needs anything, I'll hear her."

"I thought we had Guards staying in that room."

"They can sleep on pallets in the living room with the rest of them."

For several moments, Lyon met his gaze, silently considering Wulfe's words. After six hundred years of working together, Wulfe knew his chief well.

With a sigh, Lyon ran his hand across the back of his neck. "She's your responsibility. I want you, another Feral, or one of the stronger women with her any time she's out of that room, no exceptions. And I don't want her anywhere near electronic devices—computers, phones, etc."

The coiled tension in Wulfe's body eased. "Thank you."

Lyon turned a hard, uncompromising gaze on Natalie. "You must understand, we don't kill humans without cause, but we *will* destroy anyone who threatens the anonymity of the immortal races. When we first realized that Xavier was blind, and his memories of us couldn't be stolen, I wanted him put to death."

Natalie stiffened, and it was all Wulfe could do not to put his hand on her shoulder and promise her he'd protect them both, now.

Lyon folded his hands on the desk in front of him. "You *know* what would happen if the press, human law enforcement, or the military found out about us. At best, we'd be run out. More likely, we'd be attacked with weapons that can destroy even immortals. And if we die, the Daemons rise. It's as simple as that. And then it's game over for both of our races. Until we can figure out what was done to you, reverse it, then steal your memories of all you've seen, we can't send you home, and we can't let you escape. The risk is too great."

"And if you can't figure it out?" Natalie asked, her voice even and professional, despite everything. "Or you can't reverse it?"

"Let's take it one step at a time. But you must understand that if you betray us in any way . . ."

"If I betray you, you'll kill me. I understand."

Wulfe's muscles bunched, a low growl rumbling in his throat.

Lyon glanced his way but didn't deny it. "We'll have no choice. What's more," he said, turning back to Natalie. "If we're forced to take your life, we'll instantly lose your brother's loyalty, and we'll no longer be able to trust him either. So both of your lives are in your hands."

Natalie was silent for a moment before finally nodding. "You've made your point."

"Good."

Esmeria circled Wulfe one more time, eyeing him critically. "Did I get them all?"

Wulfe nodded. "Thank you, Esmeria." He opened the door for her, then closed it again after she left.

"Go," Lyon said, glancing from Wulfe to Natalie and back again. "Get the locks installed on that bedroom and get some sleep. Both of you."

Natalie rose from her chair and faced the Chief of the Feral Warriors. "Thank you for sparing Xavier's life, Lyon. Thank you for sparing both of ours. I won't betray you." She held out her hand to seal their bargain.

Lyon eyed her thoughtfully as he shook her hand. "Your brother is a good person, Natalie. The better I get to know him, the more certain of that I become. It would seem the trait runs in the family."

"Thank you."

As Wulfe ushered Natalie out of Lyon's office, he glanced back and met his chief's gaze, reading the unspoken warning clear in Lyon's eyes. *Don't fuck this up.* If he did, if Natalie found a way to escape with her brother in tow—because he knew she'd never leave without him—all their lives might be over. He wasn't going to let that happen.

Chapter Seven

Wulfe opened the door and stepped back, allowing Natalie to precede him into the hallway. Despite Lyon's warnings, or perhaps because of them, the feel of Wulfe at her back sent a frisson of warmth stealing through her veins. There was safety in that warmth, and goodness. And something more.

"Wulfe," Lyon called after him. "Send in one of the Guards. They can be emptying the room while you install the locks."

A pair of Guards overheard the command and one of them nodded to Wulfe and went to join Lyon.

As they crossed the mammoth foyer, Natalie considered Lyon's words. If he'd meant to scare her, he'd succeeded. His was no idle threat, she knew that in her gut . . . a gut that felt like it had been filled with cement. Xavier's warning made sense, now. There was honor in these males, and goodness. She was fairly sure of that. But they were warriors, first. Soldiers battling an enemy who could not be allowed to win. If she and Xavier got in the way, they'd be removed. As simple as that. Collateral damage.

She understood the ways of war, understood that sometimes a few had to be sacrificed to protect the many. The Ferals wouldn't hurt them if they had a choice. And she'd do nothing to betray them, just as she'd promised. But with her glowing like a nuclear reactor, they might not have that choice, no matter what she did.

Agitation simmered low in her blood even as she fought it back. She might not be able to control her glow. But she could accept her fate, cooperate, and pray it was enough to keep Xavier and her alive.

As they started down another hallway, Wulfe stopped and opened a door, revealing a stairwell that looked as if it disappeared deep beneath the Earth.

Natalie eyed the long flight of stairs warily. "Is this where you sleep?"

"My room's on the third floor. This is the way to the workroom, with the tools and spare locks." He motioned her forward. "I'm right behind you."

Taking a deep breath, she started down, her head beginning to feel unattached. Never could she remember feeling so physically and emotionally drained. No, that wasn't true. She'd felt worse in the days after her release, when she'd feared Xavier might really be dead. But there was no denying she'd experienced shock after shock tonight. And her mind and body wanted nothing more than to simply shut down.

"Wulfe, how long until we know if Tighe got to my house before the police?"

"Let me check."

She glanced over her shoulder to find him pulling a phone out of his back pocket. A moment later, Tighe's voice filled the stairwell.

"Hey, buddy."

"You're on speaker, Tighe. I'm with Natalie. Are you there?"

"We are. You left a bit of a mess. Nice work."

A hint of a smile flitted across Wulfe's face as his gaze met hers. "The situation's contained?"

"Best I can tell. There were no humans around when we got here, and while I'm not the best tracker, I circled the house in cat form and didn't catch fresh scent of any humans in the yard other than Natalie. We've got the place warded, now, so no one will see any blood if they do pay the place a visit. Melisande and her mist warriors have already disposed of the bodies."

"Good. Thanks, Stripes." Wulfe shoved the phone back in his pocket and glanced at her. "Feel better?"

"Yes. Very." She turned and continued down the stairs. No one would find the blood or the bodies in her house. But when she failed to show up for work, people were bound to fear the worst. "Wulfe, I know Lyon said to keep me away from phones, but it would help both of us if I could make a couple of calls to cover my tracks. One to my mom, the other to my office manager. Think of the firestorm my disappearing again will create in the media." Her mom didn't deserve that. Nor did she want her patients making the trip to her office only to be turned away.

"What about your fiancé?"

"We broke off our engagement this morning." Right after Wulfe left, she realized.

"Do I need to beat the shit out of him?"

At the anger in his low words, Natalie looked over her shoulder to find him watching her with righteous fury. Affection welled up inside her, hot and fast.

"No. I was the one who broke it off, but he wasn't surprised."

Slowly, the anger drained from his face. "Why not?"

She started to answer, then hesitated, thinking it through. "I suppose we'd both begun to realize he wasn't the man for me."

Wulfe turned still as stone. "Is there another?"

She hesitated. "No." But as she stared into those dark eyes, something soft fluttered inside of her. A wish. A longing. *There could be.* But she didn't say the words out loud. He was a godlike immortal, and she was merely a human caught up in something she should never have known existed. If all went as hoped, soon she wouldn't even remember him. Or that Xavier lived.

Her heart plummeted.

"I'll talk to Lyon about those phone calls," Wulfe assured her. As she started back down, he asked, "What will you tell them?"

She thought about that for a moment. "I'll say that I need to get away for a little while. I don't think anyone will judge me considering all that's happened. And if they do, so what? It's better for them to judge me than to search for me."

When they finally reached the bottom of the stairs, Wulfe moved past her, leading the way down a wide hallway lit by mock-gas lanterns, giving the space an old-time, atmospheric feel. A feel that quickly dissipated as he opened one of the doors along the hallway and, flipping a switch, illuminated a huge workshop filled with every kind of power tool known to man.

Wulfe pulled open a drawer in a wall unit filled with them, digging out a handful of small items.

"Here," he said, and dropped several pieces of dead-bolt hardware into her palm before grabbing a screwdriver and drill.

"Ready?" he asked, and headed back for the door.

As Natalie followed him out, she heard people on the stairs and watched three enter the hallway a moment later, two males and a female. The males were dressed just like Wulfe, naked except for a pair of workout shorts. The woman wore only a sports bra with her shorts. All three eyed her with friendly curiosity.

"Need help?" one of the men asked Wulfe. He was a nice-looking male with a long face and steepled brows. His hand curved across the shoulders of the woman, and she leaned into him as if the pair were two parts of a whole. The woman was cute, with dark, blue-tipped hair and a winning smile.

"Boyo," the third in the group said, striding forward and greeting Wulfe in the same manner Lyon and Jag had. This male was startlingly handsome in a cover-model kind of way, his hair falling to his shoulders in golden waves, his features utterly perfect in his strong-boned face.

"Fox," Wulfe said to the golden warrior, a smile lifting his mouth. He turned to the first male and greeted him in the same manner. "I'm good, Hawke. We're going to put some locks on the door and windows of the bedchamber beside mine. Lyon's orders, if Natalie's to avoid the prisons this time."

Hawke turned to her, his expression surprised, but

kind. "Hello, Natalie." He held out his hand, and she shook it. Glancing at Wulfe, he lifted one of those steepled brows. "She's here."

"Ten Mage sentinels broke into her house tonight."

Fox whistled. "Ten against one and yet here you are, boyo. Wish I'd been there to see that." His voice held an unmistakable Irish brogue.

"I wish you'd been there to help," Wulfe replied. "Inir wanted her."

A dark look passed between the men and the woman.

"Hi, Wulfe." The woman thrust out her hand to Wulfe and he greeted her as he had the men, though without the same ease. She turned to Natalie, smiled, and extended her hand. "I'm Faith." She gave her head a little shake. "Falkyn. It's nice to finally meet you."

"Finally? So we haven't met before."

"No, but your brother talks about you constantly. He's very proud of you."

Natalie smiled. "As I am of him."

"He's a good chap," Fox said, smiling. "Welcome, Natalie." And he shook her hand, too.

Lyon might not trust her, entirely, but the other shape-shifters were openly warm and friendly.

"Doing a little training?" Wulfe asked.

Hawke nodded, sending Falkyn a look of such deep adoration it made Natalie's heart ache a little. Had Rick ever looked at her like that? If she were perfectly honest, no. Nor had she ever felt that deeply about him. They'd gotten along famously, enjoying many of the same pastimes. But he'd never been necessary to her, she knew that now.

"Falkyn's skills are improving by leaps and bounds, but I want her to be the best fighter among us."

Falkyn rolled her eyes with a grin and met Natalie's curious gaze. "I'm the first female Feral Warrior in centuries, and I shift into a falcon. Not exactly Godzilla. He's determined to make me invincible anyway."

Hawke smiled. "I am."

Falkyn gave Natalie a little wave and headed past them, deeper into the underground, the two males following.

"How many of you did I meet on my first visit here?" Natalie asked as she started up the stairs, Wulfe close behind. "I got the feeling Hawke, Fox, and Falkyn were all meeting me for the first time."

"They were. None of them were here last time. The only ones you met were Lyon and his mate, Kara, and Paenther, Jag, and me."

"Because you kept us in the prisons."

"Yes. You were unconscious most of that time. We figured the less you saw and learned, the easier it would be to take your memories later."

She stiffened at the implications of that. "How difficult will it be to take my memories this time?" He clearly wasn't minimizing what she was seeing . . . or learning.

"Natalie," he said quietly behind her.

She stopped and turned to him, only a single step between them.

He met her gaze, his eyes at once soft and fierce. "I'm not going to let anything happen to you."

They'd both heard Lyon. Wulfe knew as well as she did that her life hung in the balance.

"I'm not," he repeated quietly, his gaze like steel, ordering her to believe him.

Warmth fluttered in her chest on wings of a rising affection for this honorable, enigmatic man. An unruly lock of hair hung across his forehead and her hand itched to reach for it, to brush it back, to touch him again as his words and actions touched her over and over. But he hadn't welcomed her kiss to his cheek, and she feared he wouldn't welcome her touch.

"Thank you," she said quietly, revealing her growing affection with a smile instead.

An answering warmth flared in his eyes, his own endearing smile making a small, quick appearance, filling her with a sharp and unexpected joy. With the soft lamplight half illuminating, half shadowing his face, his scars faded to nothing, and the raw male beauty of the man all but took her breath away. His was a strong face, strong-boned, in perfect counterpoint to the body upon which it was attached. His warm, masculine scent wafted over her, pleasing her, drawing her, turning her body soft and warm with wanting. The heat that licked inside her startled her, setting her pulse to flight. And he saw it. She could see the awareness in his eyes. And the disappointment.

Cheeks heating, Natalie turned and resumed the climb, dismayed and embarrassed, because it was clear Wulfe didn't feel the same. It wasn't right that she felt anything for this man when she'd been engaged to another just this morning. But Wulfe called to places inside her that Rick never had, places in her heart, in her mind, that were beginning to awaken and unfurl. Places so deep, so new and untouched, that their awakening scared her on a primitive level. If she wasn't careful, Wulfe, despite his promises to never hurt her, would. Without ever meaning to.

They reached the main floor, crossed the foyer, then, at Wulfe's lead, started up one of the curved stairs, side by side. Neither said a word.

As they walked down the third-floor hallway, the high yip of an excited puppy echoed suddenly from the other end. Natalie watched, amused, as Wulfe squatted, holding out his big hands as a small black ball of fur came hurtling toward him, tongue out, tail wagging a hundred miles an hour.

As the little black schnauzer pup reached him, Wulfe scooped the tiny creature up and held her in front of his face, chuckling as the pint-sized canine licked his chin and wiggled with happiness. His laugh was a wonderful sound.

"Are you being good, Lady?" Wulfe asked, his voice soft as fleece.

"She's a doll, aren't you, Lady?" A woman strolled gracefully down the hall toward them with a kitten held in one arm, a white cockatiel on her shoulder. Beneath a short cap of dark hair, she smiled at Natalie. "Lady thinks Wulfe's her pack mate. You should see her when Wulfe's in his animal. They're adorable together."

Wulfe grunted and set the puppy on the ground. "Back to your mom, you scamp."

"I'm Skye," the woman said, reaching out to shake Natalie's hand with the one she had free. Her eyes were fascinating, the irises ringed in a shiny band of copper. "I'm Paenther's mate. You must be Natalie."

"Word travels fast."

"I just saw Xavier."

Natalie grinned. "Xavier's mouth travels faster."

Skye laughed. "We love Xavier."

Wulfe started down the hall, the puppy fast on his heels. Natalie and Skye followed, side by side. Natalie reached over and stroked the kitten, smiling at the other woman. "You have quite a menagerie."

"Wulfe gave me Lady as a wedding present a couple of months ago. Jag gave me Tramp, the tabby, and Hawke gifted me with Princess, my cockatiel."

"They must have known you like animals."

Skye's smile was soft. "I'm drawn to animals, and they to me, in a way far beyond human understanding. I don't really understand it myself, I just know that it is."

"Then it seems like you're in the right house."

"With shape-shifters, you mean?" Her expression turned wry. "You would think so, and yet, if you knew a little more about our world, you would think not. I'm Mage."

Natalie jerked with surprise.

Skye's mouth twisted ruefully. "I see you know what that means."

"Ten of them broke into my house tonight."

Skye blanched. "But you're okay."

"Wulfe was there. He . . . took care of them."

Skye nodded. "Too many of my people have had their souls stolen. We're not all like that."

"I can see that. And I'm glad."

"You're human."

"Yes." Natalie cocked her head. "Can you see my glow, too?"

Skye nodded. "It's faint—I don't usually see auras—but it's there. The colors are beautiful."

"Thanks . . . I think. From what I gather, it's Daemon-related, which is probably not good."

Skye frowned, looked at Wulfe. "Is the Shaman going to take a look at her?"

"He already did," Wulfe told her. "All he can say is that it appears to be Daemon energy. But he doesn't know what that means." Wulfe strode into one of the rooms, a large room with a massive poster bed sitting in the middle. Against one wall sat a dresser with a mirror. But other than a single nightstand, that was it. The walls were white, there was no rug on the hardwood floor, and only a single sheet covered the bed. Against one wall sat a pair of plain army green duffel bags.

A woman . . . presumably one of the Therian Guards, poked her head out the bathroom door. "I'm gathering up our toiletries. I'll be out in a minute."

"Is Natalie going to stay here?" Skye asked, surprised.

Natalie responded without rancor, "Wulfe's been ordered to put locks on the windows and door as a precaution. It's odd to be considered dangerous among immortals who could end my life in an instant, but I get it."

Skye's eyes darkened with sympathy. "I'm glad you're not angry about it."

The woman strode from the bathroom, her hair short, her body toned and strong beneath her tank and fighting pants.

"Sorry for running you out," Skye said.

The woman grabbed the duffels and turned to her with a smile. "Thank you, but a bed is a luxury we don't need." She nodded to Natalie and Wulfe as she left.

Skye set the kitten down to scamper over to the puppy. "You're going to need fresh linens," she said and began stripping the bed. As Natalie stepped forward to help, another woman strode into the room, her arms laden with sheets and towels, a small canvas bag slung over one arm, a gun strapped to her waist.

"I've got them," the newcomer said.

Melisande walked in behind her. "Tighe wants to know if you want him to bring anything back for you, Natalie."

"I'd love him to, but I don't know if he'll be able to find them. I had to drop my purse and a yellow suitcase in the woods behind my house when the Mage started chasing us." She glanced at Wulfe. "I'd love to have my laptop, too, but I'm not sure that's allowed."

"Where is it?" Melisande asked.

"On the sofa in the family room, where the battle took place. The power cord is on the desk in the kitchen."

"We'll bring them. Lyon can take it from there." A second later, Melisande disappeared.

Natalie stared, nonplussed. One moment she was there, the next . . . gone.

"You'll get used to the Ilinas popping in and out," Skye said softly. "The rest of us have."

As exhaustion trembled through her, Natalie wondered just how many more surprises she could take in one day.

The woman with the linens and the gun plopped the pile down on the dresser, then grabbed a couple of sheets and came to join them.

She eyed Natalie with interest as she shook out one of the sheets. "I'm Delaney, Tighe's mate. I used to be human, too."

Natalie's brows lifted. "Used to be?"

Delaney smiled. "It's a long story that still gives me nightmares, but the result was worth it. I've got the hottest, sweetest male on the face of the planet for all of eternity."

Skye laughed as she grabbed one end of the sheet. "I could argue that. Mine happens to be the sweetest. And the hottest."

Delaney grinned. "We'll call it a draw."

Natalie helped the pair make the bed, her gaze drawn to Wulfe as he moved to the window and began screwing bolts into the frame.

"Wulfe, you should give Natalie one of those cell phones that Tighe gave me when I first got here." Delaney looked at Natalie. "The only calls I could make from it were to Tighe or Lyon. They didn't want me calling the FBI, which I'd been trying to do." She glanced back at Wulfe. "Load Skye's number, and mine, in case you're not around and she wants company. Being locked up is no fun, even with a comfy bed."

Wulfe just nodded but continued to concentrate on his task.

Lady began to bark and ran toward the door.

"That's her *gotta pee* bark," Skye said, hurrying after her.

Delaney met Natalie's gaze. "If you need anyone to talk to, have Wulfe call me. I'm on lockdown, too, if in a different way." Her smile turned beatific. "I'm pregnant with Tighe's child and he barely allows me to leave the house, let alone join in the fighting."

"He's right," Wulfe said.

"I know. But it doesn't mean I'm not going stir-crazy. I'm barely even showing yet." Her gaze turned serious. "They're good guys, the best, but if you betray them, there's nowhere you can hide," she said, echoing Xavier's warning. Despite the harshness of her words, Delaney's eyes were sympathetic as she grasped Natalie's hand and led her toward the door.

"Delaney . . ." Wulfe called, a note of warning in his voice.

"We need a moment of girl talk. She won't be out of your sight." Delaney led her into the hallway just outside the room. When Wulfe turned back to his task with a nod, Delaney met Natalie's gaze, her own piercing. "When you were here before, Wulfe became your protector. He watched over you like a mother hen, and he hasn't stopped."

Natalie nodded. "He's visited me as the wolf."

"He cares about you, Natalie. But there are other factors. A lot of them. You've never appeared put off by his scars, and that's huge. But tread carefully, please. In many ways, he's the strongest, fiercest of the shifters. But in others, he's vulnerable. I wouldn't want either of you to get hurt because either of those scenarios will wind up hurting him. Just tread carefully."

Natalie watched her. "You do realize you've given me only enough to make me intensely curious."

"I know. The rest isn't mine to tell. If you need someone to talk to at any time, I'm here." She squeezed Natalie's hand, motioned Natalie back into the room, and left.

Wulfe glanced at her as she approached, then turned back to the window without asking any questions.

"Here you go!" a feminine voice called from the doorway.

Natalie turned to find Melisande holding her purse and suitcase.

"I'll leave them right here." The Ilina set them by the door, then disappeared again before Natalie could thank her.

With a mind-clearing shake of the head, Natalie turned back to Wulfe, intrigued by the play of muscles across his broad, broad shoulders and back. He really had the most incredible build. Watching him did funny things to her insides, hot, quivery things. And she was just tired enough to not care if he knew it.

She moved closer, leaning against the wall beside him. "I've never seen you with a shirt on. Not that I remember."

He glanced at her with dismay. "Do you want me to get one before I finish?"

A smile fought to escape. "I rather like you without clothes on."

His hand stilled, his eyes changed, slowly darkening, watching her with an intensity that snagged at her breath, that made her body heat and soften.

Longing filled his eyes. "*Natalie.*"

For one charged moment, she thought he might drop his tools and reach for her. And she wanted that. Badly.

Instead, his eyes filled with frustration and he returned to his task. "Why don't you unpack while I finish here?"

For a moment, she just watched him, her brows drawn with confusion. He'd reared back when she kissed his cheek, as if her touch was anathema. But just now, she'd seen longing in his eyes, she knew that. She read eyes too well to doubt herself. And yet . . .

"All right." She got such mixed signals from him. Or maybe she just didn't know how to read a were-wolf. And, honestly, she was probably too tired to get anything straight right now.

Unpacking quickly, she laid her clothes in the dresser drawers and set her toiletry bag on the sink in the small private bathroom, then hung up the towels Delaney had brought with the sheets. Last, she opened the little canvas bag Delaney had left behind and found hand soap, body soap, a toothbrush, toothpaste, shampoo, conditioner, and half a dozen other female necessities including a fat Toblerone candy bar and an index card with a handwritten note across it. *If I forgot anything, just yell. D.*

Natalie smiled at the offering. They were treating her far more like a welcome guest than the un-expected problem that she was. Probably because she was Xavier's sister and they were clearly fond of him.

Her heart tightened, tears burning her eyes, as the joy of finding him well and happy rushed through her all over again. A single tear escaped, and she swiped it away.

"Natalie?"

She turned to find Wulfe watching her with con-cern in those dark, gentle eyes.

"I'm fine." She smiled. "The best I've been in weeks. I have my brother back, even if only for a little while. You have no idea what a gift you've given me."

He watched her intently. "There's nothing I want more than for you to be happy."

Sincerity throbbed in his words. And she wondered what he'd say if she told him that his taking her into his arms would make her very happy indeed. She wouldn't put him on the spot like that. Nor did she want to find out it was the last thing he wanted.

But the thought of being that close to him tantalized.

"**I**s there anything I can do to help?"

Natalie's voice, low and sexy, stroked Wulfe's senses. *I rather like you without clothes on.* Goddess, had he ever received a clearer or more welcome invitation? Her eyes had beckoned without coyness. Natalie wanted him. She wanted *him.*

And he had nothing to give. The severing of his mating bond had ruined him in that way. In a lot of ways. His senses had dimmed—his eyes losing their ability to see color as brightly, food losing its taste. Only his sense of smell had yet to fail him, but his libido had disappeared altogether. He could still get an erection if he needed to, but it required hard physical effort on his part. His body hadn't risen on its own in six months, not for any woman. And he feared it never would again. Even Natalie, as pretty as she was, failed to stir him in that way.

With not quite steady hands, Wulfe picked up his tools and strode past her. The windows were done. All he had left was the door.

"Have you ever installed a dead bolt?" His arms ached to grab her and haul her close, his wolf howling, urging him to do just that. But he refused to go down that path with her. No good could come of it.

"I've never installed one from scratch," Natalie said, falling into step beside him. "But I replaced one once."

The faint scent of her arousal nearly drove him to his knees.

"Then you know what we're doing. I could use a hand." *Goddess*. The thought of where he wanted her hand . . . Yeah and how much fun would *that* be when she found him flaccid and soft?

If he were smart, he'd send her to the other side of the room where her nearness wouldn't tie him into knots of longing and of wanting something he couldn't have. But he wanted her near him so badly, it was worth any amount of torture to watch the play of light on her creamy skin, to smell the tangy scent of shampoo in her hair, and to watch her full, lovely mouth draw up in those soft, Natalie smiles.

She followed him to the door, and he handed her the lock pieces, screws, and screwdriver, his fingers brushing hers as he laid them in her palms, the simple touch sending electricity buzzing beneath his skin and down into his body. But not far enough. Not nearly far enough.

Eyeing the door, he mentally marked where he wanted to drill, then picked up the tool and made the holes with a noisy whine. Then he grabbed the chisel and hollowed out a space for the faceplate to fit, all the while intensely aware of Natalie's nearness, of her gaze. And of the attraction thickening the air between them. Goddess how he wanted to haul her against him and bury his face between her breasts. How he longed to feel her fingers in his hair as he had in his fur.

He imagined holding her close, stroking her soft cheek as she reached up . . .

The thought of her touching his scarred excuse for a face burst the sensual bubble, snapping him back to reality. His life was too fucked up to even think about getting involved with a woman right now. And never a woman like Natalie, one who deserved laughter and beauty, safety and happiness. He'd thought she'd found those things with her human fiancé. The fact that she hadn't made the jealous male inside of him keenly satisfied. But not the part of him that just wanted her happy. Because he, with his damaged mating bond, his worrisome Daemon blood, and his waning immortality, had absolutely nothing to offer her.

As Natalie watched the muscles ripple across Wulfe's beautiful back, her hand itched to reach for him, to stroke his flesh, to know if he felt as hard and strong as he looked. His hair gleamed in the lamplight, a rich blend of browns of every shade, and she yearned to touch it, to feel its softness between her fingers.

Standing so close to him made her breath unsteady and turned her pulse erratic. She'd never felt like this with Rick, ever. She hadn't even known she *could* feel this way—this jittery, rubbery warmth that had her imagining the feel of his flesh against hers.

As he plucked one of the screws out of her palm, he glanced at her face and stilled. His nostrils flared, his eyes dilating as his gaze at once softened and sharpened, as hunger leaped into his eyes.

"Wulfe . . ."

He shook his head and turned back to his work, leaving her completely confused. Tilting her head back, she looked up at the ceiling and willed her thoughts elsewhere. Anywhere but on the too-appealing male in front of her, a male who, for whatever reason, didn't want what she offered. But she couldn't ignore him, not even for a moment.

As she watched him screw in the faceplate, her left cheek began to tingle oddly as it had as they'd ap-

proached Lyon's office earlier. As before, it slowly
began to sting. But where before, the sensation had
died as quickly as it had begun, this time it worsened.
She touched it, brushing at it in case there was something there, but she felt nothing.

All of a sudden, her cheek began to burn, and she
gasped, dropping the lock pieces onto the floor.

Wulfe straightened as if he'd been struck, rising
to his feet, grabbing hold of her arms. "What's the
matter?"

"My face." She lifted her hand, afraid to touch it.
"*What's on my face?*"

"Nothing." He grabbed her jaw with careful fingers, turning it as the fire ripped through nerve end-
ings, sending tears cascading down her cheeks.

"*It hurts.*"

"Where?" When she showed him, he covered the
spot with one hand, pressing his palm against the
fire as he cupped the back of her head with his other.
Almost at once, the pain began to fade. To her surprise, she felt his lips against her forehead, a quick,
soft kiss that melted her heart. Moments later, the
pain was gone.

Natalie sagged with relief. "Thank you."

Slowly, he released her and stepped back. As her
gaze cleared, she saw, clearly, the dismay in his eyes,
the worry.

She frowned. "What just happened?" Lifting her
own palm to her cheek, she felt nothing but smooth
skin, as if it had all been her imagination. "Earlier,
just before we went in to see Lyon, I felt the same
sharp pain. It wasn't nearly this bad, and disappeared almost as soon as it started, but it was in the
exact same spot."

He looked away before she could read the answers in his eyes. "It's probably nothing."

But the quickness with which he'd turned away made her suspect otherwise. It wasn't *nothing*. And though she couldn't be certain, she suspected he knew that very, very well.

Wulfe returned to his work, the drill's whine tearing at his eardrums as he dug out the place beneath the strike plate where the dead bolt would burrow. But while his hands worked, his mind spun. Why had Natalie suffered pain in the exact spot the Daemon had clawed her? She didn't remember the wound, not consciously. Was it some kind of subconscious recollection? He'd never heard of such a thing.

Another thought stopped him cold. What if this was the fault of his Daemon blood?

He turned off the drill and stared at the hole, unseeing. Goddess, what if he'd done this to her? What if, thanks to his Daemon blood, he'd accidentally hurt her by taking that wound?

It wouldn't be the first time he'd hurt a woman he'd only meant to help. The thought made him ill.

A buzzing erupted suddenly in Wulfe's ears. As he frowned, red smoke began to curl around the edges of his vision. Rage barreled through him from out of nowhere. His confusion disappeared, drowned beneath the rush of red smoke that ignited a full-blown fury in his mind. The drill that had been in his hand suddenly shattered against the floor beside him and he felt his fangs dropping, his claws erupting. He leaped to his feet with a roar, searching for something . . . *anything* . . . to bear the brunt of this sudden, ferocious anger.

His gaze caught on the female who was backing away from him, terror in her eyes.

Natalie.

As quickly as it rose, the smoky haze dissipated from his vision, his mind clearing, leaving him stunned. Shocked.

Natalie's eyes took up her entire face, her skin pale as new snow as she stared at him, at the monster he must appear.

His wolf howled with misery.

"I won't hurt you." The words came out deep and nearly unintelligible.

But, *goddess.* What just happened? He'd lost himself. Even furious, that shouldn't happen.

His fangs and claws retracted as he stared at her. The need to reassure her swelled in his mind and chest, yet he was clueless how to do that because he didn't know what the fuck just happened.

"I'd never hurt you, Natalie," he said, his voice still gruff. "I need you to believe that." But was he certain? He could have killed her with a single swipe of his claws, and he wasn't at all sure he'd have known what he was doing until it was too late. The thought turned his blood cold.

If he were smart, he'd hand her over to someone else, right here, right now. Except the first thing anyone else would do was lock her up in the prisons, and he couldn't stand the thought of her down there again.

Slowly, the color returned to her face, the terror easing away. "Did I do something to make you mad?"

"No! Goddess, no." He turned away from her, pressing both hands against the wall. His gaze fell to the floor, to the disintegrated drill, and his knees went weak. What if he hadn't come back to himself in time?

"I don't know what set me off. It wasn't you. The situation maybe—that you're in danger. But not you."

"You . . . changed." Her voice wasn't steady, and it broke him.

Slowly, he straightened and turned back, forcing himself to meet her gaze. "I went feral. All the Ferals do from time to time. In that in-between place, half-way between man and animal, we can fight as equals, no matter which animal we shift into. We enjoy fighting that way—it's like a Feral form of wrestling, and we usually beat the shit out of one another. But we don't lose control like I did. I don't know what happened."

Natalie watched him, her mouth tight. "I'm very good at reading people, Wulfe. And animals. I knew the first time I met you in your wolf form that you were a friend, and that you'd never intentionally hurt me. I still believe that to be true."

He nodded. But he'd caught the word *intentionally,* and that was what worried him, too. Because there was clearly something wrong. And the thought made him ill.

He swiftly finished installing the dead bolt, then turned to where Natalie now sat on the bed, exhaustion written all over her face.

"Do you want to see Xavier tonight or wait until morning?"

Her eyes snapped open, her spine straightening. "Tonight."

"I'll bring him up."

Natalie nodded, and Wulfe left, locking the door behind him. His body felt leaden as he descended the stairs, as he saw again, in his mind's eye, the terror on Natalie's face. She'd stared at him as if he were a monster.

He had to tell Lyon. Maybe his loss of control was due to the dark charm, but so far no one else had suffered such a breach of control. No, he feared the cause lay at the feet of his recently triggered Daemon blood. And if he was right?

He might soon turn into a monster for real.

*Chapter
Eight*

Natalie could barely keep her eyes open, but she fought the pull of the soft bed as she waited for Wulfe to bring Xavier up to her room. The evening's events had begun to take on a dreamlike, perhaps nightmarelike, quality. And yet here she sat, for all practical purposes the captive of shape-shifters.

Good *grief*. Wulfe's face, as he'd changed, had turned terrifying with those fangs and eyes that were not human, yet not quite wolflike. Especially when he'd first turned toward her, furious, staring at her without recognition. She'd honestly thought he was about to attack her.

Then he'd recognized her. She'd seen the moment it happened. He'd looked so confused, so horrified, chagrin and shame filling those dark eyes. And she'd ceased to be afraid despite the fangs. Wulfe had returned, regardless of the face he wore.

She heard the click of the dead bolt and rose from the bed as the door opened and Xavier entered, cane first.

"Nat?"

"Here, Xave." She strolled to him, speaking as she moved. "I'm glad you weren't already asleep." As her hand slid around her brother's arm, her gaze met Wulfe's. Her heart clenched at the misery that still swam in his eyes.

"I'll wait outside," he said, then closed the door, leaving her alone with her brother.

Natalie led Xavier to the bed, then sat cross-legged while he stretched out on his back, his hands behind his head.

"How are you holding up, Nat?"

She laughed, a single burst of air. "I can't decide if I feel more like Dorothy in Oz or Alice in Wonderland."

Xavier grinned. "It's a lot like that, isn't it?"

Natalie reached for him, her hand on his shoulder. "Are you okay here, Xave? You're safe, right?" She knew her brother would tell her the truth. If he didn't, she'd know it anyway. He'd never been able to hide his expressions, certainly not from her.

"I love it here." He took her hand and held it, the Xavier equivalent of meeting her gaze. "The moment the Mage found us in Harpers Ferry, our death warrants were signed, Nat. Your friends and Mary Rose's brother died for real, killed by the Mage and the Daemons. It was a miracle that you and me and Christy survived. But all of our lives ended that day, at least the lives we had before. In a way, all our lives belong to the Ferals now. If not for them, we'd have died. You don't remember what happened on that battle-field, which is good, but I do. The things I heard and smelled and felt that day still give me nightmares, Nat. If the Ferals lose this war, we'll all be living in constant terror. People will be dying by the thousands. And every doomsday prediction about civilization's collapse will come true."

Xavier sat up and turned to her, his face older and wiser than she'd ever seen it. "This might not be what I'd have chosen for my life. Cook's helper to a houseful of shape-shifters wasn't exactly in the career-options manual I read in high school. But I have a purpose here, a purpose I never had at home. Pink needs me. Even if she thinks she can do it on her own, she needs me. She's so cool, Nat, and the guys are great. Sure, they're kind of scary sometimes, like when they go feral and draw claws and start ripping into one another. But they're good guys. And their wives are really nice. If I could have chosen this life, Nat, I would have."

His face fell. "I just wish I didn't have to give up everyone at home to live here. I miss you and Mom. I love that you're here now, but I don't want you to get stuck here, not when you have such a great life outside. Rick has to be worried about you."

Natalie sighed, hating to have to break the news. "Rick and I broke up this morning, Xave."

Xavier frowned. "What happened?"

"I thought I was in love with him, but I wasn't. He wasn't the man I wanted to spend my life with."

"I'm sorry, Nat," Xavier said.

"Don't be. I'm just glad I figured it out before we got married." Even if nothing ever came of her attraction to Wulfe, the very fact that she'd discovered it—that she'd awakened to the possibilities within her—made it imperative that she find someone with whom she could feel that kind of excitement. Someone who, like Wulfe, would stir both her body and her emotions. And as much as she'd enjoyed Rick's company, she knew now that he'd done neither.

Natalie and Xavier talked for a while longer until a huge yawn caught her midsentence.

Xavier smiled. "You've had a crazy night, Nat. Get some sleep. We'll talk again tomorrow, and I'll introduce you to Pink."

Together, they climbed off the bed, and Natalie gave her brother another big hug, emotion welling all over again as she marveled at the miracle of his survival. "I'm so glad you're okay," she whispered.

Xavier hugged her in return. "Better than okay. You're going to be fine, too." But as he pulled back, a frown pulled at the flesh between his eyebrows, and she knew he wasn't certain of that last statement. She was in a precarious position, a pawn in an immortal war. A dangerous place to be.

And they both knew it.

As he paced the hallway outside Natalie's room, Wulfe heard the soft rap of knuckles, the signal that Xavier was ready to return to the kitchen apartments. He unlocked the door and Natalie pulled it open, meeting his gaze with a soft, tired smile.

"Thanks for letting us visit, Wulfe."

He nodded, struck speechless as he was every time he saw her, every time he fell into the calm gray of her lovely, lovely eyes.

Xavier kissed his sister's cheek. "Sleep tight, Sis."

Then he smiled in Wulfe's direction, a worry in his eyes that dug at Wulfe's gut. Because it was a worry he shared in spades.

He was still shaken by what had happened, by the way he'd lost control . . . lost *time* . . . when he'd gone feral. And by the fact that Natalie was feeling pain from a wound he'd taken from her completely. None of it made an ounce of sense.

As he accompanied Xavier downstairs, his skin crawled with the sick suspicion that it was somehow all his fault.

Entering the dining room, he found Kougar and Paenther sitting at the table, sharing a bottle of whiskey with Kougar's mate, Ariana, the Queen of the Ilinas. The two males rose when they saw him. As Xavier headed back to his room behind the kitchen, Wulfe greeted his friends warmly and was greeted in return. He nodded at Ariana, who flashed him a smile and pushed a plate of ham sandwiches toward him.

"Help yourself," she said. "Pink brought them out a little while ago, and we've already had our fill."

Wulfe sat beside Paenther. "How's Kara? Any change?"

Paenther shook his head and poured him a finger of whiskey. "She's no worse, thank the goddess, but she's no better, either. The Shaman's convinced she won't recover until she brings a good Feral into his animal."

A month ago, Inir managed to free seventeen animal spirits that had been trapped for centuries, unable to mark new Feral Warriors. Seventeen animal spirits he'd infected with a dark magic meant to force them to mark the worst, most evil of the line, not the best.

An infection passed to the ones marked, trapping them beneath Inir's spell.

Some of the animal spirits had succeeded in thwarting the dark magic to mark good men. And Falkyn. Others hadn't. Wulfe and his Feral brothers had been ecstatic as their ranks began to swell after centuries of being only nine—until the first batch of new shifters rose up against them and tried to kill them. Almost too late, they'd realized Inir's plan—to destroy the good Ferals and order the evil to free the Daemons in their place.

With the help of Ariana and the Shaman, they'd managed to cure a few of the new Ferals from the poison passed to them through their infected animals, but they had no way of knowing for certain which of the males were the ones meant to be marked—good men—and which were, deep down, evil. The only one they were one hundred percent certain of was Falkyn, the lone female among them, and Hawke's new mate.

They'd thought Grizz and Lepard to be honorable until the pair escaped. Six of the new Ferals belonged to Inir still, firmly under his spell. The rest were locked up in the Ferals' prison or hadn't shown up yet. No additional new Ferals would be brought into their animals until, and unless, the Ferals found a way to tell, conclusively, which were good men and which were evil, because bringing the evil ones into their animals was slowly killing Kara. One more, and they'd lose her for good.

Wulfe grabbed a sandwich and turned to Ariana. "Have you found anything?"

In a T-shirt and jeans, her dark hair pulled back into a ponytail, Ariana looked far too human to be

Ilina, a race whose Crystal Realm castle sat, literally, in the clouds.

"I've found a couple of ancient Mage rituals for dispelling Daemon magic that might *possibly* help reverse the dark charm that's turning all of you mortal."

"They won't work. There's another one you need to be looking for." Wulfe blinked, as startled by the words that had come from his mouth as his companions appeared to be.

"How do you know that?" Paenther asked evenly.

"I have no fucking idea." But as he turned his thoughts inward, he knew he was right. He *knew* that no ancient Mage rituals would help them. No Mage had ever used this particular magic before. It was Daemon magic last used against the Nyads millennia ago. He turned back to Ariana. "The ritual you need to find is one the third Ilina queen witnessed near the end of the second Nyad War." His heart was beginning to race because not only was he starting to lose control, now alien knowledge was somehow invading his mind.

Ariana watched him carefully. "All right. I'll try to access that memory."

As his friends watched him in contemplative silence, Wulfe returned to his food, devouring his first sandwich, then reaching for a second. By the time Kougar finally broke that silence, Wulfe was about to crawl out of his skin.

"I hear Xavier's sister is back with us."

Wulfe nodded. Just what he wanted, the discussion turning from his own increasing weirdness to Natalie's. "Something's up with her," he told them. "She's acquired an odd aura. And a little while ago, the wound I healed on her face started hurting like the Daemon had just clawed her again."

All three of his companions frowned.

"What would cause that?" Paenther asked, sipping his whiskey.

"I wish I knew."

Ariana reached halfway across the table, laying her palm flat on the gleaming surface. "I'll add that to my search, Wulfe. If I come up with anything, I'll let you know."

"Thanks." Wulfe finished his second sandwich, then said good night and left them before he started spouting more Daemon history. Goddess, he *hated* this.

No light shone beneath Natalie's door when he reached it, so he knocked lightly. When she didn't answer, he unlocked the dead bolt and opened the door wide enough for the hall light to illuminate her sleeping face above the sheet that covered her to the neck.

A rush of emotion swamped him—tenderness, protectiveness. Possessiveness. *Mine.* She'd been through so much, yet remained as solid and strong as hammered steel. She'd make a fine mate for a warrior.

For the right warrior.

He stepped inside and closed the door behind him. Stripping out of his clothes, he shifted into his wolf and curled up on the rug beside Natalie's bed, as close as he could get to her without actually joining her. He didn't want to risk waking her.

Please, goddess, don't let Natalie suffer more pain when I'm too far to hear her distress.

He shouldn't have taken her wound a month ago. He hadn't planned to. Despite days in their prison, she'd remained brave and stoic and so damned beautiful. And that wound on her cheek had made him ache every time he'd looked at it. Finally, he hadn't been able to bear it any longer.

He remembered the moment so clearly. She'd awakened and greeted him with a smile that had turned him on his tail. They'd talked as she ate the meal Kara brought down to her, but then it had been time to try again to steal her memories of all she'd seen. He'd hesitated, knowing that once he took her memories, he'd have to send her home. And he'd just gotten the chance to talk to her again.

His gaze fell to that jagged cut on her cheek, his thumb lifting to trace it lightly.

Natalie flinched.

Wulfe jerked his thumb back. "It still hurts."

"Not too much."

Which was a blatant lie.

Her brows drew down. "How bad does it look?"

"Not as bad as mine."

A genuine laugh escaped her throat, utterly delighting him. She caught herself with a groan, though wry humor continued to light her eyes and tug at her mouth. "I'm sorry, but that wasn't quite the reassurance I was looking for."

He grinned at her, amazed at how easy she was to be with.

To his surprise, she lifted her hand, almost touching his face, before lowering it again. As she did, her smile died, her expression sobering. "I'm sorry for all you must have suffered."

He grunted. "It was a long time ago." Without thinking too much about what he was doing, he made a decision. "Hold still. This may be uncomfortable for a moment, but I won't hurt you." When her eyes gave him the go-ahead, he said, *"Close your eyes."*

She hesitated only a moment before doing as he asked. He opened his hand, covering her wound and half her face with his palm.

"What are you doing?" she asked quietly.

Beneath his palm, her heart beat, throbbing beneath the surface of her skin. Once more, her scent wrapped around him like a warm summer breeze.

"I'm something of a healer." Sometimes. His own cheek began to burn and throb with surprising misery. How did humans stand the pain that took so long to go away? *"How do you feel?"*

"The pain's gone." Her voice held a note of wonder. Lifting his hand, he peered at her cheekbone with keen satisfaction. The wound was gone completely now, her cheek unblemished.

She opened her eyes, blinking. *"How did you . . . ?"* Her gaze locked onto his cheek, onto the throbbing, aching wound he knew to be there, now. Her hand flew to her own cheek, then rubbed, as if seeking . . . anything.

"What have you done?"

Wulfe shrugged. *"What's one more?"*

But he saw no gratitude in her eyes, only a keen dismay. *"No, no, no."* Her brows knitting, she grabbed his face between her hands without fear, staring at him, at the cut that would mark him as all the others had. To his amazement, her fingers slid gently over his scarred cheeks. *"You took it."*

Her voice was breathless, stunned. She stared up at him, pain in her eyes. *"Why?"*

He frowned, confused by her reaction. The last thing he'd meant to do was upset her. But the truth was, he didn't have an answer. He wasn't sure why he'd done it. Maybe he just didn't like seeing her suffer when he could help. Or maybe he hadn't liked the sight of that ugly scar on her pretty face.

What difference did it make? Women were so damn hard to please.

He turned away, breaking her soft hold on him and ending the discussion. "Lie down." The words came out harsher than he'd meant them to.

But when he turned back to her, she was still standing where he'd left her, still staring at him. Although her brows remained drawn, her eyes no longer flashed with pain but something infinitely softer.

"Will you heal?"

"Of course."

"But it'll scar you."

"Like I said, what's one more?"

"Plenty." The softness in her eyes deepened, a fine film of moisture making them shine like diamonds. "That may have been the most unselfish thing anyone's ever done for me. And I don't even know your name."

"I'm called Wulfe."

Understanding lit her gaze, the memory of watching him shift, he was certain. "I suppose that makes sense. Thank you, Wulfe."

He nodded, his jaw tight. Then he slid his hand to her neck and pressed beneath her ear, feeling a need to close those eyes that saw too much. As she fell unconscious, he caught her, then laid her down carefully on one of the pallets someone had brought down for the prisoners.

Straightening, he stared down at her, clenching his jaw at her now-unblemished beauty.

With a burst of self-disgust, he'd turned away, because nothing good had ever come from his healing gift.

Now, a month later, he was more worried than ever that in taking her pain, he'd inadvertently hurt her more.

He sank his chin on his paws and gave a low, miserable whine.

Chapter Nine

Natalie woke to the sound of Wulfe's calling her name. Blinking against the brilliant sunlight pouring into the room, she turned her head to find him filling the doorway, watching her with those liquid eyes.

A small flutter of pleasure filled her chest, making her smile. "Good morning."

"Morning."

A smile tugged at his mouth, and that flutter of pleasure intensified. She was coming to love those smiles of his. And, oh, he was a sight to wake up to. He wore a T-shirt today, tucked into his jeans, the first time she'd seen him fully dressed, but the soft fabric did nothing to hide the fine, fine shape of his broad chest, narrow hips, and thick, muscular arms. His golden armband curled around his biceps just below one sleeve.

If only he'd join her in the bed. If only he wanted to.

In one hand, he held a small silver laptop. She sat up, letting the sheet fall to her waist. "Is that mine?"

He nodded. "Hawke modified it, disabling the GPS along with your ability to get online." He gave her a rueful smile. "Sorry. Lyon's rules." His gaze dropped briefly to her chest, to her sleeveless cotton nightgown, then rose again all too quickly. If the sight in any way intrigued him, she couldn't tell. "Lyon says you can make the calls to your mom and your assistant, but not alone, and not here. We don't want the signal tracked."

"Fair enough. I assume you have my phone?" It was no longer in her purse.

"We have it."

She didn't blame them for being so cautious. No good could come of humans' getting involved in the Ferals' war. She was certain of that.

Wulfe crossed his arms over that powerful chest. "We'll be doing a power raising soon. I thought you might enjoy watching it. We'll be shifting."

"All of you?" At the thought of watching them change into all those marvelous animals her eyes went wide, and she found herself grinning. "I'd love to watch." Flinging back the sheet, she swung her legs over the side of the bed and stood up. "How much time do I have?"

Wulfe's gaze made a slow, gratifying trail down her body to her legs, bared beneath the hem of her short nightie. Pleasure shimmered through her that he was at least looking.

"Are you going to wait here while I dress?" she asked, striding to the bathroom.

"No." The word snapped out, his expression turning almost pained. "I'll be back for you in thirty." He disappeared out the door, half slamming it behind him.

Natalie glanced at the closed door, bemused. Perhaps the man wasn't as uninterested as he appeared. She could only hope.

Wulfe leaned back against the wall outside Natalie's bedchamber, searching for his breath. The sight of her in that nightgown, the soft cotton skimming her curves, hiding, teasing, enticing. *Goddess*. His mind was on fire even if his body was too damaged to respond. With her cheeks pink from sleep, her golden hair a tousled halo about her head, she'd looked like an angel—a sexy-as-hell angel. At one time, he'd have been burning to pull her beneath him. His cock would have been thick and throbbing, his pulse racing. Now it was only his mind that imagined, and longed, and wanted. And, goddess, how he wanted. He shoved himself away from the wall and started down the hallway, that vision of long, long legs and slender curves caressed by soft cotton burned into his mind.

With effort, he turned his thoughts back to the situation at hand. So far, Ariana had been unable to find any reference to the second Nyad War in the storage facility that was her Ilina queen's brain. Of course, perhaps there had never been a second Nyad War, and he'd dreamed up the whole thing. How was he supposed to verify the veracity of information he shouldn't even know? The whole thing made his gut cramp.

As he approached the dining room, Fox strode out through the doorway, a pair of large cloth bags hanging from each of his fists.

"Give me a hand, boyo?" Fox asked with a smile. "I've drawn short straw for the prison run."

"Sure." Wulfe backtracked and opened the door to the basement, then took one of Fox's bags. He knew from experience they were filled with food and drink for their prisoners.

"Have you seen Jag this morning?" Wulfe asked as he followed Fox down the stairs.

"Aye. He seems to be fine. No change."

Wulfe nodded, more relieved than he wanted to admit. None of them knew how long they had to live once they lost their animals.

"Did you hear about the female watching the place?" Together, they crossed the gym toward the hidden door at the back.

"Mage?"

"No. Either human or Therian. She parked her car along the road and was just starting up the drive when Vhyper spotted her. Before he could call for backup, in case it was some kind of trap, she lifted her hand, and yelled, 'Wrong house,' then backtracked to her car and drove away."

Wulfe looked at him as he followed Fox through the door and into the long stone passage that led to the prisons. "What about that set off Vhyper's alarm bells?"

"Nothing in particular. Not until he asked one of the Ilinas to follow and see where she went, and she drove straight out of the neighborhood."

Wulfe frowned. "If she'd really approached the

wrong house, she should have searched for the right one."

"Aye, boyo. Precisely what Vhyper thought. We're wondering if she's a newly marked Feral who lost her nerve."

"Did the Ilina stay with her long enough to know where she went?"

"No. Apparently tailing a vehicle while in mist form is extremely taxing. Lyon's ordered the Ilinas to notify him immediately if either the vehicle or the woman are spotted again."

Together, they entered the prison block where three newly marked Ferals languished in separate cells. None had been brought into his animal. They didn't know any of the three well enough to be able to guess whether or not they were the ones their animal spirits had meant to mark. They could be either good or evil, and choosing wrong would sign Kara's death warrant.

Wulfe set down his bag in front of Castin's cell and pulled out three individually wrapped foot-long subs. Straightening, he handed them to the male through the bars.

"Any news?" Castin asked. Of all of the prisoners, Castin seemed the most accepting of his fate. From what they could tell, he was by far the oldest among them, possibly as ancient as the Shaman. He'd helped in the rescue of Kara from Inir's stronghold, then returned to Feral House willingly, expressing his displeasure at being locked up with a tight jaw and little more.

When they'd first dragged this latest group of new Ferals down here, they'd discussed whether they should keep them in the dark about what was going on. The trouble was, they empathized with these men. And if the day came when they could free this group, bring them into their animals, and call them "brother," they wanted to know they'd treated them as fairly as possible under these very trying circumstances.

"Inir is attempting to turn the blood he stole from Kara into unascended Radiant's blood," Wulfe told Castin. If their situations had been reversed, he'd be hungry for information, too. "It's the prime ingredient he needs to open the Daemon Blade once the Ferals cease to register, but you probably know that as well as anyone."

Just as a Feral had to be brought into his animal through ritual, so too did a new Radiant have to be ascended to her power. Months ago, Inir had arranged for their previous Radiant, Beatrice, to be killed so that the new one could be blooded before she was ascended, and that blood used to open the Daemon Blade. Not until the last minute had the Ferals figured out what was happening and thwarted that scheme.

"What are you doing to stop Inir?" Rikkert demanded from the next cell. The male had been bad-tempered from the moment he'd arrived.

"We're working to get our immortality back, boyo," Fox answered. "Jag lost the shift, or didn't you hear? He can no longer access his animal. Inir has us over a barrel until we can reverse the effects of his dark charm."

Wulfe passed three sandwiches to Rikkert, then moved to the last cell. The third male had arrived at Feral House a little over a week ago, hailing from Kenya. He'd said little when they'd explained the situation and forced him into the prison. He'd said nothing since. Wulfe didn't even know his name.

The male rose and took the sandwiches with a nod, his dark eyes piercing, his expression enigmatic.

"One other thing," Fox said as he handed out water bottles to the three prisoners. "We got a call from Lepard. Apparently he and Grizz are out West somewhere hunting for a woman who's said to be able to see into a man's soul. If they find her, they'll bring her to us. Hopefully, she'll be able to tell us which of our new Ferals were meant to be marked."

Wulfe looked at him with surprise. "So they didn't run."

"No. They're helping in their own way."

"Good. That's good."

Castin said something in a language Wulfe didn't recognize, a fervent string of words that sounded like a prayer of thanksgiving. Rikkert just grunted. The newest Feral said nothing, as usual.

Wulfe led the way back upstairs, feeling more hopeful for the males in the prison than he had on the way down. Being marked to be a Feral Warrior, to finally, after a lifetime, be able to shift as you were born to do, should be the greatest of honors. Wulfe himself had found absolution and salvation in his own marking.

"*Daemon?*" The word brushed across Wulfe's mind, startling him.

"What is it, boyo?" Fox asked behind him.

"Nothing." *Fuck*. He waited for it to happen again, but he heard nothing more. What in the hell was happening?

The only thing he knew absolutely, positively for certain . . . it was far from *nothing*.

Natalie stood at the window, gazing at the vehicles that lined the Ferals' circular drive—a bright yellow Hummer, a white Land Rover, and a low-slung sports car that she thought might be a Lamborghini, among them—as she waited for Wulfe to collect her for the spirit raising. Beyond the drive, the woods rose on all sides, and not far beyond them, she knew, lay the Potomac River and the horizontal falls for which Great Falls had been named.

She wondered if she'd ever be allowed to leave the house, to see them again. Xavier's days of freedom were over, and the knowledge made her ache. No matter how happy he seemed to be, he was trapped here, unable to leave for fear of being recognized. He might never leave this house again.

But he was alive. Dear God, her brother was alive. Despite her concerns, her heart soared. She'd awakened to a bright, sunny day, to the sight of a gorgeous male with the sweetest smile, and in the house where Xavier now *lived*. It was a glorious day, and she would rejoice in every single moment.

The rap she'd been waiting for finally sounded on her door.

"Come in," she called, turning away from the window. She was halfway across the room when the door swung open.

Wulfe's gaze skimmed her body, taking in her jeans, her green T-shirt with the pretty detailing, and her sandals, setting off little flares of warmth along the way. Slowly, he looked up, meeting her gaze, a smile in his eyes that burrowed deep down inside her. Other men had looked at her over the years, but never before had she felt as if they really saw her. And Wulfe did.

"Ready?" he asked, a smile pulling at his mouth.

"Ready." Natalie returned his smile as she joined him. The warmth of his body wrapped around her, his masculine scent filling her nostrils. As they started down the hall, side by side, electricity arced through the air between them, making Natalie catch her breath. Glancing at Wulfe, she found him watching her with eyes that leaped with an answering awareness.

Natalie swallowed.

Wulfe frowned and took her arm, gently pulling her around to face him. Slowly, he lifted his hand, his knuckles caressing her cheek, making her pulse race and her body melt with longing.

"I can't give you what you want," he said, his voice low, rough, aching. With fingers shaking ever so slightly, he stroked her neck. "I can't make love to you."

"Can't?" she asked breathlessly. "Or don't want to?"

"Can't." He leaned in, his nose brushing the curve of her neck, his soft, fragrant hair caressing her cheek, sending her pulse into overdrive. He made a sound deep in his throat, half-human, half-wolf, a low rumble of pleasure. It took every bit of control she possessed not to weave her fingers into his hair and lift his face for her kiss.

He pulled away suddenly with a look of chagrin. "They're waiting for us," he said gruffly, and started back down the hall.

Natalie caught up to him, more confused than before, yet elated. Wulfe wanted her. Something was holding him back, but he wanted her. And that was all she needed to know.

Her step was light as they reached the stairs and started down. "After this ritual, do you think we can scare up a cup of coffee?"

"We'll grab it on the way out."

As they reached the foyer, they had to merge with the steady stream of people passing by.

"Quite a crowd today," she murmured.

One of the women heard her and smiled. "The Guards have been invited to watch the Ferals shift. We wouldn't miss it."

Wulfe and Natalie joined the stream, following the others down the hall and into the dining room. Through the back windows, Natalie caught a glimpse of a brick patio and heavily treed yard quickly filling with people.

"Do I have time to say hello to Xavier?" she asked.

"Sure. They won't start without me. And Lyon hasn't brought Kara down, yet."

Wulfe led her to the swinging door she'd watched Xavier come through last night, and into a first-class kitchen with granite countertops and gleaming appliances. Xavier was busy kneading dough. The joy that pulsed inside of her as her gaze took in his beloved, contented face was so great it was a moment before she noticed the extraordinary creature standing behind him, stirring a pot on the stove. The woman appeared to be part human, part bird, with . . . *my God* . . . pink feathers instead of skin.

The bird-woman turned and stared at Natalie. In unblinking bird-shaped eyes, Natalie saw a terrible self-consciousness, an almost palpable fear of rejection. Empathy curled around her heart. This was clearly Pink.

"X, your sister's here," Wulfe said.

"Hey, Nat!" Her brother turned toward the door.

"Hey, Xave." But her gaze remained riveted on those tense, unblinking eyes. Natalie smiled. "You must be Pink. You have quite a fan in my brother. I'm happy to finally make your acquaintance."

Xavier reached for the bird-woman without hesitation, his hand clasping a feathered arm. "Pink, this is my sister, Natalie. And, yeah, I'm a fan. Pink does all the cooking and cleaning around here, or she used to when there weren't so many people. I'm her helper, now."

Natalie met Pink's gaze with a rueful look. "This place is mobbed. I don't know how you do it all, even with help."

Pink's stiffness eased a little. "Most of our guests are temporary, and we're managing. It's a pleasure to meet Xavier's sister."

"The pleasure is all mine. I'm delighted that Xavier has you as a friend, Pink." The truth of that statement hit her hard, because it was more than clear that a good deal of the reason Xavier radiated such contentment with his captivity was due to Pink. She met the woman's gaze, letting her see her thoughts and emotion. "You have no idea," she said quietly, and smiled.

"Are you going to watch the Ferals shift this morning, Nat?" Her brother launched into one of his dear and familiar rambles. "It's so cool when they shift, though a little scary when they fight like that, but then they're best friends again, usually, except for the evil Ferals, but they're all with Inir, now, or maybe in the prisons below Feral House. We're not sure about those guys. It was scary as shit when the evil Ferals attacked. We weren't sure what they were going to do. Pink and I hid, then the bad guys ran to Inir, and the good guys finally healed and came back."

Natalie shook her head with a smile. "You must be a good listener, Pink, because my brother can talk the ears off an elephant. Mom likes to tease that he came out of the womb talking, that she had to buy him a pacifier just to get a little quiet."

Xavier laughed at the old joke. "What can I say? Active mind, active mouth."

As the two women's gazes met, Natalie watched a small smile form on that remarkable face. "I enjoy Xavier's thoughts. He's my friend."

Gratitude welled up inside Natalie, and she started around the island that separated her from the pair, talking as she went so that Xavier could follow her movement. "It's no wonder you're happy here, Xave." Natalie gave her brother a hard hug, meeting Pink's gaze over his shoulder. *Thank you,* she mouthed, earning a sweet smile.

As she released her brother, Pink held out her hand to her. "I am very pleased to meet you, Natalie."

Natalie took that soft, feathered hand between both of hers. "The pleasure is all mine."

"We need to go," Wulfe said from the doorway. "Later, X and Pink."

Natalie followed him back to the dining room. As the kitchen door swung closed behind them, she glanced at Wulfe. "She's amazing."

He watched her with eyes like velvet. "So are you."

"Natalie," a woman's voice called softly from a short distance away.

Wulfe turned. "Kara."

Lyon slowed his walk through the dining room, the woman in his arms holding out her hand toward

Natalie. She appeared wan, with dark circles under her eyes, her blond hair pulled back in a lifeless ponytail. But as she gazed at Natalie, she smiled warmly.

Natalie took the proffered hand. "You must be Kara. Wulfe says we met the last time I was here, but I'm afraid I have no memory of that visit."

Kara's smile turned rueful. "That's what they were hoping. I'm sorry you've been pulled back into all this."

"I'm not." And she realized that was true. "I know I probably won't be able to keep these memories, either, but it's worth everything to see my brother again and see him so happy." She glanced at Wulfe, a welling of pleasure filling her chest. "This is turning out to be quite an adventure."

Kara laughed. "Everything the Ferals touch turns into an adventure."

"Funny," a Feral she hadn't met said, joining them from the hallway. "I'd say everything we touch turns into a goat fuck."

"Jag, watch your language," Lyon snapped.

The shaggy-haired warrior grinned unrepentantly. "Sorry, ladies. I just call 'em like I see 'em. Are we ready to start this war dance? The sooner Kara stops looking like death warmed over, the better."

"Thanks, Jag." Kara met Natalie's gaze with a wry smile.

Jag leaned over and kissed Kara's cheek, his gaze turning stone-cold serious. "I mean it, little lightbulb. I want you getting better. That's an order."

"Yes, Jag." Kara looped her free arm around his neck and pressed her cheek to his. "Thank you."

When Jag had stepped back, Wulfe reached for Kara's hand and brought it to his lips, earning himself a sweet smile. Then Lyon started forward again, heading for the back doors. "Let's get started."

Wulfe grabbed Natalie's hand and led her to the sideboard laden with coffee mugs and industrial-sized coffeepots. "First things first."

"Mmm, thank you." She threw him a grin as she grabbed one of the cups and was rewarded with a pleased smile.

"How many will actually take part in this?" she asked, pouring herself a cup of the steaming brew.

"Ten Ferals and Kara since the purpose of the power raising is to strengthen her."

When Natalie had filled her mug, Wulfe ushered her out the back door and onto a wide brick patio ringed by azalea and forsythia bushes growing in abandon. The morning was warm, the humidity reasonably comfortable, and the sky bright blue above the trees. In the middle of the open yard, a male with a close-cut mustache and goatee lifted his hands to the sky and murmured words too low to hear.

"Kougar is calling a feral circle," Wulfe told her. "The entire back of the house will be warded once he does, so even if one of the neighboring humans walks through, they'll neither see nor hear anything. Wait here." He stepped forward, joining the other men, all of whom were incredibly well built, though not a one held a candle to Wulfe.

"Hi, Natalie." Delaney came to join her, along with another woman, an attractive brunette with eyes almost as bright a blue as Melisande's. "Natalie, Julianne," Delaney said, by way of introduction.

"Hi, Julianne." Natalie shook hands with the woman, but her gaze immediately returned to the

Feral who'd caught her eye—a male currently stripping out of his clothes, right there in front of everyone. Lyon was doing the same.

"The nudity takes a little getting used to," Delaney murmured, amusement in her voice. "Just one of the many perks of life with a bunch of shapeshifters."

Natalie snorted, her gaze following Wulfe's movements, admiring the perfection of his now-bare back and shoulders and watching with fascination as he pulled his jeans down and off. Her breath caught. His butt and legs were like sculpted marble, truly glorious to behold. How could a flesh-and-blood male be so beautiful, so perfectly formed?

"Admiring the view?" Delaney asked.

"Oh, yes. Every time I see it."

Delaney made a sound of surprise. "Something already going on between you two?"

Lyon had settled Kara on a lawn chair, and now all the males, either shirtless or naked, made a wide circle around her. Each of them had a golden armband snaked around one thick biceps, Natalie realized.

"When the Mage attacked, he shifted a couple of times," she told Delaney.

Julianne groaned. "And you're human. That must have been a shock."

Natalie smiled. "You could say that. I'd met the wolf before and had already fallen in love with him. Finding out he was really a man, a shifter, was definitely a shock. But at least I'd already come to trust him. He saved my life, attacking the Mage sentinels who'd been sent to capture me."

"I'm officially a fan, Natalie," Delaney said quietly, seriously. "If you can handle all that and not fall apart, you're rock solid."

Natalie looked at her thoughtfully. "I've been having some strange dreams since . . . the incident—the Daemons. I'm beginning to think I've been dreaming about that day even if I don't remember much of it. What happened last night was shocking of course, but I didn't have much trouble accepting it. I suppose, subconsciously, I already knew about shape-shifters and the Mage."

Delaney nodded. "That makes a lot of sense."

"Here they go," Julianne said breathlessly. "I've never seen a Feral shift."

All three women turned their attention back to the shifters. Natalie watched as Kougar pulled out a wicked-looking knife.

"Small cuts only," Lyon commanded. "And to your palms, not your chests."

Several of the shifters made sounds of disgust.

"They're not healing," Delaney said, her voice low and tight.

One by one, the shifters cut their palms, then thrust those fisted hands into the air. As Wulfe cut his own, his gaze found Natalie's and held, a look in his eyes that, for once, she couldn't read. A touch of pride, perhaps, that he belonged in that elite, mythic circle. Or perhaps a pinch of concern that she might be put off by the strangeness of it all. Maybe a little of both.

"He likes you," Delaney murmured beside her.

"I like him, too."

"Do you?" It wasn't a casual question.

"He's a good man."

"He is. He absolutely is. But he's been dealt a rough hand."

Natalie met the other woman's gaze. "Are you ready to tell me more, now?"

Delaney watched her assessingly. "When a new Radiant is marked, one of the Ferals is chosen as her mate. It happens during a ritual, all very mystical. Wulfe was the one chosen for the previous Radiant, Beatrice. From what I've heard, Beatrice was selfish and shallow and threw a tantrum that the goddess chose the scarred Feral for her."

Natalie winced. "Oh, Wulfe. That's terrible."

"Tighe says Wulfe loved her, at least at first. The goddess gave him no choice but to love her. But he suffered for almost a century and a half with a mate who . . ." She didn't complete the sentence, but Natalie heard the rest. "Nine months ago, Beatrice died, leaving Wulfe in even worse shape."

"He misses her."

"No, I honestly don't think he does. But the mating bond between immortals is a real, physical bond that, when broken, often damages, if not destroys, the one left behind."

"He seems . . . okay."

Delaney nodded. "I'm not sure in what way it hurt him. Only that Tighe says it did."

"Is there no healing from such an injury?"

"I don't know."

Natalie watched Wulfe as he thrust his hand into the air alongside his companions, aching for all he'd been through. "How could Beatrice not see past his scars? I barely see them anymore, and I've known him less than a day. He is so beautiful," she breathed. "Inside and out."

Delaney's hand landed on her shoulder. "I'm glad you're here, Natalie. Very, very glad."

Natalie met the other woman's gaze with a smile. "Me, too." Though her being there might be a very short-lived thing.

As the last of the Feral Warriors thrust his fist in the air, the bearded Feral began to chant. "Spirits rise and join. Empower the beasts beneath this sky."

The other Ferals joined in the chant, their voices low at first, then louder and louder. Goose bumps raced along Natalie's arms. Lightning flashed. The ground beneath her feet began to tremble.

Eyes widening, Natalie glanced at Delaney and Julianne.

"Watch, Natalie," Delaney whispered.

She did, turning back to the Ferals as excitement and energy pressed all around her.

"Empower the spirit of . . ." they called in unison.

"The wolf!" Wulfe yelled.

His brothers . . . and sister . . . all named their own animals. "The hawk! The falcon! The tiger! The cougar!"

Suddenly, most of them disappeared in that familiar explosion of sparkling lights to be replaced, seconds later, by incredible, magnificent animals—a glorious African lion, a magnificent Bengal tiger, a sleek black panther, and a huge red fox. Two birds of prey sat among the larger animals as their animal kin would never dare. And the wolf she was coming to adore stood with them.

But the bald Feral—a male she hadn't met—shouted with a mix of fury and agony and remained human. Kougar, too, threw back his head, his body going rigid as he failed to shift. And Jag stood, fully clothed, eyeing the other two with frustration and misery.

"It's getting worse," Delaney said beside her, her voice laced with real fear. "Kougar and Vhyper now, too."

Remain in your animals. Lyon's voice rang in Natalie's head as Wulfe's did when he was in his animal. *Concentrate on your Radiant. Share your energy with her.*

The animals milled about the circle, several nudging Kara or laying their heads in her lap. Finally, Lyon shifted back to human and the others followed, one by one. Natalie watched Wulfe shift back, then walk over to clasp the bald Feral's shoulder. A pall had fallen, dark and heavy, on the gathering. Lyon lifted Kara into his arms, then approached the two warriors who'd failed to shift, his eyes filled with a throbbing regret.

"I never thought the ritual would do harm."

Kougar's face was pale. "It wouldn't have if our connections to our animals weren't already close to shattering. This wasn't your fault, Roar."

Lyon nodded, but his mouth remained tight.

"It's more than just losing their animals, isn't it?" Natalie asked quietly.

"Ferals who can't shift, ultimately die." Though Delaney's words were matter-of-fact, Natalie heard the underlying thread of fear.

Natalie reached for Delaney's hand and gave it a squeeze, her gaze finding Wulfe where he stood with his friends. How could so much power and beauty, so much goodness and gentleness, be snuffed out just like that? It was wrong on so many levels. The Feral Warriors, these powerful immortals, might soon be no more. And while she understood that the ramifications of that were far greater than the loss of a handful of fine, strong males, that was the only part of it that she could truly wrap her mind around.

As she watched Wulfe pull on his jeans, then grab his T-shirt and turn to her with eyes as deep as the ocean, she knew her loss would be far, far more personal.

*Chapter
Ten*

Wulfe pulled his T-shirt on over his head, the summer sun caressing the back of his neck through the trees even as his heart pounded with misery. And dread. Kougar and Vhyper, like Jag, were now cut off from their animals. Three Ferals unable to shift.

Deep inside, Wulfe's own animal howled with anger and fear that he'd soon be next, and Wulfe had no words of comfort to offer. Because, for all he knew, the animal was right.

All around him, his brothers' mates flocked to their sides. As Ariana took form at Kougar's, the stoic, often silent male pulled her hard against him, burying his face in her hair. Olivia slid into Jag's arms. Of the three now-nonshifting Ferals, only Vhyper stood alone without a mate to offer comfort. Without a mate to leave behind in pain and misery, if the worst happened. If they all died.

Beside him, Fox wrapped Melisande in his arms.

Two more Feral lights have gone out, my lord. Soon all will be doused, and the Daemons will rise.

Wulfe froze at the now-familiar sound of Inir's voice in his head.

Hail the Daemons, my lord.

Hail the Daemons.

A chill rippled over Wulfe's flesh, his gaze seeking Natalie, where she now stood beside Julianne and Zeeland. Behind them, the Therian Guards returned to the house, heads down, their mood respectfully somber.

Natalie watched him with worried gray eyes—eyes filled with compassion and strength. The sun sparkled on her hair, turning it to spun gold, the brightness making her aura pale by comparison. She was so pretty, it made him ache. Especially when she flashed him a soft gray-eyes smile that arrowed straight to his heart.

"She's into you, boyo," Fox said quietly beside him, Melisande in his arms.

"I saved her from the Mage."

"I know a thing or two about female smiles, Wulfe, and that one is as warm and welcoming as any I've seen."

At Fox's grunt, Wulfe turned to find Melisande looking up at her mate with an eyebrow raised, yet softness in her eyes. "As any?"

"Except for your smiles, my love." Fox lifted his hand and stroked his Ilina wife's cheek.

Wulfe turned away, the raw tenderness between

them too private. Instead, he gave in to the need to be close to Natalie. As he neared, she reached for him, and he took her hand.

"Are you okay?" she asked, squeezing her fingers around his.

"I'm still shifting."

Frown lines formed between her pretty brows. "I'm sorry this is happening, Wulfe."

"Me, too."

"Vhyper, wait," Lyon called. Wulfe glanced up to find the warrior turning back a few feet from the door. "The Shaman would like to examine you, Jag, and Kougar."

With a curt nod, Vhyper returned to the yard and the others, coming to a halt before the Shaman. But, while Vhyper towered over the much smaller male, the Shaman had never been intimidated by any of the Ferals, and he waved his hands, reaching up to touch Vhyper's bald head. With a frown, the Shaman turned to Kougar and did the same, then to Jag.

By the time the ancient male turned to face Lyon, all eyes were upon him.

"Their animals are not gone," the Shaman explained. The hope his words created were dashed with his next utterance. "As yet. A wall has been erected between each man and his animal spirit, a wall that is disintegrating the connection and will ultimately sever it permanently."

And once those connections were broken, the men would die.

"How long do they have?" Lyon asked.

"I don't know. Jag's connection feels no less strong

than the other two, so I would venture to say there's been no significant deterioration during the past hours. It might be months. Or only days."

"And when we're gone," Hawke said, his expression bleak, "Inir will free the Daemons."

"Maybe before then." Still holding Natalie's hand, Wulfe moved toward them, pulling her with him. "Inir and Satanan are feeling our lights go out, as they put it. They know that three of us have ceased to register as Ferals. They're waiting for the rest of us to do the same."

Low murmurs of surprise and dismay peppered the group.

"So they don't even need our deaths to free the Daemons," Vhyper growled. "They just need us to lose our animals."

"At this rate, that could happen before nightfall," Tighe muttered.

Kougar stroked his beard. "They still need unascended Radiant's blood."

"Which they're working to create," Paenther countered. He looked at Wulfe. "They haven't succeeded?"

Wulfe shook his head. "Not that I've heard."

Lyon turned to Ariana, who stood tight against Kougar's side. "We need that ritual."

The queen of the Ilinas nodded. "I'm working on it, Lyon." Her expression turned resolute. "I will find it."

Lyon nodded, but Wulfe saw the fear in his eyes, the fear that Ariana would be too late. A fear they all shared.

The mood was somber as Wulfe and Natalie entered

the dining room again. Wulfe led her back to the kitchen, where Pink and Xavier worked.

Pink looked up as they entered, her expression tight. "What happened, Wulfe? I heard Vhyper's unhappiness."

"He and Kougar have both lost their animals, now, too."

Odd bird eyes filled with misery. Natalie wouldn't have thought such eyes would be so expressive, but she had no more trouble reading them than she did anyone else's.

Xavier frowned. "Dude, that's not cool."

"No, it's not. Natalie needs some breakfast, X."

Xavier's expression changed lightning-fast as it so often did. "I made Mom's banana-nut pancakes for Pink this morning, and I have some leftover batter, Nat. They used to be your favorites."

"They still are. So you're cooking for the chef, now?" she teased.

"Hey, someone has to. She's so busy cooking for everyone else, she forgets to eat." Xavier poured the batter onto the griddle. How he knew where things were when he couldn't see them, she'd never understood. "So, what did you think of watching the Ferals shift into their animals? You should have been here when Maxim shifted into a saber-toothed cat. That was *awesome*. The noises he made weren't anything like you'd expect from a cat. He's dead now—he was a seriously evil dude—but there will be another saber-tooth. Eventually, there will be twenty-six Ferals in all."

She watched Wulfe as Xavier talked, saw the way his mouth tightened at *twenty-six* and suspected she knew what he was thinking. Twenty-six new Ferals.

All of them new, because the current ones might soon cease to exist.

"Give me something to do, Pink," Wulfe growled.

Pink looked like she wanted to argue . . . until she glanced at Wulfe's face and saw the barely controlled despair. Instead, she handed him a carving knife. "The ham in the refrigerator needs to be sliced, Wulfe. Thank you."

As Xavier regaled Natalie with what he'd learned of the different Feral animals, Wulfe pulled the ham from the fridge, placed it on a cutting board, and began to cut the slices with quick precision. The man knew how to use a knife. But the tension in his shoulders told her he was imagining carving up something else. Or someone. Like the Mage behind all their troubles.

Xavier flipped the pancakes. "You should see Grizz. He's a giant even in human form, but he shifts into a bad-ass grizzly bear." A moment later, he scooped the pancakes onto a plate, added a fork and knife, and handed it to her. "The butter and syrup are right here," he said, motioning to the counter in front of her.

As Natalie sliced herself a pat of butter, Xavier leaned closer, his expression softening. "What do you think of Pink?" he whispered. "She is so amazing, Nat. You have to get to know her." Her brother's face was alight with infatuation. Maybe something deeper. Without a doubt, he was falling for that girl.

"She seems very sweet. I'm glad you're friends."

"Me, too." His voice rose to normal volume, and he began to regale her with stories of Feral House as she ate her pancakes and watched Wulfe butcher the ham.

The way the thick muscles of Wulfe's arm contracted with each slice of his knife, making his wolf's-head armband bob and gleam in the overhead light, was truly a sight to behold. As he worked, he glanced up, and their gazes met. His knife stilled and in his eyes, she saw such a mix of worry, anger, and misery that it made her chest ache. With his gaze, he clung to her, need and warmth beckoning her forward like a night ocean she could too easily drown in.

The breath trembled in her chest, and she forced herself to break the eye contact. Taking the last bite of pancake, she turned away, looking for the dishwasher and realizing that there were three of them lined up beneath the rich granite countertop.

"Do you guys have a system for which dishwasher to put the dishes in?" she asked her brother.

Xavier smiled. "Have you ever seen anything like it? Every kitchen needs multiple dishwashers."

"It was Jag's idea." Pink's soft, high-pitched voice was filled with affection. "When the Ferals undertook my kitchen renovation a few years ago, Jag demanded they fill the room with dishwashers so that I would never again have to wash anything by hand. I told them it wasn't necessary, but Jag was adamant. In the end, they managed to fit three."

Natalie smiled. "That's brilliant."

Xavier nodded. "Right? We're loading the middle one now."

Natalie placed her plate and utensils into the appropriate dishwasher and turned back to her brother. "The pancakes were delicious." She kissed him on the cheek. "Better than Mom's, though if you tell her I said that . . ." She winced. "Xave . . ."

Her brother looped his arm around her shoulders

and pulled her close. For once, he didn't say any-thing, but his sorrow was clear and open on his face. "I miss her."

"I know. The words just came out."

"It's okay. It's right to talk about Mom when we're together. I just wish . . ."

Natalie turned toward him, hugging him. "I love you, Xavier Cash. Everything's going to work out the way it needs to." She met Wulfe's gaze as she said the last. "We've got to believe that."

Xavier hugged her back. "I'm really glad you're here, Nat."

"Me, too." Nothing was right about her current situation, and yet, as she held her brother in her arms and met Wulfe's gaze over his shoulder, there was no place, at this moment, that she'd rather be.

Wulfe hung the hand towel he'd used to dry his hands on a decorative hook, watching her. "Ready to make those phone calls?"

"Yes, absolutely." Natalie gave her brother a peck on the cheek. "I'll come see you later." As she passed Pink, she reached out and gripped a soft, feathered forearm, giving a light squeeze and a smile of thanks, then followed Wulfe through the swinging door.

"Is Pink a Feral?" Natalie asked quietly as she and Wulfe crossed the dining room. Several people were sitting at the huge table, though none Natalie thought were Ferals. She didn't recognize them, and Wulfe didn't greet them. Instead, he led her into the hallway, answering her question as they walked.

"Pink was supposed to have been a Feral, yes. A few of the passive ancient animal lines survived through the centuries, though all eventually died out. The flamingo was the last, one of the oddest, I'll admit. But that particular Feral was never a warrior. The animal spirit always marked women and gave them the ability to connect with the Earth's energies as mystics, healers, seers, etc. The flamingo Feral was a big asset. But the animal spirit can only mark a Therian with the DNA of that animal—someone whose ancestry includes shifters of that line. And we believe the flamingo line had all but died out when Pink was marked. She was newly conceived, just an embryo. The problem was, the embryo split into twins and the animal spirit was destroyed. Both girls were born half-animal, half-human. Pink's sister was killed in hopes of reuniting the animal spirit, but it was too late."

"That's terrible."

"It is. For her and for the Ferals since with the animal spirit dead, so too was the gift. Pink possesses none of the mystical strength she should have."

Natalie's mouth compressed in sympathy. "She has to remain hidden from human eyes."

"Yeah. She stays with us. Even though the animal spirit within her is dead, she needs radiance just like we do. Besides, we're the only ones she's safe with. She works her tail off, trust me. She earns her keep many times over."

"Has she been with you long?"

"Centuries."

Centuries. She looked at him. "Are you all centuries old?"

He met her gaze, a glimmer of wry humor in his eyes, and nodded.

Together, they passed through the foyer, then followed the hall to Lyon's office. They found him seated at his desk, Paenther and Tighe seated on the chairs facing him. Curled up in the chair by the window was Kara.

"Hi, Natalie," Kara said with a weary smile that didn't quite reach her eyes.

The mood in the room was heavy and grim. And Natalie felt suddenly selfish for bothering them with something so trivial.

"Natalie's ready to make those phone calls," Wulfe told them.

She shook her head as she looked at him. "They can wait. You have much bigger problems."

Lyon glanced at Tighe. "Natalie wants to make a couple of calls to let people know she'll be out of town for a few days," he told the tiger shifter. "If she's careful, I suspect it's a good idea, but I want her away from here when she makes them. Leesburg area, maybe."

"I'm taking her, Roar," Wulfe said.

Lyon shook his head. "I don't want to take a chance on the Mage tracking you two again."

"Roar . . ." Wulfe argued.

But Lyon's expression brooked no argument.

"I'll take you, Natalie," Tighe said. "This place has become like a morgue. I could use a drive."

"Me, too," Paenther said, looking to Lyon for agreement. When Lyon nodded, he turned to Natalie. "Are you ready now?"

"I'll need my cell phone."

Lyon pushed back his chair, opened a drawer in his desk, and pulled out her phone. "Keep your eyes open, all of you."

Paenther took the phone and rose. "Let's go."

As they started out of the office, Tighe clasped Wulfe's shoulder. "We'll take good care of her."

Wulfe nodded. "I know." But he clearly wasn't happy.

As they reached the foyer, Jag strode in from a different hallway.

"Road trip," Tighe told him. "We'll be gone an hour or two, tops. Natalie wants to make a couple of phone calls and needs an escort. Want to come?"

"Hell, yes."

Natalie felt Wulfe's hand on her shoulder. He turned her to face him fully, his frustration clear, but mixed with such worry, such protectiveness, that she longed to step into his arms.

"I'll be fine, Wulfe," she said quietly. He was the one she was worried about. And his friends. If the Ferals didn't catch a break soon, one by one, they were going to start dying. She saw that knowledge in Wulfe's eyes, that fury, that grief. And she felt it herself.

"I'll be waiting for you," he said.

And she prayed that was true.

*Chapter
Eleven*

Wulfe followed his brothers and Natalie down the front walk to Tighe's Land Rover, then saw Natalie settled safely in the backseat. He didn't like her leaving without him, not at all. But as he prepared to close her car door, their gazes met, and something raw and electric arced between them, a fullness, a warmth, that pressed against his chest, squeezing his heart.

Was he imagining that he saw the wonder he felt mirrored in her eyes?

"Nothing's going to happen to her, Dog," Jag said from the front seat. "But we can't return her to you until you let us leave."

Wulfe closed the door and stepped back as Tighe drove off with Wulfe's heart tucked in the backseat of his vehicle. He stood there, the sun beating down on the back of his neck, as he watched the Land Rover traverse the circular drive, turn onto the residential road, and disappear. And he stood there for minute after minute more, half-tempted to remain where he was until she returned.

Finally, with a sigh, he started back to the house. As he stepped onto the brick stoop, familiar voices began to speak in his head.

The female leaves the fold.

Yes.

Wulfe's heart plummeted, his pulse racing.

But not my Daemon.

It is no matter. If we take her, he will come. Then both will be yours, my lord. As you wish.

Wulfe leaped toward the door and into the house, then shifted, giving no thought to the clothes he'd never see again.

Tighe. Paenther! Dammit, they were already too far to hear him telepathically. *Roar! Inir knows she left.* Shifting back to human he grabbed a pair of gym shorts out of the basket in the foyer, yanked them on, then reached for the bowl of car keys, grabbing the first one his fingers came in contact with. "They're going to try to take her!"

"Stay here," Lyon commanded as he came tearing down the hall from his office. "I need an Ilina!"

A second later, Melisande misted into the foyer. "You called?"

"Mist Natalie back here at once." Lyon quickly told her where she was.

No sooner had the Ilina disappeared, then Olivia's voice echoed from the upstairs hallway. "They've been attacked!" she cried, running down the stairs.

Wulfe whirled toward the door.

"Wulfe, stand down," Lyon barked.

"Roar." Impatience tore at Wulfe's nerves, every muscle in his body straining with the need to reach Natalie.

"The last thing we can afford is a Feral-Mage war in the middle of a heavily traveled suburban street in broad daylight. What in the hell were they thinking?"

"They weren't thinking," Wulfe snapped. "Or they don't care. Satanan's the one calling the shots now, and he doesn't give a damn if the humans find out about us. He *wants* the humans terrified. His Daemons will feed all the more easily once they're freed."

"They're not getting free."

"No?" Wulfe wasn't at all sure anymore.

Finally, Melisande appeared, a swaying Natalie in her arms. "They were hit by two cars, one on either side. They must have been waiting for them on the cross streets as they traveled down Georgetown Pike."

Wulfe grabbed Natalie, pulling her tight against him. "Are you hurt?"

"No. Just . . . dizzy."

"Ilina travel will do that." He cupped the back of her head, pressing her face to his bare shoulder as he held her, as he drank in the feel of her body, whole and warm, against his.

Her arms slid around him, and his heart sighed with pleasure and rightness and relief. They stood like that until Tighe, Jag, and Paenther walked in the front door about ten minutes later. None of them appeared the worse for wear. Reluctantly, Wulfe released Natalie as she pulled away and went to sit on the stairs a few feet from him.

"The fuckers sandwiched us," Jag growled.

"They trapped us good," Tighe confirmed. "The car in front of me spun sideways, blocking me just as I came even with the intersection. The moment I stopped, the two vehicles flew at us from either side, slamming on their breaks at the last minute, pinning the doors closed."

"So you weren't injured," Lyon confirmed.

"No. They barely tapped the Rover. And the moment Melisande disappeared with Natalie, they backed up and drove away."

Wulfe glanced at Natalie. "Satanan can sense us."

"All of us?" Tighe asked. "Or just you and Natalie."

"I'm not sure. The latter, I think. He knew I was at her house. He knew she'd left just now. And that I hadn't."

"How?" Lyon demanded. "You, I understand. You have Daemon blood. But how is he sensing Natalie? Does she have some kind of tracker on her?"

"You have Daemon blood?" Natalie asked, her voice low and shocked.

"Just a little." But apparently too damned much. He turned back to Lyon. "My instincts say it has something to do with her aura. Whatever it is, he wants us. Both of us." Wulfe growled low. "And he's not going to succeed."

"Neither of you is to leave this house, again," Lyon said. "Paenther, increase surveillance. I want to know where those Mage are, and I want someone watching them every moment. They're too damn close if they were able to set up a trap within minutes of your getting into the vehicle." He turned back to Tighe. "Any witnesses?"

"Hard to say, but I didn't see anyone snapping pictures. It happened fast, Roar. A minute, tops." Tighe glanced at Natalie. "And you still haven't made those calls."

"I can mist her out of the area," Melisande said. "We'll be in and out of there before the Mage can follow." Without Ilina allies, the Mage still had to travel the old-fashioned way—cars and planes.

Wulfe met Lyon's gaze, a hardness in his eyes he'd rarely turned on his chief. "Natalie goes nowhere without me."

Lyon just stared at him, the need to argue clear in his expression. Wulfe understood all the logical reasoning against their both leaving together, but it didn't matter. Inside, his wolf growled in agreement.

Lyon's jaw clenched, then he turned to Melisande. "Take them somewhere that's far enough that the Mage won't be able to reach them in time, but close enough that Natalie might have logically driven there herself."

"Cape May is nice this time of year," Natalie said, rising to her feet.

"New Jersey?" Lyon nodded and turned to Wulfe. "All right. Take backup. And get her in and out of there fast."

Something brushed across Wulfe's mind, a voice, a whisper. *"Daemon?"*

Wulfe blinked, dropping his gaze before anyone saw his dismay. As his head began to pound, he realized the voice . . . *this* voice . . . didn't have the same feel as Satanan's and Inir's. He felt no . . . malevolence. Just a demand of sorts, to answer. To reply.

Why couldn't the fucking Daemons leave him the fuck alone?

"Wulfe?" Lyon asked sharply.

Shaking his head, he forced his attention back on the situation at hand. "Cape May, it is," he said. "I'll grab some clothes and be right down." As he climbed the stairs, his stomach clenched. His Daemon blood was awakening, and goddess only knew what that meant. Nothing good. Of a certainty, nothing good.

"**A**gain."

Zeeland put his troops through their paces in the gym below Feral House, watching the hand-to-hand combat with satisfaction. There was a tension in the room that hadn't been there this morning, a new gravity in the eyes of every Therian Guard who'd witnessed the ritual in the backyard a short while ago.

They'd watched three of the Feral Warriors, the guardians of the race, fail to shift. And for the first time, most finally understood the desperate situation they could soon be facing. He could see the knowledge in the tightness of their jaws and the fierceness of their focus as they trained.

Many had viewed this assignment as a rare opportunity to visit Feral House and meet the Feral Warriors. Now, they finally understood that Inir was close to winning. And if the Ferals fell, the Therian Guard would be on the front line of a brand-new Daemon war.

It was enough to make the blood run cold.

"Zee."

Zeeland turned to find Olivia standing in the doorway. He'd worked with the petite redhead on and off for decades and knew her to be one of the finest warriors in the Guard.

"Lyon wants a word."

Zeeland nodded and turned back to his troops. "Ryland's in charge." He followed Olivia up the steep cellar stairs and through the foyer. When they reached Lyon's door, the Chief of the Ferals motioned them to enter.

"Close the door, Zeeland," he said. "Both of you have a seat." Lyon folded his hands on his desk, his eyes grave, his expression pinched as he met Zeeland's gaze. "If the worst happens, and the current Ferals cease to be, Feral House and her occupants will be in your hands."

Zeeland started, his gut cramping at the thought.

"Olivia will be your second," Lyon continued. "If she's able to fulfill that role."

If she was able. Understanding washed over him slowly. Olivia was a strong, capable leader, and had been for centuries, but she was now mated to one of the Ferals. And if Jag died, there was no telling what the severed mating bond might do to her. She might not be capable of leading at all.

"There are many things our replacements will need to know." Though Lyon's words were calm and contained, a thread of desolation lent them a flatness that weighed on Zeeland. "Hawke is writing it all down and will go over everything with the two of you plus two or three others of your choosing— Therians you trust above all others, Zeeland. You must learn everything—our rituals, our ways, all the secrets we've amassed over five millennia. With us gone, you'll be the only ones who can pass it on."

The terrible responsibility settled heavily on Zeeland's shoulders. Misery clawed at his guts. The Ferals—a couple of whom were close personal friends—might soon cease to exist, leaving their wives to suffer their loss for an eternity. All of them had been only recently mated, from what he understood. A month ago, not only had Fox, one of Zeeland's oldest friends, not yet met Melisande, he had yet to be marked a Feral. By everything that was right, the male should be on top of the world. Yet just as his life had taken this pair of rare and wonderful turns, the Mage and their evil threatened to rip it all away.

The thought of leaving his beloved Julianne alone, damaged and unprotected, was beyond bearing, and he knew the Ferals must be feeling that same excruciating dread.

"We'll do what must be done, Lyon. Nothing will be lost."

"Protect our mates and Tighe's child, Zeeland, as if they were your own. See to it that they're safe, above all else. If we fail, we'll be leaving you a hell beyond imagining. I don't intend to fail," he added fiercely. "But neither can I bury my head in the sand and risk leaving our replacements defenseless. You, hopefully with Olivia's help, will train them, guide them. I know I can count on you."

"Absolutely."

Lyon stood, dismissing him. But as Zeeland rose to leave, Lyon extended his hand, too far. Zeeland took the gesture—the Feral greeting—for what it was, a show of respect and a heartfelt thank you.

The two men slapped forearms, exchanged nods, and parted. All his life, Zeeland had dreamed of someday being marked a Feral Warrior. But as he left Lyon's office, Olivia close behind, he thanked the goddess that dream had never come true.

Wulfe stood in the shade behind a B&B near the beach in Cape May, New Jersey. The four Ilinas who'd brought them had turned back to mist and kept silent watch. Paenther and Jag had each moved to opposite sides of the yard.

Natalie stood a few feet in front of Wulfe, talking to her office manager in the crisp, professional manner of the medical professional she was. He liked watching her like this, imagining her in her white lab coat peering into the eyes of her human patients. Maybe she didn't wear a white lab coat. He'd have to ask her. Though he knew what an optometrist did, he'd never been to see one himself. Therian eyes never required glasses. Except sunglasses, of course.

"I'll be out all week," she said, then glanced at Wulfe. "Yes, I'll definitely be back in the office next Tuesday." Uncertainty twisted her pretty mouth despite the certainty in her tone. "Thanks, Cheryl. Cell service is spotty here, so if you need me, leave a message. I'll get back to you when I can." She hung up, taking a deep breath and letting it out slowly.

Wulfe could see the tension in her shoulders.

"Now my mom," she muttered, clearly not looking forward to the prospect. "Mom, it's me. I'm taking a little much-needed vacation. No, I'm fine, I promise. I just needed . . ."

As Wulfe watched, Natalie's face began to contort in pain. Wulfe realized what was happening and knew she wasn't going to be able to finish this conversation. Reaching her, he slid the phone from loose, slender fingers, disconnected the call, and shoved her phone in his back pocket as he pulled her into his arms.

"My cheek," she gasped.

"I know." His hand covered half of her face as he tucked her close against him. Her sweet scent filled his lungs, her hair brushing his chin, her lush curves an exquisite temptation as they pressed against his body. One part of his mind erupted in thoughts of touching those curves, of exploring every inch of her sweet flesh. But her body was still rigid with pain. The only touch that mattered didn't seem to be working.

His pulse began to hammer. "It's still just your cheek?"

The tears were starting to leak from her eyes. "Yes. It feels . . . like it's on fire. *Wulfe.*"

He pulled her closer, concentrating harder on easing her misery, feeling helpless. And furious. *Come on, you son of a bitch pain. Leave her alone!* Finally, *finally,* the rigidity began to ease from her body.

"There," she gasped.

"Better?"

"Yes. *Yes.*" She sagged against him, the tension draining out of her.

He lifted his hand from her face and pulled her tighter against him. "You're okay, now?"

She took another deep breath and released a long, shaky sigh. "It's gone." Stepping out of his embrace, she brushed the tears from her cheeks. "That was no fun."

No fun. He smiled at her understatement and tucked a lock of hair behind her ear. "Let's get home."

She jerked. "Wulfe, I can't leave my mom wondering what happened to me. I have to finish the call."

Even as she said the words, her phone started to vibrate in Wulfe's back pocket.

With a sigh, he handed it back to her.

"Hi, Mom. Sorry. I accidentally disconnected us, then had trouble finding a signal again. Cape May," she said after a short break. Her gaze met his. "I'm going to soak up the sun, enjoy the scenery, and get some badly needed rest. No, I'm fine, Mom. I promise."

As she met his gaze, a look of helplessness in her eyes, a familiar buzzing erupted in Wulfe's ears. Red smoke rushed in to cloud his vision. Before he could say a single word to warn Natalie or his brothers, the darkness once more swept him up and away.

"Mom, why don't you stay in Birmingham with Aunt Deb a little while longer? You might as well."

Natalie saw the instant Wulfe's eyes changed. One moment he was watching her with soft sympathy, the next, the cold indifference of an unpleasant stranger. Her pulse leaped as she remembered the last time.

"Mom, I have to go," she said suddenly, struggling to keep her voice even. "Love you!" She hung up quickly. "Paenther!"

But even as she yelled, Wulfe scooped her up and slung her over his shoulder hard enough to knock the breath from her lungs and send the phone flying from her fingertips.

"Wulfe!" Jag shouted.

"*Melisande*," Paenther called, low. "Get them out of here. Backyard of Feral House. And warn Lyon!"

A moment later, Natalie's vision flipped end over end, the landscape disappearing into darkness, then bright sunlight as she found herself staring at soft grass beneath her hands and knees. Half a dozen yards away, Wulfe knelt, retching in the grass. Seconds later, Paenther and Jag knelt on either side of him.

The back doors of Feral House burst open, Lyon racing out, followed closely by Kougar and Tighe.

"What happened?" Lyon demanded.

"He wasn't himself," Melisande stated. "He grabbed Natalie hard enough to hurt her and started running with her over his shoulder."

As the Ferals surrounded the three retching Ferals, Lyon looked to Natalie. "Are you hurt?"

"No. He just knocked the breath out of me."

Lyon nodded, his attention back on Wulfe as the shifter leaped to his feet, his eyes still those of a stranger as he looked around, spied her, and started toward her with long, determined strides.

Lyon and Tighe stepped into his path, blocking his way. Wulfe snarled, his eyes changing to animal eyes, fangs sprouting from his gums.

"Wulfe, dammit," Tighe growled. "We're not immortal!"

If Wulfe attacked them with his claws and fangs, he could injure them badly. He might even kill them, which would destroy him in turn.

Natalie pushed to her feet and ran toward the confrontation. "Wulfe, no!"

Even as his muscles bunched as if to spring, his gaze snapped to her, and he stilled, the coldness slowly disappearing from those animal eyes, swept aside by confusion, dismay, and dawning horror.

"You didn't hurt anyone," she assured him, watching with relief as his fangs disappeared, as his face returned to normal.

Lyon stared at him. "What the hell happened?"

Wulfe swung away, his shoulders hunching with shame. "I lost it. That was the second time."

And both times . . .

With a bolt of understanding, Natalie strode through the circle of Ferals, moving in front of Wulfe, forcing him to face her, even as he continued to stare at the ground. "Both times, my cheek hurt. Both times, you took the pain. Then, moments later, you turned into Wolfman." She frowned, thinking. "The first time I experienced the pain, I didn't tell you. And none of this happened."

"Where were you taking her?" Paenther asked. "In Cape May, he snatched her up and started running," He explained for the others' benefit.

"I don't know." Wulfe shook his head as if trying to clear it. "I don't know."

"Inir has found a way to get his claws into him," Kougar murmured. "I wonder if we're next."

The look that passed between the shifters was one of raw disbelief. And horror.

"We are so screwed," Jag muttered.

Lyon watched his wolf shifter consideringly. "I don't think Inir's controlling us. I think this is just another factor of your Daemon blood. And, somehow, Natalie's involved. The next time her cheek hurts, call for backup immediately. And don't touch her." His amber gaze swung to Natalie. "The moment you feel the pain, or the moment you notice Wulfe changing, yell. And don't stop until we come."

"All right."

The Chief of the Ferals turned toward the house, and the others followed.

Wulfe hesitated, watching the sky instead of the ground. Finally, he turned to her, misery in his eyes. "I hurt you." His voice throbbed.

"You were rough with me, but you didn't intentionally hurt me. I'm fine."

"Bruises?"

"Maybe. Nothing broken. Are you okay?"

For moments, he said nothing, his gaze returning to the treetops and the sky. "I don't know what's happening." He scowled and started forward, then paused and held out his hand for her. "Let's go inside."

Taking his hand, she followed him through the back door, through the dining room, and into the hallway.

Wulfe glanced at her. "I need to work out. The fury is gone, but I still feel this need to fight. I'm going to work it out in the gym. Do you mind spending a little time in your room? I can get you some books."

"Books would be good." Honestly, she needed a little time alone, if only to process everything that had happened over the course of the past day and a half. And to get her emotions back under control after talking to her mom.

Wulfe led her down yet another hallway to a beautiful room lined, ceiling to floor, with bookshelves. A huge fireplace took up most of one wall, comfy-looking reading chairs scattered about.

"Books," he said with a flourish.

"Wow." As she perused the shelves, she found every manner of book imaginable, most quite old, most nonfiction, though one entire section was lined with twentieth- and twenty-first-century best-selling novels. As she perused the titles, she thought of the hours her mom had read to her when she was little. Natalie had never tired of the stories.

At the thought, tears burned her eyes. That brief conversation had thrown her more than she'd like to admit. Despite Wulfe's assurances otherwise, she was terrified that, like Xavier, she might end up stuck here. She might never see her mother again.

"You're afraid of me," Wulfe said, his voice low and stricken.

Natalie's gaze snapped to his even as she had to blink back the moisture. "No. I was thinking about my mom."

"You miss her."

"Yes, of course. And she's having such a hard time with Xavier gone." Her gaze sharpened on his, a plea, a demand. "I can't go missing again, too, Wulfe. She's already lost both of my brothers, if in different ways. She can't lose all of us. It would destroy her."

He nodded, his eyes deep wells of determination. "I'll get you home, Natalie. I'll make it happen." But within that declaration she detected a thread of uncertainty. As much as he might want to, he couldn't promise her anything, and they both knew it.

And truth be told, she was torn, and becoming more so by the hour. Going home meant leaving Xavier behind once more. Never seeing him again. Or Wulfe.

He reached for her, his eyes as tender as she'd ever seen them as he traced her jaw with the pad of his thumb. As she stared into those dark, fathomless eyes, adoration spread through her chest, sharper and more piercing than ever before. She could hardly breathe and didn't care. She didn't need oxygen, didn't need anything but his touch. Though she'd only just met him, she felt as if she'd known him always.

How could she walk away from him, knowing she'd probably never see him again?

Her heart thudded, liquid warmth sliding through

her veins, weakening her, strengthening her, awakening every cell in her body.

Wulfe lifted her hair, letting it slip through his fingers, then leaned forward and kissed her lightly on the forehead. "Pick out a few books."

As he turned away, she stared at his back, at his broad shoulders, the pressure in her chest so great she feared it would never be contained.

Heaven help her, she'd fallen in love with a shapeshifter.

Chapter
Twelve

As Wulfe waited for Natalie to choose a few books from the Ferals' extensive library, he watched her, his chest heavy as lead. She wanted to go home, back to her world, to her mother. He got that. He understood, and he would do absolutely anything to make her happy, even if sending her home was the last thing he wanted for himself.

He just prayed he could keep her safe that long.

Finally, she turned to him, three books tucked against her chest—a Jane Austen novel and two others whose titles he couldn't see.

A small smile lifted the corners of her lovely mouth. "I'm ready."

Together, they left the library and started back down the hall toward the stairs. As they approached the foyer, he overheard Paenther and Vhyper talking.

"So what I don't get," Vhyper muttered, "is whether the real Satanan, the Daemon still trapped in the Daemon Blade, knows what the lost piece of his consciousness—the one that infected Inir—is up to. Are they working together, or as completely separate entities?"

"I don't know," Paenther replied.

"Separate entities," Wulfe told them, as he and Natalie entered the foyer. He joined his friends. "One has no idea what the other is doing, but it doesn't matter since both are fully focused on freeing the Daemons from that blade."

Vhyper's eyes narrowed. "And you know that how?"

Wulfe stilled. "I have no clue." He scowled and started to turn away, but Paenther stopped him.

"Wulfe . . . what else do you know about Satanan, or at least about the piece of his consciousness inside Inir? We need all the insight we can get."

"You already know most of it."

"Humor us." Paenther's steady gaze demanded cooperation.

Hell. He didn't know how he knew this stuff. If he could unknow it, he would. But, yeah, maybe it could help.

"During the years of the Daemons Wars, wraith Daemon consciousness shattered fairly frequently, the wisps hiding in rock crevices, in objects, and in the ground until a person—usually human—came in contact with them. The wisp, what we call dark spirit, would turn the host evil for the course of his or her short life, then both host and wisp would perish."

As he spoke, Lyon and Kougar walked up, joining them, listening.

"But of the true Daemons," Wulfe continued, "only the strongest ever left behind a piece of consciousness, and only in times of fierce desperation. The sliver of Satanan's consciousness within Inir sheared off when he was being pulled into the Daemon Blade. He resisted the pull so strongly that part of him was actually left behind. Not until Inir accidentally came in contact with it did that piece of Satanan's soul find a host and come awake again."

Hawke and Falkyn joined them. Wulfe saw the surprise on his brothers' and sister's faces, but Paenther nodded for him to continue, and he did.

"In such cases, the lost sliver is usually never found, and the Daemon himself, though aware of the loss, is rarely incapacitated by it. He may feel the loss as one might feel grief for a long-dead loved one. A literal missing piece. If the missing sliver *is* found after it has infected someone, the two pieces can be reunited only by destroying the host."

Silence descended over the foyer as his Feral brothers and sisters stared at him with a mix of interest, surprise, and shock.

"How do you know all that?" Hawke breathed.

Wulfe shrugged. "Daemon blood." He ushered Natalie toward the stairs, through with revealing his weirdness for the day. But he couldn't help but wonder what other odd Daemon knowledge now resided in his head. And why.

"The woman Vhyper saw earlier is back." Melisande's voice erupted in the foyer behind him. "She's coming up the drive."

"Keep an eye on her." Lyon leaped into commander mode. "If she leaves again, follow her. Everyone else, remain inside. I don't want to scare her off, but she's not getting away this time. I want to know who she is and what she wants with us. If she's another newly marked Feral, she's going straight to the prisons."

Jag grunted. "Ten bucks says she winds up in the prisons no matter what she is."

"She's parking the car," Falkyn called from the living room. "She's getting out and starting for the front walk."

"Move away from the door," Lyon ordered. "Out of sight until we have her in the house."

Wulfe took Natalie's hand and hurried her up to the second-floor landing, where they had a clear view of the foyer over the railing. Fox, Hawke, and Falkyn joined them while the others melted into one or another of the hallways that fed into the foyer.

A moment later, the doorknocker rang on the wood with hard, confident taps, an interesting counterpoint to the apparently tentative nature of the woman's initial arrival.

Lyon swung open the door to reveal a woman of medium stature and girl-next-door looks, dressed in hiking boots, knee-length shorts, and a lightweight vest covered in pockets over a light brown tee. Dark hair, corkscrew curly, fell well past her shoulders.

The woman stared at Lyon with a combination of wariness, awe, and that surprising confidence as she thrust out her hand. "I'm Dr. Vivian Mars, Assistant Professor and Director of the International Center for North African Archaeology at Boston University. I believe you have a Daemon in your midst, and I'd very much like to talk to him."

Wulfe jerked.

Lyon, to his credit, showed no obvious surprise as he shook her hand and stepped back. "Come in, Dr. Mars. I'll be very happy to talk with you."

The woman didn't move. "Before I come in, let me explain who I am and why I'm here."

"It's safer if we talk inside."

The woman's expression lit with wry amusement. "Safer for whom?" She lifted a hand, palm out. "Let me at least tell you that I'm human. Two years ago, during a dig in the East Sahara, I became the unwitting, if not entirely unwilling, host to a wisp of Daemon consciousness who'd been separated from his body sometime ago. He doesn't know how long. His name is Strome and he desperately wants to know what happened to his race."

Lyon turned toward the nearest hallway. "Dark spirit or something more?"

Kougar strode into the foyer and joined him. "From my experience, dark spirit craves violence, not answers. I'd like to hear more. Wulfe may *know* more."

Lyon glanced up to where Wulfe stood watching, but Wulfe shook his head. He didn't have a clue.

"Strome has sensed that you're shape-shifters and wants your guarantee not to hurt me," the woman stated. "He's sensed the strengthening of a powerful force within the Daemons and seeks to warn those who might be able to stop it. About a month ago, he felt the awakening of an honorable Daemon consciousness. It's taken us all this time to track him down. And we tracked him here."

"You came by earlier today."

"Yes." She smiled ruefully. "Strome realized he was leading me into a den . . . a house . . . of shape-shifters and ordered me to leave at once. It's taken me hours to convince him I'm willing to accept the risk, given all that's at stake. We'd both appreciate it if you'd listen to what Strome has to say and not shoot the messenger, as it were."

She looked up suddenly, her gaze finding Wulfe's. "It's you." She smiled, stepping into the foyer suddenly, without hesitation, her gaze glued to Wulfe's. "It's you he's been trying to contact, you he needs to talk to."

Wulfe's pulse began to pound. This was his worst nightmare come true. Not only was Satanan getting his claws into him, but now Daemons were starting to come out of the woodwork looking for him. Or slivers of Daemon souls, at any rate. A thought snagged him.

"You . . . is he the one who's been whispering *Daemon* in my head?"

"Yes. He was hoping you'd answer and tell him where you were."

"Call the Shaman," Lyon ordered. He clamped his hand around the woman's upper arm. "You won't be harmed, but neither am I taking any chances. You'll wait in the prisons until the Shaman can determine what you really are."

"I think it's a little late, pal," Vivian muttered.

Lyon stilled, his face turning hard as granite.

Vivian looked up at him suddenly. "I wasn't talking to you. Strome told me to leave at once, and I told him it was a little late. Am I wrong?"

"You are not."

"I didn't think so. I still answer him out loud most of the time though he seems to be able to read my thoughts well enough. Keep that in mind, please. It might be a difficult habit for me to break."

As Lyon steered the woman out of the foyer, toward the door to the basement, Wulfe turned to Natalie. "I'm following them. Do you want to come with me or go up to your room?" This might be his worst nightmare, but he wanted to know what in the hell that Daemon knew.

Natalie set the books on the floor. "With you."

Wulfe took her hand, pleased. He needed her close right now, her calm strength.

Together, they descended the stairs to the foyer, then the longer stairs to the basement, following the others through the gym and into the prisons.

"Is this where I stayed when I was here before?" Natalie asked quietly.

"Yes. Don't go near the cells," Wulfe warned her. "I don't think any of the men will hurt you, but I can't be certain." He clasped her hand tighter.

Lyon opened one of the empty cells for Vivian and the woman walked in without complaint, then turned as he locked the door on her.

"How did you know about Wulfe?" Lyon demanded, his arms crossed over his chest.

"Strome sensed him, as I said." Her confidence didn't appear to have slipped an ounce despite her imprisonment in the shape-shifters' dungeon. "He has so many questions, questions I've been unable to answer since humans didn't know that Daemons . . . or shape-shifters, for that matter . . . ever existed."

She moved to the door of the cage, gripping one of the bars in a casual manner, her gaze finding Wulfe's. "What happened to the Daemons?"

He felt her intense gaze like an unwanted spotlight, but she didn't pause long enough for him to answer.

"When Strome first glommed onto me, he sensed

no other Daemons at all," she continued. "That was almost two years ago. I've been researching like crazy, trying to find any reference to the people or events of his time, but I've found nothing. Then a few months ago, he sensed something, a hint of an old enemy, the Destroyer, he calls him. Satanan. Very faint, like a soul not fully formed."

"We're aware of Satanan," Wulfe snapped.

She nodded. "Then, suddenly, three Abominations flew free into the world but disappeared within days. About the same time, a bright new Daemon light awakened. Yours. Your awakening wasn't like a birth, exactly. More like a bloodline triggered—one of the old, honorable lines—and he knew he had to find you, to learn what had happened and to warn you."

Wulfe's jaw hardened. Though he wanted to hear what she had to say, his muscles tensed with the need to turn and leave. Why did she have to stare at him alone? It was bad enough that he was some kind of Daemon freak. Did she have to flash it like a neon sign over his head?

"Please." Vivian grasped the bars with both hands, her gaze imploring him. "Strome is desperate to know everything you can tell him. The last thing he remembers was Satanan claiming the souls of his people. Daemon souls. Strome fought as long and hard as he could, so hard that a piece of his soul sheared off and became lost, the piece that I inadvertently recovered and that now shares space inside of me."

Lyon finally answered her questions since Wulfe had no intention of doing so. "Satanan and his horde nearly destroyed the other races, the humans included. The shifters and the Mage joined forces, and with the help of the Ilinas, managed to incarcerate them in a magical prison, the Daemon Blade."

"So they're not dead," she asked, turning to Lyon. Finally.

"We don't think so, no. We believe that the current Mage leader, Inir, became possessed by a powerful wisp of Satanan's consciousness some years ago and began stealing the souls of his own Mage in order to begin a campaign to free the Daemons. They're very close to accomplishing that."

"So Satanan isn't yet free, but he's becoming very strong within his host. Strome can feel that." Vivian paused and looked away. "All right, let me try." Meeting Lyon's gaze again, she said, "He wants to speak to you directly. I'm not sure how it's going to work, but I'm going to try to let him borrow my mouth." She grinned suddenly, a woman's smile. "Behave, Strome."

Vivian closed her eyes and took two long, deep breaths, then went still. When her eyes opened, they turned to Lyon, a hardness in their depths that hadn't been there before.

"If you hurt her . . ." The voice was Vivian's, yet not. That hard gaze tightened with frustration. "I can do nothing. So I will entreat you . . . do not harm her. She is light and beauty and goodness, and poses no threat to you whatsoever. I will help you defeat Satanan's rise in any way that I can so long as you vow to protect Vivian Mars. Satanan's evil knows no bounds. He has destroyed or enslaved more immortal races than you probably knew existed, including his own."

"If Satanan doesn't rise, neither do you." Tighe lifted a single pale eyebrow. "Why would you want to keep that from happening?"

Vivian/Strome turned his way. "Even if the Daemons fly free of the blade, my true self and I cannot be reunited without destroying the vessel in which I reside. Without killing Vivian. That would be a poor way to repay her kindness. And it is unknown if the male I have become is still worthy of this world after being enslaved by Satanan and incarcerated in that blade for . . . *how long?*"

Lyon answered. "Five thousand years."

Vivian's eyes widened. "Five *thousand?*" Her voice suddenly became her own. "No *wonder* I couldn't find a trace of the places or people you knew. They were prehistory in most of the world. Okay, okay, I'll give you back the mic." She closed her eyes, and when she opened them again, Strome was back.

That intense gaze turned to Wulfe. "You are only part Daemon."

Wulfe glared at him for several seconds before answering. "A fraction. At most."

"You are a son of Ciroc. I knew him and his shifter mate quite well. She was a beauty and much in love with her Daemon husband, as he was in love with her."

Wulfe shook his head, one eye narrowing. "We've seen Daemons. They're feeding machines, pure evil. And they sure as hell don't have the equipment to father children. So how . . . ?"

"You don't speak of Daemons, shifter, you speak of Abominations. If the Daemons were imprisoned five millennia ago, perhaps you've never seen a true Daemon, only the three Abominations I felt fly free."

"Wraith Daemons," Lyon said. "That's what we call them. The Mage managed to free three from the blade a month ago. We killed them."

"I've seen real Daemons," Kougar said. "I was born before the defeat of Satanan." He turned to the others. "A true Daemon is much like an Ilina, in that they can become pure energy or take fully corporeal form. Unlike Ilinas, their natural state is corporeal, and they generally look quite human."

Vivian/Strome frowned. "Satanan created his Abominations to empower him. Through their terrorizing of others, the Abominations feed him the rancid energy that makes him stronger than any other Daemon—than any other creature of any race. It is why we could not stop him."

"You would claim that not all Daemons crave death and destruction?" Kougar asked tightly.

"I would. I do. The Daemons I knew were not evil. Some of us were warriors, certainly, but ours was a great and varied society. We lived in peace with our human and immortal neighbors. As a race, we were once in perfect synchronicity with the earth's energies—solar, magnetic, heat—giving as well as taking, in a natural cycle that once stabilized the Earth, that healed and strengthened the living beings in our vicinity, humans included. It's a cycle that has . . . or had . . . existed for hundreds of millions of years.

"Satanan, alone, fed on human suffering. And he, alone, possessed the powerful ability to tap into the life force of others, stealing our strength. An ability we learned of too late. Once he'd weakened us, he began to control us until we were unable to do anything but what he commanded. I watched it happen to my friends and brothers as they fell under his control. I fought the same fate. And lost."

"What's going to happen if the Mage free Satanan from that blade?" Lyon demanded.

"I don't know. Those imprisoned with him will likely be free as well, but it's impossible to say what state they'll be in or whether he'll still control them after all this time."

Vivian shook her head, her voice slipping through. "*Five thousand years.*"

Tighe stepped forward. "How many Abominations did he make, Strome? How many are in that blade with him?"

Strome was back in an instant. "By the time I was enslaved, he had created hundreds. Since I do not know how much time passed between my enslavement and Satanan's defeat, I cannot begin to guess. Nor do I know how many were captured by the blade."

"More than seven thousand Abominations . . . wraith Daemons . . . were captured in that blade with Satanan," Wulfe told them, "Along with the captured souls of fourteen other races, including Satanan's own Daemons." *Why* did he keep opening his mouth and letting this crap come out?

His brothers stared at him as if he'd grown a second head.

Vivian/Strome watched him with interest, then slowly nodded.

"How many Daemons left part of their consciousness behind like you and Satanan?" Lyon asked.

"I don't know. From the moment I broke away until Vivian found me, I was lost, inert. I came awake inside her and will live until she dies. If other wisps of consciousness survived as I did, they are likely long gone by now."

Vivian/Strome's gaze turned back to Wulfe. "Why have you endangered your effort to keep Satanan from escaping?"

Wulfe frowned, his muscles tensing, the need to do battle leaping inside of him. "What do you mean?"

"Why did you make a channel key?"

Wulfe frowned, then slowly turned to granite. "I didn't."

"You did." Vivian/Strome's gaze turned to Natalie. "Her."

"**What?**" Wulfe stared at Vivian and the Daemon consciousness shining from her eyes, then gripped Natalie's hand tighter. Fuck that. He curved his arm around her shoulder and hauled her tight against him, the fierce need to protect her barreling through him. "I did *not* make Natalie a channel key."

"Is that why I'm glowing?" Natalie asked quietly.

Fuck, fuck, fuck. Wulfe's head began to pound. "I couldn't have made her a channel key. I don't even know how!"

Delaney had been made into a channel key by Tighe's evil clone and . . . *goddess* . . . he'd infected her with Daemon essence, then carved a pentagram into her chest that would have killed her if not for Tighe's intervention and the miracle that Tighe's animal spirit orchestrated, making her immortal in the process.

He had *not* done that to Natalie. He hadn't. But inside, his wolf began to howl.

Vivian/Strome watched him steadily, sympathy in hard eyes. "It can only happen in one way. A connection must have been opened between the two of you, and dark energy, primal energy, allowed to fill it."

"I didn't . . . I would never . . ." But he had. With a slam of understanding, he knew what had happened. "She was cut by a wraith Daemon. I took her wound for my own."

Vivian/Strome began to nod slowly. "That might do it. How long ago was this?"

"A month."

Hard eyes narrowed. "About the time I sensed your awakening. In making her your channel key, you must have triggered your own dormant Daemon blood. What's more, I now understand the source of the energy that is strengthening Satanan. He's empowering himself through your connection to your channel key, pulling primal energy through both of you, probably without your even feeling it."

This just got worse and worse.

"How do we stop him?" Lyon demanded.

Wulfe's neck muscles felt twisted like a rope. He pulled Natalie in front of him and wrapped both arms around her, the need to protect her screaming through him even as the scent of her, the feel of her warm body against his, calmed him, if only a fraction.

"How do I unmake a channel key?" Because he had to undo this. He had to make it right.

Vivian/Strome glanced from one of them to the other. "I'll share no more with you until you've freed Vivian. The rest will be over the phone."

Lyon shook his head. "She'll not be harmed unless we deem her . . . or you . . . a threat. But she'll remain in this cell until I say otherwise. I want the Shaman to examine her. You've nothing to fear from him. He's an ancient and honorable soul who will not harm her."

"Pal," Vivian said, clearly back in the fore, clearly talking to Strome, now, "I've already told them exactly who I am and where I work. Unless I run away from everything I know, they'll be able to find me within hours. I think we should trust them. I think we *can* trust them." She turned to Lyon, her expression rueful. "I'm sure you can understand how hard it is for an alpha male and former commander to ride in the passenger seat. He wants so badly to protect me. But he can't." Her gaze sharpened as she eyed Wulfe. "I hope we didn't make a mistake in seeking you out."

Wulfe glanced at Lyon. He wouldn't speak for his chief.

"If Strome is what he says he is, an honorable spirit," Lyon told her, "then neither of you has anything to fear from us. We're at war with the Mage who are trying to free Satanan. You'll forgive us if we're overly cautious. But we would welcome a genuine ally, especially one who can help us to better understand our enemy."

Vivian nodded. "Strome wants the mic." She closed her eyes, and, a moment later, the Daemon was back in control.

"I will help you because she is inclined to trust you." His gaze turned to Wulfe. "And because it would please Ciroc for me to aid his progeny. But, if you harm this woman in any way . . ." He shook his head, his expression dark with frustration. "Don't. I have never in my existence begged, but I will beg of you now. Do not harm her."

"We don't harm innocents, not if we have any choice," Lyon said. "What will happen if Wulfe were to pull the primal power for himself?"

"*Roar.*" How could Lyon even ask such a thing? "I would *never*. I'd have to cut a pentagram . . ." He swallowed back the bile that tried to rise. "*In her chest.*"

Vivian shook her head, her expression—Strome's expression—horrified. "Why would you *ever* cut a pentagram into the chest of a human? You'd kill her."

Wulfe stared at him. "That's what Tighe's clone did to Delaney when he made her his channel key."

"His clone?"

"Long story," Wulfe muttered. "Suffice it to say, he was evil, through and through."

Strome watched him thoughtfully. Slowly, his eyes turned hard. "In the early days, before I understood what he was about, I watched Satanan pull the primal energies. I know how it's done. For you to accomplish it, I believe you would need only to fully open the channel you triggered when you healed the human female. You would have to give her back the wound you took. Through that cut, the primal energies will flow. But I warn you, pulling that darkness corrupts even the most honorable of souls. Should you choose that path, you will quickly become too powerful for your friends to stop. You'll kill them."

"No."

"I've seen only one other ride that wave of energy and not let it consume him. And even he eventually lost the battle because in the end he could not bring himself to give up the power he'd acquired."

"So once the primal energy is pulled, it can be released?" Kougar asked.

"Yes. The ritual in reverse. The problem is, no one who knows that kind of power has the strength to give it up. *Absolute power corrupts absolutely*." He turned back to Wulfe. "I should warn you that even if you don't pull the primal energies intentionally, the moment Satanan is free, he will seize control of you as he has the rest of the Daemons. And when he does, you *will* pull the power. And you'll do it for him, without the ability to claim it for yourself. You, too, will become a pawn of his evil as so many have before you."

"How do we stop him?" Wulfe demanded, holding Natalie tight against him. "How do I keep that from happening?"

"There is only one way. The connection must be broken. You, your channel key, or Satanan's host . . ."

"Inir."

"One of you must die."

Natalie jerked within Wulfe's hold.

"I won't let anything happen to you," he whispered fiercely. But, *goddess*. To break this unholy connection he'd inadvertently created without endangering either of them further, he had to kill Inir. Not that he didn't want to. Hell yes, he wanted to, but they'd been trying to find and kill that sucker for months, now, with no success.

"The Shaman's here," Tighe said.

As the youthful-looking ancient entered the prison block, accompanied by Fox, Wulfe straightened. Slowly, he relinquished his hold on Natalie, his head pounding with regret over what he'd done to her. And with shame. How could he have fucked up so badly *again*? Nothing good ever came of his gift. *Ever*.

As he stepped away from her, she looked at him with eyes filled with confusion and worry.

If only he hadn't touched her, hadn't healed her.

The Shaman walked over to the cell where Vivian stood and peered at her with interest. "I understand you're host to a Daemon consciousness, one who claims to be an enemy of Satanan's."

"Yep. His name is Strome, and he's one of the good guys," Vivian said. "You look young to be a shaman."

The Shaman smiled. "Looks can be deceiving when you're dealing with immortals. Many things can be deceiving. I've never heard it said that Satanan had enemies among his own. If true, this is enlightening."

"It's true." Vivian scowled, and it was clear that Strome was back in control. "Satanan had nothing *but* enemies. He became too strong before we ever knew the power he possessed. By the time we realized the threat, it was too late. We were already being pulled under his complete control. At the point in time I became lost—and I don't know how long that was before—"

"Four hundred years," Wulfe said, unable to stop himself when the knowledge was on the tip of his tongue. "Satanan gained full control over the entire Daemon race four hundred years before they all became trapped in the Daemon Blade."

Vivian/Strome looked at him with interest. "How do you come by this knowledge, shifter?"

"I don't know. It just started happening today. I suddenly know things."

"You've tapped into Satanan's consciousness. Or his memories and knowledge. How?"

Wulfe shook his head.

Beside him, Natalie placed a slender, yet strong hand on his forearm. "When you touch me when I'm in pain, Satanan gains some control over you. Is it possible that that connection is going both ways? That you're tapping into him, too?"

Wulfe froze. He was starting to perspire. He hated this. *Hated it.*

"It's very possible," Strome said evenly. "And quite dangerous. If such a small portion of his consciousness is already gaining this kind of connection with you, you'll stand little chance of escaping Satanan if he becomes free of that blade. You'll quickly fall under his complete control." The Daemon's gaze traveled from Feral to Feral. "This is something you must be prepared for. Once Satanan has him, there will be no getting him back. I lost many a friend that way. Good men. Honorable men."

"Satanan's not getting him," Tighe growled.

Wulfe stared at the woman, meeting the gaze of the Daemon. All his life, he'd believed Daemons to be evil incarnate. For the past month, he'd been horrified that such evil might be living in his blood, lurking inside him, waiting to come out. But if what Strome said was true, that might not be the case at all. It was a revelation, if confusing as hell. Unless this was all a ruse, an act by the woman, an ingenious way to infiltrate their ranks and gain their trust. But for what purpose?

No, he didn't think so. His instincts told him Vivian Mars and the Daemon, Strome, were legit. Either way, he and Natalie were in a shitload of trouble.

The Shaman held out his hand to Vivian. "Let me touch you, please." When Vivian slid her hand between the bars, he took it and closed his eyes. Finally, after several minutes, he opened them again. "I sense no darkness within this woman. On the contrary, I see only brightness and light, and a deep, abiding love." He cocked his head as he looked at Vivian with surprise. "You've fallen in love with the Daemon who infected you."

Vivian's eyes snapped with feminine pique. "He didn't *infect* me. He found me. We're a team. And, yes, I care for him." Her expression softened. "He's my best friend."

The Shaman nodded. "Unless I'm mistaken, he cares for you equally."

"You are not mistaken," Vivian's voice snapped in Strome's distinctive way.

The Shaman turned to Lyon. "I'm no expert on Daemons, but I sense no darkness."

Lyon nodded. "Strome claims Natalie's become a channel key."

Youthful-looking brows shot up. "Who made her one?"

"I did," Wulfe snapped, wishing his brothers would take their claws to him for it. Rip him to shreds. "I did it when I took her wound."

As the Shaman turned to Natalie, Wulfe tensed even as he knew the ancient would never hurt her. The Shaman took her hand, once more closed his eyes, then shook his head. "No darkness, no shadows. I sense nothing amiss."

"And yet the Daemon claims Satanan is gaining strength through her," Lyon said. "Through her and Wulfe both."

The Shaman's eyes opened, and he dropped Natalie's hand. "It's possible. I know little about Daemons though I've heard it said they're connected to one another far more than most races." He looked at Wulfe.

"Can you sense Satanan's hold on you . . . on either of you?"

Wulfe shook his head.

The Shaman turned back to Vivian/Strome. "Can you explain?"

Strome's hard gleam flared in the archaeologist's eyes as Vivian turned to Lyon. "I can, but I won't. Your Shaman has declared Vivian without darkness, therefore you will release her. I'll share what I know when she is free of this dungeon."

Lyon's jaw tensed. "I'll give you an answer shortly." As he turned to leave, Kougar, Tighe, Fox, and the Shaman followed.

Wulfe motioned Natalie to precede him, then brought up the rear.

The small band weaved their way through the Guards in the gym, but when they reached the hallway that would lead to the stairs, Lyon turned into the ritual room instead, flipping the switch to light the electric sconces. The others started to follow, but the Shaman hesitated.

"If you've no further need of me, Lyon, Ariana and I have work to do."

"Of course. Thank you, Shaman."

Wulfe led Natalie into the room behind the others and closed the door. Wulfe had always liked this room, with its high, arched ceiling and dark walls that mimicked the feel of the ancient caves in which the Ferals had long ago performed their most primitive rites. While Natalie stood against the wall on one side of the door, Wulfe moved to the other.

She glanced at him, a wealth of shadows and questions in her eyes. Questions he wasn't sure he knew how to answer.

"Do we trust Vivian Mars?" the Chief of the Ferals asked, turning Wulfe's attention back to the problem at hand.

"That tale was too bizarre to be anything but true," Tighe muttered. "My instinct tells me Strome sought to protect Vivian, not himself."

"If we kill her, he dies," Lyon countered.

"I think Tighe has the way of it," Fox said. "The Daemon's demands felt like a male protecting his woman."

"He's in love with her," Natalie said with certainty, surprising Wulfe, and pleasing him that she had no compunction about speaking up around his brothers. "I'm very good at reading eyes," she continued. "In Vivian's, I see intense curiosity, but also a total lack of cunning. When Strome takes over, I see fierce honesty. And honor. And the love the Shaman sensed. I absolutely believe Strome, or at least this piece of his consciousness, is in love with Vivian Mars."

"So do we trust them?" Lyon asked. "Do we let Vivian go or keep her locked in the prison?"

"If the Daemon is evil and/or in league with Satanan," Kougar said thoughtfully, "letting him go might be a risk, but keeping him here could be more of one. Killing him would be, by far, the safest course."

"But if he's not in league with Satanan," Tighe countered, "a Daemon could prove a powerful ally."

Wulfe grunted. "I think he's telling the truth. I think he hates Satanan's guts."

"I agree," Tighe said. Kougar and Fox concurred.

Lyon nodded. "So we've decided to trust him. Do we keep him here or let him go?"

"Imprisoning one's allies is a certain way to turn them against you," Fox murmured.

Tighe nodded. "I have to agree. We let him go."

Lyon opened the door. "Then we've reached a decision. We'll reconvene in the war room in ten. Fox, call the other Ferals. I want them all there. Wulfe, see Natalie to her room. Tighe and Kougar, escort Vivian upstairs."

As Wulfe led Natalie back to the foyer, he braced himself for her questions or accusations. Both practically danced in the air around her. But she said nothing, climbing beside him without meeting his gaze.

She had every right to be mad at him for what he'd done to her. Mad and scared. Goddess, he'd never meant to hurt her. That was the last thing he'd ever want to do.

When they finally reached her room, she walked inside then turned to him, her expression calm and enigmatic. "When you're through with your meeting, you owe me some explanations."

"I know."

With that, she turned away. Wulfe hesitated, then slowly pulled the door closed and locked it from the outside, consumed by the fear that in making Natalie his channel key, he'd irreparably damaged her chances of getting out of there alive. If she paid the ultimate price for *this* mistake, he might as well die beside her because it would destroy his soul.

Natalie stood at the window, looking out over the circular drive. The sun shone on the cars and trucks, filtering through the woods beyond to dot the grass. But though she saw what lay outside, her mind was wholly turned inward. And she was scared.

She'd tried to get into one of the books she'd brought upstairs with her, Jane Austen's *Emma,* but though she'd always loved the story, her thoughts wouldn't settle long enough for her to make any sense of the words marching across the page. Finally, she'd given up and come to stand at the window.

How could any of this be happening? Shape-shifters and Daemons, odd glows and channel keys. How on Earth had she wound up smack-dab in the middle of it?

Wulfe blamed himself. She'd seen it in his eyes, felt it in the way he'd held her so wonderfully tight, then released her as if he couldn't bear to touch her. And maybe he was to blame. But that hardly mattered now. All that mattered was making certain she didn't somehow hurt the Ferals in their battle to stop Inir and Satanan.

Oh, Wulfe. What have you done?

Whatever it was, he'd never meant to cause harm. She'd known the wolf but a matter of weeks, and the man but a day, but she saw the honor and goodness inside him so clearly. It radiated from him, a golden soul, at once fierce and gentle, and oh so beautiful.

It was no wonder she'd fallen in love with him though what could possibly result from her feelings she couldn't begin to guess. What if he came to love her in return? Would she willingly give up every-thing she'd worked so hard for to stay here with him? Could she really turn her back on her work and her mom, and go into hiding for the rest of her life? Was the love of any man worth that?

She honestly didn't know. And now that she'd ap-parently been turned into a pawn of evil, she wasn't sure it mattered. There was a good chance she wouldn't have a life of any kind when this was over. So many things could go wrong. So many things had already gone wrong even if she didn't yet understand the ramifications of any of them.

Turning away from the window, she crossed to the bed, where she'd left her book, and idly traced the title with her fingertip. She might not have a lot of choices, she mused, but she definitely had some. One always had choices, if only whether to fight or submit.

Long ago, she'd decided that her life's goal was to make a difference in the lives of others. She'd always believed she'd do that through her work, by helping people, especially kids, see better. Then she and her friends had been captured by Mage and attacked by wraith Daemons, and everything changed. Everything.

She wasn't the woman she was before. Instead, she'd become some kind of conduit to terrible power. A pawn, perhaps. But even a pawn could take down a king, under the right circumstances. With the right allies.

There were always choices. But to make the right decisions, one needed to understand the game. Up until now, Wulfe had been her protector. And, to a lesser extent, her jailer. But they were in this together now, far more than even he had realized. Things were going to change.

She had a feeling it was the only way they were going to survive.

Ten minutes later, all the Ferals were sitting or standing around the war room. Vivian, who'd been released from the prison and led upstairs, sat at the head of the table where all could see her and, if necessary, question her. Lyon quickly brought the others up to speed.

Wulfe stood against the side wall, glaring at his brothers and sister as Vivian's story unfolded and their gazes kept cutting his way.

"So Wulfe-man made his very own channel key," Jag mused. "Do we even know what a channel key is? Or does?"

Wulfe looked at the jaguar shifter with surprise because he suspected they didn't. All they knew, they'd learned from the clone. But it didn't make one bit of difference because he wasn't pulling the power through her. Ever.

"Strome?" Lyon asked, turning to Vivian.

The woman sat in her chair, ramrod straight, her gaze . . . the Daemon's gaze . . . watchful and cautious as he kept an eye on every male in the room. Wulfe marveled that he could so easily tell who was in charge—Vivian or the Daemon. And he sympathized with the male, who so clearly needed to protect his female yet had absolutely no ability to do so.

"A channel key is a corruption of the ancient process of transforming a female into a Daemon." As Vivian/Strome began to speak, the room turned silent, every Feral riveted. "We are not entirely flesh and blood, as one of you stated. Daemons are energy creatures. And born exclusively male. The only way for us to reproduce is by converting a female of another race into a Daemon. This change does not harm her, and at one time, could not be accomplished against the female's will. It was part of the mating ceremony.

"All that changed . . . *everything* changed . . . when Satanan learned to tap into the primal energies. He found that human females, with their earthly physiology, could be used by almost any Daemon to reach that dark power. Satanan taught his most loyal and encouraged them to empower themselves in this way, for when they did so, they, in turn, empowered him."

Wulfe frowned. "Then how did I turn Natalie into my channel key by accident?"

Vivian/Strome watched him thoughtfully. "You have feelings for her. Strong feelings."

Wulfe's mouth compressed. It wasn't any of the Daemon's business. And yet, maybe it was. He gave a nod.

"And you say you healed her."

"I have a gift." A curse. "I can take the wounds of humans if I want to badly enough."

"A rare gift. I cannot be certain, shifter, but I be- lieve that in activating your gift with your heart open, you initiated her transformation. However, because it was done through the site of the Abomination's wounding, it was the corrupted process that took place instead, making her a channel to the primal energies."

"Is she in danger?" Wulfe demanded.

Strome nodded, his expression turning sympa- thetic. "I am afraid so, yes. Making her your channel key probably would not hurt her if you never used her as such. But Satanan *is* using her. The more energy he pulls through her, the quicker she will die. I'm sorry."

Wulfe let out a roar of fury and anguish and turned, ready to plow his fist through the wall.

"Wulfe," Lyon warned. "You're not immortal."

Fuck! He pulled his punch at the last minute, going feral instead. Goddess he needed to kick someone's ass and get his own kicked in return. He needed the outlet!

Turning back, he captured the Daemon with his anguished gaze. "How long until it kills her?"

"At the rate Satanan is pulling the power through her now, months. If you open that channel fully and start drawing them yourself, she'll survive a day, at most. Perhaps only hours."

Natalie was *not* going to die. Even as the furious need to protect her drove him to pace the room with hard, angry strides, the truth of the situation unfolded in front of him. The way things stood now, she had months. And he might only have days.

With effort, he pulled himself back under control. Nothing had changed. Inir had to die, and that evil wisp of Satanan along with him. That was still the only acceptable outcome even if it appeared to be slipping through their fingers more and more each day.

"Does anyone have any more questions?" Lyon asked.

"I do," Kougar said. "If the time comes that Wulfe must pull those energies, we need to know how."

"You just heard what he said! I'm not doing it," Wulfe growled. "I'll kill her."

"He must give her back the wound he took . . ."

"How?" Kougar pressed.

Vivian/Strome turned to Wulfe. "What did you do to heal her in the first place?"

Wulfe remained mute until Kougar pinned him with a hard gaze. With a sigh, he said, "I covered her cheek with my hand and called the wound to me. Just that."

Vivian/Strome nodded. "Do the reverse. Once that's done, stand her in the middle of a pentagram and say the words to call the power."

"What words?"

"The words that are written on every Daemon's soul. Daemon magic cannot be shared, it must be called on from within, and the words are part of that. They are as individual as a fingerprint and will come to you if you want them badly enough." Vivian's brows drew together, Strome's intensity still in her eyes. "I warn you, shifter, if you pull the darkness, it will try to claim you. There is a possibility, because of the tender feelings you hold for your channel key, that she might be able to tether you, to keep you from falling into that darkness, but it will not be easy. It has, to my knowledge, never been done."

All were silent for several moments before Lyon asked again, "Any more questions?"

"A thousand," Hawke murmured. "I'd love to hear about Daemon society before Satanan."

Vivian/Strome nodded. "I'm happy to share what I can. Vivian already knows the story, but I see now that it's important for the immortal races to know the truth of what the Daemons were before the Destroyer, Satanan, came into his power."

Hawke fired questions and Strome endeavored to answer them, but Wulfe heard none of it through the pounding in his head, the rhythmic, furious need to get in his truck, drive straight to Inir's stronghold, and rip his enemy's heart out.

Finally, Strome stepped aside, giving Vivian back the helm. She rose, shaking hands with each of the Ferals with a smile. "You have no idea how exciting this has been."

"You're aware you can never reveal our existence to anyone?" Lyon pressed.

"Fully." She snorted. "They'd lock me up if I told

anyone I've got a Daemon in my head. I understand what's at risk, Lyon. Thanks to the horror stories Strome has told me of Satanan, I understand, as few possibly could, what the world faces if you fail to keep him from getting free. Strome and I will do anything in our power to help you win this battle, which is why I risked everything to find you in the first place. Satanan must be stopped."

Lyon took her hand. "If you need anything, in any way, let us know. You have an ally in the Ferals."

Vivian grinned. "Cool."

Hawke exchanged phone numbers with her. As Hawke and Tighe escorted her out to her car, Kougar turned to Lyon.

"I'm not advocating this, but I'm going to say it because it has to be said. If Strome is correct, we have it in our power to not only break Satanan's control of Wulfe but to keep him from growing stronger."

Wulfe growled, low. "*No.*" He knew where this was going.

Kougar turned to him, something close to compassion in his eyes. "She's already being harmed by the energy flowing through her. And each time Satanan snatches control of you, you risk killing her."

He was talking about ending Natalie's life. *Now.* Breaking the connection that way. No. Fucking. Way.

"If, during one of those episodes, Satanan forces you to pull those energies fully, you'll likely turn on her and almost certainly kill one or more of us as well. It's a terrible risk to take when the one you seek to protect has such a small chance of survival."

"*No!*" Wulfe drew fangs and claws, the need to rip Kougar to shreds a fire within him.

Lyon grabbed one of Wulfe's arms, Paenther the

other. "No one's going to touch Natalie but you, Wulfe," Lyon said evenly. "Kougar brought it up because we need to consider every angle, but not a male among us would harm another's female. Not even Kougar."

Though the fury boiled hot, Wulfe allowed himself to be steered out of the room and toward the foyer.

"Work it out, Wulfe. Go down to the gym and find a Therian willing to give you the fight you need." The Therian Guards might not be able to draw fangs and claws, but they were, at least, still immortal.

"If anyone touches her, I'll kill him."

"No one's going to hurt her."

But Wulfe heard the unsaid words. No one would hurt her as long as he remained one of them. In control. But if he ever let the darkness, the primal energies, take him, he knew his brothers would do whatever it took to bring him back, including destroying the connection that caused it. Natalie. Assuming he hadn't already killed her himself.

Goddess help him.

With a furious roar, he slammed his fist through the plaster, then started down the basement stairs to find an immortal to fight. If only he could rip out his own Daemon soul instead.

*Chapter
Fourteen*

Wulfe climbed the stairs to the third floor with heavy steps. He'd kept his claws and fangs sheathed and taken on five Therian Guards at once, pounding the crap out of them as they'd pummeled him in return. Though, dammit, they'd kept their punches light so as not to badly damage the *mortal*. He was beginning to think he understood how humans felt as they aged, as their younger comrades started treating them as old men.

He rubbed his jaw where he'd caught an elbow and squinted out of one eye that was starting to swell on him. Yeah, he'd taken almost as good a beating as he'd given, but he felt two hundred percent better. Not good, of course. Not when his world was still so fucked up. But he felt like he could handle it again without going berserk.

At least as long as Satanan kept his evil claws out of his mind.

But as he approached the door of Natalie's room, his steps slowed. He'd promised her answers, and he wasn't sure what he was going to tell her. What was there to say? *I played God and fucked up your life. I'm sorry.*

He rapped on her door.

"Come in, Wulfe."

He unlocked her door and let himself in, wincing at her look of dismay.

"What happened?"

"I needed to fight. I sparred with some of the Therians."

She dropped her book on the bed and strode toward him. "You need an icepack for that eye." As she reached for his face, he grabbed her wrist, holding her back.

"I'm fine."

Though she looked like she wanted to argue, she said nothing more, just watched him, her eyes alive with a dozen emotions, a hundred questions. The air sprang to life between them.

"I need to understand what's going on, Wulfe. All of it."

Slowly, he released her arm. "I know." Pressing his lips together, he walked to the window. Peering out over the drive, he began to relay everything said in the war room. Several times, he swallowed back one truth or another, then forced himself to spit them out, sparing her nothing. Sparing himself nothing. He'd made her a tool of evil. The least he could do was be completely honest with her.

As he spoke, as his voice rang low in the silent

room, he heard the faint squeak of mattress springs and knew she'd sat on the bed. Keenly aware of her behind him, he told her how Strome believed he'd made her a channel key when he took her wound with his heart open. His feelings were his problem, not hers, and she didn't need that burden, too. But she wanted the truth, and he gave it to her.

When he'd finished, he continued to stare out the window for several more minutes, the regret and shame thick as mud in his stomach. Finally, he forced himself to turn around, to face her.

Natalie watched him with troubled eyes, her brows drawn, tiny frown lines marring the flesh between them. Part of him itched to stride from the room and lock the door behind him. Part of him longed to pull her into his arms. If he thought she'd find any comfort there, he might have. But he'd done this to her.

For long minutes, she said nothing, just watched him with that troubled frown.

"You have more questions," he murmured. "Ask them, Natalie. I'll tell you anything." He owed her that much.

"How did I get the wound that made me a channel key?" she said at last. "If you won't give me back my memories, at least tell me what happened."

He sighed heavily. "Do I have to?"

To his relief, she smiled, if all too briefly. "Yes, my wolf, you have to."

My wolf. He liked those words. The animal spirit inside of him gave a low bark of agreement. They both liked them.

"Do you mind if I sit?"

The soft welcome that suffused her features as she

patted the bed beside her eased his heart as nothing else could have.

As he sat on the edge of her bed, his hands between his knees, he turned to her. "What's the last thing you remember before . . . everything happened?"

She looked away, her gaze unfocused. "Two high school friends of mine and I wanted to spend the day playing tourist and catching up. We decided to drive out to Harpers Ferry. One invited her younger brother and his girlfriend to join us, so I asked Xavier to come along, too. The last thing I remember—and I've told the police this a dozen times—was walking through one of the old cemeteries. A woman walked up to us with coupons for free ice cream in town. I vaguely recollect her placing that coupon in my palm, but nothing more."

"She must have been a Mage. The moment she touched your hand, she enthralled you and led you away."

Natalie turned to him, shadows in her eyes. "Why, exactly? Were we supposed to be the Daemons' food?"

He turned away, the memories of that day far too clear. Memories she didn't need to share.

"Don't, Wulfe. Don't hold anything back. I need to know."

With a pained sigh, he told her. "They needed bait. The wraith Daemons are drawn to pain and suffering."

"How did they make us suffer?"

"Natalie . . ."

"How, Wulfe? You don't have to share every gory detail, but I need to know *some*thing."

He looked down at his hands. "The Mage . . ." *Goddess*, he didn't want to share this with her.

"Wulfe . . ."

"They injured your two girlfriends. Cut them . . . badly. The Daemons never touched them, Natalie. Your friends fell into the spirit trap when the Earth opened and died because of that. But it's unlikely they could have survived what the Mage did to them."

He hazarded a glance and met her pained gaze.

"What about the rest of us?" she asked quietly, her voice still strong as steel despite its softness. She would spare herself nothing. The least he could do was find the courage to give her as much of the truth as she demanded.

"Humans don't see the wraith Daemons until one has made them bleed. You were clawed in the cheek, Christy across her chest. The other male . . ." He shook his head. "He died of his wounds, and I'm not describing them to you. Yours and Christy's injuries were both shallow, and I was able to stop the bleeding on the battlefield."

"And Xavier?"

"Was never touched. I'm not sure how, but the wraith Daemons must have known he'd never be able to see them."

Natalie lifted her hand to her unblemished cheek, to the spot where she kept feeling the pain. "The Daemon cut me here."

"Yes." Deep inside, his wolf growled, as angry as the man that she'd been hurt by such a creature.

"You say you stopped the bleeding on the battle-field. Mine and Christy's both." Confusion clouded her eyes.

"I did. I didn't take your wound until later."

"How did you take it? Why?"

He looked away. "I don't know why. You were too pretty for such an ugly gash. And it hurt you. I didn't like seeing you suffer."

"Wulfe?" When he turned back to her, she watched him with stubborn eyes. "Tell me how you made it disappear."

"I'm a healer. I took it." He shrugged. "I just did."

Sudden understanding leaped into her eyes. "You *took* it. You literally took it for your own." Her calmness shattered, and she leaped to her feet, whirling on him.

Lifting a single finger, she traced the path from his left cheekbone nearly to the corner of his mouth. He jerked back.

"That's the one, isn't it?" she said. "That's the scar from the wound you took from me. It's yours now. When you take a wound, you keep the scar." Her eyes widened. "*Your face . . .*"

Wulfe grabbed her hips, lifting her out of his way as he stood and brushed past her.

But she followed. "My god, Wulfe, *how many people have you healed?*"

"It's not important."

"You must have healed *hundreds.*"

He turned on her. "I didn't," he snapped. "I'm no hero. I healed two. Just two."

She stared at him, her mouth slowly dropping open. "Out of all those scars, only one is mine?"

His jaw clenched hard, but he nodded.

"The other person . . ." Her eyes filled with pain. "Who was it?"

He didn't want to talk about it. He'd never talked about it, not with another living soul, and he wasn't starting now. She'd demanded truths, and he'd given them to her, enough for one day. More than enough. With long strides, he headed for the door.

"I hadn't figured you for a coward, shifter." Natalie's cool words stopped him cold, and he looked at her over his shoulder, everything inside of him clawing to reach the door.

"It's none of your business." He'd meant to sound fierce, or at least certain, but he heard the plea that rang in his voice.

As she moved toward him, he found himself unable to turn away, not when the annoyance slipped out of her eyes, leaving only pain.

"*Wulfe.*" Natalie stepped in front of him and reached for him, laying her palms against his scarred, miserable cheeks.

"Don't touch me," he whispered. But he couldn't pull away.

"Tell me what happened. The story is festering inside you. It's poisoning your soul. Share it with me."

"I can't."

"You can." Her thumbs stroked his cheekbones, a featherlight touch that raked furrows in his mind even as it caressed his heart. With one hand, she pushed a lock of hair back from his forehead, her touch like the softest down, and his wolf whined with pleasure.

She said nothing more, made no more pleas, no more demands, as she stroked his face and his hair, pulling him completely under her spell, shattering his defenses. He didn't want to tell this story. He didn't even want to think about it himself. But he was helpless to deny her when she stared at him like that, with a softness bordering on adoration. And when she stroked him so tenderly.

"Her name was Liesel." The sound of her name after all these years felt like a punch to the gut. He pulled away and stepped past Natalie, needing to put some distance between them before he spilled this miserable tale. Moving to the window, he gripped the frame with both hands, looking out over the front yard, seeing only the past.

"Long before I was marked to be a Feral Warrior, in my early years of adulthood, the mortal daughter of one of the Therians came to live with the enclave where I'd been born. Liesel was pretty, though not as pretty as you. And I . . . I wasn't scarred in those days. The women thought me beautiful."

"You're still beautiful," Natalie murmured.

He didn't know what to say to that obvious lie. "All of the males of the enclave became smitten with her. But I was the only one who interested her. And my interest in her was primarily . . . physical. One day she cut her hand, a small cut across the palm, and I stopped the bleeding as I'd done with mortals a few other times. But it still hurt her, so I held it tight and willed it away, completely away. Suddenly, it was on my hand, but it healed within moments, leaving a scar as no other wound before it ever had. I was stunned. I spoke to the enclave's mystic and was told I had a rare Daemon gift. Any strange gifts in my enclave were called Daemon gifts. The mystic told me the gift would only work on mortals and that I should never use it. No good would ever come of it."

Wulfe ran a hand—the one that still had that faint scar—across the back of his neck, feeling the dampness of perspiration. The words felt like glass in his throat. He heard Natalie's soft footfalls as she crossed to the window, then felt the light pressure of her slender hand on his back, stroking him. He tensed, wanting her to move away, to put distance between her and this ugliness. But her sweet scent filled his nose, easing the terrible pressure, calming him. And all he wanted was for her to stay.

His gaze glued to the trees outside, he continued his tale, keenly aware of the woman at his back.

"Liesel was too young for sex, only eighteen, but she enjoyed my kisses, and I enjoyed kissing her. Several times, we snuck into the woods together. She was a pretty thing, but my mind was on more important matters. Despite my own relative youth—I was in my thirties—I was not only the biggest male, but the finest fighter in the enclave, and our clan chief had told me I had what it took to be a leader.

"One afternoon, I promised to meet Liesel in the woods after the midday meal at our usual rendezvous point. But before I could slip away, our chief took me aside and told me he wanted to make me his second-in-command, a tremendous honor. I followed him into his hut, where we talked for hours." He shook his head. "I was so full of myself and my own self-importance that I completely forgot about Liesel."

Strong, slender arms wrapped around him from behind as a soft body pressed against his back, filling him with a tenderness he thought might crush him.

"While Liesel waited for me, three young human males found her. Even a Therian female is as strong as a human male, and Liesel knew how to fight." His mouth twisted wryly. "The girl hadn't possessed an ounce of caution. When the males appeared, she'd likely welcomed them as friends until they'd proved they had less friendly sport in mind. Then she undoubtedly fought like a wildcat. When I found her . . ." He had to suck in a breath against the stark picture that still throbbed in his mind six centuries later. "She was still conscious. Her only words, 'I cut his face. He cut mine more.' Goddess, but he'd cut her, Natalie. They were just shallow cuts, but he'd slashed her everywhere, every which way. And not just cuts. He'd hit her repeatedly, shattering her nose. The blood . . ."

He loosened Natalie's grip on him and turned within the circle of her arms, needing to face her. "You can see exactly what he did to her by looking at me. I was desperate to make it up to her, so I used my gift. She was so pretty, Natalie. All I could think about was that I couldn't be the reason she lost her beauty. I took wound after wound, feeling the burning cuts erupting all over my face, then the misery of her broken nose. Finally, I got them all. With the hem of my tunic, I wiped the blood from her face, once more as lovely as it had been at noontide. For one perfect moment, she opened her eyes and looked at me with such sorrow. And then she died."

Natalie's brows furrowed. "Why?"

"They'd raped her. She'd hemorrhaged. I never even thought to look, never noticed that she was lying in a pool of blood, that her skirts were soaked with it. While I'd been intent only on restoring her beauty, she'd bled to death."

"Could you possibly have healed internal wounds?"

"I don't know. It doesn't matter because I never even tried. I'd sought only to preserve her beauty."

"I don't believe that."

"I was vain, Natalie. I was full of my own beauty and strength and self-importance. And the goddess punished me for it, turning me into a monster none could stand the sight of."

He pulled away from her, unable to bear her sorrowful gaze. "I didn't learn. There you were, so beautiful, even with that wound, but I couldn't handle it. I couldn't let you suffer. So I took your injury and made you a pawn of evil."

He felt her hand on his back again, as if she hadn't heard a word he said. He shuddered beneath her touch, hating it. Needing it.

"Wulfe, turn around." Natalie's words were so quiet, so gentle, he had to close his eyes against the aching tenderness of them. Slowly, he did as she asked, forcing himself to meet her gaze. In those gray depths, he found the same quiet gentleness he'd felt in her touch and heard in her voice.

She reached up as if to press her hands against his cheeks again, but he grabbed her wrists and stopped her.

"You didn't hear anything I said."

A sad smile breached her mouth. "I heard everything you said and much you didn't say. I heard the story of a young man who knowingly destroyed his own handsome face in order to try to help a young woman he had only a passing interest in."

"I let her die."

"You didn't know she was dying. You had no idea she'd been raped."

"I should have. Her clothes were torn, her arms were scratched and bruised. *I should have.*"

"Maybe subconsciously you suspected, but such a fate for a virgin, one you cared about, was more than you could wrap your mind around, so you healed the wounds you could see. You tried, Wulfe. You sacrificed everything to try to save her."

She pulled her hands out of his softening grip and

reached for his cheeks again, and this time he didn't stop her. "You view your scars as punishment for what you failed to prevent, marks proclaiming your guilt. I see them as marks of compassion, a reflection of the selfless nature of your soul."

"It was my fault she died."

"It was the fault of the men who attacked her. The only mistake you made was in missing an appointment, an assignation. If you'd believed she might come to harm in those woods, you wouldn't have let her meet you there. You'd have escorted her out there."

It was true. "The humans never came that far into our woods. Ever, until that day." And they never did again. He'd tracked them down, every one.

"Exactly. The very fact that you've taken that guilt and owned it for so long proves what a good, unselfish man you really are."

He shook his head even as her fingers traced the ruined shape of his mouth.

"You are the kindest, most gentle, most extraordinary man I've ever known."

Wulfe stared at her. She didn't understand. How could she be watching him with such softness in her eyes after what he'd told her? His hands found her waist, whether to push her away, or hold on to her, he wasn't sure. But the next thing he knew, he was pulling her closer, needing her closer.

Natalie smiled and continued to stroke his face, her fingers tracing his crooked nose. "You're a part Daemon, shape-shifting immortal. How do you even exist? Yet I'm so glad you do."

"You'd be safer if I didn't."

"Not true. If not for you and your friends, I'd

be dead. Daemon bait." Soft fingers traced his eyebrows, making his heart clench, making his arms ache to lock her against him and never let her go. But he forced himself to do nothing, to simply hold on to her waist as she explored his ruined face.

"You're beautiful, Wulfe."

"You're blind." He sucked in a breath, afraid he'd offended her. But the sweet smile she gifted him with melted him instead.

"There's so much more to you than your scars. I wish you could see that. I wish you could see what I see, the gentleness, the fierceness in defense of the vulnerable, and the honor, and valor, and goodness. Your skin may be scarred, but it doesn't dim your beauty, not even a little."

So mesmerized was he by her words and her soft touches that he barely registered what she was doing until the fingers she'd burrowed into his hair suddenly gripped his head and pulled him toward her.

Natalie kissed him, full on the mouth.

Wulfe shuddered at the sweetness of her warm lips brushing his, closing his eyes against the torrent of emotion that flowed into him through that small joining, lighting him up inside. He gathered her closer, kissing her back, gentle, tender kisses on her lips, her soft cheeks, her eyes, her forehead. Tenderness welled up hot and full until he felt as if his chest would crack open from the pressure of it.

Beneath his hands, she began to tremble. He heard the soft catch of her breath and felt the tension coiling in her body. The musk of her desire wove around him, filling his mind until his own hands began to shake. She wanted him. Her rising passion transmitted itself to him through the fingers still burrowing in his hair. But his body refused to respond, and it saddened him beyond measure.

Slowly, he pulled back, meeting her gaze, slain by the heat in gray eyes turned silver. He stroked her cheek, then caressed her silken hair. "I can't give you more, Natalie. I wish I could."

A shudder escaped her on a hard, pent-up breath. Disappointment pinched her eyes, and she dropped her gaze. "You're not into me in that way. That's too bad, but I understand."

Gripping her chin, he forced her to look at him. "Then you understand nothing. Mentally, I yearn to strip you naked, toss you onto that bed, and follow you down."

"*Wulfe.*" Her eyes went molten with desire, and he kicked himself for a moron.

"But my body and mind are no longer connected in that way. I was mated . . . married . . . to our previous Radiant, Beatrice, for over 140 years. She died nine months ago in a Mage attack. It damaged me, Natalie, in many, many ways. I no longer . . . rise . . . with desire, not for any woman. Food has lost its taste, colors their brilliance. My senses and my libido are shot, and I don't think they're ever coming back."

"It's more than . . . you know . . . ?"

"Impotence?" He snorted. "Yeah. I can get it up manually. And I can get off . . . pardon my crudeness. But I can't feel. I can't *want.*" He stroked her hair, loving the springy feel. "If I could, I would want you. Only you."

The disappointment in her eyes slipped away, turning them incandescent. "Do you enjoy touching me? Holding me?"

He nodded slowly, a smile tugging at his mouth. "I love touching you."

The smile she gave him was nothing short of brilliant, stealing his breath. Had the goddess ever created a woman more beautiful?

"Good," she said. "Even if you can't give me more, I'd very much like for you to touch me, or hold me. Do you like to cuddle?"

He grinned. "I'm a wolf." His heart rose, feeling lighter than it had in a long, long time, as if a terrible weight had been lifted. And maybe it had.

She laughed. "I want whatever you can give me."

"I could bring you pleasure." The thought tantalized.

Her lashes swept down, her breath turned ragged. When she looked at him again, her eyes were smoking. But she shook her head. "Maybe later. For now, just hold me, Wulfe."

His animal whined with pleasure.

"There's nothing I'd enjoy more." He lifted her into his arms in a move that felt as natural as breathing, then deposited her on the bed, and joined her. As he pulled her into his arms, his world righted itself, the terrible tension escaping his limbs as he cradled her against him, her precious head on his chest. He stroked her silken hair, filled with an incredible sweetness, marveling at the miracle of her acceptance, and vowed that if he managed to do nothing else right, he would keep her safe.

But deep down, he feared that he'd already failed.

*Chapter
Fifteen*

Natalie reveled in the feel of Wulfe's strong arms around her as they lay together, fully clothed, on his bed. His body was like granite, his arms as thick as tree trunks, yet he held her so gently, as if she were made of the most fragile glass. He smelled of dark forests and sunlit meadows, and his warm, masculine scent intoxicated her. His jaw rested against her head, her cheek against his shoulder, and nothing had ever felt so intimate, so right.

She'd lain like this with Rick from time to time, but she'd never felt as if they shared the same air, as if their hearts beat in time. And she did with Wulfe.

Her arm curled tighter around his waist as love, pure and bright, rushed up inside of her, stinging her eyes. Nothing would likely ever come of it. Certainly nothing physical. But she longed to pull off his shirt and rub her cheek against his bare chest. She longed to feel his nakedness pressed against hers. The thought shattered her breath. But he didn't feel the same, he *couldn't* feel the same after the damage he'd suffered.

If she could just be something to him, make a difference to him in some way. Sliding her hand across his chest, she looked up at him. "Wulfe, I know what Strome said, that pulling the primal energies through me could be dangerous. But if you ever need to, if it's the only way you're going to beat Satanan, don't hesitate."

Rolling onto his side, he levered himself onto one elbow and stared down at her with vehement eyes. "I will never use you in that way, Natalie. *Never.*" He stroked her cheek, his fingers as gentle as rain despite the intensity of his look.

"If the time ever comes . . ."

"No."

"I'm willing to make sacrifices, too."

He covered her lips with his finger, his eyes luminous. "I know. But I will never be okay with anything that harms you."

He tensed suddenly, going still as a frozen pond.

"Wulfe?"

"Shhh," he said quietly, his gaze rising to the ceiling even as he stroked her hair.

Impatiently, she waited for him to explain, loving the sweet feel of his hand on her head. Finally, his body relaxed on a deep breath and an exhale. His head dipped, resting lightly against her temple and she stroked his hair in return, thrilled to finally be able to do so.

"I heard Inir and Satanan again," he murmured.

"Anything important?"

He lifted his head and stroked her cheek. "Yes and no."

His fingers traced her nose, her eyebrows, her ear, his touch so gentle, so sweet. Her heart contracted even as her pulse kicked up, her breathing turning shallow. If only touching her affected him in the same way.

"Satanan's mad that the Mage keep failing. I'm kind of amused. Inir started out the one in charge, with Satanan nothing more than an advisor, but Inir's starting to get pushed aside." He grunted. "That should probably scare the crap out of me."

"Do you need to tell Lyon?" She stroked his cheek, her finger tracing one scar in particular, the one she knew to be hers.

He watched her, his body tensing slightly as she traced that scar. "I'll tell him when I go downstairs. It doesn't change anything."

"Good. I don't want you to leave."

His gaze sharpened slightly, his nostrils flaring, and he buried his nose against her neck. "You smell like heaven." Slowly he lifted his head, longing filling his eyes. "I want to touch you."

Her breath trembled out, heat racing straight to her core. "Anywhere. However . . . *wherever* . . . you want."

She felt him shudder, watched his eyes fill with soft wonder as his warm hand burrowed beneath the hem of her shirt to palm her abdomen.

Her breath caught. Mesmerized, she watched his face lower, felt his lips on her jaw, then her neck. She turned her head, giving him full access, gasping with pleasure as his tongue stroked her pulse point.

As heat suffused her body, she buried her fingers in his hair, trailing them down his neck to his broad shoulders. "Does it bother you that I'm so affected by you when you can't . . . reciprocate?"

His lips brushed her jaw. "I'm in awe that you're affected by my touch." The truth rang in his words and throbbed in the tenderness of his lips as he rained kisses on her cheek, her temple, her brow. "I love the way you smell, the way you taste." His hand slid up and over one breast. His breath hitched. "The way you feel."

As his strong fingers caressed her breast through her bra with infinite tenderness, he rose to look down into her face, his eyes shining with a soft need that lacked a carnal sharpness. "I want to see you."

Arching her back, she reached behind her and unhooked her bra. Pulling her shirt off over her head, she tossed both onto the far side of the bed, then lay back. With a shiver of excitement, she watched as Wulfe reached for her, the most reverent expression on his face.

His big hands stroked her with featherlight touches as he gazed at her breasts as if they were the most beautiful things he'd ever seen. His thumb traced one tight nipple, making her gasp. With a flick of his gaze to hers, he lowered his face, tracing that same bud with his tongue. Sensation shot straight through her, making her gasp and arch into his touch. Her hands slid into his hair and she cradled him close as his lips explored her, tasted her, sucked her flesh into his warm mouth.

By the time he lifted his face and met her gaze again, her body was flushed with need, her breath a wreck. In his eyes, she saw joy tempered by uncertainty.

"What's the matter?" she asked, caressing his cheek, running her thumb across his bottom lip.

He kissed her thumb but continued to watch her with that intent gaze. "Will you let me pleasure you?"

Her limbs went weak. "I'm yours, Wulfe. All I am, all I have, is yours. In any way you want me."

A small frown appeared between his brows as if he didn't precisely know what to make of that. And perhaps she didn't either. All she knew was that it was true. In some strange, elemental way, she'd been made for this moment, for this man.

She reached for the button of her jeans. "Will you tell me how I can pleasure you, too?"

His fingers moved hers aside. "You are pleasuring me."

With slow, easy movements, he unzipped her jeans and removed them, leaving her in nothing but a pair of white lace panties. Then, with gentle hands that belonged more to a man admiring a fine piece of sculpture than to a male in the throes of passion, he stroked her legs, one after the other, ankle to thigh, then her abdomen, and again, her breasts. Pleasure drenched his features, if not in the carnal way she might have liked.

Finally, his fingers dipped beneath the waistband of her panties and he pulled them down and off, tossing them aside.

His gaze found the juncture of her thighs, his body stilling. "Let me see you."

Lifting her knees, she let them drop, opening herself to his sight, to whatever he wanted. Fire licked between her legs as he gazed at her, as wonder once more lit his face.

"How I wish . . ." he murmured with a sorrowful

shake of his head. He looked up at her, meeting her gaze. "You are the most beautiful woman ever created."

It was flattery in its finest form, but she saw truth in his eyes and knew he believed it. Holding her gaze, he slowly lowered himself between her thighs to kiss her belly, then lower still, finding the place where her need coalesced.

At the first brush of his tongue on that sensitive spot, she cried out.

She heard him growl, a low sound of male satisfaction and stroked her again, a long stroke that traced the full length of the place she longed for him to fill. If only . . .

As if sensing her need, he slid one thick finger into her, and she moaned with satisfaction. As he stroked that finger in and out, he licked and sucked and tugged with his lips and teeth until she came with a startling crash, convulsing around him, gasping.

Slowly, he pulled away from her. As she tried to reclaim her breath, he lay down beside her and gathered her against him.

"You're so beautiful," he murmured against her temple, then kissed her there.

As she laid her head on his chest, she heard his heart beating, strong and steady. Far too evenly. "That didn't excite you." She sighed. "Not at all."

"It delighted me."

But there was something wrong about taking from a man to whom she couldn't give. As she lay beside him, naked and sated, while he remained fully dressed, she felt suddenly awkward. Pulling away, she sat up, reached for her clothes, and dressed quickly.

"I'm sorry, Natalie."

"It's not your fault, Wulfe." Down the hall, she heard voices and the sound of a barking dog. Skye must be upstairs.

"I know." His mouth twisted ruefully. "I'm sorry for both of us."

"Would you shift for me?" she asked, slipping on her shoes. "I miss my wolf buddy."

He smiled slowly. "You do realize he's just me."

She laughed "Of course. I still want to see you like that again."

"Are you sure you're not just trying to get me naked?" He was teasing, yet a gleam entered his eyes that she found too endearing.

She grinned. "I love you naked."

Without hesitation, he stripped for her, and she thoroughly enjoyed the sight. Then, in a spray of sparkling lights, the man disappeared, the wolf taking his place.

A different kind of pleasure burst within her at the sight of her old friend. Kneeling on the rug, she opened her arms and he ran into them, licking her neck as she wrapped her arms around him and rubbed his fur. Joy vibrated through his wolf body.

"I don't entirely understand where you, your wolf, and your animal spirit begin and end, but the spirit is stronger in you in this form, isn't it?"

Hmm. I'd say no, but my animal's disagreeing. At least, where you come in. He feels closer to you in this form. He feels that he's yours. Or perhaps thinks of you as his. Definitely the latter. You're his. Ours. I think he adores you as much as I do.

She stroked him, looking into those intelligent eyes. "Do you . . . adore me?"

You know I do.

A rap sounded at the door. "Wulfe? Is Natalie in there with you?"

Natalie glanced at the door. "Can I let her in?"

Sure.

Rising to her feet, she crossed the room, the huge wolf all but pressed against her side. She opened the door to find Olivia and Skye. Both women grinned and reached for Wulfe, stroking his head.

In Natalie's head, Wulfe chuckled. *There are advantages to being a canine.* Even the puppy, Lady, went crazy, trying to greet her oversized pack mate.

"We're having happy hour in Lyon's room with Kara," Olivia said, smiling at Natalie. "Come join us."

Natalie grinned. "I'd love to." She glanced at Wulfe, stroking his back. "Do you mind?"

A smile lit those dark wolf eyes. *She can come if you take responsibility for her, Olivia. Lyon's orders.*

"I've got it," Olivia said, lifting her hand solemnly. "I promise not to let her glass get empty."

Wulfe snorted. *That's not the responsibility I meant.*

Olivia threw Natalie a quick grin.

Natalie bent and kissed Wulfe's furred head. As she stepped away, he lowered himself to the floor, lying flat where the puppy could finally reach him, yipping and pouncing with delight. All three women laughed.

I'll bring her to you in a few minutes, Wulfe assured Skye. *We need a little playtime.*

Natalie watched the huge wolf and tiny puppy romp for a few moments, grinning at the sweetness of it, then followed the two women next door. Lyon's room was no bigger than hers or Wulfe's, which surprised her considering Lyon was the chief and Kara the Radiant. Then again, it didn't surprise her at all. Kara, especially, was as unpretentious as anyone Natalie knew.

The room had been painted a rich orange-gold, the curtains dark brown. Paintings covered most of the walls, an eclectic mix—everything from sailing vessels to jungle animals to landscapes.

In the center of the massive bed sat Kara, lounging against half a dozen pillows, dark circles under her eyes.

"Hi, Natalie," she said cheerily despite her less than healthy pallor. She patted the bed. "Have a seat."

Falkyn, Delaney, and Julianne strode into the room, Falkyn carrying two bottles of wine in each hand, Delaney holding a large water bottle and corkscrew, and Julianne a platter of canapés, which she placed in the middle of the bed. A row of pretty hand-painted wineglasses sat on the dresser.

Olivia and Skye each uncorked a bottle of wine and began filling the glasses.

"Melisande popped out for a minute, but she'll be right back," Kara told them. "She decided we needed chocolate-covered strawberries to go with the Chardonnay."

Olivia lifted a brow. "Where's she going for those?"

"California."

Delaney smiled. "Only an Ilina could pop across the country and back in ten minutes. Well, ten seconds. The minutes will be for the actual purchase. Sit," Delaney commanded. "All of you. I'll serve the wine."

"You should sit," Skye countered. "You're the one who's pregnant."

"Yes, which is why I'm not drinking the wine. It makes perfect sense for me to serve it."

Skye shook her head with a smile. "Yes, ma'am. Thanks, D."

Natalie joined the others as they climbed onto the bed to sit cross-legged in a semicircle around Kara and the platter of food. Delaney handed them each a glass, then joined them with her water bottle.

"We do this every afternoon," Olivia said. "It's our way of thumbing our noses at the Mage, even if those pricks don't know and don't care. We refuse to give in to the fear of what might happen. And if worse comes to worse, we're going to continue this ritual of sisterhood. Because we'll still have each other."

As one, Delaney and Olivia gripped Falkyn's knees, one on either side, their expressions pained. "Most of us." Falkyn would share the fate of the Ferals.

Movement caught Natalie's eye on the far side of the room as Melisande appeared suddenly, a white box in her hands.

"Success!" Melisande announced. "I bought three dozen because they're *exquisite*."

"Strawberry. *Now*," Delaney moaned. "I'm suddenly having a massive craving."

Melisande grinned and joined them on the bed, placing the box beside the tray of canapés, then taking the extra wineglass Skye held for her.

When they were all seated, Olivia lifted her glass. "To sisterhood."

"To sisterhood," the others replied.

Natalie lifted her glass with a smile, saying nothing, and noticed that Julianne did the same. The pretty brunette with the bright blue eyes was a wife, but not a Feral wife, if Natalie remembered correctly.

Yet both of them had been included in this extraordinary group.

As Natalie took a sip, her gaze roamed the circle, and she marveled at the welcome she'd received from every single one of them. They were a wonderful group, women she'd love to keep as friends. When and if the day came for her to return home, for Wulfe to take her memories again, she was going to lose so much.

As the women shared wine and strawberries, the talk steered resolutely away from the topic that Natalie knew must consume them all—the Ferals' waning immortality. Soon, she found herself the focus of their attention.

Olivia eyed her curiously. "So . . . what's up with you and Wulfe? You like him. Maybe more than 'like'?"

Natalie looked down at her wineglass, startled by the sudden rush of emotion. She loved him. But that was a foolish thing to admit when it was still all too likely she'd be sent back to her world with no memory of him. It was best for both of them if he never knew how she felt.

"I do like him," she said evenly, looking up to meet Olivia's gaze. "Wulfe is one of the finest men I've ever met. Wolf eyes or human, his soul shines through, and it is truly beautiful. He's beautiful."

Olivia smiled. "I like you, Natalie. You're the real deal."

Natalie smiled. For several moments, they sipped their wine in silence, but the pall they'd pushed to the corners of the room began floating forward to hang, once more, heavily over their heads.

"There has to be something we can do to stop all

this, to stop Inir," Kara murmured. "There is so much cruelty, so much evil in that man. And he's nothing compared to Satanan."

Natalie opened her mouth to ask more, then closed it. Then decided if anyone would tell her the truth, these women would. "Will you tell me about the Daemons?" Natalie asked. "At least the wraith Daemons. I was attacked by one, but I have no memory of it. I keep hearing that life will be terrible if they're freed, but I need to understand." For a moment, the others were silent, shadows in their eyes, and Natalie regretted bringing it up. "This wasn't the time or place, was it?"

Delaney patted her shoulder. "You have every right to ask. The guys keep trying to protect us, but if the Daemons rise, we need to know what we're facing. All of us."

Skye nodded. "Our silence wasn't because you shouldn't have asked, Natalie. It's because it's hard to know where to start or what to say. I saw the three wraith Daemons who were freed in the caverns. I saw them feed." Her eyes flinched with remembered horror.

Natalie took her hand. "I'm sorry."

"Don't be. You need to hear this. They're truly terrible, monsters who feed on the pain and terror of their victims. Imagine the worst torture your mind can come up with, then multiply it by a hundred. That's the way they kill."

Natalie's stomach clenched, her forehead turning hot.

Kara nodded. "Kougar says that in the old days, before they were captured in the blade, they tortured human children. By the thousands."

"They did," Melisande concurred. "They'd round them up—"

Natalie lifted her hand. "I get the picture."

"The wraith Daemons have no consciences," Olivia added. "I'm not at all sure they're even sentient beings."

Falkyn nodded. "From what Strome said, they were created by Satanan for the sole purpose of creating the pain and fear that empowers him. Wulfe says that over seven thousand of them will be set loose upon the world if that blade opens. They can't be freed."

"The Ferals won't let it happen," Kara said fiercely.

No one contradicted her, but the looks that passed between them told Natalie that none of them were certain of that, Kara included. And the Ferals were running out of time.

*Chapter
Sixteen*

After checking on Natalie and sending Lady back to her two-legged mom, Wulfe headed downstairs. As he descended the final steps, Lyon strode into the foyer, followed by the Shaman, Paenther, Tighe, and Kougar.

"Join us, Wulfe."

He did, falling into step beside Tighe. "What's up?"

"We just got another call from our escapees, this time from Grizz. They found the woman they were searching for. Apparently, she's half Valkyrie."

"*Valkyrie?*"

Kougar glanced at him. "Valkyries were members of the Nyad race, one of the races destroyed by Satanan early in his rise to power. This woman, Sabine, apparently survived, thanks to her mixed blood."

"And she's willing to help us?"

"No, she's not willing at all. She's an empath, far too sensitive to be around others. Grizz is bringing her anyway."

Wulfe frowned. "And why does he think she'll cooperate? If she's being forced, we won't be able to trust a thing she says."

"A Valkyrie can't lie, not when proclaiming a soul good or bad."

Lyon opened the door to the basement and started down, the others following. "Grizz asked for Ilina transport, and Ariana's sending it. The Ilinas are about to deliver them directly to the prisons."

The implications spun in his head. "This is great. If the woman can tell us whether the new Ferals are good or bad, we can bring the good ones into their animals, which should heal Kara. And since the new Ferals haven't been affected by the dark charm, there's no danger of their losing their immortality. Inir's plot to free the Daemons fails."

"That's what we're hoping," Tighe said, but while his voice contained a measure of relief, it lacked true jubilation. Because the original Ferals were still in trouble. None of this would solve the problem of their waning immortality.

"Has anyone else lost the ability to shift?" Wulfe asked.

"Hawke did," Tighe said, glancing over his shoulder as they descended the last of the stairs. Tighe waited for him to join him and met him with a bleak, somber gaze. "About twenty minutes ago, so did I."

"Fuck. I'm sorry, Stripes." If Tighe ever saw his unborn son, it would be a miracle.

They strode through the gym, the Therian Guards parting like a disciplined sea. At the back of the gym,

Lyon opened the hidden door in the glass that led to the prisons, releasing a woman's cry of agony.

Lyon took off running, the others close behind. They burst into the prison block to find six cells full. Three new Ferals and now Grizz, Lepard, and Sabine. The Ilinas who'd transported them stood outside the cells, waiting for Kougar's or Lyon's dismissal.

Lyon held up his hand for them to wait, then turned to Grizz ,who was cursing a blue streak.

"What the *fuck*? You fuckheads! I said transport, not prison." Grizz grabbed the bars, shaking them hard. "She's a fucking empath! What part of *empath* don't you understand? I told you she wouldn't be able to tolerate this without touching me. Let me go to her. Now!"

Sabine leaned against the bars of her own cage, her head caught in her hands, keening with pain.

The place was in chaos.

"I can help her," Grizz said, reining back his temper with obvious effort. "Touching me eases her."

Lyon swung to the nearest Ilina. "Put the woman in Grizz's cell."

The Ilina disappeared, and a moment later deposited Sabine beside Grizz, as directed. Grizz swept her up, cradling her against him as Sabine curled into him, burying her face against his throat.

"I'm sorry, I'm sorry, I'm sorry," he whispered, over and over.

But despite the way she clung to him, Sabine's response was harsh and pained. "I hate you."

Grizz lifted his head, glared at them through the bars of his cage, and snarled, "Get this done and send her the fuck home. I don't know how long she can take this."

The Shaman stepped forward. "Remarkable. I've not seen a Nyad in well over five millennia. I believed you all dead, Sabine."

"We're going to be," she gasped, "if you don't free me soon."

"Will you help us determine the souls of the males in these prison cells?" Lyon asked.

Sabine lifted her head and met his gaze, pain bracketing her mouth. "Do I have a choice?"

For a moment, Lyon said nothing. "If you lie about what you find, my wife may die. And not only will my own heart cease to beat, but without our Radiant, the Ferals will be unable to keep the Mage from freeing the Daemons. I imagine you're familiar with the Daemons?"

Sabine glanced up, looking at Grizz with such a depth of fury that Wulfe suspected she'd happily yank his heart out of his chest if she didn't need him to manage the pain.

"Let me down," she snapped.

Grizz set her on her feet, keeping one arm tight around her, an arm she gripped with both hands.

"I am called the Shaman, Sabine," the youthful-looking male said, stepping close to the cage. "I am ancient, despite my appearance, and once knew Nyads. I would touch you, if you'll allow it, to verify you are what you say and that you've not been infected with the darkness that plagues the world."

She stared at him. "If my pain at being near others is terrible, touching is ten times worse."

Lyon stepped forward, his expression determined if not unsympathetic. "I'm afraid I must insist you cooperate with the Shaman, Sabine. You understand my concern."

Sabine closed her eyes, her mouth tight, as if trying to gather her courage. She stepped out of Grizz's embrace, but took his hand and gripped it tight as she walked to the bars of the cage and thrust her hand through.

The moment the Shaman took her hand, she threw her head back, her back bowing in pain. Grizz pressed himself against her, holding her as closely as possible, his jaw rigid. The male might have anger-management issues, but he was clearly suffering at the woman's misery.

"*A good soul,*" Sabine cried.

The Shaman dropped her hand and stepped back gingerly. "She is Nyad, as she claims. And pure. There is no darkness here, I'm certain of it."

Sabine sank against Grizz, and he pulled her tight against him. Wulfe could almost see the grizzly shifter flaying himself alive for hurting her.

"Why is she calmed by your touch?" the Shaman asked.

Grizz looked up and met the male's gaze. "I have no fucking idea."

"Finish this!" Sabine cried. "And then let me go. *Please.*"

Lyon strode to the door of Grizz's cage and opened it. Grizz stared at him for a moment, then swept Sabine up into his arms and carried her into the open space.

Lyon motioned him to the cage where Castin watched with piercing eyes.

"Your hand."

Castin pushed his hand through the bars of the cage.

Sabine hesitated, shaking now. Wulfe could see

her terror of the touch to come and imagined being told he had to reach into the fire and grasp hold of a red-hot iron. Considering her reaction, he thought it might be just that bad for her.

Grizz, clearly thinking the same, shuddered, tipping his head against the top of hers. "I'm sorry," he whispered again.

Slowly, Sabine reached for Castin's hand and held on until she was quaking violently. "Old," she gasped. "So much death, so much suffering. *A good soul,*" she cried at last and released the hand.

The Ferals watched the proceedings with a mix of fascination, hope, and unhappiness. Not a one would let a woman suffer needlessly and it cut at every one of them that they were forcing this woman to suffer now.

At Lyon's direction, Grizz approached the cage of the silent, dark-skinned male with the watchful eyes. As the male extended his hand, Sabine took it weakly, and screamed. "Death. *Pain.*" She was trembling, now, shuddering. But her declaration was strong and sure. "*A good soul.*"

Goddess, how much more of this could she take? How much more of this could any of them take? Wulfe was ready to declare *enough*! They already had two they should be able to bring safely into their animals. But to leave the others in limbo, when they had this opportunity to learn the truth, was unthinkable. There was no choice but to force Sabine to press on, and Lyon did just that.

Grizz turned to the cages across the aisle, to where Lepard stood, his hand extended, his brows drawn.

Sabine didn't reach for him. She was shaking so badly, Wulfe wondered if she could even if she wanted to. Grizz lifted her hand, his face lined with misery, and handed it to Lepard.

Sabine screamed, her body bowing in agony. But her pronouncement was the same as the others. "*A good soul,*" she announced in that singular voice that was hers and yet sounded almost a thing apart.

The moment she spoke, Lepard released her, and she fell against Grizz's chest, gasping for air.

Grizz cradled her as gently as a child. "I'm sorry, Sabine. I'm sorry."

"One more," Lyon said. "Then yourself."

"Can't," she gasped. "Can't read Grizz. It's why I can touch him."

As if dragging leaden feet, Grizz turned toward Rikkert, who glared at him with a raw hatred the Ferals had yet to understand.

Grizz lifted Sabine's hand to him, and the male took it carefully. Sabine's scream was terrible, enough to shatter eardrums.

Finally, in that same, strong voice, she declared, "*A good soul.*" A moment later, she fell limp in Grizz's arms.

Grizz whirled on Lyon. "It's done. Send her home."

"Get back in your cage first."

Grizz glared at the chief of the Ferals but did as commanded. As the door clanged shut behind him, he dipped his head close to Sabine's.

"I'm sorry."

"I hate you." Her words were barely audible even to Feral ears, and broken.

"I know."

As Wulfe watched, one of the Ilinas appeared in Grizz's cage, and in the blink of an eye, Grizz once more stood alone.

"Are we going to perform the Renascence, now, or wait for nightfall?" Tighe asked, a thread of excitement weaving through his words.

Kougar stroked his beard. "She claimed every one of them a good soul."

Paenther nodded. "And Kara's told us she was wholly unimpressed with the two Ferals she was forced to bring into their animals by Inir. Neither revealed much courage, let alone honor. It makes sense that the honorable ones were drawn to us, the evil ones to Inir."

Lyon turned and strode out of the prisons, his expression grim. Glancing at one another, Wulfe and the others followed silently.

"My office," Lyon said, as they reached the foyer.

A moment later, Paenther roared, "*No.*" The male turned ashen, his eyes filling with anguish. "My panther . . ."

Another one down. Wulfe clasped him on the back and they followed, single file, into Lyon's office. As Lyon rounded his desk, his hand went out to steady himself.

"Roar?" Kougar reached for him, but Lyon reared back with a shout of agony and despair, and Wulfe knew he'd lost his animal, now, too.

They were falling like flies.

"You still have yours?" Tighe asked.

Wulfe nodded. As far as he knew, there were only five of them who could still shift now, himself and the four newest Ferals—Falkyn and Fox, Lepard and Grizz. How long until their lights, too, went out?

Deep inside, his wolf howled in misery.

Lyon sank onto his chair, burying his face in his hands. The others took seats or stood silently, waiting for him to grieve and to gather his thoughts. Finally, he looked up, his expression more than fury, more than grief. In that strong visage he respected above all others, Wulfe saw fear.

"It's critical that we bring the new Ferals into their animals as quickly as possible." Lyon's jaw turned hard as granite, his voice dropping to an anguished whisper. "But what if Sabine was wrong?"

"A Valkyrie can't lie," Kougar said.

"And the animals always mark the strongest, most honorable Therians to become new Ferals," Lyon countered. "We believed that, too. What if both are wrong?"

Kara would die.

Paenther sighed. "We only have to bring one new Feral into his animal to stop Inir."

"Which one?" Lyon turned to him, his eyes as bleak as an arctic storm. "Is there one of the three you would stake Skye's life on?" His gaze swung around the room, pinning them in turn. "Or Ariana's? Or Delaney's? Or Natalie's?"

Wulfe's reaction was fierce and immediate, his hands fisting at his side. He didn't care what the hell Sabine had claimed, there was no way he'd risk Natalie on the word of a stranger. And no way they could risk Kara. Yet the fate of the world might ride on this decision.

To a male, they looked away, unable to hold their chief's gaze.

Lyon shot to his feet with a furious roar. "We *must* bring one of them into his animal. We *must*." His voice fell to nothing as he leaned on his desk, palms flat, his head bowed. "But goddess help me, I can't. I can't risk Kara, even to save the world." Slowly, he lifted his head, staring at them, one by one, his expression a mix of guilt, desolation, and belligerence, as if he expected a fight. As if he wanted one.

But not a male there had it in him to argue. Not only would they have made the same decision in Lyon's shoes, but every one of them adored Kara. None would risk her life.

"Grizz is going to be furious when he realizes his efforts were all for nothing," Tighe murmured. His gaze turned to Lyon. "Now what?"

"The same as before. We figure out how to get our immortality back, then we go after Inir and stop him before he can free the Daemons."

So very simple.

So fucking impossible.

Wulfe climbed the stairs, his heart heavy with worry and dread, his nerves frayed. He needed to see Natalie, to settle his wolf and quiet his own desolate soul. He found her sitting on the bed with the other Feral wives, sipping a glass of wine as Kara talked about her time as Inir's captive. If this was meant to be a party, it was a failure, in his estimation. Then again, every woman there was as sharp as the tip of a spear and knew exactly what the Ferals were facing. It only made sense that they'd discuss their worries among themselves.

His gaze followed Natalie, watching her as she listened somberly to Kara describe the cruelties she'd seen in that place, and how she'd been forced to bring two new Ferals into their animals, two males she believed were evil. As he watched, Olivia picked up the box in the middle of the bed and offered it around the circle. One by one, the women pulled out a chocolate-covered strawberry, but it was Natalie he watched, his gaze following the sweet fruit as she lifted it to her mouth and closed her teeth and lips around it.

Something stirred deep inside of him, a surprising rush of heat that flowed down through his body and into his loins, making them grow heavy and full. He sucked in a startled breath at the unmistakable feel of his first hard-on in months, maybe years. Why now? There were too damn many things happening to him!

He pulled away from the door before anyone even knew he was there and went in search of advice. He found Kougar in the library talking to Hawke, and shut the door behind him.

Both Ferals turned, concern in their eyes.

Hawke sighed. "You lost your animal, too."

"No. Hell, no. I've got a woody."

Kougar said nothing, made no indication he'd even heard him.

Hawke merely lifted a brow. "What caused it?"

"I just watched Natalie eat a chocolate-covered strawberry."

Hawke nodded, all seriousness. "You like her."

"Yeah, but I'm damaged, Wings. I haven't gotten a woody without effort since Beatrice died."

"Maybe you're healing."

"How can you heal from a broken mating bond?" He whirled to Kougar. "Is it possible?"

Kougar stroked his beard. "I've heard of its happening before, but only in cases where the original mating wasn't right. And only when the right person came along."

"And your mating to Beatrice was never right, buddy," Hawke said. "We all knew that. If it had been . . ." Hawke shook his head, his eyes glowing. "What I feel for Falkyn, my Faith, I have trouble vocalizing, because finding the words for such depth of emotion stymies me every time. She's the world to me—my heart, my life, the breath in my body. There are no words to express such overwhelming love. A love I'm almost certain you never felt for Beatrice."

He hadn't. He'd thought he'd loved her, and he might have if she'd ever cared for him at all. But what Hawke described resonated inside of him. Because of Natalie.

"Did something happen?" Kougar asked. "Did you kiss her?"

Wulfe hesitated, then decided he might as well come clean. "She kissed me."

Hawke smiled. "That must have been a hell of a kiss."

"It was as chaste as they come."

Kougar plucked at his beard. "It may have been chaste, but the emotion behind it was powerful indeed."

"You think my feelings for her did this?"

"And her feelings for you."

Wulfe blinked, confusion colliding with joy. She liked him, he knew that. But Kougar had used the word *powerful*. "I have no idea what she feels for me."

Hawke clasped him on the shoulder. "Whatever the reason for your woody, it's a blessing. Go find her and kiss her back."

As if he hadn't already done that and much, much more.

Wulfe nodded. His friend was right. With his body stirring like a summer storm, he could finally share the intimacy with Natalie they both wanted.

The question was . . . should he, when everything was so screwed up?

Wulfe was halfway up the second flight of stairs, his blood on fire with dreams of pulling Natalie into his arms and stripping both of them bare, when the sound of pounding footsteps had him glancing back. Lyon and Tighe were running up the stairs, taking the steps two at a time.

"Wulfe," Tighe called.

"What's going on?"

Lyon's mouth compressed. "Natalie. Melisande found me."

Hell. Natalie was in pain and the women had sent for Lyon, not him. Turning, he ran up the remaining stairs and started down the hall.

"Don't touch her!" Lyon called from behind.

Wulfe strode into his chief's bedroom to find Natalie hunched over on the bed beside Kara, her hands clenched against her knees, tears glistening on her cheeks.

The women looked up as he entered the room, Delaney and Falkyn scooting aside to give him access. But as he reached Natalie, as he pulled her into his arms, she threw up her hands, blocking her face.

"Don't. *Please.* It'll stop." She grabbed his hand. "Just hold me."

"Always." But it flayed him alive to see her in such pain and not do what he could to end it.

Lyon and Tighe rushed into the room, coming to a standstill halfway to the bed. Lyon began issuing orders. "Melisande, move Kara to the Radiant's room. All non-Ferals out of here. Now."

Olivia stood her ground. "Let me help, Lyon. I can weaken him if you need me to, and he can't hurt me. I'm still immortal."

Wulfe felt like a fucking wild animal on the verge of going rabid.

Lyon nodded, then turned to Melisande. "I could use you, too, once you have Kara settled."

One Ilina couldn't mist an unwilling Feral Warrior, but one Ilina could call half a dozen more in two seconds. And half a dozen Ilinas could mist him to the North Pole, if they wanted to. Or the Crystal Realm, for that matter.

"I'll be right back." A moment later, Melisande and Kara disappeared.

Wulfe's jaw worked as he swallowed the need to yell at them all that he wasn't going berserk, dammit! Because, hell, he didn't know what he might do. Even if he managed to keep from easing Natalie's pain, for all any of them knew, he might still go crazed. Because none of them really knew what the fuck was going on with him.

In his arms, Natalie's shaking grew worse, the tears a steady flow down her cheeks, now. How much more of this could she take? How much more could *he* take?

He pulled her tighter, his big hand stroking her hair, her back. "Natalie, sweetheart . . ."

"Don't, Wulfe. I'll get better."

But he wasn't so sure. "Roar, what if each time Satanan tries to set up a steady flow of the primal energies through us, I disconnect it by closing the loop and stealing Natalie's pain? If I don't do that this time, her suffering might never end. Satanan might just get stronger and stronger."

Lyon frowned. "We don't know that's how it works."

How the fuck were they supposed to tell?

His hand shook with the need to cover that wound and end her suffering. And she was suffering. Goddess, she was in pain. He could feel the tension in her muscles, the trembling. Her skin was damp with perspiration, her cheeks wet with tears.

Small cries began to escape her throat, tiny, strangled screams that tore at him.

"It's not stopping, Roar. It's not going to stop." And he'd taken all he could take. Lifting his hand, he pressed his palm against her cheek, closed his eyes, and willed the pain away. But like before, it fought him. *Satanan* fought him, struggling to keep the connection intact.

"Get two more Ferals up here, ASAP," Lyon barked.

Wulfe gritted his teeth, growling low in his throat as he pulled at the pain, as he battled back the Daemon's hold on it. On her. Finally, *finally*, he felt it give way. Deep inside, his animal whined with relief.

Natalie sagged against him. *"Thank you."*

Wulfe shuddered with relief, cradling her close. She felt so good, so *right*, in his arms. Her sweet scent warmed the air between them, weaving through his senses, lighting tiny fires in his blood. Now that she was no longer in pain, his body sprang to life, suddenly, intensely aware of the touch of her hand where it clung to his wrist, and of the press of her soft breast against his arm. His own hand traced the contours of her slender back, her spine, her elegant neck, his fingers sliding into the spun-gold silk of her hair. It was all he could do not to bury his face in the clean, feminine scent of it.

His hands began to shake with need. With every beat of his heart, the desire to pull her closer, to taste her again, grew more intense, more difficult to control.

His pulse quickened, his breath becoming increasingly shallow. The last time, he'd felt her silken flesh beneath his palms and lips, he had not been moved. Never had he been physically moved in her presence.

Until now. He throbbed with the need to slide deep inside of her.

Natalie pulled back. Their gazes caught, locked, and he watched lovely, if tired, gray eyes light with wonder, then fill slowly with dawning passion. Her own breath hitched.

"Oh, Wulfe." Her words were the barest whisper.

"Wulfe," Lyon barked. "We need to get you out of here. Down to the gym."

All he wanted was to sweep Natalie into his arms and into his bed. Instead, he stroked her hair with a shaking hand. "Go. Melisande will take you back to your room."

Without warning, the familiar buzzing began in his ears. A split second later, the red fury swept across his mind, stealing his will.

"Wulfe!" a male yelled.

Enemies. He drew fangs and claws, leaping from the bed and whirling toward the ones who would attack him.

"Watch his claws! Get Natalie away from him."

Two males tackled him to the floor. "Jag, Fox, give

us a hand." Two more locked his wrists against the hardwood. "Olivia, weaken him. Not too much!"

Wulfe fought against their hold, struggling against the four who held him down, but lethargy began to steal through his limbs.

The sound of shattering glass had him turning to find the female he'd been holding now wielding a broken wine bottle like a weapon, a wildness in her eyes that gut-punched him.

"*Natalie.*" The name tore from between his lips and fangs. "Natalie, *no.*"

"Hell, not her, too," one of the males muttered. "That bastard has his claws in both of them."

As Wulfe fought his captors, struggling to reach her, to reach Natalie, the darkness and fury dissolved and he came back to himself in a rush.

"Let me up," he snapped, his fangs and claws retracting. "Let me go to her!"

The hands holding him down disappeared, and Wulfe leaped to his feet as Natalie struggled in Jag's far stronger hold.

"She tried to cut me," Jag told him. "I think she was trying to protect you."

"*Natalie.*" Wulfe reached her, gripping her jaw carefully, forcing those wild eyes to meet his. "Natalie, come back to me."

She stared at him, the wildness slowly sliding from her eyes, and she blinked with confusion.

"Wulfe?"

He took the broken wine bottle from unresisting fingers and handed it to Jag before pulling her into his arms. "It's okay." But as he said the words, his gaze rose to his chief's, and he knew the words for the lie they were. Because it wasn't okay. Nothing was.

"Is it the primal energies or Satanan that's affecting them?" Tighe asked, his gaze meeting Wulfe's. "Do you know?"

"No." This connection needed to end, and soon. Goddess help them. He curled his arm around Natalie's shoulders and ushered her toward the door. "We'll be in my room." Not only did he need time to think, but he needed to get away from the wary, worried eyes of his brothers.

"Do you think that's a good idea?" Lyon asked evenly.

"I'll call you if anything happens." His head was beginning to pound, his body about to implode.

He needed Natalie Cash in his arms.

Natalie followed Wulfe out the door of Lyon's room and the few steps to her own. What in the heck had happened? One minute she'd been watching, terrified that Wulfe would attack his friends with those deadly claws. The next thing, Wulfe was holding her, taking a broken wine bottle out of her hand, and everyone was staring at her as if she'd grown a second head.

Wulfe ushered her into her room, then closed the door and pulled her around to face him. His hands caressed her shoulders as he studied her with soft, worried eyes. "Are you okay?"

"I don't know." Her pulse was pounding. Her hand slid up to cover her chest. "My heart's racing."

"You're no longer in pain?"

"No, not at all. Thank you for that. But, Wulfe . . ." She shook her head. "We can't let that happen again." Her brows drew together. "What if, next time, you knock me out?"

His brows lifted, his expression turning thoughtful. "I don't know. It's possible that would disconnect you. We can try it."

"Okay. Good." The tension began to ease from her shoulders. "We have a plan." For now. Until that didn't work, either. And then what? She'd heard Strome as well as Wulfe had. The only way to break this connection was through the death of one of the three of them. And while it might be heroic to offer to give up her life, Wulfe would never go for that. He'd blame himself for it, hate himself for it. Besides, she liked her life, thank you very much, even as strange as it had become. No, Inir was the one who had to die. For both their sakes.

Wulfe lifted a hand and stroked her cheek. "Let me hold you." Something in his expression crumbled for the barest second. "I need to hold you," he said quietly.

She wasn't the only one shaken, she realized. Sliding into his arms, she pressed her body against the hard, muscular planes of his and knew that nothing had ever felt so right. Wulfe pulled her closer still, locking his arms around her, brushing his chin against her hair on a deep, heartfelt sigh.

As her arms went around his waist, she pressed her cheek to his T-shirt. "It's all going to be okay," she said quietly. "It's all going to work out."

He kissed her hair. "Do you know something I don't?" His voice almost teased. Almost.

"No, but it's the only acceptable outcome." Slowly, she pulled back and gazed up into his beautiful, beloved face. "We're going to beat Satanan and Inir, Wulfe. We're going to win because I know you. Your soul is too honorable, too filled with light for darkness to ever cling there for long. Satanan will never control you. You're going to beat him."

The look he gave her was at once filled with wonder and doubt. "I wish I could be so sure."

"I wish you could be, too. But I'm certain. No matter what happens, you won't hurt me. Evil won't take you. It won't win."

The wonder flared in his eyes. "You're a miracle." Tenderness drenched his liquid gaze. His lashes swept down, his hands falling from her shoulders to her hips. Strong fingers encircled her waist, gripping her flesh, kneading her hips with what, from another man, would indicate rising passion. He pulled her closer, tight against his hips and the thick protrusion in his jeans.

"Wulfe?" She stared at him, remembering the desire she'd imagined seeing in his eyes just before he lost it.

His lashes swept up, revealing dark eyes ablaze with a wondrous heat. Her heart began to pound, her body melting in response.

"What happened?" she breathed.

His hand rose, his warm palm cupping her throat and sliding slowly downward until it rested firmly against her upper chest. His pulse, quick and un-steady, pounded so hard in that hand that she could feel it.

He wanted her. And her own body flushed with answering desire.

"You," he breathed, sliding his hand up to her jaw. "You happened." His head dipped, and he kissed her with all the fierce need, all the tender passion she could have dreamed of. His lips brushed hers, warm and firm, his tongue traced her lower lip. She opened for him and he dove inside, his tongue stroking hers, twining with hers, sending a fireball of heat exploding in her chest and rushing lower, a storm of need and sensation, chaos and wonder. He tasted like summer rain and winter forests, clean and fresh and wholly, wonderfully male.

One of his hands slid into her hair, the other down her back to pull her hips tight against his and she felt, again, the very massive evidence of his desire.

As her breath trembled out, she found herself smiling.

He pulled back, looking down at her with passion-drugged eyes and a gleam that made her chest ache with tenderness. "What's so funny?"

"Not funny. Wonderful. You really do want me."

His lips brushed her cheek, trailing down to her neck, licking, nipping, making her shiver with delightful longing. Her breasts tingled, her knees weakening as, deep within, her body began to pulse and contract, begging to be filled.

"I want you," he groaned against her neck. "I want you so badly . . ."

Slowly, he rose again, pulling back, his breath ragged, his gaze hot and troubled.

"Wulfe . . ."

His gaze roamed her face, his eyes incandescent with heat and tenderness. "You are so lovely." Unsteady fingers slid into her hair, his thumbs stroking her cheekbones.

With her own hands, she stroked his chest, then began yanking his T-shirt out of his jeans, the need to feel his flesh against hers a monstrous thing.

"Make love to me, Wulfe." Her hands slid under his shirt, against his warm, solid flesh. Electricity arced between them, making her gasp. Between her legs, she began to throb. "*I need you.*"

His big hands rose to her breasts, making her cry out with pleasure and frantic desire. "I'm afraid I'm going to hurt you."

"You won't. You won't ever hurt me." Her fingers moved to his waistband, and she began to unfasten his jeans.

His hands stopped her. "I'm big, Natalie. And you're human." His voice shook. His forehead tipped to hers, his breathing ragged. "I'm afraid I'm going to lose control."

She reached up, gripped his face, and kissed him hard. "I want you to do that, Wulfe. I want that."

He resisted for all of a second and a half, then he was hauling her tight, kissing her madly, doing precisely what she'd asked him to, at last. In the same fierce, tender manner that Wulfe did everything, he lost control.

Chapter Eighteen

Wulfe was going to die if he didn't soon slide inside the woman in his arms, his Natalie, his heart. Fire and beauty and laughter, she was everything to him. Everything.

He tore at her clothes as she tugged at his jeans and T-shirt until they were both breathing hard, both wild with need. They came together in the middle of the room, mouths fusing, her sweet breasts tight against his chest, the skin of her back, her rear, like warm silk beneath his shaking fingertips.

Her nails dug into his shoulders as he kissed her, inhaled her, her tongue rubbing against his with as much desperation as her hips rocked against his thick erection. Never had he known such a violent need to join his body with another's.

His hands roamed her back, her flesh, her hair. He couldn't get enough. He would never get enough of her. Swinging her into his arms, he carried her to the bed and tossed her into the middle, tearing a husky laugh from her throat. As she grinned at him, watching him with eyes that gleamed like polished silver, his heart contracted tight and hard. When had he known such exhilaration, such pure joy?

With a low laugh, he followed her down, his mouth finding her neck, her breast, sucking hard as his hand burrowed between her legs. The moment he touched her in that sensitive spot, she cried out and rocked against him as if desperate for his touch. She was open, wet, *ready*.

Wonder barreled through him that this woman, this beautiful, marvelous, brilliant woman wanted him. *Him*.

He lifted his head from her breast and looked at her, meeting her incandescent gaze.

"You take my breath away."

"As you take mine."

His hand fisted gently in her hair, and he kissed her with an urgency that bordered on madness even as he shoved a finger deep inside of her. She moaned into his mouth, then began to whimper with need, rocking against him, kissing him like a wildcat, shattering with the sexiest, throatiest of cries.

She pulled back, desperate, her fingers clawing at his shoulders. "Come inside me. Please. *Now*."

His body tensed, terrified he'd be too much for her. But she wasn't a small woman, and maybe, maybe it would be all right. His cock found her moist welcome, and she surged up, swallowing the tip of him with a moan of pure pleasure. Wulfe held back, holding on to his last thread of control, but Natalie was having none of that.

Her hands gripped his head. "*Don't tease. I need you.*"

Oh, goddess. With a groan of pure pleasure, he sank deep into her wetness, into her tight, slick channel, amazed when he felt no resistance to his width. He was a tight fit, but she was big enough. And far more importantly, ready for him.

Rocking against him, she swallowed him deeper, and deeper still, until he'd sunk up to his balls. Goddess have mercy, she'd taken all of him. With a growl of pure need, he pulled almost free of her and sank all the way to the hilt again.

Natalie's back arched, her mouth falling open. "It's perfect. You're perfect. Make love to me, Wulfe. Hard."

As he drove into her, his vision became bathed in a golden light, a light that seemed to settle inside of him, warm and wonderful. *Love.*

Natalie's eyes widened as if she felt it, too. Then she smiled and threw her head back, moaning with pleasure. "Harder, Wulfe, *harder.*"

He ground his hips into hers until sweat slicked their bodies, until they were both grunting and groaning, racing to the top of the highest peak. And beyond. Far, far beyond. As they approached that far-flung precipice, their gazes met, locked, and Natalie smiled as her orgasm began to roll through her, an arrow straight to his heart.

With her body contracting around him, her low, sexy cries filling his ears, he came with a roar, the beauty of the moment, the *perfection*, beyond words, beyond imagining.

And then she began to laugh, that throaty laugh that shot straight to his groin, as he collapsed, spent, on top of her. Not wanting to crush her, he forced himself to roll, taking her with him, still buried to his balls inside of her. Her golden halo of hair flew around her face as she righted, and she laughed again, then covered his mouth with hers, kissing him as if he'd just given her the world.

His heart swelled until he thought it would burst from his chest.

With his hands tight on her sweet ass, he kept them fused below while their mouths joined above. Goddess, he didn't want to let her go. He wanted to stay like this, just like this, forever. Or at the very least, for days and days and days.

As one hand gripped her soft, perfect rear, his other slid up and down her slender back, love barreling through him, hard and fast. A golden thread began to weave around his heart, a thread that flowed outward to hers. The beginning of a mating bond.

Deep inside, his wolf howled, Wulfe's own need echoed in the lonely sound. *Mine.* She was his, dammit. *Theirs.* His and the wolf spirit's. And they weren't letting her go.

Unless he couldn't convince her to stay. The prospect tightened his hold, making his soul cry out. But he would never force her to remain with him against her will. Never. That would be tantamount to holding her captive.

The moment they figured out how to disentangle her from this mess, he'd give her the choice, and if she wanted to return to her world, he'd take her memories, as he had before, and send her back. What she wanted, what would make her happy, was all that mattered.

But the thought of losing her again nearly had him drawing fangs and claws. Burying his face in her hair, he held her tight against his heart, and loved her.

Wulfe was dressed, Natalie combing out her wet hair after the shower that had become far more play than washing, when he heard the rap on his door. He opened it to find Vhyper.

"Ariana thinks she's found the ritual you told her to look for. Lyon wants everyone in the ritual room, pronto."

"Praise the goddess. I'll be right there." Wulfe closed the door as Natalie poked her head out of the bathroom, a towel wrapped around her naked body. In her eyes he saw the same flare of vulnerable hope that he felt. "If the knowledge I stole from Satanan is true, this is the ritual that should reverse the damage done to us by Inir's dark charm."

"Thank goodness," Natalie said fervently.

Wulfe strode to her, cupped her damp head with his hand, and kissed her soundly. "Rest while I go reclaim my immortality. Then I'll make love to you again."

A too-wise smile lifted her mouth, but didn't quite reach her eyes. "The moment you're all immortal again, you'll be going after Inir. Just don't go without saying good-bye."

He couldn't deny her words. "I won't. I promise." Sliding his fingers through wet hair, he caressed her head. "Do you want me to ask Melisande to keep you company?"

"No. I could use a little time alone."

He respected that, but he worried, too. "I'll make sure there's someone nearby who'll hear you if you need help. If the pain comes back, yell, sweetheart. Don't hold it in. Please?"

"Okay."

He pulled her against him and kissed her again, drinking her in, certain he would never get enough. Certainly not in the few decades they might have together. Or the few days.

Finally, with a kiss to her nose, he left her, locking the door behind him.

After securing the promise of one of Ariana's Ilinas to hang out in his room where she could hear Natalie if she called, Wulfe followed Vhyper down to the basement, then strode into the cavelike ritual room, a room now lit by half a dozen ritual fires. Circling the edges of the room, the flames cast darting shadows on the ceiling and walls, giving the space an ancient, mystical feel.

Most of the other Ferals were already there, gathered in the middle, stripping off their shirts. Wulfe found his own expectant mood mirrored on the faces of his brothers. Hell, even the smoke from the fires smelled of hope. Inside, his wolf howled, the sound imploring, beseeching, as if the animal spirit begged the goddess for triumph. Or mercy.

Wulfe stripped off his own shirt, turning toward the door as Fox, Jag, and Olivia strolled in, the last to arrive.

"Take your places around the circle," Ariana commanded. The Queen of the Ilinas was in charge. She met Wulfe's gaze. "I found the words of the ritual you told me about in my memory banks. I'll feed them to Kougar through our telepathic link, and he'll repeat them. Blood is involved, of course."

"Make the cuts shallow and small," Lyon warned. "And don't cut your sword hands."

If this worked, they'd quickly heal any wound, but Lyon was a cautious leader when it came to the well-being of his troops, and Wulfe appreciated that.

Excitement pulsed in the air, heavily tempered by the failures that had come before. Wulfe knew this ritual would work. How, he wasn't certain, but deep within his Daemon blood, he knew this was the one. Still, he wouldn't breathe easily until his friends were back in their animals, their immortality fully restored.

As they took their places around the circle, Kougar lit the last fire, this one in the middle. The light from the flame glittered on their golden armbands, sending their faces into hard relief, revealing granite expressions and rigid jaws as if every male believed this ritual would succeed through the power of his will alone. They were warriors trained to take on any foe with blades and claws, but they'd been fighting an enemy armed with magic, a weapon that had nearly defeated them. They hungered for real battle. If this worked, they'd get it. Finally, they'd be able to descend upon Inir's fortress and destroy their enemies.

Kougar grabbed the ritual blade, then pulled the bowl—the top of the skull of a long-dead shape-shifter—from its shelf. He handed the blade to Lyon. The Chief of the Ferals made a small slice in his left palm, squeezed his fist, letting the blood run into the bowl, then handed the blade to Paenther, who did the same. One by one, each Feral added his blood to the bowl.

When it was Wulfe's turn, he made the requisite cut

across his palm, the sting of the blade sharp. Squeezing his fist over Kougar's bowl, he handed the blade to Fox, beside him.

Kougar was the last to add his blood, and when he'd done so, he began to chant in the language of the ancient shifters. Slowly, the rest of them took up the chant, their voices low, then building, as Kougar dipped two fingers into the blood and streaked them across the heart of each male, one after the other.

Their voices grew, the chant turning into a pulsing beat in Wulfe's blood. Magic rode the air, melding with the growing excitement.

And yet something was wrong, dammit. Something was off. He felt it deep inside.

"Radiance," the Shaman called out. "You need radiance."

Lyon's face turned to stone. He'd been trying to save the last of Kara's strength to bring a new Feral into his animal, hoping one would be marked that they were sure enough about. But that had yet to happen.

Finally, Lyon nodded, and Delaney and Olivia rose from where they watched against one wall and helped Kara into the circle, setting her on the ground at her mate's feet.

"Continue the chant!" Ariana ordered, and the males did so.

As Lyon stroked the hair back from Kara's face, she closed her eyes. But when she should have lit up like a sunbeam, she instead struggled, her face turning red, perspiration dampening her brow as she tried to pull the radiance. Wulfe felt his own muscles bunching as he willed her to succeed, hating that she was so weak, that this was so hard on her.

Finally, after long, gut-wrenching minutes, Kara went radiant. Relief flowed through the room as her soft glow slowly grew brighter and brighter.

"Touch her," Lyon commanded.

Though Wulfe had felt the life-giving energy slide through his body the moment Kara lit up, when his hand slid around her upper arm, the pure energy of her radiance barreled through him. He threw his head back, drinking in the strength that came directly from the Earth. The chant resumed, the tight knot of Ferals lifting their voices until the words pounded against the walls, hammering in his veins.

"Stand back," Kougar told them and, one by one, they released Kara to reclaim their places around the circle. As they continued to chant, Kougar poured the remaining blood into the central fire, making the flame flare and spit.

Tossing the bowl aside, Kougar raised both hands high above his head. "Reclaim your animals!"

Deep inside, Wulfe's animal suddenly howled in pain, a pain Wulfe shared as fire exploded in his head. His animal snarled and growled, howling with agony, with fury. A terrible grief raked at Wulfe's mind, wrenching a cry from his throat.

"No!"

Then all went silent. His wolf was gone. *Gone.* Wulfe roared, the cry of fury echoing back on him, suddenly the only sound in the room.

Belatedly, he realized that Kara's glow was out. The chant had gone silent.

"It didn't work," Lyon said, his voice like gravel as he knelt to gather Kara into his arms. His gaze swung to Wulfe, devastation in his eyes. "You lost your animal."

Wulfe nodded through the ice forming in his veins. His mind had turned all but numb like it often did during those first seconds of disbelief after one of his limbs was torn off, before the shock set in and the pain exploded. *Gone.* A shifter no more.

The ritual had failed.

Ariana stared at him, a hint of accusation in her eyes. "That was the ritual you told me to find, Wulfe."

Every pair of eyes in the room turned on him. Wary eyes, hard eyes filled with devastation.

"I could feel the magic trying to rise," the Shaman said. "I don't know why it didn't work."

"The words were right," Wulfe said tonelessly. "They were right." They'd fucked up in some other way. And suddenly he knew how. "We used the wrong blood."

"What blood should we have used?" Paenther asked, a thread of barely leashed fury in his words.

"I don't know."

Jag let loose a string of invectives. "It was a fucking Daemon ritual! It probably calls for the blood of virgins or firstborn children or baby bunnies or something."

"Or the blood of Daemons," Kougar said thoughtfully.

Wulfe's head pounded. "We could try it again using my blood alone." But as he turned to Lyon, he saw that Kara was asleep in his arms. Pulling the radiance had taken everything she had.

Lyon shook his head, his jaw rigid, his eyes bleak.

"Maybe it was *all* wrong." Wulfe shook his head back and forth, frustration and fury building inside of him. "What if Satanan's fucking with my head, making me think I know things? He could have told me about that ritual specifically to destroy any chance that we might succeed. *Fuck!*"

Fury barreled up and out of him on a ferocious yell of anger, grief, and pain. When he'd quieted, as his gaze slowly roamed the circle, he saw despair in his brothers' eyes, a despair he knew must darken his own.

Their last chance had failed.

Natalie stood in front of the window of her bedroom, Jane Austen's *Emma* clutched against her chest. She'd tried to read, but her mind simply refused to quiet long enough for the words in front of her eyes to register. It didn't matter that she'd already read the book three times in years past and practically knew it by heart. For a short while, she'd worked on her computer, but that had been even less productive.

She couldn't stop thinking about the fact that she'd shattered an empty wine bottle against the edge of Kara's dresser. Had she really intended to attack shape-shifters? Maybe she had. Or maybe she'd been out of her mind and would have turned on anyone within reach.

The thought scared her. Twice now, she'd lost time, though the first time her memory had been intentionally taken from her, presumably for her own good. This time she found far more disturbing because she hadn't been in her right mind. She hadn't been conscious of her actions at all. And there was a chance Satanan had been controlling her in some way.

Turning away from the window, Natalie set the book on the nightstand, then sank onto the edge of the bed and stared at nothing. She felt as if she'd awakened in an alternate universe where nothing she knew or believed was true anymore. Shape-shifters,

Daemons, magic all existed in this world. Xavier lived. And she, herself, was somehow being used to empower a Daemon, perhaps the most evil creature ever to walk the Earth.

For the first time, she thought she understood what it felt like for some of her patients, when, after years of seeing one way, of their brains processing the words on the page in a way that sometimes made the words all but impossible to read, their eyes were opened. What was once invisible or distorted finally became clear. Just last week, she'd gotten a call from the mom of one of the kids she'd taken through a full course of vision therapy. The woman was in tears because her daughter was now reading at grade level, a thing they'd feared would never happen. Words that had appeared to her seven-year-old's eyes, to leap and bounce across the page, now lined up straight and still as they were meant to.

Seeing clearly in the child's case was a blessing. Natalie wasn't so sure she could say the same. Not when her eyes had been opened to a truth she was beginning to fear she wouldn't survive.

Pushing to her feet, she walked back to the window, turning her gaze northwest, toward Frederick, toward home and the life she needed to return to. She had work to do there, still. There were too many kids at risk and too few doctors available to help them. How many times had she heard otherwise excellent eye doctors disparage vision therapy as *voodoo*? Many viewed it with the same skepticism she suspected medical doctors viewed acupuncture, unwilling to explore a specialty they knew little about, thereby leaving at-risk patients without the options that could profoundly change their lives.

Yet, returning to that life meant leaving this one and never seeing Wulfe again. Or Xavier. And the thought felt like a fist to the solar plexis.

Cut yourself.

Natalie stilled, her pulse leaping erratically at the strange thought that blazed suddenly in her mind.

Draw your blood.

To her disbelieving horror, she lifted one hand and began to claw at her opposite wrist, raking the tender flesh with her fingernails.

"No." The word was a bare whisper, uttered between clenched teeth. Pain tore along her wrist, ice filling her veins, because she couldn't move of her own free will. She couldn't call out. She could do nothing but what the voice in her head told her to do.

Satanan. This was his doing!

Suddenly, pain sliced across her cheek. *Oh, God, no. Not now. Not this, too.*

She opened her mouth to call for help, but she could force no sound between her lips. He was controlling her completely. Eyes filling with tears, heart pounding with terror, she tore at her wrist until her fingertips were slick with blood.

Finally, the words came, but they weren't her own. They fell from her lips in a whispered, frantic torrent, in a language she'd never heard. If only she could make some kind of sound, even just bang against the wall. But her body refused to cooperate. It was no longer her own.

She'd been caught fast in the web of a Daemon.

Chapter Nineteen

"I need to get out of this fucking house!" Wulfe shouted, slamming his fist into the wall of the ritual room so hard that plaster rained down on him from above. He was trapped within a body that could no longer shift, within a four-story prison from which Satanan just waited for a chance to come after him again.

Worst of all, he feared Satanan might be fucking with his mind.

If only he could take a run in his wolf, but his other half was lost to him, now. He couldn't even walk out to the goddess stone to listen to the rumbling falls of the Potomac River and feel the wind in his face.

He was so fucking angry! So frustrated. So . . . *terrified* . . . that this nightmare would never end.

Hawke clapped him on the back. "Come on,

buddy. Get Natalie. It's almost time for dinner. You'll feel better after you've eaten." Hawke grunted, the shadows from the loss of his own animal clouding his eyes. "No, you won't. But your stomach will feel better, and that's something, at least."

Wulfe nodded. But as he turned for the door, he felt an odd tug at his mind as if his subconscious was trying to get his attention. Had he forgotten something?

He shook his head. No, this tug felt external. Satanan? The thought chilled.

"Wulfe?" Kougar asked. "What's happening?"

"I'm not sure." He felt the tug again, hard and insistent. Was his animal trying to reach him? The thought lifted his heart until he realized that it was coming from another place, his heart and that gossamer thread that he'd recognized as the beginnings of a mating bond.

Down that finest of threads, he heard something, as faint as a whisper in a gale.

A scream.

"*Natalie.*" He shoved forward, pushing his brothers aside. "Natalie's in trouble."

The others parted for him, and he ran, up the stairs, through the foyer, up two more flights. But as he neared the third-floor hallway, wisps of red smoke began to seep into the edges of his field of vision.

"Roar!" He couldn't lose it. Not now, not when Natalie needed him.

"We're right behind you," Lyon said.

Wulfe ran down the hall, hearing the reassuring footfalls of his brothers following close. "She's in pain, and the darkness is gunning for me. If I don't reach her before it gets me, knock her out."

"We will."

But as he neared her door, he heard nothing. No scream, no sound of pain or shout for help. Just a perfect, terrible silence. Either the Ilina had already whisked Natalie away, or Natalie had never called out. Wulfe burst through the door, then came to a sudden halt at the horrible sight that met his eyes.

Natalie stood in the middle of the room, facing him, blood dripping from her fingertips onto the carpet, her head thrown back in agony, tears running into her hair as she whispered words he didn't understand. No, words he *did* understand. *Daemon words*.

"Satanan has her." Wulfe lunged forward, gathering her close, and watching as terrified gray eyes swung toward him with relief. Placing a kiss on her brow, he jammed his thumb beneath her ear, then swung her into his arms as she fell unconscious.

Shaking badly, he turned to where Lyon, Hawke, and Kougar stood just inside the door. "The words were Daemon words designed to open the channel to the primal energies."

"Maybe you should put her down, Wulfe," Lyon said evenly. All three males watched him as if they thought they were going to have to tackle him to the ground again at any moment.

"I'm okay. The shadows have subsided." For now.

"Is the channel open?" Kougar asked.

"Yes." He could feel a slight buzz of energy he hadn't before. Goddess, what if that darkness started to build in him? What if he lost it and never came back? But even as the worry flew through his head, knowledge followed. He wouldn't lose control to such a small amount of primal energy.

With a shake of his head, he met Lyon's gaze. "The

channel has only been opened a crack. I'm the one who needs to say the words to open it, not Natalie. But Satanan has managed to get himself a steady, if small, flow of power. It's going to strengthen him."

"Does he have complete control over her now?" Hawke asked.

"No." He frowned, his stomach full of lead shot. "I hope not."

"This connection Satanan has with you is no good, you know that," Lyon said evenly.

"I know." Wulfe's grip on Natalie tightened, and he knew what was going through Lyon's head. Probably all of their heads. The safest course of action would be to sever the connection. Here. Now.

"I love her." He met the gazes of each of his brothers in turn, men he'd lay his life down for in an instant. "I'll kill you before I let you hurt her."

Lyon's jaw tightened, but he nodded. "We risk much for the women we love."

"Without them, what do we have that's worth fighting for?" Hawke asked philosophically.

To Wulfe's surprise, Kougar nodded. "Natalie lives. It's Inir that dies."

But they were back to square one. Wulfe looked down at the woman in his arms and wished he could pack her up and take her somewhere, away from the wary gazes, somewhere that Satanan and Inir couldn't send Mage sentinels after them.

He turned to Kougar suddenly. "Would the Ilinas host a couple of corporeal visitors for a few hours? I'll go stark, raving mad . . . again . . . if I don't get out of this house."

"The Ilinas would welcome you, but I suggest Melisande accompany you."

Lyon nodded. "If you have any trouble, she and her mist warriors can either whisk you both back here, or us up there."

"You'll be safe enough there," Kougar added. "As safe as anywhere."

And that was the real crux of the matter. As long as Satanan had his claws in them, there was nowhere they could really hide.

Natalie came awake to the feel of a large, tender hand stroking her hair. Wulfe's. Even without opening her eyes, she knew he was the one who held her on his lap, cradled against his strong chest.

"Are you back?" he asked softly.

With a deep breath, she opened her eyes and met his concerned gaze, then tensed as she saw the bleakness there. Struggling to sit up, she reached for him, her hand pressing against his cheek.

"What happened? Something terrible happened. Someone died."

He stared at her, shook his head. "You amaze me with your perception. No one died, not exactly. I lost my animal." At those last words, his brow tightened, grief slashing across his eyes.

"Oh, Wulfe." This was bad, in so many ways, she knew that. But in that moment, all she could feel was his anguish, and it slew her. Sliding her arms around his neck, she pulled him close, held him tight as he buried his face against her shoulder. Fear washed through her in an icy flow because she knew that a Feral without his animal would not survive.

Her hold on him tightened until her muscles began to quake. "You can't die."

"It's not going to come to that," he said against her hair. "We're not going to let it come to that." But while he made a decent effort to reassure her, she heard no certainty in his voice.

As her gaze slowly took in her surroundings, she began to frown. They appeared to be sitting at the base of a cascade of rocks, beneath a bright blue sky. But the air . . . It was sparkling, as if filled with tiny crystals!

She jerked upright and peered around. In front of her sat a lovely pool of clear water fed by a small, tinkling waterfall. It was lovely in a stark kind of way. There wasn't a plant or flower in sight despite the fact that she smelled the unmistakable scent of pine.

"What *is* this place?" she asked, pushing off Wulfe's lap to stand and look around.

"We're safe here." Wulfe's bare feet dangled in the water. "We're in the Crystal Realm. The Ilinas' castle is just beyond the rocks."

She cocked her head at him, narrowing her eyes. "Where?"

"In the clouds."

Natalie scowled. "That's not possible."

"And a race of women who can turn to mist, disappear at will, and travel anywhere in the world in seconds is?"

Natalie stared at him a moment more, then blinked, giving up. She'd already accepted shape-shifters, Daemons, and Mage. And she'd seen the Ilinas appear and disappear, had even traveled with one. What was a castle in the clouds compared to all that?

Of far more concern was *why* they were here. "What happened, Wulfe? The last thing I remember,

you were about to perform some ritual with the
Ferals to reclaim your immortality." With a frown,
she understood. "It didn't work, did it?"

"No. Do you remember anything of what happened in your room?"

The way he was looking at her, she knew it must be
bad. "Tell me."

He held out his hand to her and when she took it,
pulled her onto the rock beside him and slid his arm
around her shoulders. "Somehow, Satanan forced
you to perform a ritual that opened the channel a
little bit." When her jaw dropped, he added hastily,
"Not far. I knocked you out and brought you here
afterward."

Vaguely, she remembered . . . something. More like
a nightmare than reality. "I hurt myself, didn't I?"

"Yes. He forced you to scratch open your wrists
and whisper a string of ritual words. I got there in
time to stop you before it accomplished much."

She lifted one of her wrists and looked at clear, uninjured flesh. With a purse of her lips, she reached
for his free arm and turned it over, eyeing the thin
scratches.

"You took my wounds again."

Eyes filled with infinite warmth watched her softly.
"I will always take your injuries. I can't stand to see
you in pain."

Love welled up, filling her chest until it nearly cut
off her breath. She lifted a hand to his cheek, lifted
her face for his kiss, and he met her halfway. Warm
lips brushed hers, featherlight. Strong arms pulled
her tight against his muscular chest, and he kissed
her with increasing urgency, with rising need and
passion. Her pulse took off, her breath growing shal-

low, then disappearing altogether as their mouths merged, their tongues twining, their limbs shaking with need and desire.

His hand slid into her hair, cupping her head, as he deepened the kiss. His need transmitted to her through desperate hands and fierce kisses, and the growing erection that pressed more and more insistently against her hip. Liquid heat slid through her, and she shook with the desire to feel him inside her again, to become one with him once more.

Wulfe's hand slid down her back, then up under her shirt to press against her warm flesh. His mouth tore from hers, his lips pressing against her cheek, her eye, her temple.

"I need to be inside you, Natalie."

"Yes. *Please.*"

He moved with swift grace for such a big man, stripping them both of their shirts and her of her bra before she could lift a trembling hand to help him. As she pulled off her shoes, he rose to his feet and divested himself of the remainder of his clothes. Laying their T-shirts on the rocks, he scooped her up and set her atop them, then quickly stripped her bare.

For long moments he sat back on his heels, gazing at her, naked except for the gleaming golden wolf's-head armband, his gaze skimming slowly over her bare flesh, setting every single inch on fire.

Watching him filled her with such happiness, despite everything, that a fleeting smile found its way to her mouth. His gaze flicked to hers, a wry, answering smile lighting his eyes as his hand reached for her, skimming up her abdomen, then cupping her breast. A moment later, she was on her back, his mouth on her breast, his hand between her legs. He drove her up, hard and fast, until she was crying out from an exquisite release. Finally, he settled between her thighs, met her gaze with an expression so full of heat and tenderness that it melted the heart in her chest, and slid thickly, deeply, *wonderfully* inside her.

Natalie reached up and clasped her hands behind his neck, holding on as she met him, thrust for thrust. Their gazes locked, her heart opened so fully she began to think their hearts, too, were becoming one.

"Do you feel that?" he asked with wonder.

The love overwhelmed her, misting her eyes with tears. "Yes." Yet neither of them had ever said the words. And then no words were possible as her body began to rise again, higher than before. Wulfe drove into her harder and faster, following her to those impossible heights, shattering right alongside her as she cried out with triumph and stunning release, and a love so deep she wondered if, within its glorious depths, she might drown.

Bracing himself on his forearms, he watched her, his eyes softer than she'd ever seen them. "I love you, Natalie Cash."

Tears misted her eyes all over again. "I love you, too, my wolf."

He kissed her nose and lifted up again, a gentle smile on his mouth. "I know. Your love is a miracle. It's healing me in more ways than I'd imagined."

She gave him an impudent grin. "Everything's in fine working order, now."

He laughed. "Thank the goddess." But his gaze turned serious. "It was the strength of your love that broke through the tangled mess of my shattered mating bond, sweeping it all away. The sweetness of your kiss." He stroked the hair back from her face.

"Food has taste, colors are back to their true, vibrant beauty. And I can *feel* again. Passion, desire, need."

As she watched him, as she loved him, her heart pinched. Because what would come of this love? What *could* come of it? Despite his words, he'd said nothing about the future.

Then again, given the precariousness of their current situation, any future might be very, very short.

Wulfe pulled out of her and rolled to her side, gathering her against him. She curled into him, her cheek on his shoulders, her arm around his waist, as he stroked her back. His mood, too, had lost its buoyancy, and she knew he had many of the same thoughts she did, the same concerns about the hours to come.

His fingers slid into her hair, and he kissed her forehead. "I'm going to keep you safe. Whatever else, I promise you that." Quietly, they lay together, enjoying the feel of one another's body pressing close. He traced the curve of her ear with his thumb. "Talk to me, sweetheart. Tell me about your life, your work. I want to know everything there is to know about Natalie Cash."

As she lay curled against him, a warm, comfortable breeze wafting over her bare skin as his hand moved to rub her back, she told him what she did, and why. How her brother James's struggle to learn to read had all but destroyed his life. How she was determined to keep that from happening to other children.

Wulfe stroked her hair. "I love that your work matters to you. That it matters, period." He brushed her forehead with his lips, then rose on one elbow to peer down at her, his gaze fervent. "I'll get you home, Natalie. I'm not sure how, but I will."

Even as she nodded, his reassurance made her ache. For the first time in her life, she'd truly lost her heart to another. How would she ever live the rest of her life without it? Without the man, the shape-shifter, she'd fallen in love with?

Together they rose and dressed. Wulfe took Natalie's hand, loving the way she instinctively brushed against his side as they wandered among the stone formations of the Ilinas' rock garden, brushing her shoulder against his arm as if she sensed his Feral need for touch—a need heightened by the empty chasm inside him that, for nearly six hundred years, had been occupied by his wolf. The silence in his head threatened to deafen him.

Yet, as empty as he felt without his animal, he knew he'd feel ten times more lonely once he'd taken Natalie's memories and returned her to her world. The thought was enough to drive a blade through his heart, yet there was nothing he wouldn't do to make her happy. Nothing.

But, *goddess,* he would suffer.

"What happens, now?" she asked softly beside him.

"I don't know." They were fucked. The ritual that should have worked hadn't, and they didn't know why. The Daemons were going to rise. And when they did, if he wasn't dead already, he'd likely fall under Satanan's control. He might turn on his friends. On Natalie.

Royally, royally fucked.

"I think you should consider pulling the primal energies, Wulfe."

His mind shut down. "No."

"With that kind of power, you might be able to beat Inir."

Shadows darkened his eyes. "You don't know what you're asking."

"I know exactly what I'm asking. More than asking. I'm demanding that you not compromise the Ferals' ability to win this battle, certainly not for me. If the Daemons are freed, Wulfe, I'm going to die. Likely in a horrific way. We all are. Please don't ever lose sight of that fact."

He turned to her, needing her to understand. "Just the little bit of that power that I consume when Satanan pulls it through us is enough to send me out of my mind. What do you think will happen if I open the channel? I'll be swamped by it. I could kill every one around me. Everyone I care about."

"I think you have more control in that state than you think. Every time you blank, you come back to me. To *me*, Wulfe." She stared at him, such certainty in those gray eyes. "I can pull you back."

"And if you don't?"

"If the Daemons rise, we're all dead either way."

"No." He dropped her hand and moved away from her, watching one of the small waterfalls, its spray welcome against the heat of his flesh. She didn't know what she was asking. He wouldn't even consider it.

He felt her arms go around his waist from behind and he slid his hands atop hers. A small shudder went through him as her welcome touch soaked into him.

"We're connected, Wulfe," she said quietly. "Beyond the channel key. I don't understand it, I just know that it's true. From the start, you've protected me. You won't hurt me. I *know* that. And just as you'll protect me, I'll protect you."

"Natalie . . ."

"Trust me, Wulfe. Far more importantly, trust yourself."

Wulfe stared at the water tripping down the rocks, his heart pounding because the Ferals' needed a miracle. But how could he possibly pull this off? How could anyone? If he lost control of the darkness, he could become the instrument of the world's destruction.

Goddess, he prayed silently. *I beg of you, don't let that happen. I know you've been disappointed in me. I know you punished me for my vanity and my mistakes all those years ago. I'm reminded every time I look in the mirror.* His hands gripped Natalie's tight. *I'm sorry. Please don't make Natalie pay for my sins, too. Please protect her through this. And protect my brothers. If a life must be forfeit, let it be mine.*

He felt a soft cheek rub against his shoulder. "I won't let the darkness take you, Wulfe. I promise."

With a shudder, he pulled her around in front of him, until he could hold her precious face in his hands. Her eyes were so calm, so sure.

"How do you have such faith in me?" he asked with wonder.

"Because I know you." She placed a slender hand over her heart. "In here."

As he stared into those gray eyes, alight with conviction, he felt a calmness beyond reckoning, a joy without bounds. "Goddess, how I love you." Pulling her close, he kissed her, drinking of her essence, her strength, even as he shared his in return.

Slowly, they pulled apart. He caressed her cheek,

subconsciously tracing the line of her missing wound, until he realized what he was doing. Strome's words came back to him, that in order to pull the primal energies for himself, to open the channel fully, he had to give Natalie back the wound he'd taken.

"How could I ever intentionally hurt you?" he whispered, tracing that invisible line down her cheek.

Her hand covered his. "You won't be hurting me, Wulfe. You'll simply undo what you did before and give me back the cut that was always mine."

"I would take a hundred to keep you from suffering that one."

"It's a small price to pay to save the world. Besides, I'd kind of like a rakish scar. A battle scar." Her smile turned impish. "I rather like yours, Shifter. I rather fancy having one of my own."

He shook his head, then snorted, remembering her as he first knew her—with her hair unwashed and tangled, that jagged wound across her cheek. From the very start, she'd never been anything but beautiful to him. From the first moment he'd spoken with her, that calm poise and courage of hers had shone through so brightly that her imperfections had faded to obscurity. He'd fallen in love with her then, wound and all. No simple scar would ever change that. A hundred scars wouldn't change it.

And he finally understood that it was the same for her. His scars truly meant nothing to her, nothing but a chronicle of past events. As hers, if the day ever came that he felt driven to return it, would become a sign of her courage and a mark of battles fought.

"You humble me." He stroked her hair back from her face and kissed her, caressing her lips with his, sliding his tongue into her sweet mouth, pulling her tight against his heart as he loved her. As she loved him in return. But as their tongues stroked one another, voices began to whisper in his head, and he jerked back, freezing.

My lord, it is done. My sorcerers have accomplished the impossible. They've created the unascended Radiant's blood needed to open the Daemon Blade. All but two Feral lights have been doused, and the last two should be choking out any minute.

Gather your Ferals.

Done. The moment the true Ferals are no more, the ritual will begin. You will be free at last.

"What's the matter?" Natalie asked, her expression worried.

"They've done it. They have what they need to open the Daemon Blade. We're out of time."

Wulfe grabbed Natalie's hand and started running toward the Ilinas' castle. "Melisande!" he shouted.

A second later, the petite Ilina materialized in front of him, her expression battle ready. "What happened?"

"Get us back to Feral House, *now*."

Wulfe raced into the Feral dining room through the back door, Natalie and Melisande close behind. Paenther, Fox, and Zeeland sat at the table.

"Roar!" he shouted at the top of his lungs, knowing his chief could be anywhere in the house. "Foyer!"

The three at the table leaped up and followed as he grabbed Natalie's hand and ran down the hall. All the Ferals, hearing his shout, converged in the foyer within a minute.

"They've created unascended Radiant blood," Wulfe told them. "Inir says only two of us can still shift. He's preparing his Ferals to open the blade the moment they can't. We're out of time."

"I've still got my animal," Falkyn said.

Fox nodded. "As have I."

Lyon's gaze snapped toward the basement door. "Grizz and Lepard?"

"I'll check," Melisande said, and disappeared. Four seconds later, she was back. "They both lost theirs within the past hour."

"So Inir was right," Fox muttered. "We're down to two."

Jag's hands fisted. "Let's go kill that bastard."

"Wait!" Olivia said beside him. "The Therian Guard should go after Inir. You're still mortal. Let us try to capture him and bring him to you."

"Not a chance, Red." Jag hauled her close. "This is our fight."

Olivia turned on her mate, her expression warrior-hard. "Kara saw hundreds of immortal sentinels. Too many for you to take on in this condition, Jag, and you know it. And that's *if* you can find your way through the warding again."

Fox joined the argument. "The Guard is unlikely to have any better luck breaching that warding, Olivia, and you know it."

Ariana appeared suddenly in the midst of them, frustration in her Ilina eyes. "I finally know what went wrong with the ritual to restore your animals." Silence dropped like a blanket over the foyer as all heads turned her way. "The ritual requires the blood of the one who made the charm. The Shaman has felt Inir's magic in it from the start. We need Inir's blood."

"Bloody hell," Fox muttered. "So there's no fecking way out of this. We're attacking that stronghold just as we are, as nonshifting mortals."

Vhyper shrugged. "Better nonshifting than dead."

"We attack Inir's fortress immediately," Lyon snapped. "The ten Ferals will head out first along with

Zeeland and Olivia and however many Guards the Ilinas can take. The rest will follow as quickly as the Ilinas can get them there. Say good-bye to your mates, grab food, and arm yourselves well since you won't be shifting." He turned to Ariana. "Once you've delivered us close to the warding, the same place you did last time, return here with your Ilinas to protect our women. Mist them out of here if you need to."

"We're all going?" Tighe asked.

"Do you see an alternative?"

"No. We're going to need every man. What about Grizz and Lepard? They delivered themselves back here, knowing we might kill them."

"They stay in the prisons. Trusting them is a risk we can't afford."

Wulfe had to agree. As much as they could use Grizz's and Lepard's help, Grizz was a time bomb with a short fuse. If Inir found a way to turn him against them, he could kill two or three of them before they realized what was happening.

"Gather your weapons and meet back here immediately," Lyon commanded. "The Ilinas will transport you as you arrive." Lyon swept Kara into his arms and ran up the stairs.

Wulfe took Natalie's hand and followed. The moment he ushered her into his bedroom, he gathered her close and kissed her with all the worry and frustration that battled inside him.

Finally, he pulled back, cupping her face. "You'll stay with the other women."

"If Satanan takes control of me again?"

He tipped his forehead to hers. "I pray that doesn't happen." Lifting his head, he met her gaze. "It's far too dangerous to take you into battle."

Her jaw hardened, a warrior's strength shining in her eyes. "If you need me, send for me. Don't hesitate, Wulfe."

He stroked her creamy cheek, then pulled away to arm himself, strapping his knife-laden hunting belt around his waist and two swords across his back, one for each hand. Finally, he slid a pair of knives into his boots.

As he straightened, shouts and whoops blasted suddenly from the foyer two stories below.

"Goddess, please let this be good news for once," Wulfe muttered. Grabbing Natalie's hand, he ran.

Zeeland stood in the foyer, surrounded by the Therian Guards, Olivia, and Fox, the shouting in his ears and the hands slapping his back barely breaching the shock as he stared at the claw marks that had erupted on his forearm seconds ago, four parallel marks, each several inches in length, that looked like long-healed scars.

His heart pounded, goose bumps rising on his flesh as understanding slowly penetrated his stunned mind.

"Lyon!" Olivia shouted beside him. "Zeeland's been marked!"

Marked. To be a Feral Warrior.

His jaw had dropped and still hung open as he met Fox's grin. Fox held out his hand and slapped forearms with him in the Ferals' traditional manner.

Julianne flew into his arms, and he held her tight against him as he buried his face in her hair.

A Feral Warrior. At last.

But was the animal who'd marked him one of the seventeen who'd been infected? It might be one of the two who'd been infected and died, an animal spirit that should be clear of Inir's poison this time. There was no way to know.

Would the Ferals imprison him now, too?

Goddess.

He looked up to find Lyon at the top of the stairs, joined in quick succession by most of the other Ferals and many of their mates.

"Is it true?" Lyon demanded.

Zeeland held up his arm.

"Hot diggity damn!" Jag crowed.

"*Praise the goddess,*" Hawke said starting down the stairs, Falkyn beside him. "Roar, I've known this male since he was a child. I would stake my life and that of my mate on Zeeland's being the best of the best. There's not an ounce of darkness in him."

"I agree," Fox said from beside Zeeland. "I've worked with him for decades, and he's as honorable as they come."

"This is what we've been waiting for," Tighe said. "A sure thing."

The Ferals were all streaming down the stairs, now, all but Lyon. When Hawke reached Zeeland, he slapped forearms with him, his grin wide and delighted. "Bringing a good Feral into his animal will reverse the damage done to Kara."

"You're our ace in the hole." Wulfe extended his arm to him, too. "The moment we bring you into your animal, we halt Inir's ability to perform the ritual to free the Daemons."

"Time for a Renascence, boys and girls," Jag said, slapping Zeeland on the shoulder as he extended his arm.

"The goddess stone, ASAP." Lyon's voice boomed

down the stairs, and Zeeland looked up to find him carrying Kara down. "Ferals only. And Julianne. Olivia's in charge here."

Kougar looked up. "Roar, it's still daylight. There will be humans all over the place."

"Go. Raise the warding. The rest of us will arrive by Ilina."

Groans peppered the foyer, but Kougar nodded as Ariana turned to mist beside him. A moment later the pair disappeared. The rest of the males stripped off their shirts, many laying knives and swords of every length into a pile against one wall. Pulling away from Julianne, Zeeland did the same, then kicked off his boots. In a few minutes, he'd be shifting, and he had no idea if he'd be able to hold on to his clothes and weapons.

The chills raced over his skin. *Shifting*.

"No!" Falkyn cried.

Hawke grabbed her as she swayed. "Faith?"

"My falcon. *She's gone*."

The Ferals' exchanged ominous glances. They were down to one.

Two minutes later, Ariana was back. "He's ready."

Zeeland grabbed Julianne's hand, meeting her bright blue gaze and the love and pride in her eyes. She grinned at him, slaying him all over again as she did every single time she smiled. Goddess, but he loved this woman.

As Ilinas appeared out of nowhere, all around the foyer, he released Julianne's hand and, a heartbeat later, was swept into a tingling, scratchy cloud that spun until he was sick with dizziness. Almost as soon as it began, the ride ended, and he found himself on the rocks overlooking the Potomac, retching his guts out. All around him, the other Ferals were doing the same. He finally understood why they complained so much about Ilina travel. What a miserable ride.

Ariana joined Kougar and began chanting, while the rest of the Ilinas gathered close to the short rock face farthest from the river below.

As Zeeland rose to his feet, he found Julianne and went to her. "Are you all right?"

She shook her head with a rueful smile. "Quite a trip."

He tucked a lock of her hair behind her ear and pulled her close. The sun was low in the western sky and would be setting soon, the day warm and bright. A perfect day to turn into a shape-shifter. His grin escaped, and he kissed his mate soundly, needing to share his joy with her.

Quickly, the Ferals gathered into a circle around the rock, Lyon depositing Kara in the middle, cupping her face.

"Take your time, little one."

"I can do this, Lyon. I *will* do it."

But, *goddess,* the woman looked like death warmed over. She swayed, dipping her head as if holding it up was too much effort.

"Roar?" Paenther asked.

"Pulling the radiance earlier took a lot out of her," Lyon admitted, stroking his mate's head. "But this is what she needs."

"I'll pull it," Kara said so softly, Zeeland barely heard her.

Finally, Lyon stepped back and took his place. "The warding will keep Zeeland from escaping if he's been marked by one of the still-infected animal spirits and the darkness takes him. If he turns into the eagle or sabertooth, both of which should be clear of the poison, now, we're good. If not, the Ilinas will whisk the rest of us out of here so that he doesn't injure anyone while Ariana cures him."

The thought that he might, like Ewan, be turned to evil, even temporarily, raked at his mind. But the Ferals had been taken by surprise by the first batch of new Ferals, unaware they'd been infected. They would not be caught unaware again.

Golden armbands gleamed in the bright setting sun as Kougar began to chant in some kind of ancient language, and the others joined him. How they expected him to learn all this well enough to pass it on, he didn't know. The thought that he still might have to be the keeper of the Feral legacy smothered his euphoria, dampening his joy. But he would do what must be done, no matter the cost or the difficulty, as he always had.

Kougar lifted the ritual knife and cut his palm, then curled his fingers into a fist around the blood and handed the knife to Lyon who did the same. Each warrior followed, one after another. Finally, Paenther handed the knife to Zeeland and motioned with his head for him to follow suit. When he had, Kougar shoved his fist into the air and the others followed.

"Little Radiant," Lyon said softly, his tone tight with worry.

From where she sat on the stone, Kara attempted to lift her arms to the sky, her face pale, her eyes dulled from the poison that had attacked her too many times as she brought evil Ferals into their animals without knowing it. But her arms dropped again, as if too heavy for her.

"Kara." Lyon's voice throbbed with misery. He knelt at her side, stroking her hair.

"I can do this," their Radiant said, her voice determined if far too soft.

Lyon kissed the top of her head and once more took his place in the circle.

"Shite!" Fox exclaimed suddenly. "I just lost my animal."

"Fuck," Jag muttered. The hopeful air disintegrated into a tight, heavy cloud of tension. The last of the Feral lights had gone out. Zeeland's own had yet to come on. Inir's evil Ferals were beginning the ritual to free the Daemons from the Daemon Blade.

The race was on.

"It'll be close," Paenther murmured.

Or not close at all, if Kara couldn't pull the radiance.

This time, Kara pressed her palms to the stone beneath her, closing her eyes, and tilting her head back, her face tight with lines of concentration. The seconds ticked by, then a minute. Two. Zeeland's pulse pounded as he prayed for her to find the strength she needed. *Come on, Kara. Come on, sweetheart.*

Silence blanketed the goddess stone as every man and woman held his or her breath, waiting. Praying. If this didn't work . . .

Suddenly, Kara went radiant, light erupting within her, a dim glow at first that quickly grew brighter and brighter until it shone through her skin as if she'd swallowed a small piece of the sun. Zeeland's mind sang with relief and excitement, his gaze finding Julianne's as she stood beside Ariana, his heart warming.

"Stay where you are, Zeeland," Lyon ordered. "If

you touch her without an armband, the radiance will kill you."

As the rest of the Ferals stepped forward, closing around Kara, clasping her arms or ankles, or pressing a palm to the top of her head, Zeeland remained still, and watched. Kougar was the first to release Kara and walk toward him. He pressed his bloodied fist on top of Zeeland's. The others joined them, Lyon pressing his fist atop Kougar's, Paenther's atop Lyon's, Wulfe's atop Paenther's. One by one they added their blood until all pressed close around him.

Kougar began to chant, switching to English as the others joined in. "Spirits rise and join. Empower the beasts beneath this moon. Goddess, reveal your warrior!"

Thunder rumbled across the clear sunset sky, a roar of powerful magic. The rock beneath Zeeland's feet trembled, as if in anticipation. Or dread. Zeeland's pulse thudded in his ears. Power raced through his body, a joy and pleasure and *rightness* of extraordinary proportions. And suddenly his vision shifted until he was staring at the belts of the males and female encircling him. His senses exploded—sights, sounds, scents. He heard the heartbeats of every person around him, smelled them individually.

A cheer went up.

"The sabertooth!" Jag cried. "So it was *you* the animal meant to mark, not that bastard Maxim."

Incredible. A saber-toothed tiger, an animal not seen in nature in ten thousand years.

"Shift back, Zeeland," Kougar said. "Choose to be a man once more, and it will be so."

Zeeland did as he was told and in a burst of colorful lights and intense pleasure, he shifted back into a man. And he still had his pants on!

The others gathered around him, clapping him on the back and slapping forearms with him.

"Henceforth," Kougar intoned. "You will be known as Zaber."

"Kara," Paenther breathed and all turned to find Lyon grinning as he lifted Kara high, their Radiant's face aglow with health, at last.

The moment Lyon set Kara on her feet again, she strode to Zeeland and threw her arms around his neck, hugging him close.

"Thank you, Zee. You just saved my life."

"It's my honor, Radiant. You may have just saved the world."

The reminder was like ice water, dousing the jubilation. As one they turned to Wulfe. But even before Wulfe uttered a word, the paleness of his skin told them all they needed to know.

Tighe scowled. "We didn't get Zeeland brought into his animal in time."

"No." A mix of fury and pain glowed in Wulfe's eyes. "For a few minutes the only Ferals who registered were Inir's evil ones. It was enough. They've begun the ritual to free the Daemons."

Chapter
Twenty-one

"**H**ow long do we have before they free the Daemons?" Lyon demanded, pushing himself off the ground in the backyard of Feral House where the Ilinas had deposited them after bringing Zeeland . . . now Zaber . . . into his animal.

Wulfe rose beside him, his mind numb, still ringing with Inir's triumphant shout. In that strange place inside him that Wulfe was beginning to think of as his Daemon soul, he could swear he felt that blade coming alive, little by little. He could feel it preparing to open.

"It's impossible to know," Kougar replied, watching them with the dispassion that had once been such a part of his nature and was now only a façade. "But I don't think the Daemon Blade will open quickly. It was never meant to open at all." He reached for his mate. "Ariana and I will mist to West Virginia, first. If Inir expanded his anti-Ilina warding, we need to know."

"And if Ariana bursts into flames?" Lyon asked. They'd lost an Ilina to the warding the last time they'd tried to reach Inir, desperate to rescue Kara.

Ariana kissed her mate. "I'm going alone. I'll test for the warding as I approach the mountain."

As Kougar opened his mouth as if to protest, she disappeared.

Behind him, the back door opened and Wulfe turned to find Natalie rushing toward him, the sunlight in her hair. His heart tumbled. He opened his arms, and she ran straight into them.

"You're going," she said quietly.

"Yes."

"Get your weapons!" Lyon called to the group, then turned to Olivia. "Is the Guard ready?"

"Ready and waiting, Lyon." Olivia threw her arms around a bright-eyed Kara as the other wives gathered around them. "I'm so glad you're okay."

Wulfe kissed Natalie's forehead. "Wait here. I'll be right back." He raced into the house, where several other Ferals were already retrieving their shirts, boots, and weapons. A minute later, dressed and armed, he strode back out through the dining room and into the sun just as Ariana returned.

"The spot we landed last time is still safe," Ariana announced as Kougar hauled her against him, burying his face in her hair.

Wulfe returned to Natalie, pulling her close. "Wish me luck."

Instead, she kissed his cheek. "Be careful." Turning to him fully, she reached for him, cupping his face with her hands, meeting his gaze with a look of such unbounded love that it made his breath catch. He reached for her hips, pulling her close, drinking in her warmth, her sweetness, her strength.

"Wulfe." His name sighed from her lips. "You are the finest man I've ever known. I know you can do this."

He stared into those calm gray eyes. "Goddess, how I love you." He kissed her, softly at first, tenderly, with wonder and care. Then more fiercely as she threw her arms around his neck and kissed him back as if staking her claim. As if sealing their fate.

"Wulfe!" Paenther called. "We're going."

With difficulty, Wulfe pulled away, but continued to touch her, stroking her cheek, sliding his head down her soft, silken hair. "Stay in the house. There are Ilinas here to watch over all of you and to mist you away if there's any danger."

She nodded, but they both knew the greatest danger to her was nothing the Ilinas could keep her safe from. It was Satanan.

"Wulfe, get us to that fortress!" Lyon called.

The Allegheny Mountains rose all around them, thick with spruce and hardwoods beneath a rose-colored sunset sky. Wulfe turned toward the direction he knew Inir's fortress to lie, the direction he felt in his Daemon blood would lead him to Satanan, and started to run. *Goddess,* he could *feel* the son of a bitch.

Behind him, his Feral brothers and sister, and the more than 150 Therian Guards, mobilized. The pounding of their feet vibrated across the mountainside, resonating deep in his blood. They were an impressive force though they'd have been far more so if the Ferals were still able to shift. At least they had one shifter among them, now. Zeeland.

Wulfe picked up speed, the knowledge that the evil Ferals were even now opening the Daemon Blade screaming like a siren in his head. For five thousand years, they and their Feral predecessors had kept Satanan from breaking free. Now they were minutes away from failure. Their only chance of success meant battling fully shifting, fully immortal evil Ferals. Goddess knew, it wouldn't be a picnic, but at this point, he didn't give a damn. He was so tired of sitting on his ass, so ready to fight!

"We've only got about an hour until the draden come out," Hawke commented, as they ran. No longer able to shift, they'd be sitting ducks.

Vhyper grunted. "If we haven't stopped the ritual in an hour, it's not going to matter. We're going to be dead either way."

"We've got company," Paenther warned. "Mage. More than a dozen of them."

"We'll take care of them," Olivia called.

As half the Guard peeled off, Wulfe pressed forward, Lyon on one side of him, Paenther on the other, the rest of the Ferals close behind.

The seconds ticked away with his heartbeats, and he felt every fucking one. They had miles to go. *Miles.* And in addition to the Mage welcoming committee, they still had warding to get through and possibly something far worse. The last time they'd tried to breach this mountain, they'd found themselves eyeballs deep in a mind fuck of a labyrinth. If not for Fox, they might still be lost in there.

As the sound of battle rose behind them, Wulfe's

muscles tensed with the need to join in. Around him, he felt the restlessness of his brothers and knew he wasn't the only one. It wasn't in a Feral's nature to run away from a fight, but the bigger battle lay ahead. And there was no time to waste.

The clouds rolled in suddenly, dark and full. The wind began to whip.

"Dead Mage," Jag murmured, his voice tight and hard. It must be killing the male to remain with his Feral brothers when Olivia, his mate, was leading the charge in that battle.

Thunder rumbled across the sky. Mother Nature got pissy when her Mage, who'd once been as close to nature spirits as any being alive, were killed. The rain began to fall, hitting Wulfe's shoulders, sliding through his hair.

Moments later, as he crested the rise, Wulfe saw what he'd been looking for—the curtain of shimmering color, blues and purples and reds, rippling and flaring across the entire landscape. In front of it sat a small, crystalline lake, its surface boiling with raindrops.

He raised his hand and slowed. "The warding."

"I still can't see it," Hawke murmured.

"Good thing we have Daemon Eyes on our side," Jag said.

"Wait here while I test it," Wulfe commanded, surprised at how comfortable the mantle of leadership felt on his shoulders. He'd been good at this once, in the old days. Until the goddess took umbrage and struck it all away. Would she do so again? The thought had his gut clenching.

The warding flowed, swaying back and forth like a sheet on a clothesline on a breezy day. "It looks thicker than before," he told the others, his voice partly drowned out by a hard crack of thunder. "Far more substantial." Energy sparked and spit as if the warding had been supercharged and was still plugged into some giant electrical outlet.

"That can't be good," Vhyper muttered.

As Wulfe neared that shimmering curtain, the hair rose on his arms and his throat began to itch and crawl. The last time, he'd felt nothing. Maybe it was just a factor of his having lost his animal. And, shit, that could be a problem because last time, they'd only gotten through it in their animals. He'd hoped his Daemon blood would allow him to breach it this time, and hand his friends through, even if he couldn't shift. If not, they were in deep shit.

They were probably in trouble either way. Neither Inir nor Satanan were fools. They knew the Ferals would be back to try to stop them. It only stood to reason they'd have beefed up the warding to keep them out this time.

There was only one way to find out.

Small pellets of hail joined the rain, stinging Wulfe's bare arms as he pressed forward cautiously, stopping a foot in front of the warding to reach out his hand. Electricity bolted through his body, knocking him back with a powerful blow, setting every nerve ending on fire. With a roar of pain and fury, he landed on his rear in the wet grass.

"Wulfe!" Lyon yelled.

"Stay back!" Wulfe pushed himself to his feet with effort, the jolt still searing the blood in his veins. He wiped the rain from his eyes and stumbled back to the others. "It's far stronger than before."

But Lyon was used to giving orders not taking

them, and strode forward to try the warding for himself. A moment later, he, too, was picking himself up off the ground.

As Lyon rose, they all stared at one another, an unspoken, *What the fuck do we do now?* hanging in the rain-soaked air.

Dammit, Wulfe thought, staring at that colorful barrier. He knew what had to be done. And he was the only one who could do it. He could almost see Inir's eyes lighting with evil glee at the prospect. Inir would know, of course, that if Wulfe pulled the energies through his channel key, he'd almost certainly be able to crash through the warding. But he'd know, too . . . or Satanan would . . . that no Daemon had ever retained control after pulling that power. The two of them were counting on Wulfe's losing it. Inir had already said it. *The Daemon shifter will come to us, my lord. I promise you. And when he does, he will be yours.*

He heard Natalie's words again. *You are the finest man I've ever known. Just as you'll protect me, I'll protect you. I won't let the darkness take you.*

Wulfe turned to Kougar, his gut cramping. "Have the Ilinas bring Natalie. I'm pulling the primal energies. It's the only way to get through."

His brothers exchanged wary looks, but Lyon nodded. "We're out of options. Satanan cannot rise."

"You can do this, Wulfe," Paenther said. "There's no better man."

He wasn't sure about that, but somehow, he had to pull this off. Every one of them was counting on him. Natalie most of all.

Wulfe began to run back the way they'd come, back to the drop-off site, knowing the Ilinas couldn't risk getting too close to the warding. Minutes later, Natalie was in his arms, rain-soaked, warm, and loving.

"I believe in you, shifter."

He stared into those calm, beloved eyes beneath lashes spiked with rain, and nodded. "I know. You're going to keep me tethered." But his heart was pounding with uncertainty and dread. He pulled Natalie tight against his chest, holding her against the buffeting wind as his gaze watched the storm play out on the now-churning lake.

Goddess, please protect this woman who is my heart, my life, against all dangers, including me. Help me stay strong against the darkness, so that I don't hurt her. And please help us defeat Satanan and Inir. I ask this not out of pride, but because so many will suffer if we fail. I beg you to forgive my errors in the past. I beg you . . .

Without warning, the sun broke through the storm clouds, a single, thick sunbeam illuminating the nearby landscape. And in that sunbeam, a rainbow appeared, running from one end of the sky to the other, a perfect, glorious rainbow beneath still stormy skies. Beauty within the darkness. A miracle. *Forgiveness.* He felt it shower him, felt his heart cleansed and lifted, buoyed with joy over this omen, this blessing.

Thank you, Goddess.

He kissed Natalie's hair, hugging her tight, and blinked back the moisture in his eyes. "Are you ready?"

With a nod, she pulled back and kissed him. "I'm ready. We can do this."

He wasn't convinced, but they were out of options. He could not fail.

As the rain pounded, Natalie ran over the wet ground, Wulfe's hand tight around hers.

"The warding is just up ahead," he told her. "Only I can see it."

All Natalie saw was grass, trees, mountains, and rain. Mostly rain. Wulfe finally came to a stop and pulled her close. Within his hold, she felt his tension and knew how much he dreaded this.

A chill shivered through her, her own muscles tensing. Despite all the times she'd urged him to do what he had to, now that he intended to call that power through her, she was scared. If the little bit of energy Satanan had pulled had hurt so badly, how much more would this? Most of all, she worried about Wulfe.

She would keep him tethered. She had to.

As his hand pressed against her rain-chilled cheek, pain sliced through his gentle eyes.

Natalie covered his hand. "I love you, and I'm not letting you go. Fair warning."

He smiled faintly and said nothing, his jaw tight. "It's not working," he muttered.

"Do you have to chant?"

"Not for this, no. Strome said I had to reverse what I did the first time. I healed you by calling your wound to me."

"Was it easy?"

"No. I can only heal a human's wounds if I want to badly enough."

"How badly did you want mine?"

"Fiercely." He blinked against the rain.

"You have to want to give it back to me just as much." She gripped his hand where it covered her cheek. "Wulfe, I *want* that wound back. I've always known I had some purpose, that I was chosen for this life because I was needed here. I believed, until now, that my purpose was to help people see better and to ensure the children can read. But I was wrong. I'm here because you need me. As your channel key. Perhaps as more. This is what I was born to do."

"Natalie . . ."

"Just as I believe that you were born for this, too. You were born who you are, what you are, because at this critical moment in time, only a Daemon-wolf could possibly stand against a consciousness as powerful as Satanan's. This is your destiny, Wulfe. Claim it. Let us both claim ours."

His gaze bore into hers, searching, finding. His big body sighed, the tension easing out of his shoulders as his spine straightened, as his shoulders fell back. Acceptance entered his eyes though the worry remained.

With a tight nod, he shifted his hand on her cheek, holding the back of her head gently with his other. "You're right."

She smiled softly. "Of course I'm right. Now give me back my wound, shifter, so that we can stop those bad guys."

His smile was fleeting as he closed his eyes. At first nothing happened. Then a throb erupted in her cheek beneath his hand, uncomfortable, but not truly painful, as his scar—the one that should have been hers—began to fade.

Wulfe pulled his hand away suddenly and peered at her with concern. "Are you okay?"

"I'm fine. Now call the power you were destined for."

"We need a pentagram."

"Here," Hawke said. Kneeling, he quickly dug a pentagram in the wet ground with his knife.

Wulfe's big hand closed carefully around hers, and he led her into the center. Turning her to face him, he cupped her face gently in his hands, his mouth compressing.

"It's going to be okay," she whispered.

In his eyes she saw dread, but also the acceptance of the responsibility that he'd been laden with thanks to his Daëmon blood. Taking a deep breath, he closed his eyes and covered her wound with his palm. Then he began whispering in a language that sounded like nothing Natalie had ever heard.

Deep inside her, something began to happen. She felt a tingling in her feet that rushed suddenly upward, through her legs, her body, her chest, her neck, then into her face, finally coalescing in the cheek beneath Wulfe's hand. As the words flowed from his lips in a never-ending stream of visceral sound, he threw his head back as if in pain . . . or ecstasy.

The words flew from his mouth, faster and louder, no longer a whisper.

The tingling in Natalie's body began to sting, then burn, but she clamped down on the groan that clawed at her throat.

Wulfe's grip on her face tightened, the words shooting from his mouth, the power rushing up through her, hot and furious, until she feared she would scream. She couldn't breathe, could barely stand. Too much. *Too much.*

Suddenly, Wulfe released her.

As Natalie fell to her knees, gasping for breath, Wulfe let out a bark of alien joy. A roar of power and strength, of invincibility and cruelty.

With dread, Natalie looked up into the eyes of a stranger, eyes glowing bright red. Eyes filled with evil.

Natalie stared, her vision narrowed from the pain, her heart pounding as the man she'd fallen in love with stared down at her as if he'd never seen her before. She's promised to keep him tethered, but she'd never had a chance to grab hold! And he was already gone.

No, he wasn't gone, he couldn't be.

Closing her eyes, she pushed past the physical discomfort to concentrate on the man she knew, the one who looked at her with such soft adoration, not this red-eyed stranger. She thought of him in his wolf, protecting her with his life. And his gentle, tender touch when he'd made love to her as a man.

Emotion rushed through her, raw and bright, and something moved inside of her, a thick, irregular beat. Not her heart. *His*. She could swear she felt Wulfe's heart, covered in shadows.

Impossible. Then again, what was truly impossible in a world with shape-shifters and Daemons?

Beneath the shadows, Wulfe's heart still beat whole, bright, and golden. She could feel it. It wasn't lost. Not yet. But the darkness attacked that core of his goodness, of his honor, and if she didn't find some way to stop it, and soon, it would steal him away for good.

Fire shot down her limbs as she tried to stand, and she gasped, sinking back to her knees.

"Natalie?" Hawke asked, warily.

"Don't move." Lifting her hand to her eyes to block the worst of the rain, she looked up. "Wulfe, I love you. You love me, too."

He didn't respond, and she sensed the shadows darkening inside him. They were already winning. Desperation rushed up inside of her. The golden light flared suddenly, the edges of the shadows curling away as if her need to save him had driven them back. Maybe it had. Maybe, within the strange connection they'd developed, her thoughts and will really were that powerful. The thought filled her with a fierce determination.

Wulfe swung toward her suddenly, his face a mask of fury. With a growl, he grabbed her by the neck, his rain-slicked fingers nearly encircling it, lifting her to her feet. The pressure against her windpipe choked. *He's going to kill me*. Her heart raced, her mind began to scream, and she struggled, clawing at his hand, his wrist. But he was far, far too strong.

"Natalie!" one of the Ferals called.

"Wulfe, stand down," Lyon shouted.

For one bright moment, she thought rescue was on the way. But all hope was dashed a moment later when Wulfe raised his free hand and the Ferals flew back as if they'd simultaneously hit warding.

The Ferals couldn't help her.

Hope died. The next moments, perhaps her last, were utterly out of her control. But it was that knowledge, that kernel of truth that stole fear's power over her, easing her panic long enough for rational thought to intrude. The man she loved would never be able to live with taking her life, if he ever returned.

The need to protect him burst within her, hot and bright. That golden glow flared, sizzling the shadows, burning the edges away. The fingers that gripped her neck loosened just enough for her to breathe— but not to escape—as if she'd somehow brushed the mind or heart of the honorable male inside. But not enough. Not yet.

With every ounce of concentration she possessed, she stared into the red eyes of the stranger and loved the man within. As she did, she watched the shadows retreat from her assault, then push back, then retreat again.

Around them, the Ferals recovered, rising to their feet. Kougar and Hawke circled behind Wulfe, and she knew they were looking for a way to take him. But her focus remained steady.

For just a moment, she saw a flicker of recognition in his eyes, a glimmer of horror, but it lasted only seconds, then was gone. *Dammit.*

But even as the darkness rushed back into his eyes, he released her, snatching his hand away as if she'd burned him. And maybe she had. Or maybe touching him gave her far more power over the shadows.

Wulfe spun, suddenly, facing the brothers he no longer recognized. "You think you can harm me?" With a flick of his wrists, he sent Hawke and Kougar flying back a second time, then turned back to her as if somewhere inside he recognized her as the true danger. Fangs erupted in his mouth, claws from his fingertips. A feral snarl rose from his throat, terrifying her at her most primitive level. But she was going to pull him back from this if it was the last thing she did.

Sweat ran down the back of her neck, melding with the cold raindrops. The primal energies ran through her, a steady, painful stream, but no longer incapacitating. Only one thing mattered—winning this battle for Wulfe's soul.

Slowly, she took a step toward him.

"Natalie, get back," Lyon warned.

She kept her gaze pinned on Wulfe. "You've never forgiven yourself for failing Liesel, Wulfe, even though what happened to her was never your fault. I know you won't hurt me. You won't fail me. Fight the darkness. Come back to me."

"Natalie, he could kill you with those claws."

"He won't."

She took another painful step toward Wulfe, then another, praying she was right.

Power swirled inside Wulfe, smoke and fire, consuming his gaze, his mind, his soul—the power to take on every one of the insects that surrounded him.

Why didn't the female cower before him?

He swatted at her, his claws coming close to her face, yet not touching her. Something inside of him growled at him not to touch her.

Rain poured down upon him, soaking his clothes. Lightning split the skies.

The female grabbed his wrist, and he pulled away, but she held on tight and nearly fell against his chest. Her scent assailed him, sweet and intolerable. *Gray eyes*. The thought rose from the smoke as her touch burned his wrist, but that snarling thing inside him ordered him to let her do what she wanted. A word burst out of the haze.

Natalie.

His head began to pound, his heart to thud. *Dangerous*. Light shone through the darkness, a golden glow threatening to burn away the shadows. A glow that was hers.

"What are you doing?" he growled.

"Loving you." There was such agony in her eyes.

"Don't." Instinct told him to pull away before it was too late, and he did, jerking his hand from her hold, catching her palm with one of his claws as he jerked free of her. A faint ribbon of blood bloomed on her flesh, and something deep inside him howled.

Fighting it, he pulled back his lips and snarled at her. She was small compared to him, female and human and should be terrified. But instead of retreating as she should have, she lunged at him, grabbing his bare forearm, pressing against his side.

"Come back to me, Wulfe. I know you're in there. *Fight* it. For me. For your friends."

Her hands shook, her warm blood smearing his arm. Lines of pain bracketed her mouth, making him ache. He didn't want her in pain.

Why did he care? The thought roared in his mind. He was power incarnate. With a swipe of his clawed hand, he could rip off her head.

The thought of it nearly brought him to his knees. *Natalie.*

Protect her. *Protect her.*

The thought, the need grew and grew, pulsing in his veins, battering and silencing the shadows that yelled for him to push her away, ripping through the power, through the darkness, through the light.

Wulfe blinked, disoriented and confused, at the woman tight against his side, clinging to his arm. Natalie. He'd drawn fangs and claws. *She's in danger.* The thought exploded in his head even as he took in the sight of his brothers, weapons drawn staring at him as if he'd become the enemy.

Understanding slammed into him like a rock. He'd lost it again. Badly. As he retracted his fangs and claws, his gaze flew to Natalie, to the agonized lines of her face, to the warm stickiness beneath the hand that still grasped his arm.

"I hurt you." The words tore from his throat, cutting like razor blades.

"You're back." Her grip fell away and she sagged against him, clearly injured.

"*I hurt you.*"

"*No.* Just a little. It's the primal energies . . . I'm okay."

The primal energies.

"Wulfe," Lyon called. "Destroy the warding."

And everything snapped back into place—West Virginia, Inir's ritual to free the Daemons, the heavy warding that surrounded the mountain that even he hadn't been able to get through.

Turning until he once more gazed upon that colorful curtain of energy snapping in the wind, he lifted his hand with a snap and willed that curtain destroyed. As he watched with satisfaction, it hissed and popped, exploding into a million bits of light that winked out, one by one, until they were no more.

Goddess, he had power.

Deep inside, he could feel that golden thread, the beginnings of the mating bond, pulsing with light. It was Natalie's love that had pulled him back, her love that had tethered him, just as she'd promised, but at what cost? She was shaking, the energies hurting her. And that golden filament was already beginning to tarnish and fade.

He pulled her around to face him, holding her up. "I have to shut off the primal energies."

"No." Natalie's voice was strong, her gaze unyielding. "Stop Inir from freeing Satanan. Only that. *Then* turn them off."

He shook his head, his heart threatening to shatter. "You'll be dead by then."

"I won't." She smiled at him through the pain with a strength that he envied. "I'm tougher than that."

Lyon strode up, joining them, pushing his rain-drenched hair from his face. "How much of the warding did you disable? Is it safe for the Ilinas to mist us closer to Inir's stronghold?" They were still miles away from the fortress. And, he remembered now, quickly running out of time.

Wulfe sent his senses flying outward, taking in the energy of the mountain, feeling the warding as if it were a part of him. And in a Daemon sort of way, it probably was. The sudden, unnatural storm had turned day to night.

"The outer warding has shattered," he told his chief. "The inner is still strong, but I can get us through. It extends two hundred yards around the stronghold in every direction. It's Ilina-proof, but the Ilinas are in no danger as long as they remain outside that."

Lyon swung to Kougar. "It's your call."

Kougar closed his eyes for several seconds. "Ariana's already on her way to test it."

"Have they freed the Daemons?" Paenther asked, striding up.

In the part of him that was connected to Satanan, Wulfe could feel the ritual proceeding. "Not yet."

Ariana appeared from mist beside her mate. "We can deliver you to the base of the hill, a short distance from the stronghold."

Lyon nodded. "Take us."

Ilinas appeared out of thin air all around them, snatching up Ferals and Therians alike.

"Hold on to her, Wulfe," Ariana said. "I can take you both."

Moments later, Wulfe was spilling his guts on the ground at the base of the stronghold, Natalie sitting a short distance away. Wulfe pushed to his feet, then helped Natalie to hers. She gasped with pain, a soft sound that stabbed him in the heart.

"I'm shutting the energies off."

"No you're not. I can handle this." She met his gaze with granite in her eyes.

A shout went up. Moments later, Mage sentinels began to rush out of the stronghold by the dozens.

"Get the Ferals through those gates," Olivia yelled to her troops.

Wulfe kissed Natalie gently. How could he leave her like this?

"I've got her, Feral," Melisande said. "I won't let anything happen to her."

Wulfe nodded, sliding his palm along Natalie's jaw, his own jaw hardening. "I'll kill him quickly."

"And I'll keep you tethered. Stay away from the darkness."

He smiled. "Deal." He kissed her soundly, then ran to join the others just as Zeeland . . . Zaber . . . shifted into a saber-toothed tiger with a furious roar.

Deep in his mind, Wulfe heard his wolf howl in answer.

Thank the goddess. His animal was back. But he felt his wolf spirit's pain, felt him at a distance. The Daemon energy might have cracked the wall the dark charm had erected between them, but it hadn't destroyed it.

He pulled on his animal, trying to shift, but nothing happened. Dammit. The wolf whined and snarled. Then pain shot through his body in a searing rush, and slowly, slowly, in a spit of dark lights, he managed to shift.

"How'd you do that, Wolf-man?" Jag shouted.

Daemon blood.

"I'm starting to envy you, Dog."

As the Therian Guard surged forward to take on the Mage sentinels, the Ferals charged. Wulfe and Zaber took point, a huge wolf and sabertooth tiger, attacking sentinels only when they had to, preferring to just run them down. This was not the battle that mattered.

The wind began to howl again, rain slashing, hail pounding, lightning bursting across the sky as Inir's evil Mage died by the dozens. As Wulfe and Zaber approached the gate through which the sentinels had rushed from the castle, the heavy metal bars of the portcullis began to descend.

Acting on instinct, Wulfe shifted back to a man in the same flare of pain and dark, spitting lights, then lifted his hand and, with the force of his mind, stopped the gate's descent, halfway down. He grunted. Daemon power was damn useful. Shifting back into his wolf, he dove under the gate after the sabertooth. Behind him, the other Ferals ducked beneath the half-lowered gate and followed them into the courtyard. Massive, steel-reinforced, wooden doors barred their access to the castle itself, but Wulfe sensed no magical warding blocking their way.

Wulfe looked at that door. *Zaber, let's take it together on the count of three. One, two, three!*

The two huge beasts made a running charge, lowered their heads, and plowed through the massive doors, splintering them.

With a triumphant growl, Zaber leaped through the opening, and Wulfe dove through after him, the other Ferals following close behind.

As more Mage ran at them, the Ferals drew their swords. "We've got these, Wulfe," Lyon shouted. "Keep going."

Come on, Zee, it's up to us. Wulfe raced forward, leading the way through the massive castle, running down one shadowed corridor after another. As he ran, the smoke began to curl in from the edges of his mind as if the darkness sought control again. His wolf snarled.

In his head, he heard Satanan's voice. *It's taking too long!*

My lord, the blood is not truly that of an unascended Radiant, so it will take time. But the ritual is working. The blade is opening.

The Daemon shifter nears, and he is not mine. His channel key interferes.

Can you tear him loose without breaking the connection?

Of course.

Wulfe's heart dropped to his stomach. *Natalie?*

No answer.

Natalie!

When she still didn't answer, he tried another route. *Melisande?*

Something's happening, Wulfe. Natalie ran, and I caught her, but she's not herself. She's fighting me.

Dammit, dammit, dammit.

Wait. I think she's snapping out of it.

Wulfe? Natalie's voice. *I don't know what happened. Satanan feels you tethering me. He's trying to stop you.*

He won't. A bright pulse of her energy flowed through the slowly tarnishing thread that connected them, a pulse layered with determination. *You battle him on your end, shifter, I'll battle him on mine.* Just the sound of her voice sent the smoke and shadows scurrying away.

He felt a fierce surge of pride and gratitude that the goddess had gifted him with the love of such a strong and glorious woman.

He wouldn't fail either of them.

Finally, he and Zaber burst through yet another thick door and into the pouring rain. They were on the back side of the castle, overlooking the cliffs behind the stronghold. On the rocks, not twenty yards below, six bare-chested men stood in a circle ringed by fires that flickered and spit in the rain. On the rock at their feet lay a dagger.

The Daemon Blade.

Wulfe recognized four of the males—Polaris, Lynks, Croc, and Witt. The other two must be the pair Inir had forced Kara to bring into their animals when she was a captive here. They knew Lynks was an asshole—a coward and a pedophile. Polaris, whom they'd known as Ewan, was a good man who they believed to be the one the animal had meant to mark, but he'd been subsumed by the dark infection carried to him by his animal spirit, and an unwitting pawn of Inir ever since. Whether the other four had honor or evil in their souls was anyone's guess.

Outside the circle, watching with eager eyes, stood a man dressed in a blood red ceremonial robe, his short hair, even wet, gleaming with a copper sheen. Deep within his Daemon blood, Wulfe sensed Satanan's consciousness in the male. With a surge of hard satisfaction, he knew he was staring at Inir.

Inir is in a bright red robe, he told Zaber and the other Ferals. *His hair's as copper as his eyes.* As Inir turned toward him, Wulfe realized his last observation was all too true. Inir's Mage eyes weren't just ringed in copper, they were copper through and through. And in them, Wulfe read dismay and a sudden, raw desperation.

His wolf howled in delight.

"Kill them!" Inir shouted, and the dozen Mage sentinels who stood between the Ferals and their targets drew their swords and started rushing up the stone walkway.

Wulfe's muscles bunched. *I'll crash the ritual while you stop Inir, Zee. Don't kill him. We're going to need his blood to reclaim our immortality, and I don't know how much. Bite off a leg or two, and he won't be able to get away. You'll enjoy the taste when you're in your cat.*

Zaber grunted. *He won't get away. Let me take lead. I'll heal.* As Wulfe, still mortal, would not.

Go.

Zaber leaped forward, the stocky, muscular cat bulldozing the Mage, taking their slashing swords without slowing. But as Wulfe followed, one of those swords caught him, slicing through his shoulder in a searing flash of pain. And with the pain, the tendrils of darkness began to crowd in on him all over again.

Natalie.

I see them. I'm here. But her voice was losing strength, and it was long moments before the shadows reacted, and they backed off too slowly, as if at any moment, they'd spring again. Natalie was weakening. And the distance between them was growing too much.

Melisande, can you bring her any closer without endangering her? Maybe the woods on the other side of the fortress?

No problem, Wulfe. I'll mist her there, now.

Thank, Mel. Hold on, Natalie. This will all be over soon. He prayed. *And keep talking, if you can. Recite the alphabet or just keep talking. Your voice grounds me.* And reassured him that she was okay.

Low, husky laughter sounded in his head, but there was a pained quality to it that made him ache. *The alphabet it is.*

Wulfe took two more wounds before he and Zaber fought past the sentinels and their blades. Finally, nothing stood between them and their targets.

Inir raised his hands, his eyes closing as if in prayer, though Wulfe suspected his intent was to draw magic.

But Inir wasn't Wulfe's problem, not yet. He turned fully to the six Ferals gathered around the Daemon Blade. With a growl, he leaped, intending to fly into the middle of the circle. Instead, he hit a solid wall of energy that threw him back, hard, onto the stones. Pain shot through his spine.

He shifted to human and the moment he did, the warding became visible—a glimmering blue dome around the evil Ferals and the Daemon Blade. Wulfe lifted his hand, willing this warding to shatter as had the last, but nothing happened. Dammit.

With his fist, he tried to breach it in human form and nearly shattered the bones in his hand. He might as well have hit a brick wall.

Shifting back into his wolf, he called to his brothers. *I can't get through.*

At the cry of a man's agony, Wulfe swung his head to find Zaber tearing off one of Inir's legs.

My lord! Inir cried. *Why are you withholding your power from me?*

Because I need it to rise!

But I am your servant, your right hand.

You are nothing, Inir. My vessel. My tool. And I need you no longer.

Wulfe grunted. After all these years, after all the death and misery Inir had caused, Satanan had forsaken him. Karma was a bitch.

Wulfe ran toward them, limping, one of his hind legs almost certainly fractured. *Try to get through the warding, Zaber. I'll handle Inir.* And, goddess, would it be a pleasure.

As the sabertooth took off, Wulfe faced the male, the *creature*, responsible for so much pain. At Wulfe's snarl, Inir threw up his hands, real terror in his eyes.

Wulfe almost felt sorry for him. If Inir had been a good man controlled by Satanan's will, he might have. But he knew better. And Inir would die. Soon.

Wulfe leaped, grimacing at the fire in his hip, and grabbed Inir's other leg. With his massive jaws, he bit it clean off, the warm blood tasting right and fine in his mouth. The blood of his enemy. The son of a bitch would not escape his fate.

I can't get through, either, Zaber said.

Wulfe limped toward him, meeting him halfway. *Let's try it together.* They leaped as one, and Wulfe felt the warding give ever so slightly. But not enough. *We need the others.* Together, they'd be able to break through, he was certain of it.

While Zaber stood guard over Inir, Wulfe turned and loped back up the path to where the rest of the Ferals dispatched the last of the Mage. The doors to the fortress swung open, and Olivia stepped out, followed by a flood of Therian Guards. In their midst, he glimpsed Kara, and he wished Natalie were with her.

Belatedly, he realized she'd stopped talking to him. *Natalie? Melisande, is she okay?*

She's fine, Wulfe. But Melisande lied. If Natalie were fine, she'd have answered him herself.

The truth, Mel.

The truth is, she's fighting Satanan with everything she has. You have to do the same.

What he had to do was help her. Concentrating, he found Natalie in his mind, in his heart, through that gossamer, fraying thread, and loved her violently, passionately, tenderly, pouring everything he had down that pathway between them, willing her to hold on.

A thin, weak pulse returned to him through that cord. Fear curled around his heart, the need to go to her clawing at his insides, but Melisande was right. They each had their battles to fight.

As the Therian Guard delivered Kara to her mate, Lyon took her hand and strode toward Wulfe. "Did you get through?"

"The warding's too strong. It's going to take more than two of us in our animals to breach it. But Inir's down and ready for the ritual."

Lyon nodded. "Quickly."

As one, the Ferals raced back to where the great sabertooth stood guard over the moaning, legless Mage. But as Zaber and Wulfe shifted back to men, and the Ferals gathered around, Inir suddenly began to laugh.

"You are fools to think you can stop me. I will rise!"

"Satanan," Tighe muttered. "He didn't protect his boy."

"He doesn't give a rat's ass about his boy," Wulfe replied. "He doesn't need him anymore." But while his gaze was riveted on the sight of this terrible enemy finally prone at their feet, Wulfe's mind was consumed by worry for Natalie. The primal energies were too much for her. They were weakening her. *Killing* her. *Please goddess, don't let her die.*

Kougar strode to Inir and, without hesitation, cut off one of his hands. As Inir screamed, Kougar cut off the other, holding both of them wrist-side up, cradling the blood. Turning toward the others, he began to chant as he had in the ritual room, repeating the words they'd used before, words that Ariana and the Shaman believed would reverse the dark charm's damaging magic.

"The ritual fires?" Tighe asked. The fires ringing the other Ferals were long out.

Kougar shook his head, a quick, silent, "not going to bother."

As the Ferals ripped off their shirts, they all took up the chant. Kougar began to swipe Inir's blood across each of their hearts, one by one. Their voices grew louder, the magic beating at the air, pounding in Wulfe's blood. A soaked-to-the-skin, yet proud and once-more-healthy Kara strode into the middle of the circle, waiting for the signal.

On the alternate goddess stone, where the evil Ferals' ritual continued, an eerie red-orange light suddenly blasted from the Daemon Blade, an unearthly scream tearing through the night like the voices of a thousand damned souls suddenly freed.

Inir began to laugh like a madman. "You're too late. It's done! The blade has been opened. Satanan rises!"

Chapter Twenty-three

The Ferals' worst nightmare had come true.

In the midst of a hurricane-like storm, the Earth screaming in outrage, shapes began to fly out of the Daemon Blade through that swirling red-and-orange energy—dozens of them, hundreds.

"*Holy goat fuck, Batman,*" Jag muttered.

The Daemons were free.

Their chant had died abruptly, Kougar and Lyon, as one, murmuring the words to throw up a powerful feral circle that should, goddess willing, keep the Daemons out. At least until they could retrieve their immortality.

Wulfe's gaze flew to Fox. "Warn Melisande. Tell her to get Natalie out of here." Only the Ferals mated to Ilinas had the ability to speak to their mates telepathically when they weren't in their animals.

"She knows," Fox assured him.

But Wulfe knew, deep inside, the women hadn't left. Natalie wouldn't leave him as long as he needed her. The knowledge both warmed and terrified him.

"Finish the ritual," Lyon ordered.

Kougar took up the chant again as he swiped Wulfe's chest with Inir's blood, then Fox's, then Zaber's.

Wulfe's pulse pounded in disbelief as wraith Daemons flew past by the dozens, their black, ropelike hair rippling back from horrific faces contorted like wax figures' left too long in the sun. Sharp fangs dripped from their mouths, claws from their fingertips, their black, cloaklike bodies rippling in the wind.

Five thousand years the Ferals had fought to keep this from happening. *Five thousand years.*

The need to reach Natalie, to protect her, thudded in his mind, in his chest. Wulfe took up the chant with the others because the sooner this was over, the sooner he could save her.

In front of him, Kara went radiant, brilliantly so. Magic tore through him, cleansing, renewing, regenerating. He could feel his wounds healing, his breath filling his lungs with life and light. Radiance and Feral energy rushed through his body, strengthening him in the way he was meant to be strong. Feral. *Immortal.*

Deep inside, he felt the last of the wall erected by Inir's poison—a wall intended to destroy his connection with his animal—some crashing down, then obliterated into nothing. His wolf howled with triumph as they were fully joined once more.

All around him, the Ferals shifted into their ani-

mals with relieved growls and whines and sighs. But
no sound of victory. Except one.

Lyon swung his heavily maned lion's head toward
Inir with a deep, rumbling growl. *This is for harming
my mate.* With a feral roar loud enough to wake the
heavens, he bit off Inir's head.

Wulfe shifted into his wolf and immediately called
to Natalie, for once hoping she wouldn't answer, that
she was too far away.

But she answered immediately. *"I'm here."*

Dammit. *The Daemons are free! Melisande, take
her to the Crystal Realm. Quickly.*

But it was Natalie who answered him. *We see
them, Wulfe.* Awe and fear wove through her too-
soft voice. *But I'm not going anywhere.*

Natalie . . .

No, Wulfe.

Goddess. *Now that the Daemons are free, Satanan
has no more need to pull the primal energies. There's
no danger.*

We don't know that. I'm not leaving.

Deep inside, he knew her caution wasn't misplaced.
The darkness could try to claim him even without
Satanan's interference. But he needed her safe!

"Look at the blade!" Hawke shouted.

They all turned. Directly above the Daemon Blade,
the colors swirled, dense and fast. At the top of that
twisting mass, the head of a male had begun to form.

All around them, flying shapes began to material-
ize. Wraith Daemons by the score, but also human-
looking men and women dressed in fur or leather
or naked, and armed to the teeth with knives and
blades of every length and size. Suddenly, the human-
looking ones—were they Daemons, too?—began at-

tacking the wraith Daemons as if their lives depended on it.

Shite, Fox murmured.

One of the leather-clad men, a tall male with thick dark hair tumbling to his shoulders and black tattoos covering nearly every inch of his body and half his face, turned to the animals, the Ferals.

"Stop Satanan before he's free! We can't touch him, but we can hold off the Abominations."

Abominations. The same term Strome had used for the wraith Daemons. The real Daemons looked human, just like the Therians and Mage.

Wulfe leaped toward the evil Ferals, who continued to chant as Satanan slowly formed in that swirling color, his neck and shoulders now visible.

It's going to take all of us to breach the warding of that circle, he told his brothers, then realized Lyon would never leave Kara to fend for herself among the Daemons. *If only the Ilinas could mist in.*

Sending his senses outward, he realized they could.

The anti-Ilina warding must have been destroyed with Inir, he told his brothers. *It's gone. The only warding now is the one encircling the evil Ferals. Have the Ilinas mist Kara out of here.*

The moment Kara was out of danger, the eleven good Ferals raced to the ritual stone. Around the edges of Wulfe's mind, the smoke began to gather again, nipping at his control, at his conscience. Concern gripped his mind.

Natalie?

I'm fine, Wulfe.

But, dammit, she didn't sound fine. She sounded as weak as a newborn kitten. His wolf whined in distress. Wulfe knew he didn't dare disengage from the primal energies yet, but *goddess,* he'd better do it soon.

The good Ferals circled the evil. Within that swirling color, Wulfe could feel the darkness growing stronger. A pressure began throbbing in his chest and head, and he imagined that swirl of color calling him, trying to drag him toward it. Or trying to yank the soul out of his body. Was this what had happened to the rest of the Daemon race? Was it happening to the newly freed Daemons even now?

If the tattooed Daemon was right, the moment Satanan was loose, he'd snatch control of them all once more. This time, Wulfe included.

Roar, Satanan's calling my soul. If he gets free, I may turn on you.

He's not getting free.

As he watched, the evil Ferals suddenly shifted into their animals, turning to face the impending attack—a polar bear, white tiger, crocodile, lynx, black bear, and giant-ass wolverine. Powerful, yes, but too few against their far more experienced and more numerous opponents. Six evil against eleven good. It wouldn't be much of a fight if the good guys could just get through the damn warding.

Spread out, Lyon ordered. *Falkyn, get the Daemon Blade.*

The little falcon shifter, their sole female Feral, was by far the fastest of the lot. *On the count of three. One, two . . .*

Suddenly, the polar bear shifted back into a man, grabbed the sword he'd dropped to the rock at his feet, and lopped off the head of the wolverine standing beside him, then whirled and took off the head of the white tiger.

Polaris . . . Ewan . . . was clearly free of the dark magic that Inir had used to control him.

Three! Lyon yelled.

Wulfe leaped, feeling the warding resist, then give with a soft, sucking pop. They were in! Falkyn zipped past him, barely visible from the corner of his eye. And then suddenly she was all too visible as she flew back onto the stone as if in slow motion.

As Hawke darted after his mate, Satanan laughed within that swirling storm of energy and color.

Inner warding. Falkyn's voice was breathless in his head. *Satanan's warded himself in the middle.*

As his brothers and Polaris took on the remaining evil Ferals, Wulfe leaped at the Daemon Blade and, just like Falkyn, flew back, slamming into the rock in a blaze of pain.

Wulfe! Natalie cried.

I'm okay. We've almost got him. But, goddess, he didn't know if that was true.

As the animals battled around him, Wulfe scrambled to four feet and shifted back to a man. Breaching Daemon energy might require taking Daemon form. And, much to his surprise, Daemon form was not all monstrous.

"The Destroyer attempts to reclaim my soul!" yelled one of those fighting the wraiths.

"Shifter, hurry!" the tattooed Daemon called. "If Satanan regains control of us, you're dead."

And Wulfe had no doubt that was true, not when he could already feel Satanan pulling at his own soul. The smoke and shadows once more began to curl around the edges of his mind.

Wulfe thrust himself into that swirling mass of orange and red, fighting the darkness that sought to ensnare him. Suddenly, the warding parted, and he was in. Standing before him with eyes that glowed bright red in a hard, if distinctly human-looking face, was the High Daemon, Satanan, the most powerful, most evil being ever to walk the Earth.

Wulfe's pulse pounded as he stared at his nemesis, at the dark hair blowing in every direction, caught in that wind of power, and at the broad shoulders covered in a silver robe. From the waist up, Satanan now appeared fully corporeal.

A smile broke across that hard mouth, a smile of such evil, such malevolence that Wulfe's skin crawled.

"You are mine, shifter."

Wulfe didn't bother to answer. Instead he lunged for the blade that lay on the rock between them, the swirling red-and-orange energy flying from its etched and enchanted steel. But before his fingers could close around it, Satanan's hand shot up, palm out, and Wulfe was slammed back against the warding. Pain tore through his back, then raced through his flesh as if he'd been electrocuted. He struggled to right himself, to pull free of that blazing current, but he couldn't move.

Inside his head, the shadows multiplied, as if fed by his pain, ready to steal his mind even as Satanan prepared to steal his soul.

Wulfe roared with frustration. He would not let this son of a bitch win! Struggling to concentrate when his mind was consumed with pain, he gathered the primal energies that continued to rush through his body, then threw the power as Satanan had. But the High Daemon only laughed, threw back his head, and inhaled it. With horror, Wulfe felt his soul, his very life force trying to follow.

Goddess, goddess, goddess. He couldn't fail. Natalie was counting on him, as were his brothers and, hell, the whole damned world.

"Wulfe?" Lyon called.

He was going to have to pull the energies harder. Which would hurt Natalie. It might even kill her.

His mind screamed in denial. His wolf howled in misery, then growled low, reminding him without words that above all . . . *above all* . . . Satanan could not be allowed to win. As he faced the greatest evil the world had ever known, Natalie's words came back to him. *You were born for this. You were born who you are, what you are, because at this critical moment in time, only a Daemon-wolf could possibly stand against a consciousness as powerful as Satanan's. This is your destiny, Wulfe. Claim it!*

As if Natalie felt his hesitation, at that very moment, a pulse of energy flowed into his heart through that wisp of a mating bond. A soft, loving energy filled with the infinite strength of Natalie's will. Her body might be weakening, but her determination to help him succeed remained as strong as ever.

Together, they would win the day. Or die trying.

The fear that he would lose her flared in his mind, but he shoved it back. Letting the world fall to Daemons would not save her. Their only way through this maelstrom was together.

Taking a deep breath, Wulfe pulled on the power, on the primal energies. They came, as they had before. And then suddenly they were rushing into him a dozen times faster and harder than before. What the fuck? *Natalie.* She was helping him, pulling them with him.

No! Instantly, he shut down the flow. It was too much. They were going to kill her.

Again, he felt that pulse of pure love, one with a decided edge of demand. Hell.

Satanan's hips had formed, now, and his thighs. Only his lower legs and feet remained trapped by the swirling mass of color. They were out of time.

With a prayer to the goddess, he took a deep breath and called once more on the primal energies, embracing the rush this time because he had to and because, woven within that swirling, terrible power, he felt Natalie's calm certainty, her courage, her love.

Calling on the power inside of him, Wulfe finally broke free of Satanan's invisible hold. But when he pushed forward to try again to retrieve the blade, Satanan's power slammed into him like a two-hundred-mile-per-hour headwind, and he couldn't move. Lifting his hand, he tried calling the blade to him, but that didn't work any better. Dammit. He couldn't push forward, let alone attack.

All the while those primal energies swirled inside him, smoke and shadows, gleeful of the darkness, of Satanan's evil. One wrong step, and he was going to become lost in that dark power, whether his own or Satanan's.

A faint pulse of soft, loving energy brushed his heart, making his gut clench with anguish. Natalie's brightness, her strength and light were almost out. Pulling the energies was killing her, yet he couldn't stop. He had to win.

Satanan began to laugh. His legs had formed, his feet were becoming visible as the red-and-orange swirl slowly died. The pull on Wulfe's soul grew stronger by ten. He could feel it being sucked out of his body!

Desperation tore through him, his muscles straining against the unnatural power. He was a Feral, dammit!

A Feral. Only part Daemon.

In a flash of insight, he finally understood. It had taken his Daemon form to breach the warding, but only in his non-Daemon animal form was he protected from Satanan's growing control. Only in his wolf would he prevail.

As the animal inside him gave a howl of approval, Wulfe shifted with ease and joy into his furred form and lunged for the Daemon Blade. As he'd hoped, his wolf's body slid through the power blast as his man's . . .. his Daemon's . . . could not.

Snatching up the blade in his teeth, Wulfe tossed the magical steel into the air, then shifted back, and caught it with one hand. Without pause, he whirled and stabbed the Daemon Blade deep within Satanan's chest.

The High Daemon roared with fury, the scream echoing across the mountain and far into the sky. And a second later, Satanan disappeared, sucked back into the blade.

Shadows began to fly at Wulfe from all directions, following Satanan, vanishing, one after another, by the score.

With a roar of triumph, Wulfe lifted the blade aloft, the wind whipping at his face and hair, energy crackling over his skin. Victory sang in his blood. And more.

Power.

The primal energies rushed through him in a torrent, no longer siphoned by Satanan. Dark, rich, and seductive, they filled him, strengthened him.

The shadows rushed in, clouding his vision and his mind as the power consumed him.

Natalie lay on the rain-soaked ground, beneath the trees, her knees pulled against her chest, her teeth grinding against the horrific pain. Wave after wave of fire rushed up through her feet, through her body, a constant, steady stream of molten energy.

On one side of her, Kara stroked her face. On the other, Melisande pressed her hand to her arm, stealing as much of the pain as she could. Not enough. Not nearly enough.

Wulfe's love caressed her mind, lending her strength, helping her heart continue to beat.

"He's won!" Ariana cried, taking form a few feet away. She'd been moving between them and the Ferals, giving the women a play-by-play as she stood ready to call in her mist warriors if the Daemons turned against the Ferals. "Wulfe stabbed Satanan, and the wraith Daemons are following him into the blade!"

"But not the other Daemons?" Melisande asked.

"No. I guess we'll find out what that means soon enough." She knelt beside them. "How's Natalie?"

"I can't keep hold of her much longer. Wulfe has to shut down the channel, or he's going to kill her."

But it was too late. As she lay there in misery, the soft flow of Wulfe's love suddenly shut off. And a moment later, a piercing cold rushed into her in its place.

"He's . . . lost," Natalie gasped. "To the darkness."

Kara made a sound of despair, but Melisande only growled. "He's not lost, yet. Get back, Kara. Natalie and I are going for a little ride."

A moment later, Natalie's world flipped end over end, then righted itself suddenly as she came to lie on her back upon cool, wet stone, her stomach turning. The rain beat softly against her face and hair, telling her she was still alive. For now.

"Natalie's dying, Wulfe," Melisande announced. "The woman you love, is dying."

With a start, Natalie forced her eyes open, turning instinctively toward the male who held her heart and her life in his hands. Electricity arced all around him as if he stood in the middle of his own private lightning storm. His eyes stared at her without recognition, once more glowing red. Around him, the Ferals circled, ready to attack him, to kill him if they had to.

Strome had warned that the darkness always won. She'd pulled him back once. But heaven help her, it was all she could do to keep breathing through the pain. Where was she going to find the strength to save him one more time?

Extraordinary, magnificent, glorious power raced through Wulfe's veins. They would bow before him, the insects. They would worship at his feet!

If only he could silence the one inside, the wolf, and his snarling, his fury, his howling.

The shifters—he'd known them once—surrounded him, their weapons drawn.

"Wulfe, buddy, don't let the darkness win," one of them said.

"Come on, Wolfman. We need you, dude."

"Wulfe, release the darkness. That's an order!"

"Natalie is going to die, Wulfe," yet another said quietly, his voice throbbing with emotion. "Don't let her die, Wulfe. If she does, you're both gone."

But the male they spoke to was already gone. Couldn't they see that?

"Wulfe." The female on the rock at his feet spoke, her voice a mere whisper. He recognized her, his channel key. Once she died, he'd gain no additional power, which was a pity. But he could barely hold all he'd claimed already, so it was no matter. *All* would kneel before him!

Something pulsed in his head, a small golden glow that flared, then disappeared, again and again, each pulse igniting the darkness of his mind, dissolving a few of the shadows, but it was no matter. The pulses grew weaker, fainter. Dying.

Natalie's dying.

The words broke through the shadows, stabbing him through the gut. The wolf trapped inside him howled with fury and desperation.

He gathered the shadows close, pushing back the words and their inexplicable pain, concentrating only on the power. But the words pushed again, attacked again, over and over and over.

Natalie's dying. Natalie's dying. Natalie's dying.

The pain grew. Emotion began to break through the wall of shadows, at first a mere trickle, slowly becoming a small stream, then a flood.

No. He didn't care. He *wouldn't* care.

He was panting as he fought it back, fought against the love that battered at the walls he'd thought impenetrable. Though he struggled to destroy all emotion and shore up the walls, the light slipped through his defenses, burrowing deep, filling him with warmth and love and fear. Scattering the darkness to the winds.

Wulfe came back to himself in a dizzying rush, his gaze dropping to the woman lying dead at his feet.

"*Natalie!*" He fell to his knees beside her, his heart

splintering as he gathered her cold hand in his warm one. And felt life. *Not dead. Thank you, goddess.* His own heart began to beat again even as he knew she must be at death's door. Scooping her unconscious body against his chest, he turned to the throngs who stood all around him, watching.

"How do I save her?" he yelled.

A deep male voice he didn't recognize answered him. "Release the primal energies, shifter. Send them back through her, back where they came from, and close the door."

"How?" But even as he asked the question, he knew the answer. He found it written on the Daemon sliver of his soul.

Closing his eyes, he began to say the words—words he'd never known yet had always known. Words that repudiated the darkness, banishing it back into the bowels of Hell.

The darkness inside him resisted, trying to seduce, to beguile, but Wulfe had no need for power beyond what he'd always had. He needed Natalie. Only that. Only her. Though the darkness fought valiantly, it was no match for the determination of a man in love and, slowly, it lost its hold on him and slipped away. He felt it flee back through Natalie, back to where it had come from. Out of his head, his blood, his bones, draining, evaporating, until it was no more.

Taking a deep, cleansing breath, Wulfe blinked, feeling odd and yet wonderfully himself again. From his mouth, slipped another string of unknown words, words he knew would close the channel once and for all. Lifting Natalie closer, tucking her head against his chest, he bent and kissed her lips.

"Come back to me. Please come back to me."

Her aura was gone, now. Amazingly, so too was the wound on her cheek.

She stirred in his arms and his heart began to beat again. Slowly, her lashes lifted. As she saw him, a small, calm, gray-eyes smile lifted her lovely mouth.

"You did it."

A shudder went through him, and he pulled her tight against him. "We did it together," he whispered against her hair. Inside, his wolf let out a howl of pure happiness.

Lifting his head, Wulfe faced his brothers. Behind them stood several dozen Daemons of the human-looking variety, each armed with a sword or knife, though none appeared to be actively threatening. In fact, unless he was mistaken, the expressions on most of their faces were a mix of gratitude and disbelief, of relief and wonder.

"I can stand," Natalie said quietly, and he set her on her feet, if reluctantly, keeping an arm tight around her.

His brothers surged forward, gathering around him, slapping him on the back. Lyon grasped his forearm. "A hell of a job, Wulfe. One hell of a job."

Wulfe handed his chief the Daemon Blade.

"Wolfman," Jag crowed. "You just saved the whole fucking world."

"Perhaps," Paenther said quietly, drawing their attention back to the dozens of Daemons watching them, reminding them that although Satanan might be defeated, much of his horde was still loose.

The tattooed Daemon stepped forward. "We are in your debt, shifter."

Lyon faced him. "You're Daemons."

"Most of us, yes. But there were many races subjugated and ensnared by Satanan, and all those who survived were freed this day."

"The world you left is no more." Lyon's voice resonated clearly across the gathering. "The humans now number in the billions, and they've acquired great power. They don't know the immortal races exist and they must never know if we wish to survive. Find a way to live in this world without discovery and without harming the other races, including the humans. Or we'll be hunting you down."

The tattooed male nodded. "Satanan's way was never ours. We wish only to return to the mountains and live in peace."

Jag snorted. "Good luck with that."

The Daemon's jaw hardened. "Many of those who were freed today have already escaped, many whose souls were long ago destroyed by Satanan. They have neither heard your warning nor would likely pay it any heed if they had. We will hunt them and destroy those who cannot be saved."

Lyon nodded. "If you need assistance—and you may until you learn the ways of this world—we'll help you. I am Lyon, Chief of the Feral Warriors, the shifters."

The Daemon male nodded. "I am Strome, the last true king of the Daemons."

Wulfe jerked. Around him, several of the others made noises of surprise.

The male eyed them curiously. "You have heard of me."

Fox gave a small smile. "You're something of a legend where we're from, boyo." None of them, it seemed, were willing to endanger Vivian's life, not when she'd risked so much to help them.

Lyon looked around. "You may remain here, in this fortress, for as long as you wish. The owner no longer needs it. But the humans inside will be set free. Leave the humans alone. *All* humans."

Strome turned to Wulfe. "You, shifter, are part Daemon."

Wulfe nodded, wondering if they'd always know he was one of them. "Apparently I have a Daemon ancestor."

Strome nodded. "Ciroc."

That was the name Vivian's Strome had given him.

A fur-clad Daemon stepped forward, his beard full, his shoulders nearly as wide as Wulfe's. "I am Ciroc."

Wulfe stared, a chill dancing over his skin. This male was his . . . how many greats? . . . *grandfather.*

Ciroc smiled with a startling pride. "You honor me and all who have come before and after me, son of my son of my son. Relinquishing, nay *shoving away* that kind of power was a sight to behold, a display of strength and nobility few men possess. Of any race."

Strome nodded. "You honor all who challenge evil. You would be most welcome should you wish to join my tribe, shifter of Ciroc's blood."

The distinctive sound track of the original *Star Wars* movie cut the stillness suddenly. All heads turned toward the door, where one of the Daemon males held a laptop like he feared it would explode in his hands. As he approached, all the Daemons stared, wide-eyed, many of them backing away.

"What is this?" Strome demanded.

"It's harmless," Lyon assured him. "Human technology. Playacting."

The Daemon moved to where he could watch the

battle on the screen, then shook his head, his eyes wide. "The world has indeed changed."

Lyon grunted. "We don't live in the Star Wars universe, but yes, it's changed. More than you can imagine."

Strome moved away from the laptop and extended his hand to Lyon. "I thank you, shifter. You and your people have freed me and mine. We are in your debt."

After only a moment's hesitation, Lyon met him halfway. "You have a lot of catching up to do. I suggest you coerce the remaining Mage into showing you how to use the televisions and computers, and learn how to live in the twenty-first century. I'll send Wulfe back to see how you're doing in a couple of days. Right now, we have other things to attend to."

Lyon turned to Ariana.

"Home?" Ariana asked.

Lyon smiled, reaching for Kara as he turned to Wulfe with a lift of a tawny eyebrow.

Wulfe's still-stunned gaze returned to Ciroc. He nodded, getting a nod and a smile in return, then glanced down to find Natalie watching him with color in her cheeks and an incandescent joy in her eyes.

The smile tugging at his mouth bloomed fully. "Home."

Two hours later, the Ferals sat or stood around the massive dining table in Feral House with their mates. Their numbers had swelled, and would continue to, it seemed, until they were twenty-six once more. The moment they'd returned to Feral House, a carafe of Inir's blood in hand, they'd performed a series of rituals to bring the new Ferals residing in their prisons into their animals. Castin, as they'd expected, had shifted into a cheetah. Rikkert, into a rhino. Kougar had declared their Feral names to be Cheet and Rhyne, respectively. The third male, now known as Dact, had shifted into a startling creature—a long-extinct pterodactyl with a twenty-foot wingspan. A one-man demolition team if he ever shifted in the house.

With each Renascence, Kara had felt stronger and better, making it clear that the souls inside these Ferals were honorable and good. Sabine had been right, and they had no more qualms about Lepard, whom she'd declared also good. Only Grizz's soul remained in question, though only, it seemed, to the grizzly shifter himself. No one else doubted the honor of a male who'd risked his life to save his brothers.

The second ritual had cleared the new Ferals and Polaris of the dark magic that had infected all the animal spirits of the seventeen. The third had cleared Lepard and Grizz of the dark charm's curse, restoring their immortality.

Now, seventeen Ferals sat or stood around the table.

Nine new Ferals had yet to come in—the ones who would be marked to replace the evil Ferals and the three who'd yet to appear. Kougar had finally revealed the ones missing to be the horse, the gorilla, and the arctic wolf.

Wulfe liked the idea of another wolf in the house.

In addition to the Ferals, all the wives had joined them. And Natalie.

She sat beside him, leaning against him, his arm around her shoulders. Her sweet scent filled his senses, her nearness, his heart. Goddess, he loved her. As if she felt that surge of emotion, she turned to meet his gaze, her eyes soft as a summer breeze, setting his pulse to flight at her loveliness. Her eyes were bright, her cheeks rosy. Pulling the energies through her hadn't injured her permanently from what he could tell. She'd recovered almost immediately. All he wanted to do now was sweep her up to his room and make love to her until neither of them cared about the future, about anything but lying in one another's arms.

But now wasn't the time. And he was dreading getting her alone as much as he was looking forward to it. Because the moment he did, they were going to have to have *the talk*. He intended to pop the question. And he was terrified she was going to kiss him and tell him that her life was in Frederick, not here.

How could he ask her to give up her work, her mom, her home? *Everything?*

But, goddess, he wanted her to stay with him.

"Victory to the Feral Warriors!" Tighe shouted, thrusting his fist into the air.

"Victory to the Feral Warriors!" the others shouted in reply, their fists rising as one. Only Grizz, standing apart, didn't participate.

"Can we claim victory?" Hawke asked, ever practical. "With the Daemons now free?"

"The wraith Daemons are gone," Lyon replied. "As is Satanan."

"And Inir," Paenther added. "Perhaps now, some of the Mage who've lost their souls will begin to reclaim them again."

"We'll have to keep a close eye on the Daemons and the others who escaped." Kougar took a sip of his whiskey. "More than one has traditionally fed on humans though I'm the first to admit I know little about most of those races. They inhabited a different part of the world from the shifters in those ancient times, and they were already firmly under Satanan's control by the time I was born. Perhaps, as Strome indicated, the evil we've always attributed to Daemons in general was only a reflection of Satanan's control over them."

"We can hope," Lyon said somberly. "If they prove otherwise, we'll have our work cut out for us."

"What about the draden?" Fox asked, his arm around Melisande's shoulders. "We always believed they were the remnants of the Daemons incarcerated in the blade, but there's no doubt they've multiplied a thousandfold since ancient times. Do you think they're gone now?"

"We'll find out soon enough."

Grizz suddenly pushed away from the wall and strode to Melisande. "I need to find Sabine."

Melisande nodded, then gave Fox a quick kiss. "I'll be right back." A moment later, she and Grizz disappeared.

"Natalie," Kara said with surprise. "Your wound. I just realized it's gone again."

Natalie reached for her cheek with a look of disappointment. "My badge of honor."

Wulfe smiled and kissed her temple. "It disappeared along with your aura once I released the primal powers and closed the door on them. I can cut you a new one."

She laughed, the sound the most beautiful beneath the heavens. "Thanks, but no."

He grinned and kissed her soundly on the mouth this time.

"I wonder . . ." Kougar murmured.

Delaney made a funny sound and Wulfe lifted his head to find her watching him with wide eyes, her hand covering her mouth. Tighe gripped his mate's shoulder, the look on his face half disbelief, half smile.

"What?" Wulfe demanded.

"Prick her finger," Tighe said.

Wulfe scowled. "*Why?*"

Tighe's smile escaped, his dimples flashing. "When Delaney was made the channel key, she became immortal. We thought it was pulling the clone's half of my soul through her body that changed her, but now I'm wondering."

Natalie's eyes widened. "*Immortal?*"

"Speculation, only," Wulfe murmured, but his heart began to pound. If Tighe was right, it wouldn't necessarily change anything. Natalie wouldn't have to stay with him, even then. She could go wherever she wanted, do whatever her heart desired. But if she did want to stay . . . *they would have forever.*

"How do we test it?" she asked, breathless, her eyes wide.

With an unsteady hand, Wulfe released her to pull a small switchblade from his pocket, then he held out his hand for her. "Just a prick," he promised, but she placed her hand in his without hesitation.

Taking a deep breath, Wulfe gripped one slender finger and nicked the very end. A tiny pearl of blood appeared. He waited two seconds, then brushed it away, revealing skin uninjured. She'd already healed.

Joy lifted inside him.

Natalie's wide-eyed gaze locked on his. "Do it again. A bigger cut this time."

"It'll hurt."

Her calm gaze bore into his. "I need to know."

So did he. This time he cut her palm, a shallow, half-inch slice. The blood welled again, and healed before their eyes.

"Immortal," Tighe crowed.

The table fell silent. Because none of them, Wulfe included, knew if this was good news or bad.

Wulfe stood suddenly. "We need to talk."

Natalie, stunned, nodded, and he grabbed her hand and led her up to his room.

Wulfe ushered Natalie into his bedroom. As he closed the door, she turned to him, her heart pounding, her mind in chaos. *Immortal*. She'd been turned *immortal*.

"What does this mean?" she asked, sounding as bewildered as she felt.

Wulfe stood as if frozen, watching her with liquid eyes. "It means you're one of us, now. In a way. You have to hide what you are from the humans. From the mortals."

"I can't go home." The thought tried to catch at her emotions, but found only small purchase, because the truth was, she didn't want to go home. That wasn't what she wanted at all.

"You can go wherever you want. We won't be able to take your memories, now, and you will have to be careful of a lot of things, but I trust you, Natalie."

She watched him, her pulse pounding. Emotions threatened to overwhelm her. "Wulfe . . . what if I don't want to go home?"

A light sparked in his eyes, hope and joy, and she knew, in that moment, that he wanted her to stay.

"But . . . your mom. Your kids with the vision problems."

Her heart caught. How could she turn her back on them? The kids would find another doctor. But her mom would never survive the loss of all three of her children. Tears burned her eyes. "I don't want to leave you."

"I don't want you to go." And suddenly she was in his arms, his hands in her hair as he gripped her head, as his gaze bore into hers. "Tell me what I can do to make you stay."

"Find a way for my mom to remain part of Xavier's and my lives."

"Done."

"How . . . ?"

"Hell if I know, but I'll fly to the moon and back if that's what it takes to make you stay."

Her heart filled, a smile lifting her mouth.

"What else, Natalie? I don't see how you can keep your practice—I'm sorry—but tell me how I can help you make a difference, and it's done."

A small laugh escaped her throat because her dreams—dreams she hadn't even known she possessed, were all coming true in one swift rush. "Maybe you can help me open the minds of a few more eye doctors to the benefits of vision therapy?"

Wulfe's smile bloomed slowly. "Start setting me up with eye appointments." His smile dimmed, his gaze turned piercingly raw. "What else do you want, Natalie? Anything. Anything at all if you'll just stay."

She swallowed the lump that had risen into her throat as she saw so clearly what he wanted her to say.

"You, Wulfe. I want you. Forever. For eternity. *I love you so much.*"

"Eternity is a long time."

"Too long?"

"*Never.*" He pulled her tight against him, burying his face in her hair as his big body shuddered. When he pulled back, moisture glistened in the velvet depths of his beautiful eyes. "I've waited for you all my life, Natalie. Even eternity won't be enough." A precious smile broke across his handsome, beloved face. "Will you marry me, Natalie Cash? Be my mate?"

"Yes, Wulfe. A thousand times, yes."

Wulfe let out a whoop that she feared might bring down the ceiling, then swept her into his arms and kissed her until she was breathless, wanting, and dizzy with love.

Epilogue

"**W**oof! Woof!"

The toddler's voice and the small, pounding feet had Wulfe turning and grinning as he strode through the foyer of Feral House.

"Hey there, tiger." He knelt as the dimpled, tow-headed two-year-old flew into his arms.

"Up!"

Wulfe rose and lifted the boy until they were eye to eye. "This high?"

"No. Up!" A chubby hand shot into the air.

Wulfe lifted him until he could blow bubbles in the boy's soft belly.

The child screeched with laughter. "Up! Up!"

Wulfe lifted him all the way over his head. "This high?" He couldn't wait until he could hold his own child like this.

"Daddy!" the boy squealed, and Wulfe pulled him down, placing a quick kiss on his forehead before he set him on his never-still feet.

"Anders, buddy!" Tighe grinned and scooped up his son. They were a pair, those two.

Little Anders, named for Tighe's Therian father all those years ago, pressed small hands to his father's cheeks and kissed Tighe's nose.

Wulfe pretended not to notice the moisture that gleamed in Stripes's eyes, as he blinked back the moisture in his own.

Delaney strode into the foyer, Kara on one side, Melisande on the other. Delaney was just beginning to show with her second child, a daughter this time. Therians rarely conceived, but apparently humans-turned-immortal conceived as easily as humans, which thrilled all of them. The more children in Feral House, the better.

"Wulfe, did you wake her?" Delaney joined her husband and son, pulled close by Tighe's strong arm. "We're ready. Everyone's here."

Wulfe grinned. "I'll go get her." He took the stairs three at a time, then strode to his bedroom, opening the door quietly. The last thing he wanted to do was startle his sleeping wife, but he found her brushing her hair in front of the mirror.

She turned to him with a smile so full of love it nearly drove him to his knees even after nearly three years of marriage.

"Am I late? You were supposed to wake me."

"I wanted to let you sleep. You girls need your rest."

Natalie laughed, her hand stroking her distended belly. "Only one of us slept. Your daughter does not like it when I lie still."

Wulfe knelt before her and pressed his hand to Natalie's pregnant stomach. A small foot pressed back. His eyes lifted to Natalie's in wonder. "I can't wait until I can hold her."

Natalie gave a small laugh. "Trust me, you're not the only one."

Wulfe pulled her against him as best he could and kissed her soundly. "You are the most beautiful woman who ever lived."

She pressed her hand to his cheek. "And you are the most beautiful man." Her words weaved deep down inside, finding truth and purchase. In all the ways that mattered, to Natalie, he was. And he would always, always endeavor to make certain she felt that way.

"Ready?" he asked.

"Of course. Is it just the Ferals and their wives?"

Wulfe smiled as he steered her down the stairs. "With twenty-six of us now, how would we fit anyone else?"

They'd put an addition on the house last spring, doubling the size of the kitchen and dining room, and adding living quarters for the kitchen staff Pink and Xavier now oversaw. They'd also added a play-room for Anders and the soon-to-be-born girls, and a far larger gathering place with sofas and tables for social events like Natalie's baby shower—a space large enough to hold them all. Plus a few more.

Wulfe steered her there now and watched with pleasure as she saw the decorations—the pink bal-loons and streamers—and the people.

"Mom," Natalie gasped, as her mother strode for-ward and enveloped her in her arms. Natalie threw him a look of gratitude. Though he hadn't told Natalie he was bringing her mom to her shower, the woman had been to visit, now, many times. He had to wipe her memory, to some extent, each time, but he'd figured out how to do it in such a way that she never forgot that her kids were okay, and she'd see them again soon. She knew the visits had to remain a secret for her children's safety.

Around the room stood twenty-five of the twenty-six Ferals, the Feral wives, half a dozen Daemons, and several others new to the modern world. Even after more than two years, they were discovering additional races of creatures who'd escaped the Daemon Blade. They'd found some strong allies among the escapees, but also made some bitter enemies. Life was never dull in Feral House.

Only Grizz was missing, on yet another search for Sabine. When he'd returned to Montana after Satanan's defeat, he'd found her house empty. Deserted. Not even the male tasked with delivering her supplies knew where she'd gone. Grizz had been trying, without success, to find her ever since.

Kara raised a toast. "To our soon-to-be newest edition. And her wonderful mom and dad. Have you decided on a name, yet?"

Natalie glanced at him, a soft smile breaking across her mouth before she made their announcement. "Liesel. We're naming her for a girl Wulfe knew in his youth, a lovely young woman whose life was cut short and who needs to be remembered."

When Natalie first suggested the name, he'd balked. The memory of Liesel still had the power to cut. But the more he'd thought about it, the more he knew his wife was right. The name would become his daughter's, no longer bound to his nightmare. At the same time, this was a fitting way to give the girl he'd failed one final gift. Immortality.

The Feral wives surged forward, surrounding Natalie and whisking her to the chaise that was already surrounded by presents of every shape and size. As the pack of females passed Pink and Xavier, Natalie grabbed a feathered hand, dragging the ever-shy Pink along with her to a peal of sweet, high-pitched laughter. More than a dozen Ilinas had arrived at Ariana's and Melisande's invitation, and they stood on the periphery of the feminine clutch, laughing and smiling.

Natalie's gaze found him through the throng. "Don't you want to help open presents?"

Wulfe laughed and shook his head as Tighe handed him a beer. He lifted the bottle. "Can't. Got my hands full."

Natalie threw back her head and laughed, then tore open the first present.

Tighe's hand landed on Wulfe's shoulder. "You have no idea what you're in for, my friend. Kids explode into your life, leaving everything you thought you knew in shambles. That daughter of yours is going to transform you. After Natalie, she'll be the best thing that ever happened to you."

The emotion in Tighe's voice had Wulfe looping his arm around his friend's shoulder. "Our daughters are going to be virtually the same age."

Tighe grunted. "You thought we had our hands full with Inir's evil Mage. Just wait until those two become teenagers."

Hawke and Kougar joined them, Jag and Fox striding up a moment later, followed by Vhyper, Paenther, and Lyon. One by one, they slapped forearms with Wulfe, congratulating him on the child that would soon be born. Then as one they turned and watched their wives.

"How did we stand this place when it was just us rattling around here?" Paenther mused.

"All those years, just nine Feral Warriors." Lyon grunted. "Compared to now, this place was like a morgue."

Tighe lifted his beer. "To the women who've brought us light and life, laughter and love. May we make them as happy as they've made us."

"Hear, hear," Jag said, taking a swig of his beer.

The women exclaimed over one of the gifts, their sweet voices raised in pleasure. But it was only one woman Wulfe had eyes for. His precious Natalie.

She held up a ruffled pink dress that was smaller than his hand for him to see, grinning with delight. But all that mattered to him was the joy that radiated from those calm, gray eyes.

And the love.

For him.

*They are Feral Warriors—an elite band of
immortals who can change shape at will.
Sworn to rid the world of evil, their wild
natures are primed for release . . .*

Missed any of Pamela Palmer's dark, sexy series?

Keep reading for a glimpse of more
of her **untamed romances**

from Avon Books!

Desire Untamed

Kara MacAllister's quiet life is transformed forever the night a powerful stranger rips her from her home, claiming she's immortal and the key to his race's survival. Lyon arouses a fierce, primal hunger deep within Kara—beyond anything she had ever imagined. But when their lives are threatened by an ancient evil, Kara and Lyon realize they have found a love they would risk their souls to claim . . . and a powerful desire that could never, ever be tamed.

The relief and welcome in her eyes as he approached nearly drove him to his knees. His hands shook with the need to pull her into his arms. For once he didn't have to fight the urge. He cupped her bare shoulders and pulled her against him, his passion igniting and flaring into a wildfire with the first brush of his heated flesh against her silken skin. Her breasts pebbled against his bare chest. Her scent rose up, clouding his mind, ensnaring him in a haze of lust that was almost too thick to breathe.

When he covered her mouth, reason fled. Her sweetness drugged him, stealing all thought but the certainty she was the only sustenance he would ever need. His hands pressed against her back, pulling her closer as her own hands swept up to catch in his hair, holding him tight.

His tongue swept inside the lush cavern of her mouth, seeking its mate, drawing small moans from her throat that grew in force until she was rocking against him. In a far, distant corner of his mind, he remembered where they were. Remembered they stood within the circle of his fellows. He should let her go and step back.

But his beast roared, *Mine!* and he increased the pressure of his tongue strokes instead, marking her, his beast daring the goddess to ignore his claim. In a trembling rush, Kara came apart in his arms, clinging to him as soft whimpers escaped her throat.

Lyon continued to kiss her, drinking in the heady taste of her release until the torrent passed, and she clung to him. Slowly, regretfully, he released her mouth and held her tight against him until she could stand on her own.

Sweet goddess, he wasn't letting her go. She had to be his. His logical mind took up the cry of his beast. *Mine.*

But she would only be his if his fingertips glowed in the mark of the true mate.

His scalp began to tingle with cold realization. Glowing fingers would have triggered a shout. A cheer. The only sounds that met his ears were the crackle of the fires and the stunned and utter silence of his brothers. He knew. Before he ever pulled away from her and looked at his hands, *he knew* there would be no glow.

Mine! his beast roared in anger and betrayal. But he lifted his hands and stared at the traitorous normalcy of his flesh.

Kara wasn't his.

Obsession Untamed

Every time FBI agent Delaney Randall closes her eyes, she suffers yet another nightmare. A brutal serial killer has found his way inside her head, and she lives each murder through his soulless eyes. Tighe, a dangerous Feral Warrior, needs Delaney and her visions to help stop the rampages of an evil fiend. As the two join forces, Tighe—who has little use for humans—falls for the intense beauty and becomes wild with an obsession as untamed as his heart . . .

"I'm not getting married without underwear. Or without my gun. Not with wild animals on the loose."

Tighe took a step toward her, his mouth compressing dangerously. "You'll do whatever I tell you to do."

She threw the gown on the floor. "Go to hell."

He lunged for her, grabbed her arm, and hauled her roughly against him. "I don't like this any better than you do, but it's either bind yourself to me or die. I gave you the choice already. You chose this. You chose me."

"I was delirious."

His jaw went hard as he released her with one hand and flicked open a switchblade three inches from her face.

"It's not too late to change your mind." The tightness of his mouth spoke of barely leashed violence, but in the agitated flutter of those angel wings in her head she sensed an unhappiness as raw as her own. He was being forced to tie himself to a woman he didn't love.

No, not forced.

He could have let her die.

Her fury ebbed as her heart began to ache for him almost as much as herself. "Would you really kill me?" she asked quietly. She already knew the answer.

The anger drained out of him as he retracted the blade and shoved it back in his pocket.

"No." He released her along with a sigh that echoed with pain. "But if you won't go through with this, I'll have no choice but to step aside while someone else does. The survival of our race is too important." He shook his head. "Not just to us. If we die, there will be no one left to keep the Daemons from returning. Imagine thousands of creatures terrorizing the human population. Creatures worse than my twin. A dozen times worse."

She shuddered and stared at him, her mind struggling to accept round after round of evidence that the world was so much more complex than she'd thought. "So I really don't have a choice?"

His mouth turned rueful. "You really don't."

"But you do. A human death can't mean that much to you. Why bind yourself to me when you could have let me die? When you don't want me?"

His mouth turned up in a wry half smile. "Who says I don't want you?"

As she stared at him, he bent down and picked up the gown, then met her gaze again, his expression softening just a little. "Come on, D. Let's get this over with."

It wasn't quite the marriage proposal she'd dreamed

of, but there had been something in his expression, something in his words that eased the ache inside her. Not much, but maybe it was enough. Especially since she clearly didn't have a choice.

"I need to get cleaned up."

He handed her the gown and nodded toward a door in the corner. "Bathroom's in there. I'll see if I can find you a brush or something."

She nodded and took the gown from him. As he started to turn away, she stopped him. "Tighe?"

He turned back to her.

"Thank you," she said softly. "For not letting me die."

His gaze seemed to search hers for several moments, then he lifted his hand and traced her cheekbone with his thumb in a featherlight touch. "You're welcome." Then he turned away.

Passion Untamed

*Though the Mage witch Skye has a gentle heart,
demonic forces have enslaved her, forcing her
to kidnap Paenther, a powerful and dangerous
immortal. Even chained and naked, he is a cunning
prisoner who seduces her, turning captive into captor.
Despite Paenther's fury over her treachery, Skye's
gentle beauty calls to his soul, calming the wild chaos
within. But when evil threatens, their only chance at
survival is to trust in one another . . . and the power
of love.*

Paenther scented violets even before the witch
stepped into the room. She returned without her animals, her hair wet as if she'd just showered, her eyes
hollow. Without a word, without meeting his gaze,
she crawled up beside him, between his body and the
wall, and lay down, curling against his hip. He could
feel her trembling.

As much as he hated her, he'd always had finely
honed protective instincts toward women and children, and they rose now. Something had hurt her.
He reminded himself he didn't care. But as he felt her
slowly calm, her breathing evening out in sleep, the
tension eased from his own body.

He wasn't sure when he'd drifted off, but he woke
to the sound of water dripping from the stalactites
into the puddles scattered across the room and the
feel of the witch's silken head on his chest. She had
one arm wrapped around his waist, the other hand

tucked against her neck. That second arm was nearly within reach of his mouth. But he'd lost the desire to hurt her. Her gentle touch and her acceptance of his fury had taken the edge off his need for revenge.

He blinked, feeling . . . strange. Almost . . . relaxed.

With disbelief he realized what was wrong. Or what was right. The rage, the ever-present rage he struggled to contain day and night, the rage burned into his soul by Ancreta nearly three hundred years ago, had inexplicably left him.

How? Was this simply more magic?

Did he care?

Chained atop this cold stone, deep in the bowels of a second Mage captivity, he felt more at peace than he had in years. Eased. Whole in a way he hadn't felt in centuries.

Had she somehow, miraculously healed him? Or was her nearness affecting him in a way he'd never imagined anyone could?

The implications rocked him. He almost hoped it was just enchantment. Just a lie. Because if it wasn't, if this easing of the torment he'd lived with for centuries was somehow coming from her . . .

A witch.

Heaven help him. The last thing he wanted was to need her. More than he did already.

Rapture Untamed

The most combative and tormented of the Ferals, Jag is a predator who hunts alone. But when Daemons terrorize the human population he partners with Olivia, a flame-haired Therian temptress as strong as she is beautiful. As their sensual dance heats up, a dark force sets its sights on Olivia, threatening to destroy everything she's vowed to protect—and the only one who can save her is the arrogant shifter she lusts for but dares not love.

"**D**id you love him?"

"You know the answer to that. As a friend, yes, but you know I didn't return the feelings he had for me." Her elbow slammed into his solar plexus. "But so help me, if you think I shouldn't care that he's dead . . ." Her heel drove hard into his knee. "If you think I can just forget the sight of that monster stripping his face away one strip of flesh at a time . . ." Her voice cracked. "So help me, Jag, I'm going to beat your cold ass to hell and back."

The bed collapsed beneath them with a crash. He rolled onto his feet, but Olivia followed, spinning and slamming her heel into his knee again, splintering his kneecap. With a roar, he collapsed onto his other knee just as the door burst open wide.

Tighe and Wulfe pushed inside, then halted in the doorway, staring at the wreckage of the bed, him on his knees, blood running down his face and his fire demon of a partner standing over him, about to drive her elbow into his skull.

Jag grinned. Goddess, but he loved a strong woman. He wiped the blood from his mouth and gave Tighe a jaunty salute.

Olivia whirled on the pair in the doorway, her eyes blazing with unholy fire. "Unless you want to join the fight, get the hell out of here."

Tighe lifted his hands in quick surrender. "I'm gone."

Wulfe, the bastard, grinned. "Don't kill him."

The respite had given his knee a chance to heal. As Wulfe pulled the door closed behind him, Jag shot to his feet, ready for another round. He loved a good fight, and this one had gotten his blood pumping, and at the same time given him an outlet for the awful tension that had been riding him ever since that goat fuck of a battle.

But Olivia's eyes showed no such relief. Deep in those gray depths, he could see her shattering. His heart clenched in his chest as he understood. She fought the grief and her own emotions more than she fought him. And while he'd gladly let her beat the crap out of him if it helped her, he could see it wasn't helping at all.

The emotion needed another way out. The sheen in her eyes told him that.

She launched herself at him again, but even as she did, tears began to run down her cheeks, seeming to make her madder. He let her get in a couple of good punches, then he grabbed her in a bear hug and pressed her face against his chest as she struggled.

"Let it out, Liv," he said quietly. "You're not going to get rid of it until you give in. Just let it out."

She fought him a moment more, her fists pummeling his shoulders until the storm overtook her. Sobs wracked her small body, her fists opening, her fingers clinging to him as grief swept her away.

He felt a deep and sudden need to comfort her and didn't have a clue how to do it. He'd always been great at causing anger. Soothing raging emotions was beyond him. He could always use the calming touch of his hand, but he sensed that wasn't what she needed right now. She needed to get it out.

He patted her back awkwardly.

She buried her face tighter against him, clinging to him harder, as if his attempts weren't that awkward at all.

He lifted his hand and cupped her small head, holding it tight against him. Deep inside his chest, he felt a cracking of the ice that had for so long encased his heart.

He didn't want that. Didn't need it. But even as the thought went through his head, his arms enclosed her in a vise of a protective cage through which nothing would ever harm her again.

Hunger Untamed

For a thousand years she has haunted him—Ariana, queen of the Ilinas. Kougar believed her lost to him forever until the truth of her betrayal left him bitter and hungry for revenge. Ariana, caught in a deadly battle of her own, is neither the soulless creature Kougar believes her to be nor the savior he seeks. And when darkness threatens to annihilate both races, the greatest danger of all becomes the glorious love Kougar and Ariana once shared. A love that has never died.

"Tell me what's going on."

She struggled against his hold, thrashing wildly. "Let me go!"

Inside, his cat yowled with distress. His gut knotted at the anguish in her eyes. But if he let her go now, he might lose his only chance to save Hawke and Tighe. He couldn't be certain where she'd go. And if it wasn't the Crystal Realm, he wouldn't be able to follow.

He tightened his grip on her jaw, forcing her to look at him. A sheen of perspiration dampened her too-pale skin. "You're not going anywhere until you tell me what's going on, Ariana."

He waited as she struggled to pull herself together though her breaths remained ragged and her lips pressed tight with a faint tremble that told him she was close to tears. She blinked hard, pulled in a shuddering breath, and met his gaze.

"Who knows?" he prompted quietly.

"A Mage." She tried to look away. "The moonstones have kept him from finding me. He'll attack us."

Kougar frowned. "I didn't think anyone knew you were alive." Those who knew the truth had a way of dying beneath Melisande's sword. Or being dragged back to the Crystal Realm to die there.

"He didn't. Now he does."

Kougar stared at her, struggling to fill in the blanks. Since when did the Mage attack Ilinas?

"He's attacked you before?" He stilled. "When, Ariana?"

She glanced at him, but couldn't hold his gaze. "A hundred years ago."

"You're lying." Goose bumps erupted on his arms as understanding crashed over him. "Not a hundred years ago, but a thousand. Am I right?"

When she didn't answer, he squeezed her jaw harder. "Am I right?"

"Yes! Yes, it was a thousand years ago." She met his gaze, truth and anguish in her eyes. "He all but destroyed us. The moonstones were all that's kept us safe. I don't know why he couldn't sense me through them, but he couldn't." Tears began to roll down her cheeks. "But now he knows."

Kougar reeled at the implications. "It was never dark spirit that attacked you, *but a Mage*?"

His breath lodged in his throat as his world flipped upside down, as Ariana rewrote thousand-year-old history in the space of seconds. Twenty-one years ago he'd learned the Ilinas weren't extinct. That Ariana still lived. Twenty-one years later, he was still reeling from that revelation. But this rocked him even more. Because if Ariana hadn't been attacked by dark spirit . . . *she wasn't soulless.* The woman he'd loved still lived.

Ecstasy Untamed

Shaken by recent events, Hawke feels his bond with his animal spirit weakening—and once it breaks, he's finished. The arrival of Faith sends his life spinning even further out of control, for although she enflames his deepest primal passions, she's promised to Maxim, the newest Feral Warrior. Little do they know Maxim has secretly bent her to his malevolent will, and Hawke is the only one who can end Faith's slavery and protect the Feral Warriors from this new threat.

She tilted her head at him, her eyes curious. "Do you have a human mom or dad?"

"My father was a Feral Warrior." He leaned in to pull out the two remaining suitcases. "He was the previous hawk shifter and my mother the Radiant."

Her jaw dropped a little before snapping shut. "You're Therian royalty."

He started, then laughed. "I've never heard it put like that."

"So why the affinity for humans? Are you really as nice a guy as you seem?"

A nice guy. He'd always been that, or tried to be. He liked people, humans and Therians alike, more than many of his brothers. He liked kids, in particular. But nice guys didn't erupt in fits of rage, endangering anyone and everyone around them. And that was something he definitely did these days. Goddess, she shouldn't be out here with him alone. For a few enjoyable minutes he'd forgotten the rage that simmered inside him.

He blinked. The rage was barely noticeable. When had that happened?

The moment Faith smiled at him.

He set the last two suitcases on the pavement. "I'm not entirely sure what I am anymore." As soon as the words were out, he wished he hadn't answered quite so truthfully. It wasn't something he wanted to talk about. "So how did you come to accompany Maxim to Feral House?"

Her eyes lost their sparkle. "I think I'm going to be his mate."

His mate? Hawke tried to mask his dismay but knew he'd failed when she shrugged.

"We're not exactly a matched pair."

Hawke tried to laugh, but the sound was forced. "Not exactly."

His *mate*? He'd feared they might be lovers. By the way Maxim had walked off and left her in the car, he'd hoped she was just his servant. Disapproval curled in his gut. Newly marked or not, the man was lacking basic manners if he could treat the woman he'd chosen to spend his immortal life with so carelessly. That Feral didn't deserve this jewel of a woman.

But it didn't matter, did it? They'd clearly chosen one another. Maxim had brought her with him all the way from Poland. Soon, Faith would be just another of his brothers' mates, living at Feral House permanently. Just one more happily ever after for him to watch from afar. Except . . . he hadn't been attracted to the others. This one he was.

A Love Untamed

The newest member of the elite Feral Warriors brotherhood, Fox is eager to prove himself. When paired with the legendary Ilina warrior, Melisande, he finds himself spellbound by a woman who's his match in every way—too bad she doesn't find him nearly as charming. Beneath Melisande's brittle exterior lies a violent hatred of all shape-shifters—a hatred that slowly crumbles as she glimpses the gentleness in her far-too-seductive partner. Their survival demands unconditional trust and their salvation surrender to a wild, untamed love.

"**M**elisande, is it?" he asked, drawing on the full force of his Irish upbringing. "A beautiful name for a beautiful woman."

Sapphire eyes snapped at him with disbelief, certainly not the usual reaction to his attention, but he played the game the way he knew how. He held out his hand to her, uncertain whether she would meet him halfway and suspecting that if she did it would be with a huff or a roll of pretty blue eyes. Either would be fine as long as he got to touch her.

"I'm Fox, Melisande. It's a pleasure to meet you."

"That's what you think." Her voice was music laced with acid. She ignored his outstretched hand, her eyes narrowing as she smiled at him, but there was nothing pleasant about that smile. Hawke's words came back to him, that he'd have more luck taming a tornado, and it occurred to him that he might finally have come across a female who was immune to his charms.

"Mel," Ariana warned.

The petite blonde flung her empty hand toward him as if it were not empty at all, as if she meant to toss a fireball in his face.

Instead, exquisite sexual pleasure rushed through his body on a blast so strong, so pure, that he nearly came right there in the middle of the hallway. On a groan, he arched his back, his eyes dropping closed as the pleasure roared through him, wave after wave of pure ecstasy.

When he could move again, his eyes snapped open, and he straightened to find the most fascinating woman he'd ever met staring at him in wide-eyed disbelief, her mouth forming a horrified O.

A grin spread slowly across his face, his gaze locking with hers. The next time he felt that kind of rapture in her presence, he'd be deep inside of her, and she'd be screaming her release right along with him.

Go to hell shimmered in Melisande's eyes as if she'd heard his silent promise, her mouth snapping closed, once more tightening into a hard line. With a low growl of fury, the beauty disappeared, misting away.

Fox began to laugh.

"What did you do to her?" Kougar asked, clearly puzzled.

Fox shook his head. "I've no bloody idea."

A Blood Seduction

Quinn Lennox is searching for a missing friend when she stumbles into a dark otherworld that only she can see—and finds herself at the mercy of Arturo Mazza, a dangerously handsome vampire whose wicked kiss will save her and betray her. What Arturo can't do is forget about her—any more than Quinn can control her own feelings for him. Neither one can let desire get in the way of their mission— his to save his people, hers to save herself. But there is no escape from desire in a city built for seduction, where passion flows hot and blood red . . .

"**T**ell me your name," she murmured against his temple.

"Master," he replied, his warm breath tickling her neck.

She snorted. "No, it's not."

He lifted his head, his eyes hot and amused. "It is to you." His steel-like arm curved around her waist, pulling her hips into contact with his . . . and with the very thick ridge that rose between them.

Quinn gasped. "*Vampire . . .*" Her body was on fire for him, but she didn't want this. The memory rose of those fangs between her legs. A shudder coursed through her, dousing the fire he'd fanned. She pulled her fingers from his hair, pushed at his shoulders. "My question."

"You've asked it." His mouth grazed her temple, making her shiver all over again.

"Your name was hardly my question. And you didn't answer it. I have to find my brother. The young man who was with me. Please . . . *Master* . . . please, help me find him."

His mouth moved, and she felt the flick of his damp tongue along the edge of her ear. She gasped, accidentally rocking forward, pressing her hips against that thick erection. The groan that escaped her throat sounded embarrassingly happy.

"Will you help me find Zack?"

"No." One long-fingered hand rose to cover her breast.

Her head tipped back, her eyes drifting shut at the wicked pleasure. This was wrong. So wrong. "Please. You must."

His lips returned to her jaw. "You are magnificent, *tessoro*. Built like the sleekest racehorse, all long limbs and lean strength." He released her, his fingers suddenly at her waist, unzipping her jeans. "There is nothing I *must* do. Except have you."

A Kiss of Blood

Quinn Lennox vowed never to return to Vamp City. But with her beloved brother's fate hanging in the balance, and her own power beginning to emerge, she chooses to risk all on yet another perilous journey back to the twilight world. When the dangerous and all-too-seductive Arturo Mazza comes for her, Quinn knows she can never trust him. But though she tries to deny it, her heart begins to hold hope that a certain ruthless vampire can learn the meaning of true love . . .

"**A**re you going to bite me?" she asked, surprised. But she felt no prick of fangs, only the cool brush of his lips. And felt an answering shiver of pleasure.

"I am going to do what I've been wanting to do for hours," he said huskily. He turned her in his arms and kissed her thoroughly, his hand sliding into her hair, the other pulling her hips tight against his. When she slid her arms around his neck and opened her mouth to his, he slid his tongue inside with a groan, pulling her closer still. Passion erupted between them, a heady, wonderful pleasure that stole all thoughts, all worries, drenching her body in pleasure.

"This isn't helping me reach my magic," she said breathlessly, as his lips trailed kisses along her cheek and jaw.

"This *is* magic," he replied, his hands roaming restlessly across her back. "I need to be inside you, *bella.*"

"There are vampires outside."

"They won't come in."

A burst of humor left her mouth on a sigh. "And you don't care if they do."

"I do not." His mouth nuzzled her neck. "I need to taste you, to feast on you, to worship your body in comfort and leisure without anyone's forcing our intimacy." As Fabian had last time.

And she needed that, too. Heaven help her, she needed him. That quickly, their kiss had stirred her into a frenzy of desire that sang in her blood, snapping and popping . . .

She stilled.

He lifted his head, peering at her with question.

"Hold on a second. Let me try something." When he slowly, reluctantly, released her, she turned once more to the chair, lifted her hand, and sent it flying into the wall.

"The passion?" he queried.

"I guess. It seems that my magic only works when *some*thing's stirring my blood."

He pulled her back against him, one hand sliding over her breast, the other between her jeans-clad legs. Quinn groaned, arching at the pleasure of his hands on her.

"All I need is you, Vampire," she gasped.

*G*ive in to your Impulses!

These unforgettable stories only take a second to buy and give you hours of reading pleasure!

Go to *www.AvonImpulse.com* and see what we have to offer.

Available wherever e-books are sold.

AVONIMPULSE

IMP 0811